D1520859

Stories Migrating Home

Kimberly M. Blaeser, Editor

A Collection of Anishinaabe Prose

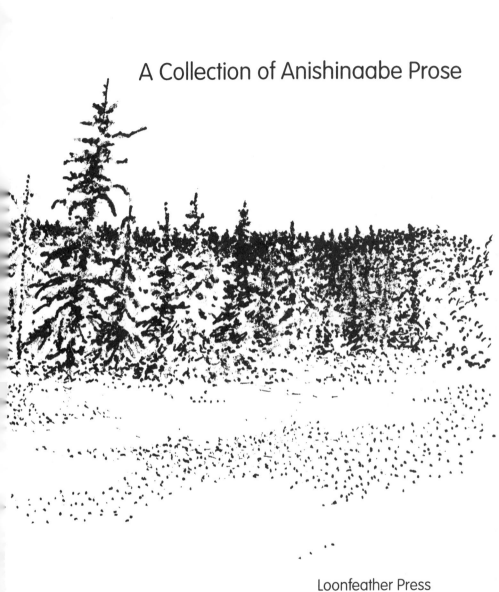

Loonfeather Press
Bemidji, Minnesota

Cover and designs by Slats Fairbanks
First printing, 1999
Printed in the United States of America by Richards
Publishing, Inc.
ISBN 0-926147-08-0

This publication is printed on recycled, acid free archival
paper made from 20 % post-consumer waste.

Stories Migrating Home was made possible, in part, by a
grant from Region 2 Arts Council through funding provided by
the Minnesota State Legislature and by the Native American
Arts Initiative, an organization supported by the Region 2 Arts
Council with funding from the McKnight Foundation.

Loonfeather Press
P.O. Box 1212
Bemidji, MN 56619

For Marlene Blaeser, 1933-1998.
Who shared with me her story heart—
whose memory will always be my home.

Acknowledgments and Permissions

"Blackbird Women" by Denise Sweet, *Buried Roots and Indestructible Seeds: Essays in American Indian Literature*, Wisconsin Humanities, University of Wisconsin Press. A version of "Ethnic Derivatives: Tricksterese Versus Anthropologetics" appeared as "Transethnic Commencements" in *Hotline Healers: An Almost Browne Novel*, (Wesleyan University Press, 1997).
"Giiwedahn: Coming Home, Summer 2000," text © Winona LaDuke, *Last Standing Woman*, reprinted with permission of Publisher Voyageur Press, Inc., 123 North Second Street, Stillwater, Minnesota, 55082 U.S.A., 1-800-888-9653. "Indian Hands" by Gail Moran Wawrzyniak, *The Beaver Tail Journal*. "Jeannette," (an excerpt), copyright 1995 by David Treuer. Reprinted from *Little* with the permission of Graywolf Press, St. Paul, Minnesota. "Looking for St. Joe" by Lise Erdrich, *Special Report: Fiction (Feb-April 1990)*. A prose version of *The Rez Road Follies* by Jim Northrup has been published by Kodansha America, Inc. The original version of "Spirit Sticks" by E. Donald Two-Rivers appears in *Survivor's Medicine*, the University of Oklahoma Press (1998), Norman, Oklahoma, and is used by permission of the publisher. "The Stone" by Anne M. Dunn, *Grandmother's Gift: Stories from the Anishinaabeg*, published 1997 by Holy! Cow Press, Duluth, Minnesota, and used by permission. "The Trap" by Armand Garnet Ruffo was previously published in *The Canadian Fiction Magazine*, Toronto, Canada.

Contents

Storied Landscapes

Survival Migrations

Dreaming Home

Wintering and Returning

Sovereign Motions

Home Tellings

Gathering of Stories

Searching for and bringing together the works in these pages, I lived many of the stories in imagination. The process of collection, the writing and telephoning of various authors, unexpectedly immersed me in other tales. I tracked graduations, publications, job changes, worldwide wanderings, health problems and even natural disasters. The mysterious, frightening, hilarious, sometimes tragic, always fascinating and generous accounts of the authors' lives surprised me with their threads of connection to my own. The inevitable exchanges of experience enriched me, but most of all they reassured me about the vitality of storytelling in far-flung Indian communities. They reinforced what I have come to understand about the necessity and power of storytelling.

Story power has always been a vital part of native lives. Indian people don't really instruct their children; they story them. That is, not only tell them stories but encourage them to hear and see the stories of the world around them, admonish them to remember the stories, and inspire them to create and discover their own stories.

When I was a child, all the work and play had memories attached. A walk to the outhouse reminded my mom of her Aunt Florence who once had a premonition which included the tilted floor of the outhouse at the farm in Beaulieu, of her Aunt Florence who everybody knew saw things, of her Aunt Florence who, she would later say, I must have taken after. The pocket of my grandma's apron must have held stories, for she would often pause, her hand in the bottom of that pocket as if fingering something, and then exhale a laugh and begin the account of someone's foolishness while hanging clothes or picking berries or gone visiting. I know the kerosene lamp gave off bright memories, for whenever it was lighted someone began to tell a Star Bad Boy story. The casting of the fishing line carried stories as it arced across the water at Bass Lake, plopped into the lily pads at North Twin, sent rings rippling from the bobber at Little Elbow. How my mom came to get her name, the bold skunks at the farm, Ivan and Bill's return from Indian boarding school— the stories rippled out from each moment until the very air we breathed seemed to fill us with history. We become the stories we tell, don't we? We become the people and places of our past because our identity is created of their stories.

The tales might tell the origin of things in the world as we know it (how the deer got its antlers, how trickster stole fire for the people), or they might tell about our relatives and the history of our people's relationship with the land. The land itself is storied. Many places have a tale associated with them that underscores our connection to them. "This is the lake that Grandpa Bunker used to believe had the best tasting rice." "This is the old Antell sugarbush. We went with a team of horses then, and camped in the woods until the boiling was done. We laid trap for beaver down by the lake there and spent hours chopping wood to keep the fire going. When the sap was running good, you could hear a pounding all through the woods." I listen carefully, then and now, as if I can still hear the echoes. And sometimes I think I do, and sometimes I think it's just my story heart beating on and on like sap falling drop by drop—*sap, drip, sap, drip, heart, beat.*

Story remains the heartbeat of Indian community. People and other beings have stories associated with them. "His mother was crippled from polio, but she used to walk four miles every day to cook for us during the time our own mother was sick with the fever." "We saw that bear for years every time we were picking berries in the patch by Little Sandy Lake, and he always let us have our spot and we always let him have his." The accounts may have morals, suggesting an appropriate action or relationship, or they may simply allude to the general or specific mystery of life, but always they reinforce our connections. By centering us in a network of relationships, stories assure the survival of our spirits. Stories keep us migrating home.

The Anishinaabe have a long and admirable legacy of both oral and written literature in many genres. Early published works include two volumes of song poems recorded and translated by Frances Densmore in *Chippewa Music* in 1910 and 1913. Later transcriptions of these songs and of Ojibwe stories were undertaken by Gerald Vizenor and appeared in several editions, the most recent, *Summer in the Spring*, published in 1993. The range of memoirs and life stories include a work authored by John Smith in 1919, *Chief John Smith, A Leader of the Chippewa, Age 117 Years, His Life Story as Told by Himself*; that of John Rogers in 1957, *A Chippewa Speaks* (reissued in 1974 as *Red World and White*); and the story of Maude Kegg, a recent, 1991, bilingual publication, *Portage Lake: Memories of an Ojibwe Childhood,* transcribed by John Nichols. Historical and cultural accounts include one written by Peter Jones (Kahkewaquonaby) in 1861, *History of the Ojebway Indians; With Especial Reference to Their Conversion to Christianity*; one by George Copway (Kah-ge-ga-gah-bowh) in 1851, *The Traditional History and Characteristics Sketches of the Ojibway Nation;* and one by William Whipple Warren in 1885, *History of the Ojibways Based upon Traditions and Oral Statements* (reissued in 1984 as *History of the Ojibway People*). Ojibwe writings are also well represented in the contemporary literary scene. Several of the authors included here have earned national and international recognition for their publications, most notably Louise Erdrich; Gordon Henry, Jr.; Jim Northrup; and Gerald Vizenor. Vizenor, who edited the 1987 collection of Ojibwe prose, *Touchwood*, has often noted that the Anishinaabe can claim "more published writers than any other tribe on this continent."

The present anthology attests to the volume, range, and voice of contemporary Ojibwe writings. It includes, for example, the personal experiences of several Native boarding school residents

in Paulette Molin's "The People of the Puckered Moccasins," a
gathering of writings by Ojibwe students who attended Hampton
Institute in Virginia. It also includes excerpts from the comic
drama, *The Rez Road Follies* by Jim Northrup, poignant
autobiographical pieces like Gail Moran Wawrzyniak's "Indian
Hands," and a wonderful gathering of fiction. Set anywhere from
Paris to California to White Earth, offering accounts of
everything from dream visions to AIM politics to repatriation,
the stories vary in voice and approach from the raw sexual humor
of Eddy Two Rivers' "Spirit Sticks" to the mythic quality of Anne
Dunn's "The Stone," the surreal signature of David Beaulieu's
"Crows," the tough realism of David Treuer's "Jeannette," and
the gentle lament of Armand Ruffo's "The Trap." And yet, the
thirty works collected here intersect and overlap one another in
rich patterns. Movements, tones, images and themes, gathered
like rushes from the fertile northwoods lakes of traditional
Anishinaabe homelands, weave colorful mats of tribal story.

Repeating motions of memory, dream, liberation, or
transformation. Repeating voices of family, vision, history, or
humor. Repeating stories of search, survival, departure, and
return. Repeating the names assigned loss, healing, origin, and
ritual. The stories construct intricate patterns of home. That
home may be only the shared memory of a vanished-from-the-
map St. Joe as in Lise Erdrich's story. Or it may be a fry bread
wagon parked at a Minnesota highway wayside, precariously
positioned, as Pauline Brunette Danforth characterizes it,
"between wilderness and civilization." But whatever the
particulars, the stories rendered here and the images cast of
home waver like bulrushes in the breeze of mixedblood reality.
They bend with the wind-weight of history, rustle with the voices
of revolution and celebration. Their variety captures in fine
design the rich expressions of Anishinaabe experience.

Of Landscape and Narrative

through every body crevice
earth moments seep in
build nests
hatch outlook
linger in cells and soul

place anchors
hold generations
evolutions of face
and history
spinning
spinning on land axis

Boundary Waters Canoe Area Wilderness
one white flash
of recognition
and gone
snowy egret
dressed for breeding
shaggy neck plumes
jutting out
woodpecker silhouette

Colorado River, California
egret egret egret
native to two landscapes
collected in casual clumps
forage in shuffle steps
line dancing
to flush their prey

people animals and stories
flung   across land and time
return
        boomerang
back to beginnings

birds redraw flight angles
stars repeat sky patterns
and we revive tellings
all chanting renewal
a whistle call
kissing memory
through pursed lips
re-re-re-re

and these stories too
follow wind paths
faint   ancient
engravings in mind
instinctual migrations
against currents
across continents

> *Brooks Range, Alaska*
> breath of caribou
> passing within feet
> of my longing
> I watch each precise
> setting of antlers
> bull thrusting
> high   this weight
> of balance
>
> small brindled calf
> muzzle open in panic
> bleating my presence
> indifferent cow
> grazing
> belly filled
> with knowledge
> of journey

gathering grounds
images of crossings
imprinted as a mother's scent

Jasper Pulaski Wildlife Refuge
against october sky
red-headed skeletons
cranes all bone
and histrionics
parachute into fields
dusk quiet slashed
with awe and tremolooo

where sandhills gather
flocks of spindly legs
fold and unfold
wings fan up
            and down
lifted like marionettes
in gangly dance

all these
carried by blood
echoes
or ghost ancestors
song poems too
roosting like swallows
in overhanging eaves
wintering and returning

memories of passages
ranging like voices
across my inner ear
distances
traced in hieroglyphics
written in swamp meadows
stories migrating home

Kimberly M. Blaeser

Storied Landscapes

![decorative ornament]

Tracks: Book Two

An Excerpt

Louise Erdrich

The House

During a brilliant thaw in the moon of little spirit, an Ojibwe woman gave birth on the same complicated ground where, much later, the house of John James Mauser was raised. The ridge of earth was massive, a fold of land jutting up over a brief network of lakes, flowing streams, rivers, and sloughs. That high ground was a favorite spot for making camp in those original years before settlement, because the water drew game and from the lookout a person could see *wausau*, far off, spot weather coming or an enemy traveling below. The earth made chokecherries from the women's blood spilled in the grass. The baby would be given the old name, *Kah si gi wit*, Born on the High Place. After a short rest he was tied onto his mother's back and the people moved on, moved on, pushed west.

From that direction, the place where the dead follow after their names, came wheat in a grasshopper year, hauled out green and fermenting to feed the working crews. A city was raised. Minneapolis. Wood framed. Brick by brick. At the base of the hill the aroma of roasting grain filled the air and made one man turn his American mind to the question whether he couldn't merchandise the smell itself, the idea, so filling and substantial. Another man dished the hot mush onto wooden slabs and tried

11

to fend off the questions of a lithe, determined woman in a featherless hat—she had a paper from a newly formed animal protection organization. *Violation, Violation!* she cried out. As the horses strained forward with the load of bricks anyway, she threw herself into their path, lay panting on the ground in her dress of buttermilk wool, waiting for the Percheron hooves and stone boat, for the whip to crack, but of course the horses stamped sideways in wonder. One stumbled, the other panicked, and to the curses of the drayer the woman was lifted, in a swoon of boneless fanaticism, by two workers who then tossed her into a drinking trough.

After her petition was passed in the city council by a solid majority, the loads were lighter, fewer horses' hearts burst, and this woman's name went into the books. Even as she penned away the first night after her dunking, however, larger stones were being quarried to the northeast. The best brownstone came from an island in a deep cold northern lake. The ground of the island had once been covered with mammoth basswood that scented the air over the lake, for miles out, with a swimming fragrance of such supernal sweet innocence that those first priests, penetrating deeper into the heart of the world, cried out not knowing whether God or the Devil tempted them. Now the island was stripped of trees. The dug quarry ran a quarter mile in length. From below the soil, six by eight blocks were drilled and handcut by verdant Italians who first hated the state of Michigan and next Wisconsin and felt more lost and alien the farther they worked themselves into this country. Every ten hours, night and day, the barge arrived for its load and the crane at the water's edge was set into operation. The Italians slept in shifts and were troubled in their dreams, so much so that one night they rose together in a storm of beautiful language and walked onto the barge to ride along with their own hewn rock toward the farthest shore—forfeiting wages. Still, there was more than enough brownstone quarried, cut, hand-finished, shipped and hauled uphill, for the construction of the house to continue.

And to the north, near yet another lake and to the edge of it, grew oak trees. On the whole continent and to each direction these were judged the finest that could be obtained. In addition, it proved easy and profitable to deal with the Indian agent, Tatro, who won a personal commission for discovering that due to a recent government decision the land upon which these trees grew was tax forfeit from one Indian, just a woman—she could go elsewhere, and anyway, she was a troublemaker. There was no problem about moving the lumber crews right in and so the cut was accomplished speedily. Half was sold. The other and the soundest of the wood was processed right at the edge of the city to the specifications of the architect.

Watching the oak grain emerge in warm swirls of lumber, the architect thought of several gestures he could make—the sleek entrance, the complicated stairwell, the curves. He saw the wood accomplishing a series of glowing movements in grand proportions. He pointed out the height of imposing windows to his decorating assistant, Miss Gheen, who took detailed notes and proceeded some miles south to procure fine lace produced by young Dakota women whose mothers had once worked the quills of porcupines and dyed hairs of moose together into intricate claw emblems before they died of measles, cholera, smallpox, tuberculosis, and left their daughters dextrous and lonely to the talents of the nuns.

Copper. *Miskwa wabic.* Soapstone. Slate for the roof shingles. A strange, tremendous crystal of pyrite traded from a destitute family of Pillagers in the autumn of no rice. The walls were raised and fast against them a tawny insulation of woven lake reeds was pressed tight by three layers, and then four, so that no stray breeze could enter. The chimneys were constructed of a type of brick requiring the addition of blood, and so, baked in the vicinity of a slaughterhouse, they would exude when there was fire lighted a scorched, physical odor. Iron for the many skeleton keys the house would take and for the griddles and the handles of the mangle and for the locks themselves and the Moorish-inspired turned railings of the entrance and the staircase was mined on the Mesabi range by Norwegians and

Sammi so gutshot with hunger they didn't care if they were trespassing on anybody's hunting grounds or not and just kept on digging deeper, deeper into the earth.

Water from the generous river. Fire trembling in beehive kilns. And sweat, most of all sweat from the bodies of men and women made the house. Sweating men climbed the hill and set the blocks and beveled the glass and carved the details and set down floors of wood, parquet, concrete, and alabaster. Women coughed in the dim basements of a fabric warehouse sewing drapes and dishcloths and hemming fine linen. One day overhead a flight of sandhill cranes passed low enough to shoot and the men on the crew brought down nearly a hundred to pluck and roast, eat, digest, and use up making more sweat, laying bricks. A bobcat was killed near the building site. One claw was set in gold and hung off the watch fob of John James Mauser, who presented his wife with a thick spotted muff made to the mold of her tender hands. She referred to it ever after as "our first housecat," and meowed at him a little, when they were alone, but she was much too well brought up to do more than that and stiffened harder than the iron bannisters when she was touched. Making love to her was for young Mr. Mauser like entering the frozen body of a window mannequin whose temples, whitened and throbbing, showed the strain. One night, he looked down at Placide Armstrong—her arms were stiffly cocked and raised, her legs sprawled, her face as he formed an apology in panic for climaxing was lean and mournful and suddenly gopherlike. He'd married Placide for money, maybe worse, and now they had this house.

They had this house of chimneys which contained the blood of pigs and calves so that a greasy sadness drifted in the festive rooms. They had this house of tears of lace constructed of a million tiny knots of useless knowledge. This house of windows hung with the desperations of dark virgins. They had this house of stacked sandstone colored the richest clay-red and lavender hue. Once this stone had formed the live heart of sacred islands. Now it stood upright and naked on a hill. They had this house of crushed hands and horses dropping in padded collars and this house of the shame of Miss Gheen's inability to sexually attract the architect to her and the architect's obsession with doorways curving in and curving out and how to get them just exactly so, eminently right. They had this house of railroad and then lumber money and the sucking grind of eastern mills. This house under which there might as well have been a child sacrificed, to lie underneath the corner beam's sunk sill, for money that remained unpaid for years to masons and to drivers was simple as food snatched outright. In fact, there is no question that a number of people of all ages lost their lives on account of this house.

That is the case, always, with great buildings and large doings. Placide knew this better than her husband, but both were nonplussed, and felt it simply was their fate to have this house of glassware sinks and a botanical nursery, of palm leaf moldings and foyers that led into foyers of leaded glass, this house of bathrooms walled with quiet marble, gray and finely veined. This house of lead plumbing that eroded minds. This house of beeswaxed mantels and carved paneling, of wooden benches set into the entryway wall and cornices and scrolls and heavy doors hung skilfully to swing shut without a sound—all this made of wood, fine-grained very old-grown quartersawn oak that still in its season and for many years after would exude beads of thin sap—as though recalling growth and life on the land belonging to Fleur Pillager and the shores of Matchimanito, beyond.

The Roads

She took the small roads, the rutted paths through the woods traversing slough edge and heavy underbrush, trackless, unmapped, unknown, and always bearing east. She took the roads that the deer took, trails that hadn't a name yet and stopped abruptly or petered out in useless ditch. She took the roads she had to make herself, chopping alder and flattening reeds. She crossed fields and skirted lakes, pulled her cart over farmland and pasture, heard the small clock and shift of her ancestors' bones when she halted, exhausted in a dead gray hopeless rage of patience. Through rain she slept beneath the cart's bed and when the sun shone with punishing heat she rose and went on, kept walking until she came to the iron road.

The road had two trails, parallel and slender. This was the path she had been looking for, the one she wanted. The man who had stolen her trees took this same way. She followed his tracks.

She nailed tin grooves to the wheels of her cart and kept going on that road, kept taking one step and then the next step, and the next. She wore her moccasins to shreds, then stole a pair of boots off the porch of a farmhouse, strangling a fat dog to do it. She skinned the dog, boiled and ate it, leaving only the bones behind her, sucked hollow. She dug cattails from the potholes and roasted the sweet root. She ate mudhens and snared muskrats, and still she traveled east. She travelled until the iron road met up with another, until the twin roads grew hot from the thunder and lightning of so many trains passing and she had to walk beside.

The night before she reached the city the sky opened and it snowed. She thought hard. She found a tree and under it she buried the bones and the clan markers, tied a red prayer flag to the highest branches and then slept beneath the tree. The next morning, Fleur pushed the cart into heavy bramble and piled brush over to hide it and then she washed herself in ditch water, braided her hair and tied the braids behind, together. She put on the one dress she had that wasn't ripped and torn, a quiet brown. And the hobnail boots. A blanket for a shawl. Then she began to walk toward the city, carrying her bundle, thinking of the man who had taken her land and her trees.

She was still following his trail.

Far across the fields she could hear the city rumbling as she came near, breathing in and out like a great sleeping animal. The cold deepened, for a new snow had fallen overnight. The rushing sound of wheels in slush made her dizzy, and the odor that rushed, hot, from the doorways and windows and back porches caused her throat to shut. She sat down on a rock by the side of the road and ate the last pinch of pemmican from a sack at her waist. The familiar taste of the pounded *weyass*, the dried berries, nearly brought tears to her eyes. Longing filled her. She wanted to sing. She could feel her dead around her, gathering. She straightened her back and kept on going, passed into the first whitened streets and on into the swirling heart of horns and traffic. The movement sickened her, the buildings upon buildings piled together shocked her eyes, the strange lack of plant growth confused her. The people stared through her as though she was invisible until she thought she was, and walked more easily then, breathing smoke, exhaling fire.

Below the heart of the city, where the stomach would be, strange meadows opened of stuff clipped and green. For a long while she stood before a leafless box hedge, upset into a state of wonder at its square shape, amazed that it should grow in so unusual a fashion, its twigs gnarled in smooth planes. She looked up into the bank of stone and brick and wooden buildings that towered farther uphill. In the white distance one mansion shimmered, light glancing off its blank window panes and turrets and painted rails. Fleur blinked and passed her hand across her eyes. But then, behind the warm shadow of her fingers, she recovered her inner sight and slowly across her face there passed her mother's haunted, white, wolf smile.

⧓⧓⧓

The Stone

Anne M. Dunn

A certain man lived near a wide field. In the middle of the field was a great white stone. The man called the stone "Grandfather" because it had been there for many, many winters.

Now it happened one day that the man was hungry. But there was no food in his house. He sat for a long time hugging his belly and moaning to himself in a pitiful voice.

Then he decided he would go to the stone and pray for food. He wrapped his old robe around him and hurried to the field.

Running to the stone, he flung himself upon it.

"Grandfather," he wept, "I am hungry. Truly, I am starving! Please give me something to eat. Provide me with good meat and save my life."

As he lay there he began to feel very warm. Then he began to perspire. He decided that he didn't need the old robe anymore. So he sweetened his prayer with an offering as he wiped the sweat from his face.

"Grandfather, I know you have heard my prayer. I know you will provide meat for me. So I am giving you my robe."

Then the man threw the robe over the stone in a grand gesture of generosity and went away.

Now Great Spirit is not a stone, but Great Spirit is in all places at all times. Therefore Great Spirit had heard and seen what the man had said and done.

As the man walked homeward, he suddenly came upon a freshly killed deer. He looked about, but he saw no one. Then he raised happy hands toward the red sky of the setting sun.

"Thank you, Grandfather," he shouted. "You have provided the meat I need. Therefore, I shall live."

Quickly the man skinned the deer and cut off the hind quarters. He laid wood for a fire and prepared to cook his venison.

But he could not light the fire. No matter how he tried, the tinder would not kindle.

By now it was getting dark and he could feel the cold creeping over his neck, his shoulders and his back. His teeth began to chatter. Still, he could not light the fire.

Suddenly he stood up and threw down the flint.

"I need my robe," he thought. "Grandfather doesn't feel the cold. He doesn't need it. Besides . . . he's had it all day. I'll go get it now."

So the man returned to the field and snatched the robe from the stone.

Now Great Spirit is not a stone, but Great Spirit is in all places at all times. Therefore, it was Great Spirit who had provided meat for the hungry man. What is more, Great Spirit had accepted the man's humble offering and the spirit in the stone had loved him for it.

Now the man wrapped himself in the robe and returned to his camp. What he saw stopped him dead in his tracks. His round eyes stared and his mouth fell open.

The venison was gone! Where the fresh deer had been, there was only a skeleton.

He couldn't believe his eyes. He touched the ribs; they were as dry as sticks.

The man sat down. He hugged his belly and moaned loudly. But instead of being sorry for what he had done, he said, "I should have eaten the meat before I took back my robe."

Although the man's foolish speech and lazy conduct had shown how selfish he was, he was blind to his own faults. So . . . Great Spirit, who still heard the cries of the lazy man, paid no more attention to him.

Then the man got up and said, "I will go to my sister. Her man is a good hunter. She will have meat. I'll trade something for it. Perhaps my robe. I won't need it tomorrow . . . when it's warm again."

So he began walking toward his sister's home, completely forgetting the lesson Great Spirit had tried to teach him.

But in the middle of the wide field the white stone mourned for the foolish, selfish, lazy, hungry man.

▸◪◪◃

Looking for St. Joe

Lise Erdrich

W hen the head nurse hands us the patient charts I'm buffaloed. It's the first time I actually looked at one, and all I understand is the thing that no one else would—the box that says Born: St. Joe, 1887. That explains about my *client,* as college-educated nurses are to call them. Not passive patients but healthcare consumers, "bio-psycho-social beings" in our textbook.

There is no St. Joe. Not anymore, except in this old person's mind. Those days have been plowed under, turned into beetfields and wheatfields. There's an empty space where nobody even knew to write ND. I don't know how to be a nurse, but I know about St. Joe. For the moment, that's a secret. I don't doubt, though, that soon enough someone will give me the accusing look that says: "You're Indian, aren't you. They're paying your way through. That's the only reason you're here."

And it could be true. Maybe I don't have any natural talent for this. The lines and graphs and numbers on the chart look threatening. The narrative notes await today's contribution. A nurse strides past the station remarking that someone is "Cheyne-Stoking." Croaking. A few doors down the hall. I'm not afraid of blood, but the name of a syndrome being used as a verb is the kind of thing that makes me nervous. The rules of English were supposed to be a useful ticket.

The head nurse of St. Patrick Home is giving us the bio-psycho-social scoop on each of our assigned clients. Our

21

instructor from the university follows up with the appropriate theoretical spin. St. Pat's head is a "trained nurse" of the hospital-school era who tries to treat our college notions with a dose of reality.

She says of my client, "Cleo's just a sweet lovable little old lady with a streak of noncompliance, doesn't want to take her pills. She's waking up lately yelling about the Sioux Indians and has this buggy thing about being a 'halfbreed,' she goes off on that all the time but her daughter says she's French-Canadian." She punctuates this with her cheerful, tolerant smirk, which is clearly an instructional device. "She needs help with ADLs. . . . " She goes on, giving me hints about the client's Activities of Daily Living, and there's a rush of blood trying to rise to my face. I tell myself there's nothing to give me away. Nothing to trouble with. I'm free, invisible, like water or air.

"You're a white girl! It's just your eyes that are Indian," this fancy dancer told me at an Oklahoma powwow. I think that's what he liked about me, too, that whole summer showing me off to his mean teasing friends who were all the color of pipestone and clay. If he got mad at me he used to pout and say, "You squaw." Just like the white boy I loved the next summer.

It's hard enough to figure out what to do next, how to do the right thing right now. I'll keep my mouth shut and my eyes open. I'm thinking that when I get home I'll have to study harder, practice things more, or I could be dangerous. This is the first day I ever had a client that wasn't made out of rubber or plastic. I got up early this morning, feeling like I didn't belong in my skin, especially as I put on these crisp white clothes and pantyhose. They feel creepy and electric on me, charged with responsibility. In the mirror was some neatly-contained tidy individual I'd never met before. Every hair tightly braided. Eyes that looked back at me with extreme caution, doubt, and clinical detachment.

Getting the babies fed and dressed and over to the sitter's on time was a rugged set of movements. My spotted 1970s Chevy bucked and snorted all the way to St. Pat's, a big old dark brick place down by the river—the kind of place for folks who are not only old, but poor. I took one last deep breath of clean cold March air and opened the door.

Snow-blind, I stood in a hot blast of steam heat that cooked the murky entrance. A queasy smell met me in the close, dark hallway. I walked right into it, trying to get used to it, following it down into the basement: greasy, soggy, mushy institutional breakfast odors, mingled with the general scent of decay.

Our orientation conference is in a corner called the Fun Room where residents play games and work on arts and crafts. A collection of sad clothespin butterflies are shoved to one end of the table. I'm thinking if I can only get through the day, then the week, year, career will go by like water.

Subjective Information on my client's chart is set off in quotes. "I can't breathe. There's no air. Let me go home. I'm a halfbreed. I don't belong in here." The student before me wrote this down; who but a college girl would? Other sheets tell me that Cleo's daughter left her in this place, that her heart, lungs, limbs, everything is failing and she "is not a candidate for surgery or therapy."

Still, my assignment is a theoretically sound written plan that motivates her to "participate in self-care and ADLs." If I don't concoct this properly I'll flunk. After orientation everyone goes up to the second floor to start in on the clients. When I find Cleo's room and look in the bed, first thing I check is her breathing—whether she's doing it, and how. Twenty-seven times a minute, shallow, quiet although the chart said wheezing. I hold her thin papery wrist in my hand and take her pulse. It's slow, feeble, irregular. While I'm standing there doing this I can see the dark line of the border water below us.

The Red River of the North. It flows north to Manitoba, past the city of Winnipeg where there's a two-tier white paddle wheel steamboat called the River Rouge. I want to be a tourist. I want to wine and dine and gamble on one of those floating cakes. There's a legend about how the river was named for blood. Even I have heard about the Chippewa and Sioux fighting over this valley from the time my many-times-great-grandfathers first came here. I think about how the river is now, clogged with the breaking ice, flowing slowly in some places and swiftly in others, winding its way into the Hudson Bay drainage. Very gingerly, I shake the old lady awake.

"Cleophile," I say. That must be her baptismal name, a favorite of the old names. "Cleophile, wake up, it's your new friend." She comes to in slow motion and reaches for her spectacles on the bedstand, frail hand fumbling, trembling. "Eh?" she quavers. "Who are you? I don't know who you are." Her manner is fearful and resigned. I help her get the glasses on, but she still looks as if she can't make sense of me.

"I'm a student nurse. I'm going to be coming in to see you every Monday and Wednesday morning," I pronounce, low and slow. She drifts for a minute. "Where did you come from?" she says.

"From the University. I'm a student nurse." She makes no response, is sinking downstream. So I look over my shoulder, out the door. All clear. "I'm from St. Joe," I tell her. She seems to startle out of her dream or into it. She leans forward, enthused. "Oh, my," she says, a big grin on her face. "How many came with you?"

"It's just me, I'm afraid. No one else could come." Maybe she thought I'd bring the whole tribe.

I help her into her wheelchair and bring the basin of water and washcloth. "I can do it," she croaks fiercely, protesting when I finally help her get cleaned up and dressed, the time factor. My grades. She's so thin and stiff I could just lay her on the bed like a paper doll and get the job done quick. Her gray hair has been cut short but she can comb it only with a struggle. At last she's sitting in her wheelchair next to the bed, all dressed, shoes and socks on, dentures in place. I go to get a breakfast tray and then fresh sheets.

When I come back the University instructor is there with a questioning look on her face. "I don't know why, but Cleo certainly seems alert this morning—excited, in fact. Have you done a cardiac and peripheral vascular assessment today?"

My own heart jumps. "Assessment" is who this person is, what she does. Something tells me that her assessment of me is none too good: single mom one step away from the welfare heap, overworked, overstressed, difficulty handling the program, possibly not interested or efficient enough, better be weeded out.

I can't let that happen. I haven't checked Cleo's blood pressure but I nod yes. When the instructor asks, I give her the same figures that I read on yesterday's notes. She takes her stethoscope and listens to the old lady's tired heart, gets out her blood pressure cuff and pumps it up.

"My readings are higher—you have to make sure the cuff isn't loose. Don't forget to listen to the heart sounds. There's a splitting sound here I want you to take note of. I'd like to see how you describe it later on. And her heart rate is slightly increased. Cleo tells me you're from St. Joe, what does that mean? The way she was carrying on."

I shrug in a conspicuous and noncommittal way. "It used to be a little town down the river. Up north."

"In Canada?"

"No, North Dakota." That's all she's going to get from me. I don't tell her the significance of that place, this valley, its forgotten people. It's not a requirement.

"Oh, and it's gone now, your hometown? Funny, I never even heard of it and I've always lived here." I start making the bed, skin crawling. Eyes on me do that. Why do they always want to know when they don't really want to know? Even if you look like the flip side of a buffalo nickel you are not a credible source unless your story fits an established frame of reference. Hollywood, the school books.

Something in my blood starts to shriek and wail enjoyably, like that crazy Led Zeppelin "Immigrant Song" in the back of my mind. I want to laugh out loud. I want to be speeding down the highway, to music. I want to run off and join the party tribes, have been that way before. But now I'm on my own.

It's not that there's no town left. There's a town. The immigrants named it after *their* version of heaven, Valhalla. They thought they were looking at the Valley of the Gods, I guess, the way it was back then. It was 1871, the year after the railroad reached and crossed the river. Before they came my great-grandpa was altar boy to the legendary missionary who named the place St. Joseph in the year of the territorial census. The Pembina Hills country was still the sort of paradise that made it usual for a native man's occupation to be listed as "Hunter" on the 1850 census. Like his father before him, great-grandpa hunted bison. He took the saint's name too: "Soozayf" in their dialect. He lived to be a farmer. "Warrior of Pembina" on the 1863 treaty document, the elder Joseph had to smoke his pipe with the U.S. Government and leave the valley of the Red without a fight. That way people could stay alive, long enough to wander into the reservation and starve.

I know about St. Joe, but that won't help me with this bed. I can't seem to get the bedmaking right, especially the part about getting the pillow out of the old pillowcase and into the new pillowcase without shaking micro-organisms around or hugging it to my contaminated person. The instructor inspects the sheets and tells me to correct them, a warning edge in her voice. The corners weren't tight enough. Finally, she goes away.

Cleo has said nothing this whole time, staring at the gray bacon on her fork as if she'd started to think of something and then forgotten what it was.

"Cleophile," I say to her, "how can you dance with the young men if you don't stoke up your furnace. Cleo, eat *sou dezhenee, li tous, li lawr boukawnee avik li zaef. Meetshou shaenmawk!* Eat your breakfast, the toast, the bacon and eggs. Eat it right now !" It's a type of French with Indian verbs. They're not the quite-right words, in fact I had to study them in college. It's not the way to use them. Yet her eyes light up.

"*Ah, baen, en vyay niya,*" she says with a grin, her finely-carved face cracking into a hundred lines. "I'm an old wreck. I will let the young girls have a chance now." Right then it's easy to see she was a beauty once, *en zhalee fee.*

"You're not an old wreck," I say. "You only look to be about ninety." That makes her cackle.

"I used to love the dance," she tells me. "T'was many days at a time, all the night. Oh, we used to go to the dance, my sisters

and I. . . . My papa and brothers played the fiddle so beautiful.
. . ." She trails off, gone to visit some log house of long ago nestled
in the green sleepy Valley, a house alive with music and dancing feet, the clear black sky and sparkling stars overhead, dancing, dancing till dawn in the lovely lonely land. I know these
tales by heart.

"Why, I bet you can still do the Red River Jig," I joke. "You
know there's some fiddle guys who made recordings. I'll bring
my tape player next time and you can show me how to do it."
It's a French and Indian dance with Scottish hornpipes doing a
Highland fling in the fiddle, something to wear the rug out.

"No, I'm pretty near dead," she says. "I'm the last one alive.
I had fourteen brothers and sisters. I had twelve children. They
are all gone now except my daughter, but she's a white woman
now. She married *an Narwayjin*." She looks up at me suddenly,
as if she just remembered something. "Are you a halfbreed?"
she asks.

"Why sure," I tell her. "Aren't you?" For all I know she's a
long-lost relative. That word has never had exactly to do with
fractions.

"I'm a *halfbreed*," she declares, very certain of what she
means. A *Mechif*, a *metis*, a mixedblood, not *li savazh*. To certain
of the vanishing generations it's an honorable distinction. Of
course all that their people built, all the help they gave to the
early settlers, all their peaceful civilized ways counted for
nothing when the land began to fill up. They were just Indians
who had to be removed.

"You're *en boun faem*, a fine lady, and it's time to take your
pills. I'll go get them and then you're going for a spin on those
wheels." She smiles, nods, settles back behind the limp toast
and bacon, slippery green eggs.

Cleo has several different medications. There's a proper
procedure for handling and dispensing them, and since I've never
done meds before, the instructor has to supervise to see if I
practice what I learned from the books and audiovisual cassettes.

Just when I'm almost done mixing and sorting the
medications correctly, I drop a pill on the floor. Now it's

contaminated, but my instructor looks the other way. These pills are expensive. I simply pick it up and put it into the little cup next to its name on the checksheet. Still, I messed up and she won't forget it.

Cleo hasn't left this wing in weeks, from what I can tell. The staff don't have time, and she can't go by herself. We move out down the hall, off the wing. Most of the residents who have been set out in the hall in their wheelchairs are vacant or unconscious. Others are clumped around the television set, in a similar condition.

There's a talk show about fat dogs and lite dogfood. The problem of overweight dogs in this country is terrible, it seems. A panel of concerned professionals is recommending individual regimens of exercise and nutrition. They have a pudgy poodle walking on a treadmill.

"Is he depressed, would you say?" the hostess springs at the pet psychologist with her microphone. She looks carefully starved and neurotic.

In the oldest, core part of St. Pat's is a pleasant surprise, a sort of drawing room. There's not a soul around. "Hey, how about this," I say to Cleo. "Let's go chat in the parlor." But she has fallen asleep.

The room has dark-polished woodwork, bookcases full of old cloth-bound gilt-paged volumes, heavy wine-colored embossed drapes, fake oriental rugs, fading parchment lamps and lumpy worn-smooth antique chairs and couches. There are framed black and white photographs of women in long white dresses and feather-plumed hats, a class of graduating nurses with birdwing headgear, men in strict suits and vests fingering their watch fobs. The room is dim except for a place by the two tall windows where sun shines in. A table with a vase full of cloth flowers catches the golden light in a dappled pattern of curtain lace. Next to it is a piano.

I park Cleo by the table and start playing "Camptown Races," watching to see if she's surprised. Slowly, ever so slowly, she wakes up and focuses. Her head wobbles on the way up, and her eyelids flutter heavily. Meds. I end the tune with a flourish and lean toward her congenially. "How do you like that one?" I ask. "Do you have any requests?"

"Are there any of those Sioux here?" she inquires, cranky. "They killed my grandma and cut off her scalp. Where are all the girls from St. Joe? How many came with you?"

They call it senile dementia, but I can see how her mind is wandering around in a necessary way, sorting and sifting through a hundred years worth of stuff. Right now she's at the Indian boarding school at Fort Totten. And I'm one of the "Mechifgirls" who was sent with her on the wagons. Probably she knew my grandma. I play along, inventing from the clues. I ask wishful futile questions, supply a sentence to her fragments—words like *souers grises*, salt pork, and AWOL. We steal raisins from the commissary, get whipped. We scrub laundry, milk cows, bake airy white bread. We pray and pray and pray. We march in lines to supper, sleep in rows at night. Our friends are sent to the infirmary with "consumption" and trachoma. Some don't come back.

"Let's just run away," I decide. "Where can we go?" It was a military post that the Bureau of Indian Affairs took over for assimilationist education, with the help of an order of sisters from Montreal, Canada.

Cleo looks at me then and I know she knows where she really is at this moment, and where she is going. She laughs at me— real foxy—and in a lucid past tense recalls how it was to go to the school of the gray nuns so long ago with her younger brother. He had long blond ringlets and blue eyes and was very small for his age, "a nangel." Cleo defended him as best she could. "T'was that way with Amable," says Cleo thoughtfully. "I remember one time when Mama and Papa came to get us. We were all traveling in the wagon." She pronounces it *waw-ginn*.

"We saw *a nanimal* running across the road. 'Papa, what is that little animal,' he said. 'Would you go and catch it for me so that I can eat it?' Oh, Mama and Papa would do anything for him. We knew he wouldn't live very long. He had TB. So we stopped right there and Papa went and got the animal for him.

It was a little beaver. Mama made a fire and cooked it for him. 'Oh, that was so good,' he said."

They were going northwest, toward the reservation, where they had relatives. By then there was too much sickness and too many settlers in the Valley. They could no longer stay on their river plot chopping wood and farming. The buffalo were long gone. Even their bleached bones that had once littered the plains so thickly had all been picked up and sold to buyers who shipped them East for some mysterious thing white people did. I have seen the photographs, skulls stacked in mountains by the railway.

"We didn't find many bones then," Cleo says, "but for that time we were happy. My brother was happy, to be traveling again. When we got to *la mootawyn* he said, 'Now I'm tired,' and he went to sleep. We buried him at the church."

On the reservation there was not enough of anything to go around, except the influenza, whooping cough, tuberculosis. There was no more escape. Once a haven of the great flocks and herds, the hills were bare of sustenance. "People started to fight then," says Cleo. "T'was no use."

The family tried raising crops in the swampy scrub before they went farther west to try their luck in Montana: "*daw li Mootanaw.*" Cleo had met a boy who was a hard worker and a good dancer and she was "already fourteen." They stayed behind, built a mud-chink cabin, scratched out a livelihood, made children. The missionary priests always said you needed twelve to gain the gates of heaven.

"I never could eat a gopher," says Cleo. "They crawl through the graves and eat dead people, you know. And everyone was eating gophers at times. And I would never eat a dog. One time I saw an old woman. I thought she was playing with the puppies but then she knocked them on the head and put them in the soup." Cleo pauses. "I guess she must of been a Sioux. Anyhow, not a good Catholic."

The way she says this strikes me funny. I remind her about when we were going past the TV. "Remember? That program with the overweight dogs. They were talking about what to do with those dogs."

Cleo says, in a little bemused voice, "*Ah baen*. The dogs are too fat?"

Then she says, "Soup," trying to recall what we were talking about, or answering that problem. I can't help laughing. I remember that my grandma once in a while cooked muskrats a certain way with lots of onions, so that everyone thought they were eating some real fancy jackrabbit.

"It's *li gravy, li rubaboo*," I conclude, smacking my lips in a foolish, exaggerated, French sort of way. "Secret of lee great Mechif chefs." Cleo stares at me with polite restraint, her eyes watering. "I'm going to bring some rubaboo and rub it on your breakfast if you don't eat it next time," I bumble on. Sometimes I just act dumb and crazy, can't help it. Cleo busts out laughing and coughing.

Just then my instructor comes barreling in with her assessing expression and tells me it's time for Report & Record.

"There you are! Cleo seems almost lively today. You've really got her going. What did you find to talk about?"

"Oh, diet, nutrition, stuff like that." The instructor looks perplexed. I wheel Cleo back to her room and join the group.

We're required to chart and share our observations. One by one, the instructor goes through the group and discusses our work and clients.

She notes how well Cleo is doing, wonders if we had a little "reminiscing therapy." I tell her yes, that's what it was. I feel better already. She ignores that and talks about short-term and long-term memory loss and atherosclerosis and dementia and the effects of polypharmacy.

"Did you hear about the Indians again?" asks the cute girl who's just nineteen or twenty. Her memory is new, her connection to this land is new, she's a full-blooded Scandinavian and probably thinks of anything Indian as being unreal, part of the remote past. "Nurses at the station were telling me about her. Pretty wild stories!" She has giggly eyes.

"Perhaps you could keep this in mind while you're working on increasing your client's level of activity and involvement," says the instructor and gives us a brief recap of Maslow's Hierarchy of Needs tied to old-age diapers etc. "Increasing self-esteem and ADLs go hand in hand. Self-esteem is learned through interaction with others; I'm not sure why Cleo chooses to express low self-esteem through calling herself a halfbreed."

Already, I can see the blank hostile stares. Yet I can't seem to stop. "Well, believe it or not—because she's proud to say so." Clumsy silence. Reluctant attention turned my way, no way to undo it.

"Because the mixedblood Indian people have lived around here for generations, because the fur trade companies intermarried with native tribes since the 1700s and formed this fur trade society that existed until the railroads and settlers and all that came in 1870, and then they sort of got left out of history because no one understood what they were all about anyway." It's out like muddy water rushing out of the dam, all tangled up with catfish.

"The Red River Halfbreeds. I mean that's what they were called then." They look shocked now, suspicious. It contains terminology known to be derogatory and uneducated. My instructor shifts in her chair as if she's ready to break in here. I quickly don't get the hint.

"Thing is, a lot of them were absorbed into Indian or white culture but others had their own lifestyle that was a marriage of Indian and European ways; in Canada they had their own flag and government and national anthem, they called themselves the New Nation and tried to defend their rights to the land and self-government, so their leader was hanged for treason but a bunch escaped to the U.S. and stayed here."

There are those who regarded him as an immortal hero, although branded a religious nut and outlaw. Even today there may be left on the reservation one or two oldtimers christened Louis-Riel in his honor.

"Most of Canada and even this area was called Rupert's Land when the Hudson Bay Company owned it, at least according to their papers, so when the Canadian government took over, the people lost their farms and everything, so that was called the Halfbreed Rebellions."

My family tree was American when those Canadians came over the border bringing all sorts of trouble. They've been feuding for a hundred years, that's why I know. The army held up Indian rations over that mess. The starvation winter followed, 151 people that the priest knew of.

"Some ended up on the reservation where the whole group is designated Chippewa Indians. But many were forced to wander—they were never able to receive legal Indian status, or find any place in non-Indian society."

Like my client, I could say. Everyone is silently indicating that I'm being quite the big pain with my nutshell history. I'm indulging myself, I'm a smart-ass.

"That's an interesting perspective," our instructor says with crisp inflection. "Where did you happen to learn this?"

"Introduction to Indian Studies class," I lie.

"Well thank you, moving ahead now—nothing you ever learn is ever wasted in your nursing careers as you can see. You will integrate it into your Knowledge Base and apply it to problem-solving situations of the Nursing Process: Assessment, Nursing Diagnosis, Planning and Implementation of Interventions, Evaluation of Care. . . . "

The days and weeks go by, and it does work that way. We gradually take on more responsibilities, extra clients. Pretty easy compared to a real nurse's job. Still I have to escape from the present, from the future, for a few minutes. Cleo and I visit when I get time. Sometimes we're back in the buffalo days, piecing the handed-down words together like an invisible puzzle even as we work on one of those standard nursing home jigsaw scenery deals. Sometimes we talk about heaven, what it might be like.

Cleo believes in the miracles that the missionary priests are said to have performed, making water squirt out of hills and so on. She thinks she could get her Treaty check pretty soon, too. My great-great-grandparents and their children and their children's children died still waiting to be paid for that spurious transaction. I wonder what it is to have such faith, the ability to keep on believing in something.

"Cleo, the government is just too slow. Let's go get that ten million acres back from those rich farmers, tell them it was all a big misunderstanding. We'll buy it back for ten cents an acre, fair and square like we got, and pay them a hundred-some years later, same deal as we got. Think they'd go for that?"

She just shakes her head and laughs, beyond thinking about the fairness of it all. If there's a heaven, they should hand her La Pay at the gates.

"Maybe it looks like St. Joe, Cleo." I know there was never any place or date where everything was paradise. Still, I want to go back in time and see things.

"Ah. Wee." Cleo sighs, not a sad sound, more like anybody taking off their shoes, home from a long day's work. She talks of St. Joe, of the dear cabin of her childhood in the leaf and sun-dappled woods by the clear running stream where she and her brothers and sisters played and caught speckled trout. There was a fish trap built into the river by the old mill. The fish are usually swimming through her dreams these days, she wakes up all wet laughing. *Lee pwesoon, lee pwesoon!* She always wanted to go back to St. Joe and have a look. I promise I'll go with her when I get a chance, and take a bunch of pictures.

"I'll get there first," Cleo says very slowly and with dignity. I can't think of anything to say to that. We just sit and accept this then.

"Send me a postcard," I say finally. She nods her head, agreed.

The last day I'm at St. Pat's Cleo and I are in the drawing room. We have talked about a lot of things, but there's so much more that I wish she could tell me. Now we sit for a long time silent, watching the light go in and out of the window at the whim of flying clouds. I get up and play "Red River Valley" on the piano, trying not to be too clumsy, sentimental. It's not elegant, but when I look at Cleo she's crying and smiling at the same time in a sudden stream of lace-filtered light. Then I notice other oldsters wobbling into the room, drawn by the music. They move like ancient turtles, their heads poked up in curiosity. I play the song again, and again, and it's improving. No one in this room cares if I sing well, but I don't do it. We all know the words. We can hear whatever good true voice is singing.

It's midnight, lights out, kids asleep. School's out for the summer, going on eight hours now. I can come back in the fall if I want to. I passed. I passed with flying colors. I'm sitting in front of the TV drinking whiskey. It's a big old bottle of spirits. I keep pouring the whiskey over the ice and waiting for a feeling of relief. You'd think it would just come rushing right in. Every time I put new ice and whiskey in it makes a cracking sound. Snap, crackle, pop.

I think of the river ice breaking up in the early spring, the loud crashing sounds. I think of the big rocks floating along, melting, through the early spring. I wonder if I feel good. I feel my brain cells getting desiccated, popping, bursting, dying, causing this sensation that we interpret as pleasure. Lately I've had a nagging fever. Now the TV is crackling and snowing. I start to get up to switch channels but instead the coffee table lurches forward, the bottle tips over. The screen is incandescent. It seeps quickly into the dark, taking on the shape of North Dakota. The right-hand side squiggles and blurs and becomes the Red River of the North, and I dissolve back into the couch with the TV snowing and the whiskey spilling and the river running and running, towards Pembina, St. Joe, Winnipeg.

Crows

David Beaulieu

Winter surrounded the city; invaded the houses, crawled under the fences, crowded onto the buses, and walked down the street as it followed John Clement Beaupre, slipping past him in a rush as he opened the door. The few patrons at the bar quickly turned and shouted insults at the flock of crows that flew past John Clement and now sat uninvited at the bar.

The cold's bitterness grew. The night fell. The city became brittle, untouchable. Lonesome cars reached for each light post, waited and then dashed to the next before they disappeared. The people who crossed the street came one at a time, covered to hide their faces. They moved quickly, looking over their shoulders as if someone were following them. As each moved from view, others would appear, look over their shoulders and rush to the edge of night from where they had entered.

The street light flickered as the wind shouted the snow into a forced dance which swirled and jumped, falling back to the street and sidewalk as if it had suddenly lost a fight. Winter crows flying without direction and arguing with each other followed John Clement as he entered the street. Lost, unable to leave the night's boundary, the crows followed John Clement as he followed their shadows, reflected from the street light, to enter the bar.

John Clement Beaupre was born across the corner and a few blocks down the street, beyond the flickering street lights.

From where he sat, he could not see past the light to the house where he had entered the world. His father had left this world one evening late in the fall in the company of crows whose shadows reflected untold stories which preceded him. John Clement's father had left, never to return, vanishing into winter without explanation. No sightings were reported, no stories were heard. Gone without a trace.

John Clement left from this place one early Spring morning in search of a man who did not exist. At each place he camped he would hear voiceless stories of tales unknown, left by his father's shadow which moved ahead of him one place at a time, into his future and into his father's past. He returned from each journey to this place, slipping under the edge of night, each time from a different direction. Entering a place where there was no past or future, with nothing but the shade and breeze of what might have been or what could be, John Clement sought the true source of the longing to be remembered. In this land he listened to wordless whispers, never able to remember the tale or tell the story.

The shadow tellers of the stories yet to be told, who held the secret to the source of such longing to be remembered, always escaped. At each place he had camped they had moved on to somewhere else; vanished without a trace. At each place he listened to the sightings not reported and the stories not told of the shadow's search for someone to cast itself in a place to be remembered.

Where the world began and blew away like leaves upon the breath of Winter, John Clement saw the shadows or the cast of crows that followed him. Something of his father remained to be found in this place; something of the tree from where all the shadow leaves blew in all directions carrying voiceless stories to remember, untold stories to create.

John Clement turned from staring at the light coming through the amber of his beer, which waited his next question, to check the weather outside. A winter storm was coming and the way home seemed too risky to take. In the morning the crows would take their shadows to late night forest motels where they would check in under assumed names and pretend to make love. John Clement plotted a reunion.

The jukebox played sad "keep the storm clouds away" songs. These songs remembered the violent late fall storms which had driven the crows into the woods to be trapped by winter, unable to leave its boundaries; trapped as if in a cage. Here they argued among themselves and plotted an escape.

John Clement had entered night; winter's cold dark light and walked the endless line against the edge of day. The crows through the frozen air heard his steps, which made a loud noise upon the sidewalk, as if his steps were the only sounds in the world. They watched as they argued among themselves for some sense of direction, not found in their debates. From their perch in a forest of leafless winter trees, the crows took flight to follow the noise of John Clement's feet as he walked straight to the bar.

The crows and their shadows began to dance to the songs on the jukebox. John Clement tapped a crow on the shoulder to cut into the dance. The shadow's body moved with the rhythm of the song, and he began to sing softly in its ear. Slow dancing with the storyteller, John Clement felt a need to hear its untold story told. As he felt himself begin to slowly enter her, John Clement asked if the shadow knew his father, and she answered, "Yes, I have missed you."

He became terrified, unable to move, as if trapped, unable to wake up. The crows began to argue and a violent fight broke out in the bar. The shadow was suddenly pulled out of his arms by an angry crow. He felt empty and it terrified him. From where the shadow had been there was now nothing and he feared he had become his father's own voiceless story, had given birth to it, with all the pain associated with the creation of such complete emptiness. He felt himself becoming a shadow and attracted to the breeze, which aroused the crows.

The crows got up and left the bar. Unable to fly, they stumbled and swerved along the sidewalk, holding up their complaining companions. John Clement followed the noise, which had entered the neighbors' disturbance calls, to watch the crows as they quickly escaped under the edge of night just as the morning and police arrived. The shadow looked back over its shoulder toward John Clement Beaupre. Alone, with nothing but the stories of his search for the shadow that had abandoned him for the company of crows, John Clement watched the shadow dragged into another night.

►♛◄►♛◄

Another Flood Story

Faith Allard

G chi Manitou put a great many things on this earth, and each one was put here for a reason. The buffalo and deer clothe and feed us, the trees shelter us and the spirits guide us.

One day Gchi Manitou was walking through the woodlands of the north by the big waters when he heard a beaver and a raccoon talking, for, as you know, all the animals can talk. Sneaky as Gchi Manitou was he sat in the bushes for a while and listened. He heard Raccoon telling Beaver that in two moons to come there would be a great rain, and so Beaver should build his dam very high and very strong. Then it would hold back all the water the rain would leave behind, so all the other animals would not get flooded out. Beaver asked Raccoon how he knew about the rain. Raccoon told Beaver that when black striped his tail a great rain would come. Well, Beaver, minding his own business all the time, didn't even realize that Raccoon's tail was always striped. So Beaver took Raccoon's word for it and worked on his dam day and night.

While Beaver was working hard, Raccoon found Beaver's winter food supply of fresh lake bottom root (which Raccoon loved but didn't like getting his paws wet digging for). When the third moon showed its face, Beaver couldn't understand why it didn't rain, so he went looking for Raccoon. He soon found him fast asleep with a round, full belly. Because Raccoon was not a very neat eater, Beaver saw bits of his lake bottom roots freshly chewed and scattered all around the sleeping Raccoon.

Beaver was very angry, so he snatched Raccoon out of the nest, dragged him to the water and tried drowning him when Gchi Manitou stopped him. Beaver objected, telling Gchi Manitou that Raccoon had lied to him so that Raccoon could eat all Beaver's winter food. Gchi Manitou was silent for a while, then he said, "I will think about this and return in one moon with my opinion.

As Gchi Manitou walked through the forest searching for a solution to the problem, he met many animals who offered their opinions. Deer said, "Take his stripes so that everyone will know that he is a trickster."

Bear said, "Paint him white so that everyone can see him coming."

Dragonfly offered to take his mouth so that he could tell no more lies. Gchi Manitou thought about it for a while and then asked Dragonfly to join him back at the water where Beaver and Raccoon were. Dragonfly was very happy to help Gchi Manitou and went excitedly. When they reached the edge of the wood, Gchi Manitou made Dragonfly swift and precise, and then he told him to go forth and quickly sew up the edges of Raccoon's mouth. So Dragonfly did, and with the quickness of a ferret sewed the edges of Raccoon's mouth, then returned to the wood. Gchi Manitou was pleased with the job that Dragonfly had done and granted him always to be swift.

Finally Gchi Manitou walked over to Beaver and Raccoon. Raccoon was begging Beaver to use his big teeth to help him cut the stitches of Dragonfly, but Beaver refused. Raccoon asked Gchi Manitou why Dragonfly had sewed his mouth so small. Gchi Manitou replied, "Big lies have a hard time coming from small mouths!"

Survival Migrations

Jeannette

David Treuer

O n my sixtieth birthday I want no more rhubarb. It was one of those wake up early days. One when you notice it's raining outside your window but it doesn't shut all the way so the wet air gets in your room. It was one of those pull your legs out from under the covers mornings to find that you have no slippers for your feet. You used them to plug the crack in the other window the night before when the rain started. Your moccasins were sold at the last powwow so there would be real oranges to eat for a whole week. Breakfast, dinner, and supper, there were real, not so fresh, but oh so orange oranges to eat. Not in a can or on a picture but full of real juice and little pulpy capsules that burst just right when you sucked them from the rind.

The first time I ever tasted an orange was when I was a little girl and a white woman from Iowa gave one to me. Ever since, I wanted that little bit of sunshine that had been passed hand to hand across the United States only to reach me. All different colored hands just so I could use my thumbnail to tear off the thick peel. Right when I peeled the orange open I checked to see if I nicked or dented the fruit and I separated it carefully. I pulled it into sections like I was separating the only three one-dollar bills I had ever seen only to forget them in a skirt pocket that got washed, the bills nestling comfortably and damply together.

I sucked the sections and let the juice roll down my tongue while I closed my eyes. With my eyes closed I could ignore whose kitchen I sat in and who actually gave me that little bit of music on my tongue. With my eyes closed I didn't have to see the pile of dishes in the sink and the china balanced on the table covered in a white-and-red checkered cloth, china that I was whipped over when I broke it.

After one whipping the hat-and-shoe ladies must have felt bad, must have felt guilty, because they gave me an orange. With my eyes closed, and my mouth full of that sweet orange, I sat and heard the grasshoppers rubbing their wings together in the field and heard the killdeer scream when the men came close to their nests in the meadows, where they tilled up to the edge of town. I sat and heard all of that as I sucked the sections until the clumps of pulp gave way and I emptied the skin until it was a dry sack that I chewed quickly and thoughtlessly because there was no flavor in it anymore.

That was the first orange I ate. But the whole bag of them that I traded my moccasins for I ate quickly, tearing them apart with no caution for juice or rind until I had jammed my mouth full and my fingernails hurt where the rind had worked its way into the flesh. I ate those with no patience because then I had Celia, my girl, and Duke and Ellis were gone working the steel mills in Sheboygan. I had my daughter and mothering sucked out all the gentleness I had saved for myself.

It rained hard and then soft and then just drizzled, frosting my window that usually doesn't have a view at all. However, with mist or light rain, if I squint hard I can pretend that it is the highest tower on Crazy Ludwig's castle in Germany. I saw a picture of it once. With a good mist and fog I can see that lake at the bottom of the valley, glittering in the sun. I read, there where I saw the picture, that the lake at the bottom was made by slaves and that Ludwig was crazy as a nut. That could be, but he sure appreciated a nice view; the way the pine trees go right down to the edge of the lake, and the bridge that goes over the gorge looks so delicate and fragile even though it's made from solid stone. Huge windows that can look out to see these things, that can see swans arching their necks on the lake, is much better than my view without fog or rain. If it's frosted over I got a good view but if it's not then all I see are the sawed-off bodies of the black spruce trees, cropped because they got too close to the electrical wires that hung low overhead. Those, and the stubby whitewashed Catholic church across the street.

It was a morning with rememberings of oranges and castles and rain that cleared up too soon to expose my view of amputated trees. It was my birthday morning, and I knew that I couldn't stay in the old-age home. I was sixty. Sixty years old in a rainy room with a disappearing view and no slippers. It's true that I signed myself in, committed myself to bad food and a bad view. In less than a year with a bad view I knew I couldn't stay there anymore. I needed a little taste of kindness on my birthday. I wanted just a little bit of orange so I could go on with the business of being sixty.

Being sixty isn't like turning from nineteen to twenty. From nineteen to twenty there was nothing but an intake of air and a quick look around to see if anything'd changed. The only difference is that you hold your cigarette more loosely in your hand and your legs are crossed a little higher up. Your casual intake of smoke can be followed by draping your arm over your crossed legs so you could drop ash on the floor.

From nineteen to twenty you wear your skirt a little shorter and put on a darker shade of lipstick. You say "shit." You complain about your aching feet, but not too loudly. You speak about what you read in the papers and you can even shrug and laugh while the word "bullshit" rides on your laughter. When you laugh you pause before it comes and in its wake you let silence fall before you take another drag on your unfiltered Camels. Cigarettes that you can now smoke one after another without getting sick.

You sit with your friends and watch the men watching you. You and all of your friends lean together conspiratorially and laugh at one of them, pretending that you haven't grown up with him and all his cousins your whole life, and that it wasn't him that you first kissed behind the honeysuckle on the south side of the clapboard reservation schoolhouse.

Turning from fifty-nine to sixty isn't anything like that. That just means that your age is easier to say and harder to hide. It means that it is expected that you have had your fill of sweetness and softness, and wetness between your legs. It means that no one will give you an orange while you sit in their kitchen ready to do their and God's work. Turning sixty allows me to walk over behind the old weighing shed next to the railroad tracks where the rhubarb still grows in weedy clumps. The red stalks are thick and the broad green leaves on top sometimes hide everything until I take hold of the base and rip them up. I tuck them under my arm and walk back to my little kitchen in the old-age home where I peel them carefully, my fingers turning raspberry red. Being sixty means that I can eat them plain and let them pucker up my whole mouth. I am allowed to enjoy the feeling of tartness.

Turning sixty also lets me know that the only reason I can enjoy the puckered feeling in my mouth is that I know that no one will bring me oranges anymore. Everyone is content to let me chew the stringiness of life while I wilt in the memory of an orange that is so simple and pure. Oranges are too simple for a woman who has turned sixty. The outside is too smooth and the inside too sticky and sweet. Save the sweet stickiness for the younger ones as the rain lifts, exposing the power lines and the church outside my window.

But on my sixtieth birthday I want no more rhubarb. On my sixtieth birthday I would give anything for the bitter peel of an orange. I would give anything for the sting of sticky acid just for a glimpse of the whole fruit underneath. On my sixtieth birthday I would like to sit in a white woman's kitchen eating an orange with my eyes closed listening to the grasshoppers and the killdeer only to open my eyes to see my beloveds standing on the other side of the screen door, to the side of the back porch. On my sixtieth birthday I would like to see them, my beloveds, standing in smeared clothing and matted hair holding a dirty loaf of bread and a torn quilt. I would like to see them, each one an exact duplication of each other. Each of them standing with those eyes wet like they were going to cry.

I was a baby, born in 1908, when some say history ended up here where the real woods used to stand. Though from where I sit now, in the last house at the end of Poverty, I see it differently. From where I sit and watch Donovan, Jackie, and Little play, streaking past the windows chasing each other, or tumbling around Duke and Ellis's Catalina I see it differently. Who would have guessed that the seeds cast and broken open by fire would have opened this way, these ways. So I watch them, and they think me mean, they think me bitter, only because there is so much they don't know. Donovan doesn't know who left him by the side of the road; Jackie knows that Lyle is her father, but she doesn't know why he left. And Little. Little knows, he knows but refuses to speak about his past, a wisdom those of us who lived through the old times, those of us who snuck through the nets of smallpox and influenza learned long ago. Long ago in 1908. And on the reservation, 1908 was a naked year, devoid of any warmth. That was the year the last big trees were knocked to the ground. The last three-hundred-year-old red pine was cut from the center of Manitou Island in the middle of our lake. All we had left was second growth and when we stood naked, the truth about us was revealed in stands of slashed poplar and scarred jack pine. The fish dove to the deepest part of the lake to avoid the logs that clotted its surface in a sticky mass, before floating down to Minneapolis where they were skinned and sliced into boards the settlers liked to use to build their houses.

The bear had left long before, but now the deer left us too. They were always so shy, them and the rabbits. The deer never made much noise and were too gentle to call attention to our condition. It was too much for them to watch us drown in the dust that settled across everything.

In 1918 the last buffalo died, and now no one believes that they ever even lived up here. It didn't die from gun or arrow, but from an intense loneliness. It staggered into the center of town and died on the streets as everyone stood around and watched through half-lidded eyes, lazy with whiskey. When its last breath left, and it lay in the dust without even its own voice, some men came to cut what flesh they could from its body. As they cut it open they were forced back by the smell of rotting flesh. The skin disintegrated under the prod of axe handles and steel-toed work boots. No one wanted to touch it with their own hands so it stayed there all night. When in the morning someone brought a flatbed trailer pulled by two logging horses to remove it, they found that it had already left. Its outline stained the sand for another half a year, until the snow came.

In 1918 my mother was dreaming of a mink wrap until all thoughts of going down to the Agency to get her rations of flour and lard were driven clear from her head. I stood there and listened as she lay wrapped in a wool blanket in mid-June. It was dark and she lay against the wall in a pile of quilts made from rotting panels of fabric that I had cut from the pants legs of drunken loggers as they lay passed out along the boarded wall of the town bar. Her eyes were closed and a sweat from hunger clung to her face as she turned from side to side.

"Baby?" She didn't open her eyes but she reached out with her voice because she couldn't lift her arms anymore.

"Yes, Mama." I sat next to her and straightened the tangles in my hair, my fingers catching in the sticks and tangles. She didn't brush it like she used to.

"All I ever wanted was a mink wrap. Your daddy never gave one to me, did he?"

"No, Mama." Daddy was long gone and we figured that he moved off with the lumber camps, the only place where there was predictable food. My hair hung down my back and it got smoother and smoother the more I picked the sticks and burrs, stuck there from the raspberry patch behind the church.

"They soft, you know. Like hundreds of feathers all close together." I nodded, my head bobbing from weakness. My stomach had been empty since the last week. The only food I'd had were the green raspberries that I picked from the one patch that still bore fruit, which was against the woodpile behind St. Mary's.

"Them ladies in Italy have 'em. But they don't grow mink over there. Mink come from right here. How come I don't got one around my neck?" Her voice was cracked and I remembered when it used to sing me songs. When we were out in the bush, collecting Indian tea which cut the hunger, or pulling the shriveled blueberries coated with dust, she would sing to me.

> Don't be sad, little girl.
> Don't cry little girl.
> Don't cry anymore little girl.
> Because the birds still love you.
> And I can hear them calling you
> tonight.

I bent my head close to hers and I wrapped my hair around her neck. It reached all the way around and I could grab it on the other side. It was oily smooth and it was thick.

"Is this how it is?" I whispered in her ear.

"Yes. You found one. That feels so nice."

I tightened my grip twisting the extra hair around my hand and turned my shoulder in, taking up the slack.

"Is this how it is?"

She nodded and a breath brushed past her cracked lips. I dug my feet into the dirt floor and pulled harder with my hand.

"Is this how it is?"

She said nothing now and her body grew tense, relaxing bit by bit as I held her wrap as tightly as I could around her neck.

"Is this how it is?" I whispered at last and hugged her.

"You don't need to cry anymore, Mama. *Gego mawiken, Gaawiin gimanezisiin jimawiyan*. You don't got to cry no more."

But she was far away so I got up and walked through the one room shack to the flapping door. I opened it and stepped out into the dust and heat of June. Not looking up at the sun I headed north, to the lumber camps where Duke and Ellis were stripping logs for one penny per stick.

West of town and along the river just north of where Poverty sits now: that's where the logging camp was; long low shacks tossed in an ever-growing clearing like matchboxes strewn across a scratched table. Every day at five the men got up and spit on their hands to seal the still-bleeding blisters and cuts. Spitting again on the floor as they stamped their feet into cracked hobnail boots, they shrugged off the morning cold.

I had never been to the camp before. But I knew where I was. In the fall when the leaves had dropped from the maple and basswood, before the ice stopped the water solid, the sounds flew down along the river and across the lake: an axe patiently nicking slivers from a huge pine, the singing of a hammer against a horseshoe and the horseshoe against the anvil. Sometimes when the wind was just right a short laugh stole to where I sat with my mother huddled in the quilt as our clothes lay drying on top of the barrel stove in our shack. Sometimes there was an explosion. A deep, trembling, soft, below the register of ice cracking on the lakes. Dynamite.

From the shack we lived in I could see the men come into town, bent and dirty men who came out of the woods and into town, loaded up on whiskey and passed out along the road or under the shallow eaves of the bar. Duke and Ellis came too, and even though they weren't older than ten, they worked the camps following the food.

They had come from one of the Indian camps where they found work even though they were so young because the old men were dead and the young ones were still busy dying overseas. Duke and Ellis left the northern camps in the winter of 1916, walking over the lake and into town. Their toes frozen, mute and identical, they were smart enough to pry open the coal chute at the back of the church and slip inside, falling asleep behind the coal furnace, sleeping off the cold while the frostbitten skin blistered and peeled. That's where I met them not in the basement of the church where they slept that winter and where they carefully pried open boxes of communion wafers, nibbling like mice, but in the coat room where they hid during the services, tapping coat pockets for forgotten change.

My mother went to church during the winter when she could still walk. Not because of God, but because of the cold. She only spoke Indian, so even though I was eight when we started going to the wooden white church I knew it was for the same reasons that we walked from the bush and lived in town: for food, warmth and company. She knew what I didn't know. She was dying and she had to find somebody to pass me off to, someone to push her only living child into the act of living.

All of her brothers and sisters had died, my father had left. I don't even remember my own brothers and sisters, though my mother told me I had three of each. I don't remember them, at least not exactly. I can bring back voices, the swish of a braid over the woven cedar-bark mat I played on in the sugar bush, a thin hand tying me tighter on the travois as we broke camp. I remember a worn trouser knee as I sat on my father's lap as he chewed venison soft in his mouth before placing it gently between my lips.

My mother never talked about my brothers and sisters, though she said my father left for the logging camps when they were still up north where the biggest trees had not yet been beaten down. She spoke about him, recalled his hands as we wove mattresses from cattail fronds, his singing voice as we struggled back to our shack in town loaded down with salt, lard, and flour. When she spoke of him then, a little more came back; the shape of his knotted calf as I clung to his leg, the weight of his palm on the crown of my head as he stood and spoke.

Since she spoke of him and not of the others I assumed he was alive and the others weren't. When I met Duke and Ellis I asked them if they knew my father. They told me in whispers between hanging coats in the church that they did, and when they last saw him he was still alive.

We left the woods when I was eight, when the game left for the most isolated swamps and the few remote stands of ancient trees. There hadn't been much food for a while, but there had been others around to help with the sugaring, to untangle the nets and rice the river. The Indian Agent had been trying to get

us to move, to get the few remaining families out of the bush
and into town, or even better, to move south where they were
opening up the prairies for us. That Agent was trying hard. He
trekked up river to where we camped, red in the face, batting
mosquitoes and deerflies. He pleaded. He begged. He brought
the priest.

"For your children's sake," they said.

"For their education."

Knowing that my mother knew no English they spoke
Indian, chopping at the words, stumbling around like two bears
in a single-seat outhouse.

"Who are they?" I asked, peeking from behind the sap-boiling
kettle.

"Evil," she said.

"What do they want?"

"Evil."

My mother wouldn't listen and I imitated her, crossing my
arms and drawing deep breaths. When we heard them coming
we hid in the sumac, under the drooping canopy of black spruce,
in tall grass, in whatever and wherever. But the high fire, the
brim-full kettle and still-gasping fish told them we weren't far.

So they left us alone. Instead they gave out annuity
payments in town. They knew we would come, that we had to
come in, caught by the gills while they slowly drained the water
away. Our numbers shrank; some made the walks to town and
back, others cashed in and moved to where there was open field,
where the trees never shouldered, and where they said grain
grew as far as the eye could see. They knew they would die if
they abandoned their lakes, but they thought they would die
with full stomachs, not knowing that they would be gnawed to
death by the wind and have their eyes go wide at the sight of
the endless open.

My mother and I were the last to leave. By that time we
were stretched tight, no longer able to pull the nets by ourselves,
to tip the copper kettle. We were being peeled back from the
land the way the skin of smoking fish curls over to expose what
is soft and white, what can be flaked away by the wind, by even

the softest, weakest hands. Finally, finally we rolled the nets and stashed them in a tree, coated the kettle in mud and turned it with a thunk on its heavy rim, put what we had in empty flour sacks and walked to town. Don't look back, don't look back.

The People of the Puckered Moccasins:
Selected Writings by Chippewa Students at
Hampton Institute

Paulette Fairbanks Molin

*I*n the old days the tribes were known by the style of moccasin they wore. We who gathered ours at the top were called
Ojibways or Chippewas, which in English means "people of
the puckered moccasins."* Thus, Stella O'Donnel, an Anishinaabe
graduate of the Hampton Normal and Agricultural Institute in
Virginia, wrote in 1911. Her article, "People of the Puckered
Moccasins," appeared in publications of the day, and is among
the writings of early Chippewa students collected here.[1]

Between 1878 and 1923, over 1,300 American Indians
representing sixty-five tribal groups attended the Hampton
Institute in Virginia. Among them were fifty-one Chippewa
students, the majority enrolled at the boarding school after the
turn of the century. Twenty-nine of these students were from
Minnesota (all but two from White Earth), twenty from
Wisconsin (primarily Lac Courte Oreilles and Lac du Flambeau),
and one each from Michigan and South Dakota. Consistent with
the enrollment patterns for the overall American Indian program
at Hampton, the majority, thirty-two of the fifty-one Chippewas,
were male. By the time the Chippewa students arrived at
Hampton (the majority after 1897), most of them were between
17 and 20 years of age, and had already attended other boarding
schools.

The Hampton Institute, in contrast to other American Indian boarding school programs, was established to educate African American students. Its Indian department, which was added ten years after the school's founding in 1868 was supported by the federal government until 1912.[2] The school was founded by Samuel Chapman Armstrong, a military veteran who had led a regiment of African American soldiers during the Civil War. He sought to train "the hand, the head and the heart" of selected youths "to be examples to, and teachers of, their people" at the private, nondenominational, coeducational school.[3] Hampton's training combined instruction in the trades, academics, and Christian religion with manual labor. The American Indian enrollment, small compared to all-Indian boarding schools, was always eclipsed by the African American majority on campus.

Hampton's assimilationist training for American Indian students included an emphasis upon replacing tribal languages and traditions with English, Christianity, and "civilization." One aspect of the training included the outing or work placement system, where students were sent to Euroamerican families, generally during the summer months in the Berkshires, to do housework or farm work at minimal pay. On campus, the American Indian students lived in separate dormitories constructed to house them, the Wigwam for males and Winona Lodge for females. By the time the first group of Chippewa students arrived at Hampton in 1897, efforts were underway to phase out a separate Indian department, which had been established to instruct American Indian students with little or no exposure to Euroamerican ways.

Student writings in Hampton's archival collections include both published and unpublished accounts. One source of publication was Hampton's Indian student newsletter, *Talks and Thoughts of the Hampton Indian Students*, which was published between 1886 and 1907. According to Hampton faculty member Cora Mae Folsom, who served as advisor, students "contributed all the material, edited and printed it, and held themselves responsible for its finances."[4] The native language subheading of the publication, *"Tahenan upi qa ounki ya biye*—Come over and help us," reflected the American Indian program's predominant Sioux or Lakota student enrollment.[5] *Talks and Thoughts* was generally published monthly in a four-page format and included news items, outing letters, folklore and poems, alumni notes or letters, and reports of campus events. Readers were often urged to subscribe by sending in twenty-five cents or enough postage to cover the cost of a one-year subscription. Chippewas George Hamlin and Anna Bender were among the student editors of the publication.

Other sources of publication on Hampton's campus were *The Southern Workman*, which was published from 1872 to 1939, and *The Hampton Student*, which flourished from 1909 to 1927.[6] *The Southern Workman* was the school's primary publication during the period and included writings by administrators, faculty, students, alumni, and regular contributors from the field. Besides chronicling the Hampton model of training, the publication's monthly coverage extended to regional, national and international issues of the day. *The Southern Workman* reported on the development of the American Indian program from its inception in 1878 until its final year in 1923, including information on student arrival groups, curriculum reports, visitors to campus, letters from parents and students, commencement and anniversary day events, editorials on federal policy, and student writings. *The Hampton Student*, as the name indicates, was a campus-wide student publication. After *Talks and Thoughts* was discontinued, American Indian news and writings appeared in that bi-monthly forum along with African American contributions.

The majority of Hampton's American Indian students did not write for publication, but unpublished writings exist for the greatest share of them, including the Chippewas. Hampton scholarship recipients were required to write thank you letters to private donors, the source of tuition and other support at the school.[7] These scholarship letters generally provide background information about family, school, and tribal group in the student's own hand. Students also corresponded with personnel at Hampton from outing assignments, job placements, other schools, and home. In the case of individuals who served in the military during World War I, some letters were written from farflung military bases in the U.S. and Europe. The amount of writing varies from student to student, some corresponding with Hampton personnel over a long period of time and others briefly, or not at all.

Some scholars attribute student writings, especially those published in boarding school newspapers, to faculty or staff thought and/or expression. However, the capability of Indian students was (and is) generally overlooked or underestimated. A number of students, including most of the Chippewas represented here, had had extensive exposure to English language instruction. Indeed, student writers such as Anna Bender poignantly comment on the length of time they spent in schools far from home. During the period, the coercive emphasis placed upon instruction in the English language, at the expense of Native languages, included complete immersion, object teaching, endless drilling, penmanship practice, daily recitations, and composition exercises. A consequence for students was that among the boarding school population were those who had acquired advanced skills in the imposed language.

Further, many students arrived at boarding school already bilingual or multilingual.[8] Once at Hampton, they continued to use their tribal language(s) to some extent, both with and without official approval. American Indian students also learned about languages other than their own from one another.[9] This linguistic diversity had an impact on learning and using the mandated language.

Because a number of the writings, especially letters, were composed in a variety of settings, this material provides a basis of comparison of writing samples over time for many individuals. The subject matter reflects the circumstances in which they were written, including boarding school influences and practices. The various writings at Hampton include instances of a student's own expression (as in letters written from home or other settings back to school personnel), instances where a teacher's editing comments are clearly indicated (as in some scholarship letters), instances where students recorded oral accounts provided by classmates (examples include some of Anna Bender's writing in *Talks and Thoughts*), instances of native language use and English translations (especially among early Dakota Territory students and their families), instances where authorship is unidentified or unclear, and instances where the influence of faculty is unstated, but evident.

The writings presented here appear in chronological order by the date they were written or published, beginning with Alexander La Rock's article on lace making in 1900 and ending with Albert Cobe's account of his trip to Finland in 1926. However, some travel through memory to a more distant time, as in George Brown's description of his childhood days and Anna Bender's account of her return home from the first boarding school she attended. I sought writings by both male and female students and representation by students from several Chippewa communities. My emphasis was upon published works, but some unpublished materials are also included. Although a few of the selections have been excerpted because of length, other editorial changes, which appear in brackets within the text, were kept to a minimum to keep the students' words intact. Published writings in this sample were done primarily by graduates, those who had spent a great deal of time in boarding school. Therefore, they represent only a small number of voices from the total American Indian enrollment at Hampton. Scholar K. Tsianina Lomawaima's words about the students represented in her book about the Chilocco Indian School hold true here: "Their voices speak to us powerfully but should not lead us to forget the voices that we do not, or cannot, hear."[10]

The selected writings speak of a period of time when home for tribal children was often a distant memory, when boarding schools separated them from their families and communities. The selections reflect a variety of assimilationist policies and practices of the day, such as missionary disapproval of tribal dancing in George Hamlin's article, "June the Fourteenth," and Alexander La Rock's account of the missionary-introduced lace making cottage industry among the Chippewas. In composing autobiographical sketches for each of the students, other factors became apparent, especially health issues. Widespread illness and early deaths, generally from consumption or tuberculosis, were pervasive among students and their families during the period. Two of Hampton's first Chippewa graduates died shortly after leaving the school, while other students lost family members and friends to early deaths.

As Lomawaima points out, the boarding school narrative has been, with few exceptions, the province of those who speak from positions of power. "What," she asks, "has become of the thousands of Indian voices who spoke the breath of boarding-school life? They have surrounded the historical narrative, speaking around it and under it, and even talking back to it."[11] This collection of writings, all non-fiction, represents an effort to add more American Indian voices to the narrative.

Although the themes of assimilation and alienation associated with boarding schools are present in the selected writings, the beauty, strength and persistence of tribal identity and culture are also reflected. Memories and observations of home and community appear in many of the selections, especially in accounts of the land-based seasonal round of Anishinaabe life. Students write of maple sugar making in the spring, berry picking and gardening in the summer, wild rice harvesting in the fall, and winter fishing. They describe, both here and in other writings, the beauty of homeland ("Your Hampton and Maine do not compare," Michael Wolf), the changing seasons ("Spring is creeping in on us," George Hamlin), and the tribal group ("The Chippewas are an agricultural people," Stella O'Donnell).

Themes of individual and group perseverence and adaptability, in the face of adversity and change, also emerge. George Hamlin, for example, describes how participants at White Earth's annual celebration prevailed over missionary interference at the gathering. Alexander La Rock comments on Chippewa women scheduling lace making around maple sugar gathering, using profits from the introduced industry to support the traditional activity. Michael Wolf demonstrates through his teaching methods why Indian teachers were (and are) desired in tribal communities. He also reflects humor, so rich among the Anishinaabe, as well as appreciation for the "beautiful philosophy" of Indian people. In short, all of these young students, "people of the puckered moccasins," speak or write their way home.

Alexander La Rock

Alexander La Rock, who arrived at the Hampton Institute from Lac Courte Oreilles in Wisconsin at the age of eighteen in 1897, wrote of his journey to Virginia as follows:

> I left home to come here at Hampton on Sept. 14, '97 on Monday evening and arrived here at Hampton Thursday evening, coming on my way I saw some of the largest cities I ever saw . . . . Coming over the Alleghany Mountains I got scared sometimes the limited we were on was going 58 seconds a mile running right on edges of the Mountains. I expect it would run off the track every minute. Anyhow I arrived safely and thank God for it very much as everybody ought to do.

Identified by school officials as the full blood son of Battiste La Rock, Alexander sought "to get a broader idea" through education. His previous schooling consisted of four years of training at two Wisconsin schools.

At Hampton, Alexander's studies included academic subjects, "elementary agriculture," and the wheelwrighting and blacksmithing trades. In 1899 he spent several months at an outing placement in Cornwall, Connecticut, where he wrote: "I like my place quite well, but not quite as well as Amherst & am three miles from the railroad station. Oh how I miss my beans and cornbread. ha! ha!" While at Cornwall, he responded to a

Hampton faculty member who had requested definitions of "Indian words": "I have written the answers in English what they mean, after quite and careful consideration, but I am steadily forgetting my 'Ojibeway or the Chippewa language.'"

After completing a three-year term at Hampton, Alexander left for home on June 11, 1901. By 1909, he was active in local town politics and had been elected chairman of the town board and served as a member of county government. During that period, his family grew to include a son and daughter. In 1918, Alexander was serving as government policeman at Couderay, Wisconsin.

The following article on Chippewa lace makers appeared in the February 1900 issue of *Talks and Thoughts of the Hampton Indian Students.*[12]

Chippewa Indian Women as Lacemakers

In 1889 Miss Sibyl Carter of New York City opened a school at the White Earth Reservation, Minn., and one at Reserve, Wis., for the purpose of teaching the Chippewa Indians the art of lacemaking. Her desire to give these Indian women a chance to be self-supporting led her to make the experiment, and their ability and skill have already justified the effort.

Uncle Sam offers every advantage to Indians of school age, but after leaving school and returning to their reservations there is but little they can do which will bring them an income. The lacemaking industry brings them a sure and prompt return for their labor and helps them a great deal.

The women vary in their degrees of skill. The greatest difficulty is in keeping such delicate material clean during the progress of working out the elaborate designs. This is in itself a step toward higher living and to bring the work up to a certain standard is another important step. Sometimes an imperfect piece has been made, but after awhile a feeling of pride grew among the women as to who should produce the most perfect piece of work; from that time on an imperfect article has been rare.

All sorts of pretty laces are made by their skillful fingers, from a tiny edging up to the most elaborate pieces that sell for from $50. [sic] up to $8.00 a yard. The lace is used by ladies for collars, cuffs, vests and fronts, and many other articles are made which find a ready sale wherever they have been introduced.

When the money is paid to them for their lace they say, "Apeeche-neshe-shi-shane" (very good). With their earnings they buy their provisions, tea and flour. Besides buying provisions they buy a great big brass kettle that holds gallons and gallons of sap. When the sugar making season approaches about the middle of March lacemaking is put aside for awhile and they take up their occupation of sugar making.

George Hamlin

By the time seventeen-year-old George Hamlin arrived at Hampton from the White Earth Reservation in 1900, he had completed eight years of training at several other boarding schools, including three in Minnesota (Wild Rice River, St. John's, and Clontarf) and one in Nebraska (Genoa). The son of Isidor and Maria (La Fortune) Hamlin, of French Canadian and Chippewa ancestry, George was influenced to attend Hampton by a Genoa teacher.

Described in school records as a fine violinist, George served as chief musician in a Hampton band, studied harnessmaking and greenhouse trades, and became one of the editors of *Talks and Thoughts*. Besides writing "June the Fourteenth," he contributed other articles on tribal life. In addition to his creativity in music and writing, he produced a few small drawings in *The Southern Workman* and was selected to speak on behalf of the seniors at anniversary exercises in 1903.[13]

At Hampton's 1903 commencement, George became the first Chippewa student to graduate from the school, followed by his brother Louis in 1905. A few months after his return home, George's father died. George farmed with family members, losing a "thirty ton hay crop to a prairie fire" in the summer of 1903. During the next year, he wrote to a Hampton teacher: "This has been an unusually severe winter. The snow is nearly all gone, yet it is safe to drive over the lakes with four-horse teams. Spring is creeping in on us, however, and I am so glad. It is so different here from spring in the South, so much more noticeable. We can see the snow go, see the returning birds led by the crow, feel the air grow warmer, and the new life and vigor creep into our bones. It is great, spring is, up here."

A short time later, in May 1904, George was reportedly hospitalized with tuberculosis. He died the following year at his home on the White Earth Reservation, shortly before his twenty-second birthday. The following excerpt is based on the June fourteenth celebration which George observed at White Earth while he was home from school in 1898. His article was published in *Talks and Thoughts of the Hampton Indian Students*, August and September, 1901.

June the Fourteenth

The treaty by which the reservation became the home of the Indians, was signed on the fourteenth of June, so that day has always been celebrated by them, at White Earth. It is always attended by great crowds of people from the neighboring towns outside the reservation. The Sioux Indians from Dakota are invited and they always come in great numbers. Three years ago I returned home from school in time for the celebration. I will endeavor to tell something about it.

At eight o'clock in the morning the little town of White Earth is thronged with eager multitudes. We hear the report of a gun followed by war whoops and yells. Presently the grand procession makes its appearance over a hill to the north of the town. It is led by the band, but who can hear the music above the noise the Indians make? They are all in bright array and are mounted on their little ponies. The ponies all dance along sideways and make as good a show as possible, though many of them give everybody a chance to count their ribs as they pass along. The long procession passes through the main street, (which is the only street) and over another hill to the south, then the Indians are dismissed.

An officer rides through the crowd and shouts, "The birch bark canoe race will take place in ten minutes."

The people gather around the lake where the Indians are to race, and watch them as they paddle swiftly but silently over the water. The men's race comes first, then the Indian women take the paddles, line up and wait for the signal to start. It is given, and they are off. At times the canoes are all huddled together and the women do not have room enough to use their paddles. All is confusion on the lake. The women lose their tempers and splash water on one another with their paddles. The people on shore send up cheer after cheer. At last the racers reached the goal with water dripping from their clothes.

The canoe race is followed by the horse race. The Sioux ponies, which are kept in trim, defeat our well fed horses. After the races the Indians of both tribes sit down together to listen to addresses delivered by their chiefs. The prominent members of the tribes smoke the 'Peace Pipe,' and bury the hatchet.

As soon as the hatchet is buried we hear the beating of a drum which calls the Indians to the dance. On this occasion something unusual happened before the dance was over. A minister who preached in one of the churches of White Earth at that time, came where the Indians were dancing and mildly reproached them, telling them that dancing was wrong. At first the Indians thought he had come to see the dance, so they danced with all their might. Some of them understood the English language and they soon told those who could not what the minister was trying to do. Many of them became angry when they found he was opposed to their dance.

"Go [a]way" said one of them to the minister. "We [will] whip you, make you dance, go away."

During the remainder of the day there are ball games and field sports.

People begin to leave very early in the afternoon and by nightfall they are nearly all gone. The Sioux Indians leave very early the next morning and the White Earth Agency is again regarded as one of the loneliest spots in all the northwest.

Anna Bender

Anna Bender, one of the five siblings to attend Hampton, was the daughter of Mary Razor Bender, a member of the White Earth Band of Chippewa, and Albertus Bender, a German-American homesteader. By the time she arrived at Hampton in 1902, Anna had already been away from home most of her life. At age six, she was sent to the Lincoln Institute in Philadelphia, where she remained for seven years. Very young when she left home, Anna did not remember her trip from Minnesota to Pennsylvania. Her first memories were of Lincoln, the "only home I can distinctly remember," where a half day was spent in school and the other half knitting and sewing. During the summer, she traveled eighteen miles outside of Philadelphia, staying in a rural area near Valley Forge, where she recalled activities such as gathering flowers and climbing trees.

After three years at the Pipestone boarding school, Anna spent a summer at home before leaving for Virginia. Besides serving as editor of *Talks and Thoughts* during her tenure at Hampton, she was active in the Josephines, a literary society organized by American Indian female students, and the service-oriented Christian Endeavor Society. She wrote down stories told by other students and composed articles, such as "An Indian Girl in Boston," an account of a trip she and her sister Elizabeth made to Boston in 1904.

The first female Chippewa student to graduate from Hampton, Anna completed her studies there in 1906. She then did clerical work in North Dakota for a short time before enrolling in a commercial course at Haskell Institute in

Lawrence, Kansas. Following her graduation from Haskell in 1908, Anna was hired as a clerk at the Chemawa boarding school in Oregon. In 1910 she married Reuben Saunders [also Sanders], an industrial teacher at the school. The following year, Anna died from "a surgical operation for the removal of a tumor." She was twenty-six years old.

At Hampton, Anna wrote an unpublished account of her life sometime between 1902 and 1906. The selected excerpt centers around her departure from Lincoln Institute and her return home.

From "The Story of My Life"

I had no reason for wanting to go home, except that other students went to theirs. I seldom heard from my parents and was so young when I came away that I did not even remember them. . . .

How miserable I felt when the time came to go! It was to me the leaving of a home instead of returning to one. The trip was very pleasant at first for there was a crowd of us returning, but when we got to Chicago I was made sad and lonely again by the departure of my friends. From St. Paul I had to travel all alone, not for long as my home was just fifty miles from there.

My mother met me at the station bringing with her my two youngest sisters and two younger brothers whom I had never seen. They greeted me kindly but they and everything being so new and strange that I burst into tears. To comfort me my mother took me into a store close by and bought me a bag of apples. As the house was only about a mile from the station we all walked home thro the woods while my sisters tried to cheer me up by telling me about places we passed and the good times they had.

As we gathered around the table later a great wave of homesickness came over me. I could not eat for the lump in my throat and presently I put my head down and cried good and hard, while the children looked on in surprise. When my father returned from work he greeted me kindly but scanned me from head to foot. He asked me if I remembered him & I had to answer no. He talked to me kindly and tried to help me recall my early childhood, but I had never known many men and was very shy of him. At last he told me I had changed greatly from a loving child to a stranger.

Stella O'Donnell

Stella O'Donnell, the daughter of a Chippewa mother from White Earth and a Euroamerican father, was the first of three siblings to attend Hampton. Her schooling began in Minnesota at the Wild Rice River school, which she attended two years, followed by five years at the Pipestone boarding school. Archival records indicate that she travelled directly from Pipestone to Hampton and had "not been home in five years" although her mother died of consumption during that period. Stella entered Hampton shortly before her seventeenth birthday, writing a year later, "I have never stayed home much. I have always attended some school." In 1907, she described the daily schedule at Hampton, which follows in part, in a scholarship letter:

> The rising bells ring at five fifteen in the morning for the students to get up (the teachers get up in time for their breakfast at eight o'clock). We have breakfast at six; after breakfast we return to our rooms and put them in order. At ten minutes of seven we go to study until eight o'clock. We each have some work assigned to us in the line of putting the house in order and we do this work after study hour. At twenty minutes of nine we go to the opening exercises which last about ten or fifteen minutes. All the middle classes discuss current events after exercises until twenty minutes past nine. By that time we are due at our classrooms.

Stella completed Hampton's training in May 1909, returning to the campus for a post-graduate course in teaching. In 1910 she was hired to teach in Bena, Minnesota.

By 1911, Stella had entered Haskell Institute in Lawrence, Kansas to take a commercial course. At her graduation in 1913, she was among the honor students in a composition contest. Stella then obtained a position as a stenographer at the Pawnee agency in Oklahoma. By 1917, she was working in Tulsa.

An abbreviated account of "People of the Puckered Moccasins," which Stella presented as part of Hampton's anniversary day celebration in 1910, first appeared in *The Southern Workman*, followed by a fuller version in the *Oglala Light* in April, 1911.

People of the Puckered Moccasins

My mother was a daughter of the Ojibways, the tribe Longfellow describes in *Hiawatha*, and I, who was born and spent my childhood among her people am, by Indian law as well as by affection, also a daughter of the Ojibways. In the old days the tribes were known by the style of moccasin they wore. We who gathered ours at the top were called Ojibways or Chippewas, which in English means "people of the puckered moccasins." The Chippewa is the largest tribe north of Mexico. Our range is about the Great Lakes, one-half being in Canada and the other half in the United States.

Early in the seventeenth century the American and French traders came into the Ojibway country, bringing beads, blankets, and firearms . . . . At first [the Chippewas] probably used the original Indian designs in their bead work formed by straight lines only, but in [an] effort to follow nature more closely they have adopted the curved line, designing leaves, flowers, and fruit. This distinguishes their work from that of all other tribes today. As a child I liked to watch the women with a broom straw, dipped in paste, draw their designs on the material, then embroider it by filling it with beads.

Only the older Indian makes his wigwam of birch bark, but

all use the soft, bright grass mats, which the women still make with great skill and taste, of rushes gathered from the hundreds of lakes in that section. The rushes are dried, died, and woven on a rude loom, much as the Navajo weaves her blankets.

The Chippewas are an agricultural people. . . . When the first crow flies, they make sugar from maple trees; when the leaves are as big as squirrels ears they put in their gardens of corn and vegetables. After this they go into woods and fields for berries or to dig snake root. By the time the berry season is over they gather wild rice and do their winter fishing. The berries and fish are . . . put up in airtight birch-bark boxes called *mucox*, and kept for the long cold winter during which the men are logging and trapping.

What the Chippewas need most are intelligent examples on the farms and in the homes. Our men and women are too much like fire, kindled then easily dampened. We who are educated must go back to those people with something definite to do, and then we must do it with a willing, loving, and sympathetic heart.

George Brown

George Brown (*Metawagwen,* Sounding Feather), a nineteen-year-old fullblood from Wisconsin's Lac du Flambeau Reservation, enrolled at Hampton with two cousins in the fall of 1908.[14] At that time, his father, Busweweigigig, was still living, but his mother, Ogimawabigokwa, had died "long ago." George had already completed eight years of schooling at the Lac du Flambeau Indian Training School, where the motto was "A-no-ki-win ni-tum (Duty first)" at his commencement in 1908. At Hampton, he earned a trade certificate in carpentry in 1910 and an academic diploma in 1913. During his tenure in the east, George spent a year (1910-1911) in Amherst, Massachusetts, working for a contractor and builder at union wages to gain practical experience at his trade.

In 1912, when the U.S. government cut off support to the

American Indian program at Hampton, George was among the group of students referred to as "Hampton's Plucky Indians," for choosing to remain at the school without federal aid. He commented: "you still see thirty-six of the very best Indians here. The Indian has been a problem which the white man has not yet been able to solve." He and other Indian students had to attend Hampton as work students and/or obtain support from family, tribe, or other sources.

After his graduation in 1913, George returned home before leaving for Greenwood, South Dakota, to work as a general mechanic. From 1915 to 1917 he worked as a carpenter at the Pipestone boarding school in Minnesota, where he also directed a faculty orchestra and played the flute. During the summer of 1917, George married Sadie Norris, who worked as a cook at the school. By the following year, they were living at Lac du Flambeau and George's carpentry wages under contract were reportedly twice his Civil Service wages. By 1921, the couple had two children.

The following selection is from a 1913 account, "Some of George Brown's early memories, dictated to C.W. Andrus [Caroline W. Andrus, a Hampton faculty member] as part of a possible speech." George and other students frequently did public speaking at various locations.

Some of George Brown's Early Memories

I was born in a wigwam twenty-five years ago. The wigwam stood on a peninsula where the Lac du Flambeau school now stands. I was born in the spring, in the maple sugar season.

The very first impression that I recall was that of three or four wigwams on the shore of the river that opens into French Lake, and there I stayed for some time. I had one brother older than I, and two sisters younger. The occupation of the older people was trapping and fishing. I remember this very well, for they used to bring a lot of otter, musk rats, and such animals. The nearest trading post was two days journey south. I do not know surely, but I think it was at the city of Wausa[u]. They went in a canoe, but of course they had to make some portages on the way. Generally when they came back they brought beads, fire arms, blankets and food, mostly flour and pork. The beads were used by the women for ornamenting the garments they made, and took the place of the porcupine quill embroidery, which is now practically a lost art. There was always great rejoicing when they returned. After the third day we began to watch for them, and if they came in the day time the person who first caught sight of the canoes would run back to the camp and we would hurry to the shore to wait for the landing. Like all children we were very curious to see the things they had brought and looked forward anxiously to the time when we should be old enough to take such trips.

After the return from trips like these feasts were always held. This is just the same as you would do if some of your friends had been away and you asked them to supper. Usually on such occasions the oldest man present is asked to preside, and a pound of tobacco is given him. He is asked to sit in the place of honor. This varies according to the construction of the lodge. If it has two doors he sits on the west side. If there is only one door he sits opposite it, near the centre of the lodge. All the food is brought in by the women and placed in the centre of the lodge. First the tobacco is passed around among the men, and they smoke for a short time. Then the old man who is presiding begins to talk, slowly begins to beat his drum, gradually he enters into a song, and after he has chanted his prayer the feast commences. There are always two men appointed by the one who gives the feast, to divide the food after this prayer . . . . If there is a drum in the wigwam a dance is always held after the feast, a short social dance. If not then stories are told by the old men. These stories are generally of their past experiences, and of the history of the tribe. It is in this way that the children learn the history of the tribe.

I never saw a white man until I was about five years old. I was born in a wigwam, and I was in a wigwam when I saw him. He was a French trapper, and came there with my grandfather. We lived on the shores of French Lake in Wisconsin. He stayed and had one meal with us. I had heard of white people before, although we never said white man, we called them all [*Wemitigoji*], which meant Frenchmen, or [by another expression], which means man with a beard.[15]

The life of the Indian was a very busy one, and varied according to season. In the very early spring they moved to their maple sugar groves and made sugar. Usually the women put up the wigwam, but in the sugar groves it was built differently, and it was the work of the men. While he was putting up the wigwam the woman was attending to the birch bark receptacles which they had made for catching the sap. After the wigwams were finished the men tapped the trees, the women following after them with birch bark holders for it. They usually stayed in the camp a month or more, putting away enough syrup and sugar to last a year. After the sugar season was over they went home and planted corn and potatoes. Corn must be planted when the leaves are as big as a squirrel's foot.

Michael Wolf

Michael Wolf (*Widonique*, Still Cloud), the son or Peter and Angeline (Roussam) Wolf from the Lac Court Oreilles Reservation in Wisconsin, entered Hampton in the fall of 1909 at the age of eighteen.[16] Michael previously attended Indian schools in his home state, two years at Odanah and seven years at Hayward. In a 1910 scholarship letter, he wrote that his parents, a full blood and a mixed blood, had four children. The *Southern Workman* described Michael as "a descendant of the interpreter and guide of the early French explorer, Pere Marquette," and as "familiar with the old-time festivals and dances of the Chippewas." His sister Susie also attended Hampton, from 1910 to 1912.

Michael wrote that his goal was "to finish school so I can go home and help my people." A student leader at Hampton, he won a second place prize of three silver dollars for an essay he wrote on Wisconsin Chippewas in 1913, the year he graduated.

Following commencement exercises, he and fellow Chippewa graduate George Brown, stopped in Chicago on their way home and spoke on behalf of Hampton at an exhibition, "The World in Chicago."

Although Michael had planned to continue his education at Mt. Hermon in Massachusetts, he became ill enroute to the school and had to return home. By the fall of 1913, he had obtained a position as disciplinarian among the Kiowas at Rainy Mountain School in Gotebo, Oklahoma. Michael later worked on the Rosebud and Cheyenne River reservations in South Dakota. In 1914 he married Emma Sherer, a member of the Lake Winnibigoshish Chippewa band from White Earth and another former Hampton student. Michael also continued his education, including taking a law course while teaching in Oklahoma and training to be an officer in the military during World War I. He later served in a variety of leadership roles at Lac Courte Oreilles.

The first selection by Michael Wolf is an excerpt from an address he made at the Carlisle Indian school on April 2, 1913 and published in the *Red Man,* Carlisle's student publication, the following month. The second two are brief excerpts from letters he wrote to Hampton faculty members, the first to Caroline Andrus, dated January 27, 1914, and the second to Cora Mae Folsom on February 14, 1914, both regarding some of his teaching experiences.

Address by Mr. Michael Wolf

Brothers and sisters, let us realize the fact that we are living in an age of progress and history-making; that upon our shoulders rests the destiny of our people and the solution of the so-called Indian problem. I cannot see why the white people call this the Indian problem. Before the advent of the white people we had no problem. Ever since they landed they have been the problem of this country, and yet they put it on us. My friends, it is up to you and up to me to go out and convince these people that we are the ones to solve this problem. They can't do it. They have tried for the last four hundred years. Think of it! And where have they gone? Every day we are gaining new experiences and making new friends, so let us lay by for future use a knowledge and enthusiasm that we cannot help using for the benefit of our race, if we have any love for it whatever. We, too, have our ambitions and ideals like other people, and as education and experience teach us to sift the good from the bad, to know the right from the wrong, we can hardly escape being a help to our people. Not all men can lead to any great extent, but we can all show by our daily lives that this country holds more for the Indian than can be found within the borders of the reservation, and that education is free to those who want it enough to reach out for it. To be a leader of power one must understand it and respect it, even as we understand and respect the white man and his civilization.

The trouble with some of the boys and girls who return to the reservation—I mean those who have had the chance to live with the white race and see its system of industry and development—when they go back to the reservation they do not respect the old Indian at all. They seem to have lost their Indian hearts in their absence; they have seen too much of the white man to see beneath the shabby exterior. From our ancestors we inherit honesty, bravery, sympathy, religious instincts, and many of the noblest qualities known to mankind. If we can cultivate this our inheritance, while educating our brains and training our hands in the white man's knowledge, we shall be in a better position to understand our people and to help them. When I recall the people who have influenced me the most, I find they are not the ones who talked the most, but those who with singleness of purpose have proved their love and respect for the laws of God and man in their daily lives. I learn from them that to succeed I must have and keep to a strong, steady purpose, have ambition to inspire me, and great faith to carry it out.

My friends, we realize that we have too often been running after shadows and have lost the real meaning of education as it should be applied to civilization. There is a great deal of work to do on our reservations. You know the conditions of those loved ones out [sic] home, as they feel their way through the dark shadows of ignorance, while trying to understand this new life. If there is anything in you or me of service, that is where it should go. Let your deeds prove what you are. Be proud that you are endowed by the All-Wise Creator with the same instinct of life, the same hopes and aspirations as any other man. The white people are watching us from all sides. There are those who know the manhood of the Indian, and who admonish us with paternal voices; and there are those who do not know the integrity of our fathers, but who only see the picturesqueness of our lives. They think our fathers were nothing but savages; they do not know the beautiful philosophy that has been taught us in our teepees by our grandparents.

In the first letter, dated January 27, 1914, Michael wrtote to Hampton faculty member Caroline Andrus of some of his experiences teaching at Rainy Mountain School in Gotebo, Oklahoma:

I have my hands full here at Rainy Mountain. These boys (Kiowas) have been very good, and I am proud of them. Before my time, these young men got in trouble with everyone. They were abused and kicked around like dumb creatures. No one would say to them, "I am your friend." Time and again they tell me how glad they are because I am here. Surely I know what responsibility is now; when I was in school I always looked for a good time and did not pay much attention to my teachers and instructors, but I do wish that, some day, one of my Hampton teachers would walk in and see me at work. When I took charge of my department, the employers told me time and again that the Kiowa boys could not be trusted and that I ought to carry a whip and use it. My method is very simple, and it is not anything more than letting the boys go on their honor, and not one has gone back on his trust. I told the boys and girls (in front of the employees), that I was here to protect and to help them, and I am trying mighty hard to live up to that statement. Of course, there are those folks who think that I am wrong in handling my boys, but the principal likes my way and he says that this is the most pleasant year that he has had.

In the following letter, Michael wrote to Hampton faculty member Cora Mae Folsom on February 14, 1914, about his experiences working with youngsters while at his home [Lac Courte Oreilles]:

My life at home was filled with joy and hard work. I had a class of youngsters that could not be excelled in swear words when I first started to work with them. These youngsters, twenty-two in number could rattle out lumberjack talk just about as fast as a horse can trot. It was a proposition for one to begin, but I finally beat them out by reading athletic stories. My first reading was about Walter Johnson, the star pitcher of Washington, and it was not pleasant to hear one yell out, "The son ___ ___ must have been raised in h__." The next evening I used my wits by using some of the *language*, but of course, it wasn't as tough, then I said, "Let us form a club!" They agreed. I, of course, made the rules. Swearing, tobacco, liquor and gambling were prohibited. And as long as I was home nobody broke his pledge. It was and is remarkable how these chaps changed. We had outdoor sports and rowing when we were not splitting wood for some old people or plowing in our fields. The club is still alive and the president, who was the worst in the lot, writes to me every month. There are only six members at home, the rest are off to school. People at Hampton would be shocked to know that I, a Hampton graduate, swore and used tough language to convert others, but my scheme worked anyhow. You must not tell on me, Miss Folsom, because nobody at Hampton knows and "I would be jumped." Western phrase.

Albert William Cobe

Albert Cobe (*Nachewanaquad*), the full-blood son of Joseph Cobe from Lac du Flambeau Reservation in Wisconsin, was one of the last Chippewa students to enroll at Hampton.[17] Influenced to attend by Hampton alumnus George Brown, he arrived at the school in the fall of 1920 with Thomas Cross, another student from home. By then, Hampton's historic American Indian program, which ended in 1923, had dwindled to a few students.

Albert, who had completed seven years of schooling at the Lac du Flambeau government school, stated that his goal was "to be a farmer." He remained at Hampton until July 19, 1921, when he left "without permission, discouraged because Thos. Cross went." In the fall of that year, *The Southern Workman* reported that the two students were attending the government school at Mt. Pleasant, Michigan.

By 1926, Albert had been attending Haskell Institute in Lawrence, Kansas, for at least two years. At Haskell, he was selected to be a delegate to a World"s Conference for Older Boys in Helsingfors, Finland. In search of financial assistance to cover the expense of supporting "one Indian student delegate, representing the Indian race" at the conference, the supervisor of religious education at Haskell sought a contribution from faculty member Caroline Andrus at Hampton. In his letter to Andrus, the supervisor indicated that Albert, who had attended a statewide conference in Kansas and gave a "remarkable report" on his return to school, was elected president of the "Senior Hi-Y" and had served as a willing worker for the previous two years. The Haskell official further indicated that approximately four-hundred dollars was needed to have Albert travel to Finland with a special tour, which included sightseeing in Norway and Sweden on a forty-day trip.

The selection that follows is an excerpt from an article he authored for the *Y.M.C.A. Bulletin* at Haskell Institute on his return from Helsingfors. In December 1926, Albert wrote Caroline Andrus that he was in his last year at Haskell, completing a teacher's training course. At that time, he hoped to continue his education at an eastern college.

An Indian's Impression of Helsingfors:
Haskell Student Reports on Parliament of Youth

From Haskell Institute YMCA Bulletin XVI/II (November 1926) in Albert Cobe file

Two months ago I was in the midst of 1600 men, a group composing every nation and practically every race of people in the world. The occasion of which I speak was the 19th World's Conference of the Y.M.C.A., held at Helsingfors, Finland, last August.

I was proud to be one of these men as a representative of a great race, the American Indian, not simply as an antique, but as a living, striving human. The Indian being pictured as an antique is fast fading from the horizon and we are more and more being looked upon as being a part of the great march of civilization, regardless of the fact that we are often thought of as not being the result of the long process of evolution according to the theory of Darwin. On one occasion, when attired in my Indian regalia, I was approached by a young German fellow, who, after securing my confidence, stated: "I still do not believe you are a real Indian, because the feather you have on your head is not yours—only tied on." This was one occasion I found it necessary to explain that we Indians came from monkeys as all other human beings— not from chickens.

What results we have achieved from this Conference we cannot say at this time, but this we know; we came to understand the young men of other lands better through our associations in those few short days at Helsingfors. This conference will go far toward uniting the world into a brotherhood, a result which the Y.M.C. A.'s of every land are striving for.

Endnotes

[1] All of the student writings collected here are from the files of each respective student, courtesy of Hampton University Archives. The Chippewa tribal designation used by and about these early students at Hampton is retained in this collection for consistency. Names or terminology in the tribal language, indicated for some of the students, are spelled as they appear in Hampton's archival records. When translations are provided, they are also included.

[2] After the loss of federal support in 1912, Hampton's historic American Indian program continued until 1923. Between 1912 and 1923, students had to work their way through the school and/or obtain support from other sources.

[3] Helen W. Ludlow, ed., *Ten Years' Work for Indians at the Hampton Normal and Agricultural Institute at Hampton, Virginia* (Hampton: Normal School Press, 1888).

[4] Cora Mae Folsom, who had a forty-two year tenure at Hampton, served multiple roles, including teacher, director of pageants, museum curator, and Indian corresponding secretary. Many Indian students corresponded with her and her assistant and eventual successor, Caroline Andrus.

[5] According to the count in the Hampton University Archives, 473 Sioux [Dakota/Lakota] attended the school between 1878 and 1923, the largest tribal group represented. The subheading eventually gave way to inspirational quotations, such as, "A smooth sea never makes a skillful sailor," from numerous sources, including Plato and Shakespeare.

[6] Before *Talks and Thoughts* was established, an Indian student column was published in *The Southern Workman* as part of a page called "Hampton Students' Own," beginning in December 1880.

[7] Private contributors paid for tuition and other training expenses for both African American and Native American

students at Hampton. The school's federal allocation of $167 per American Indian student was applied to board, clothing and related costs.

[8] Both full-blood and mixed-blood students represented linguistic diversity during the period. Among the early Dakota Territory students were those who had learned to write in their tribal language and knew sign language and/or other languages. Cracking Wing, a full-blood Mandan student who arrived at Hampton in 1881, spoke four or five native languages. The evidence suggests that his linguistic skills carried over to his study of English, which began at the school. The Bender siblings had a German-American father, who had learned to speak the family's tribal language. Anna and Elizabeth Bender sang Chippewa songs to audiences in connection with fund-raising efforts on behalf of Hampton. The Hamlin brothers had a French-speaking mother and learned that language as well as Chippewa and English. Early students also served as interpreters in a variety of settings, including Hampton.

[9] Early students also learned English skills from African American students on Hampton's campus.

[10] K. Tsianina Lomawaima, *They Called It Prairie Light: The Story of Chilocco Indian School* (Lincoln: U of Nebraska P, 1994) xvi- xvii.

[11] Lomawaima xii.

[12] See also Kate C. Duncan, "American Indian Lace Making," *American Indian Art Magazine* 5/3 (1980): 28-35, 80. Duncan indicates that Sibyl Carter, an Episcopalian missionary, began teaching lace making to Ojibwe women on the White Earth Reservation in 1890. The enterprise, a cottage industry, expanded to other tribal groups and lasted into the 1930s.

[13] Three of George's drawings appear in Leigh Richmond Miner, "Art-Teaching at Hampton," *The Southern Workman*, XXXII/5 (1903): 219- 224.

[14] For additional information on George Brown and Michael Wolf, see Tim Pfaff, *Paths of the People: The Ojibwe in the Chippewa Valley* (Eau Claire: Chippewa Valley Museum Press, 1993).

[15] The Anishinaabe spelling for Frenchman is taken from R. R. Bishop Baraga, *A Dictionary of the Otchipwe Language* (Minneapolis: Ross & Haines, 1966). Tribal language translations were left out of the original manuscript.

[16] Michael's surname also appears as Wolfe.

[17] Albert Cobe's mother, unnamed in Hampton's records, was identified as Chippewa with "no English name."

►◄►◄

Feather in Hand

Paul M. Kinville

Leon could feel the sweat dripping down his neck where the tie he wore pulled the collar of his shirt tight against his skin. He was standing at the head of the church with his fiance and three other couples, two on their right, and the last on their left. Leon heard his mother call it the Publishing of the Bands. Once received, they would be engaged and then married.

As the priest came forward, his white robes slipping across the marble floor, Leon saw himself in the mirror at the back of the altar. Hair cropped nearly to his scalp, hands folded in front of him. The tie at his throat was choking now, and his dress shirt, the only one he owned, was too small. Still, his girl friend had insisted, and now they were here.

It was a spirit in the window that started it.

He could see, reflected in the mirror, a window in the back of the choir loft. An eagle was circling on the other side of the window, and Leon could see it clearly. He watched it turn three lazy circles and land on the small ledge outside the window. It stood a moment, then sailed up and out of the window's gaze. As it passed from sight, a feather fell, fluttering by the window and out of sight.

He paused a moment, then turned and walked down the aisle. The shocked stares of friends and family crossed the church with him. As he passed, a whisper grew louder behind him and swept him straight through the massive church doors and out into the sunlight.

He walked below the window, outside the choir loft, and scanned the ground for the feather. It was lying ten yards from the church, on the sunlit lawn. Leon bent down and picked it up. A wing feather. He tucked it, quill down, into his shirt pocket, and as he crossed the church parking lot, he pulled the tie from his neck and unbuttoned the collar of his shirt.

When Leon returned home, he found his mother in the kitchen. She was sitting on a stool, speaking into the telephone. "He just came in, I'll call you later." She set the phone down slowly, deliberately and spun in the chair to face him. "You mind telling me what the hell is going on? What were you thinking, just walking out of the church like that?"

The words spit at Leon, and he involuntarily took a step back. His mother slid forward on the stool, ready to spring from her seat. "What happened in there?"

"I saw something that made me change my mind."

His mother's eyes were coal, and her skin was a smoldering red. Thin, angry lines stood out at the corners of her mouth. "What kind of gibberish is that? You saw something? How is that girl gonna feel, how does she feel now, you walking out on her like that? Her father was going to give you a good job at the factory in town!"

"You left her standing there, waiting for you to come back. How do you expect the priest to let you marry her when you walk out in the middle of mass?"

The black dress that she wore was angry, like it had been sad before. Leon remembered the cemetery, when his father died. The weight of his brother, only a baby, in his arms. His mother had sat in front of him, her back shaking slightly, wearing that same dress.

Leon stood, looked out the window above the sink, then back to his mother where she sat on the edge of the stool. She was watching him, waiting. His head fell and he stared at his feet, a pair of old but solid black loafers. He could see the spot on his right toe where a patch of leather had been scuffed off and blackened over with polish.

"I saw a spirit in the window of the church."

His mother shook her head slowly. "She was a nice girl, and her father was going to give you a good job. Are you telling me that you are throwing that away because of something you saw in the window?"

She climbed down from the stool and moved across the kitchen toward him. Leon backed against the sink, his hand gripping the counter behind him. He watched her eyes move across his chest to the feather, poking out of his pocket.

"An eagle left this, at the church. The pipe carriers have always said how important the eagle feather is in council." Leon carefully drew the feather from his pocket, holding the quill gently in his hand. He held it between himself and his mother, like a shield. "This will let me talk, and speak my mind. I want to go back to college and finish school. I think Pop would have liked that."

She reached out and took the feather from Leon and turned it in her hand. "This is an eagle feather. Did your father give you this?"

He told her what he had seen at the church. She stood there silently as Leon explained, and he watched the anger slide off her face. The lines were no longer severe, but Leon could still see their mark, etched onto her face. She stood without speaking, looking down at the feather.

His mother looked at him. "Think hard, Leon. What happened last time, that was terrible. As disappointed as I was, I never blamed you for leaving. But this is a big decision. Make it with your head. And your heart."

She looked away from him, feather in hand. "I think I have some leather left from the bracelet I made for your cousin. If you let me get out of this dress, I'll show you how to tie that feather up, nice."

She handed the feather back to Leon and walked from the kitchen. She paused where the kitchen tile turned into the carpet of the dining room. She said, "Call the girl, Leon."

He watched his mother disappear down the hall, then followed her, turning into the bedroom he shared with his younger brother. He set the feather carefully on his desk and opened the top drawer. He took out a folder, and sitting in the chair, opened it and looked at the top of the first page.

It was a short story he had written for his freshman English class. Scrawled across the top, in angry red ink were the words, "Good. Yours?" He set the first story on the desk and looked at the top of the second. "I cannot give you credit for this. The academic integrity code is very strict about plagiarism," was scrawled in the same red ink. Leon remembered how angry he had been, sitting there in class, reading those comments.

After class, he had followed the professor to his office, confronting him at the door.

"What's this?" Leon showed him the pages.

The professor looked at the pages in Leon's hands and said, "Probably something you copied. I should tell you, I am going to be speaking to the Academic Advisory Council on this matter."

"I wrote these myself. These are mine," Leon had told him, but the professor hadn't believed him.

Leon hadn't known how to type when he entered college, so many nights had been spent sitting up with his father, dictating assignments while his father tapped away on the old typewriter they had picked up at a garage sale. He could remember his father, wearing an old threadbare robe, hunched in the dining room chair, typing the stories out and telling Leon to slow down so he could catch up. Though his father had been sick at the time, the two had stayed up late on many nights, typing out Leon's assignments.

When his father heard what had happened, he called, then visited the school, protesting the entire incident. The last trip his father made to the university had also been the last time his father left the house without assistance. The professor finally retracted his accusation and gave Leon credit for the stories, even apologizing to him in front of the class.

This had been enough for Leon. As his father's health had declined, Leon withdrew from the university, staying home to help take care of him.

Leon put the two stories back in the folder and slid the folder into the drawer. He looked down at the eagle feather lying on the desk, and he imagined the eagle again, circling slowly outside that church window.

The Trap

Armand Garnet Ruffo

When Hammil went to live in the abandoned caboose at the edge of town Lillian Bow didn't think twice about it. Those who knew Hammil saw it coming. Lillian said she never could understand how Hammil could bear to live in that house under those rules. Lillian lived down the street from Hammil's parents and knew what the boy went through as well as anybody. How many times had he come to her front door, only to reappear again exactly one week later. And not by choice, certainly not.

Hammil, thin as a willow, straw yellow hair always immaculately combed, shoes polished and repolished, Sunday clothes always a size too small, shirt cuffs hanging out of his jacket sleeves, wrists hanging out of his shirt cuffs. Hammil, son of Alfred and Rita Schumacher. Lillian remembered the time she'd coaxed him into her house after he'd shoveled the driveway. Mr. Bow had been out on the road, him being a railroad man, and there'd been a snowstorm. She couldn't remember exactly why she'd needed the car, but thinks it was to pick up the sewing machine she'd ordered from Sears. She'd been anxious to try it out.

Must have been a Saturday, about 8 o'clock. She'd been looking out the kitchen window that morning, checking on how much snow had fallen during the night, which was difficult because of the frost on the glass. And there was Hammil with his head bent as if looking for something in the snow walking past in his grey nylon parka, no hat, no mitts, walking in the direction of his home, but like he wasn't going home, like he wasn't going anywhere.

So she tapped her window until her knuckles turned white. Hammil heard the noise, stopped in his tracks, and went over to investigate. She in the meantime had run over to the side door and called.

"Hammil, what are you doing out so early on such a cold morning?"

"Nothing," he said.

"How would you like to earn some money and shovel the drive for me."

"O.K.," he answered, showing no sign of emotion one way or the other, as though his face was frozen shut. She'd lent him a pair of beaded moosehide mitts she'd made herself and a matching scarf and toque she'd bought for her husband at the carnival.

After the work was completed, Hammil knocked a couple of times on the outside porch door without even making an effort to get inside out of the cold. Lillian wasn't sure how long he'd been standing there before she decided to check to see how he was coming along. Even so, it took a lot of coaxing on her part to get him to step into the house.

"Hammil!" she said, "I'm not going to stand out here and argue with you. If you want your money then come in!"

And that was that, he really had no choice. So she made him take off his coat and boots and sit down at the kitchen table for a cup of hot chocolate. She felt bad about him standing outside. Once he'd taken the first sip, she figured he wasn't going anywhere too quickly, especially when he began to ask about the mitts. He'd wanted to know how she made them and where she got the hide. She told him that one of her sons had shot the moose a couple of years ago and that she'd tanned the hide herself, same way her Cree grandmother had taught her. Lillian made it known that she was proud of her traditions.

"But my goodness what a time I had just to get him to sit down," she told her husband over a cup of tea. "And then the moment I paid him he gulped down his drink and said he had to go home. He was polite, mind you."

Mr. Bow didn't say much, only that the boy had done a good job. He often saw Hammil around town but had never spoken to him. And when Lillian finally mentioned the boy's fascination with the mitts, all he said was that the boy could use a good feed of moose meat; he needed some meat on his bones.

Bow was a quiet man who liked flannel shirts with two pockets, one for his tobacco and one for his pens, and who spent all his leisure time outdoors either fishing or hunting. His son Charlie had been his partner in the bush until he'd moved away to Toronto to take a job with Social Services. Bow now went out alone. Stan, his other son, he never saw and often never knew where he was held up. Bow used the word "held up" when he spoke about him, even though Lillian, herself, didn't particularly like it. Stan was a drifter. The odd letter they got usually came from somewhere out west. The last time he'd written, a year come September, he'd made it all the way to Victoria. They'd received a postcard with the picture of the Empress Hotel on the front and the message, "Got a good job. Will send money for family," scratched on the back. Lillian liked to say Stan was unsettled, even troubled. Mr. Bow said nothing.

Lillian supposed the reason that Hammil felt so uncomfortable sitting at her table was because of his weekly campaign on behalf of the Jehovah Witnesses. Something she could not understand. Some of the kids who came to her door were undoubtedly enthusiastic about what they did, no less than the adults, but for Hammil she could tell it was pure torture. He'd stand back, a little behind the others, until one of the older men or women would quickly turn and whisper something in his ear. Only then, as if suddenly jabbed by a cattle prod, did he take a step forward. Once at the door he'd try to get his lines right, "Have you heard the word . . . huh, mankind will only be saved when . . . huh, the word of God . . .

huh . . . ," but he would often stumble over them. Red faced, he would avert his eyes and attempt to start again. "Don't get me wrong," Lillian said. "You know I value a good religious upbringing as well as those people down the street but when a child is clearly sick inside and can't . . . " Here she halted because she was remembering when she made her own two young children go to church no matter how much they protested and resented it. That however was different—never did she make them peddle their religion.

"I'd never do that sort of thing," she added pensively, knocking her cup against her saucer and spilling a bit of tea on the table, and then jumping up to get a dishcloth, her bottom swinging under her flowery printed smock, this heavy woman considered by the community a good woman, a credit to her race.

"We were raised Catholic. I can still remember the village priests coming round and knocking on the door of every Indian and Metis family that happened to miss a mass. I still go," she said. "Feel kind of guilty when I don't."

Mrs. Bow once asked her husband about Alfred Schumacher. She was told that he was a nice enough guy, but doesn't much associate with the other men. A Roadmaster for the C.P.R., Schumacher's job was to make sure his section of the track was maintained. He told the men what they were to do and supervised the work. Over lunch he usually sat in his office with the door closed. The only time he went to the lunchroom was to get a cold drink from the vending machine. Most always he brought coffee in a thermos. When he went out to inspect some track and rode the motor car with the other men, he usually didn't say more than he had to. Mr. Bow said he thought it was because of his poor English.

Mrs. Bow thought it was because religion can make a person self-righteous. Although she didn't really know much about their kind or their religion, she made it clear she didn't care for what she saw.

"It's the way they look at you! Kind of reminds me of those old crows, I mean the old priests. Did I ever tell you about Father Marchland from our village? Now he was one stern priest, a little wizened man who made sure to get his share of sacramental wine."

Lillian herself didn't drink alcohol or at least not very often. When she did have the odd glass of wine on special occasions, such as on birthdays and New Years, one glass usually led to another. Mr. Bow made sure to watch out for her when she got in one of her moods, as he called them. When Lillian thought of drink, she thought of Stan and pictured him passed-out, or yelling at her, or leaving his wife and daughter. Slowly polishing the trophies he won playing hockey and baseball for the town team, she often found herself standing with her eyes closed watching a husky young man with deep brown eyes, nineteen years old. A long time ago.

"Imagine, they won't even let their children have blood transfusions. Afraid they'll go to hell. Seems rather odd, doesn't it?" she said, pouring herself more tea. Once two older Jehovahs managed to talk their way into Lillian's home. She ended up buying two of their little magazines, paid 25¢ a piece. After reading them, she used them to light the fire. Never left much of an impression on her. She did have a few questions, but by the time they came around again she'd forgotten what they were.

That summer when Hammil moved into the caboose, Lillian decided to go pay him a visit. She knew where the railway siding was because each August she went that way to pick blueberries. And since it was now nearly blueberry picking time, she thought that in visiting him she could check on how the berries were coming along. On the table she carefully placed a bag in which there were two jars of her raspberry jam and one she called Heavenly marmalade, made with strawberries and oranges. She quickly scribbled a note to her husband in case he got home while she was still out, stuck it to the fridge, and then put on her walking shoes, as well as her nylon jacket, just in case it got windy or wet.

To her pleasant surprise the afternoon sun broke free of the cloud just as she passed the last house on the road—the one

with the lawn full of javex-bottle weather vanes. There she came
to a stand of birch. The birches brought to mind her grandmother's
sturdy baskets and how she used to soak the strips of bark to
make them pliable and then sew them together.

Between two large trees lay the path. She noticed the rain
had washed away the soil that had been heaped over a metal
culvert, forcing her to make a little leap to get across to the
other side. Once over, her bag of preserves clamped tightly in
her hand, she puffed and patted her chest lightly. Around her,
the birch and pine cut the afternoon into a blend of shadow and
light; soon, however, she came to an opening and proceeded to
walk alongside the tracks. She smiled at the thought that in a
couple of weeks she would return with her plastic pails. She
wondered if her niece, Stan's daughter, would be available to
help; maybe she could even get Charlie's family from Toronto to
come, though this was highly unlikely.

Lillian didn't often think of Charlie. When she did she simply
acknowledged that he was doing well. Since his move he'd had
three promotions. Two years ago she had gone south for a
gallstone operation and had spent a week with Charlie and his
family. She'd been surprised to discover that one family would
need such a big house. Charlie also had two cars and a boat for
Lake Ontario. He wore a suit and tie to the office even when it
was scorching hot outside. After work he came home exhausted
and spent the rest of the evening watching television. He rarely
called.

In the near distance, she spotted two brown boxcars and an
old wooden caboose; all three were pulled off onto a rusty siding
used as a depot for junked equipment. In flaking white paint,
one of the boxcars said C.P.R., the other Algoma Central. As she
neared them, she began to call Hammil's name, but her voice
sounded shrill so she stopped and swallowed.

Now that she had arrived, her enthusiasm waned and she
wondered if she was even doing the right thing by coming out
here. Maybe Hammil wanted to be left alone? Maybe she should
have waited until she'd heard from him? In her confusion, she

stumbled and nearly twisted her ankle on one of the hunks of slag strewn on both sides of the tracks.

As she drew closer, she heard Hammil's voice. At first she thought he was talking to someone, until she could hear him better and realized that he was singing, or at least trying to. What she heard she would later describe as almost a plaintive chant. It was strange coming from him, because it was like hearing the past, something Lillian might have heard as a little girl but from voices who knew the music and its meaning. She moved cautiously past the two boxcars and towards the caboose. The sound stopped.

"Hammil," she called. "It's me, Mrs. Bow!"

There was silence. Finally he called out to her.

"Come in, Mrs. Bow." The door facing her swung open.

"Hammil, you've got to help me. I can't make it up on my own. It's too high," she said. The boy now made his appearance on the small platform of the caboose. He looked much the same as he had the winter before, except that his hair was now longer. There was a red hanky tied around his forehead. He bent down, first relieved her of the bag in her hand, and then took hold of one of her arms to help hoist her up onto the platform. He led the way inside.

She noticed pictures from a calendar tacked on the walls: a bear, a wolf, a moose. She was impressed. "You've turned it into a little home," she said, between gulps of breath. She dropped herself onto one of the wooden benches that lay on both sides of a little table tucked under a window.

"Nice place you've got Hammil. It reminds me of the cabin I used to stay in when I went trapping with my father. Many years ago." Lillian wasn't sure exactly what she should say to the boy because she really didn't know him. She did know, however, that he couldn't possibly live in a caboose. Maybe she could help him cope with his parents and, in so doing, convince him to return home? "I've brought you a few things. Hope you like jam." she said.

Hammil thanked her. He too wasn't saying much, besides asking her if she wanted something to drink, pop, maybe. He offered to make a fire in the little woodstove in the corner and boil water for tea. She said a drink of water would be nice.

"Why'd you come," he asked unexpectedly, bringing a canteen to the table and taking a seat.

"I wanted to see how you were getting along," she answered. "You know I've got two sons and they come to visit me."

"What about you, Hammil? Are you going to visit your mother? Why did you run away? If you tell me, maybe there's something I can do to help?"

"Just didn't want to stay there anymore."

"Well there must be a reason?" she asked.

"Because I know I'm going to hell so what's the use," he blurted out.

Lillian immediately recollected those Sunday scenes which the boy had been forced to go through on her front step.

"What do you mean you're going to hell?"

"That's what they told me."

"Who told you?"

"Everybody. But I don't care. I'm not going back," he added defiantly.

Mrs. Bow wasn't surprised. She'd heard the story many times before, as loud and repetitive as the cawing of a huge bird. "When I was a little girl they used to say that to me too, Hammil."

"So what did you do?" He now pointed up to his bow and arrow hanging behind her, over the door she had entered. "See that, I'm going to learn how to trap and hunt and live in the bush. So what did you do?" he repeated.

Mrs. Bow now stared through the window. For a moment she saw the little cabin that had once been part of her childhood, marten and beaver pelts stretched across the front of its walls. That image quickly faded and her eyes settled on a patch of shadow clinging to the branch of a birch tree, which immediately brought to mind an ominous crow, wearing what looked like a white collar, craning its neck towards her, aware of her presence.

In thought, she instinctively fidgeted with the brown bag on the table. The rustling like a spring snapped her attention back to Hammil. She turned back towards the boy and asked him if he knew how to set a trap. "I can teach you," she said. "Yes, you must learn about traps if you're going to survive." There was no way to tell the boy that, just as so many others before her, she had paid heed to the word of the crows.

Sage Dreams

Danielle M. Hornett

The tired, rusty bell over the door clunked her arrival. The reservation's only mini-mart was empty except for the two elder cribbage buddies huddled over a beat-up card table at the back of the long room. Amanda's uncle glanced at her and waved.

"Saving on electricity?" she asked Winky. "Or is that game so exciting you hadn't noticed it was getting dark?" She found the light switch. The fluorescent hummed and blinked a few times before catching. Taking a Coke from the pop machine and grabbing a chair that had seen better days, Amanda joined the men.

"Turn them on," Winky grumbled pointing his lips toward the lights, "and folks'll think I want their good business. Can't ya see we're busy?" He scratched the stubble of his day-old beard and studied his cards.

"Howdy gal, " Uncle Dan said. "What'cha been up to? I called earlier but ya musta been bummin'." He peered at her over his glasses. "Ya ain't been out slippin' around with your new admirer now, have ya?" He turned to his sidekick, "Don't know if I mentioned it, Winky, but Punky Jakes was droolin' over my niece here like a love sick puppy over at church last Sunday." He chuckled.

"Ya mean a *St. Bernard* puppy, don't ya?" Winky came back. "Remember what a string bean that young-un was. Wouldn't know it to look at him now, would ya?"

"You guys are disgusting!" Amanda scolded. "I came by 'cuz I wanted some company, but now I'm not so sure." The old men hooted. "As a matter of fact," she continued, "I've been at Annie's. But knowing the rez hot line, you already knew that." Dan and Winky snorted confirmation. "Noah is doing a healing tomorrow night at her place and wants to know if you two'd like to come. He wants Ben and Yemmy to come too."

"Lord, help me," Winky wheezed a laugh. "Been a long time since I been to one of them things. "Course we'll go. If Noah needs us, we'll be there . . . right, Dan?"

Dan grunted his surprise. "How'd that happen?" he asked. "Can't imagine Annie agreeing to anythin' like that. She never was one for Indian ways,"

"JR talked her into it. I saw him and Winnie last night. They're worried sick and so am I. JR said that his ma's been going downhill even after the doctor assured her they got all the cancer. I almost didn't recognize her the first time I stopped by." She took a long sip of Coke.

"Good for JR," her uncle said. "Annie never could say no to that boy. Guess 'cuz he's always been the man of the family. His pa's been drunk and not worth a shit since day one." Amanda winced. Her uncle usually didn't talk about people, even if they were Neil Butler. "That man could make babies," he grumbled, "but not take care of 'em. I always felt sorry for that Annie girl."

Both Winky and Amanda waited for Dan to continue. When he didn't Amanda told the old men about the spirit at Annie's and what she knew of Noah's plans to send it away.

"He said you shouldn't fast because of your diabetes," she told her uncle.

"I know. I know." Dan folded his hands, any interest in the game lost for the evening. "Winky, why don't you donate some corn and I'll fix menomin. I still got enough to feed a hungry dozen or so."

"I got fruit too," Winky said. "Dang, if this ain't the most excitin' thing that's happened to me for a long time." He smiled his lopsided jack-o-lantern smile and leaned back in his chair and lit a cigarette. Amanda left the old men trying to outdo each other with stories of past ceremonies; she doubted they even knew she was gone.

Miss-Never-Late had spent more time than she should have looking for cloth for the tobacco ties Noah wanted. Finally she ran into WalMart for remnants and arrived at his cabin by seven thirty. As she stepped into the small porch, Niijii opened his eyes, then closed them again without barking. Amanda guessed she'd been accepted by the shaggy no-breed guarding the door.

In an uncommonly serious mood, Noah smudged each of them, the cloth, and finally the tobacco before they began working on the ties. After tying up her fingers a few times, Amanda learned to twist her wrist, just so, in order to secure the tobacco solidly into the cloth squares. While they worked, Noah told her what she needed to know to help him at sunrise and in the afternoon. When they finished he insisted they rest, saying she could sleep in his room and he'd take the couch.

"I'll wake you just before sun-up," he said between yawns.

Amanda's body was ready for sleep, but her mind raced with thoughts about the ceremony and her place on the reservation after fifteen years in Milwaukee. The sage smoke smell in her hair reminded her of Great-uncle Hobo, and her grandma, . . . and of the first time she'd visited Noah. He'd walked her to her car and his braids had slipped into the open window—was that really just a few weeks ago? She could still hear Niijii snoring softly outside the bedroom door. He'd adopted her this evening after Noah let him back in.

"Is this it, Gramma?" the little girl asked as she picked up a piece of sage. She studied its wooly, greenish-blue leaves before handing it to the old lady in the red flowered dress and faded blue shawl.

Her grandmother took the sage with one hand and reclaimed the hand of the five-year-old Amanda with the other. They continued down the rutted path behind the cabin.

"Yes, Manda, that's it. Isn't it beautiful?"

"It don't smell so boo-tiful," the little girl said. Because she loved these times when Gramma and Hobo would take her to the woods with them, and they always smelled of burnt sage, it made

her feel safe. Sometimes the sage was used for smudging or medicine, she knew. But often her grandmother would tie it in small bundles with réd string and put them on the window sills in the house—for protection, she'd say. Gathering new sage was an important chore and Amanda was proud to be part of it.

Slipping her free hand easily into her Uncle Hobo's crinkled, dry one, Amanda squinted up at Gram's brother. He was the oldest person she knew—probably even as old as God, she thought. Hobo never made her feel like a bother like some grown-ups did. And he had such a wonderful face—all wrinkled like Gramma's prunes. Amanda scrunched up her face, wondering if she'd look like that some day.

The two elders spoke only in Ojibwe. That was okay even if Amanda didn't understand what they were saying. She knew it was hard for Hobo to speak English. He'd try, but his words got all mixed up with Indian. When she couldn't understand, he'd smile his toothless smile and make hand gestures that sometimes helped.

Hobo was very thin, stood ram-rod straight, and always walked as though he was on his way to someplace special. Amanda tried to walk like him, stretching her little legs as far as she could. His long white hair was tied at the back of his neck in a pony tail and held by a brown leather strip. As he walked, she watched the tail bounce with a life of its own. Amanda tossed her head from side to side, feeling her braids hit against the sides of her shoulders. Sometimes she could talk Mom into a pony tail like Uncle Hobo's, but not too often. Her hair liked to slip out of the tail and look "lazy," as Mom called it. Better to have braids so it would behave.

Sometimes just she and Gramma would gather sage, then Gram would tell stories of "the old days" as they walked slowly over the dirt road that led from the back of the pond to the place where the sage grew. As hard as she tried, Amanda couldn't imagine her old grandmother as a young girl and Uncle Hobo as a young boy riding horses through these woods. What her mind saw were child bodies with the heads of her gramma and Uncle Hobo as she knew them now. Even at her age, Amanda recognized this as a silly picture, and stifling a giggle, she'd struggle to act grown up, knowing that's what Gramma'd want.. At times like this Gram would look down at her and smile, like she was reading her mind. Hobo could do that too. Amanda thought that probably was something all old people could do.

She woke to rapping on the door. "Amanda? Time to get up." She struggled to respond, the dream world and the real world confused in her half-sleep state. Noah tapped his knuckles against the door again and waited until she grunted. "Dress warm, it's chilly out there." He paused, "Are you awake?"

"Yeah . . . be right there." The faint smell of sage filled Amanda with longing for her grandmother and great uncle. It didn't feel like thirty years since she'd seen them or twenty since she'd left the rez for college. Jumping out of bed, she threw on jeans and a sweatshirt. As she ran her fingers through her hair, the screen door slammed. Noah was already back outside.

She brushed her teeth with her finger and gulped down a glass of orange juice, then grabbed her jacket and followed Noah. A fire flickered in the small pit he'd dug in the back yard. He was warming his hands over the flames. Amanda tripped, nearly falling over pieces of sod he'd removed to make the hole.

"Careful," he said not looking at her. "I'll put that back when I'm finished. You'll never know we dug here. That way we won't scar mother earth. The sun will be up in fifteen minutes," he said, looking at the still dark sky in the east.

Amanda watched the sky begin to lighten, remembering how Hobo had explained that the space between the spirit world and the human world was thinnest now—the best time to communicate with the spirits.

"Pray with me," Noah said.

He pulled a pipe from his bag. "My tools," he grinned at her. "This bag holds everything I need." He handed her the pipe while he dug in the bag again. "Got special tools for special jobs," he grunted and squinted into the bag. "I can't always find what I need right away . . . but . . . everything is in here . . . someplace." He finished digging and sat back on his heels. "Ah . . . asemaa, special-made from red willow for ceremonies." He held some out to her. "Hobo taught me how to make it. Someday I'll teach you."

Amanda was filled with wonder at the connection between her and Hobo, and Hobo and Noah; that Noah's teacher had been her great uncle and in turn, Noah was teaching her. The circle continued.

He put the other things away and took the pipe from her. He held it skyward and prayed in Ojibwe. He gave the pipe back. "I want you to fill it."

"I don't know how." She shivered, sweat peppered her forehead despite the cold.

"Then it's time you learn," he said in that old-time voice that went with all important instruction.

The sky began to lighten behind the pines as he led her through each step. She repeated what he told her to say in English while he prayed in Ojibwe; their breath pierced the cool, predawn air with ghostly puffs of punctuation.

First they thanked the Creator for their lives and the new day. Then they prayed for clear minds and good thoughts to help them face the duties ahead. They asked for their spirits' helpers to come. They explained, each in their own language, what was happening at Annie's and what they planned to do. They prayed for help to send the lost spirit home. Noah pulled the other tools out of his bag and asked blessings for each of them. By the time they finished the prayers, red streams of morning sun filtered through the trees.

"Can you feel the spirits?" he asked. "They're all around us."

"I felt the air pressure change," she whispered. "Did the spirits do that?"

An eagle called from overhead. Noah smiled. "Migizi just answered you," he said. They watched the Grandfather's messenger circle twice before moving out of sight behind the tall pines. Amanda saluted the Grandfather's sign—his messenger.

"You're gonna do okay," Noah told her.

Amanda added a silent prayer for courage—and hoped she looked more sure of herself than she felt.

Noah added wood to the fire. "We'll keep this going all day and take the coals to Annie's. Fire's an important part of the ceremony."

Amanda looked around, took a deep breath and choked on the morning-crisp air. "I don't remember if I was ever up this early," she laughed and cleared her throat. "We almost beat the birds up." She nodded toward a red-winged blackbird watching them from his perch on a thin reed at the edge of the trees. Its new-day whistle filled the air.

"You'll be happy to know I saw a couple of robins in the yard last week," he said. "They looked like scouts to me." She returned his grin. His humor was returning; this was the Noah she knew.

By noon Amanda was exhausted. She sat by the fire resting her head on her up-drawn knees.

"Go take a nap," Noah said. "I'll get you up in an hour or so."

Too tired to argue with him, she went inside, kicked off her shoes and threw herself across the bed. Niijii stood next to her, his head on the covers, eyes begging. She fell into a dreamless sleep before she could put her hand out to pet him.

Amanda woke three hours later and looked outside. Noah still squatted near the pit. The fire was almost out. He looked up when she pushed the screen door open

"Get that bucket near the door there," he directed with his chin. "That's how we'll carry the fire to Annie's."

She did as she was told, ignoring the concern that nagged at her. Noah should know what he was doing, she hoped, as he shoveled the hot coals into the bucket.

"Here." He gave her the keys to the Bronco. "Go open up the back for me."

"Won't that start a fire?" she asked.

"I hope so, that's why we're taking it," he said. "Or do you think the Bronc needs a heater?"

"Noooooo. I mean in the car. The bucket's hot, won't it start the carpet on fire?"

"Run grab that piece of plastic from under the stoop. That should take care of any problem."

Amanda dug under the small porch and found a broken piece of carpet protector, the kind she used under her chair at the office. She put it on the floor in the back of the Bronco and eyed it warily as Noah put the bucket on it. Even with its wide bottom, she was sure the bucket would tip when they went around the corners. Noah shook his head and grinned.

"Don't worry," he said. "The spirits are with us."

"Maybe so, but . . . do they want us taking foolish chances?" she asked.

He laughed at her and went to the unused garage out back, returning with an old washtub. "This won't tip," he said. Carefully, he poured the coals from the bucket into the tub. She shook the edge of the tub—it sat solidly in place. "Satisfied?" he asked.

"Satisfied," she told him.

They arrived at Annie's just as Dan and Winkie were walking up the rickety steps, each loaded down with a large box. The Vincents' and JR's cars were already there. Dan walked by the door to give Amanda a hug.

"I'm proud of you," her uncle said. "And Hobo would be too," he added, as though he were reading her concern about her place in the ceremony.

Amanda blushed and hugged him back. "And I'm proud of you."

"Hey, what about me?" Winky cried.

"I'm proud of you too," she said and smiled at him.

"No, I don't care about that," he groused. "Where's my hug, gal?"

She hugged the old man. The tic in his eye was worse this afternoon. It was one long, continuous wink.

JR met them at the door. The kitchen smelled of meat, pies and fry bread. Annie was sitting at the table staring out the window. Butts smoked down to the nubs overflowed the stained glass ashtray in front of her. She was dressed; no torn chenille robe and blue plastic beach thongs today. Annie's hair had been brushed but still hung dull and stringy around her thin face. Dark circles emphasized her green eyes and classic cheek bones.

Her fingers worried the top button of the oversized denim shirt she wore.

"Might as well get started," Noah said. "Sundown in about twenty minutes and we better be ready. I'll get the coals for the fire. Come on, Amanda. JR?" JR nodded. "We'll meet you out back," Noah said.

As she came around the corner of the house, Amanda stopped. A replica of Noah's pit was dug into Annie's yard—same shape, same size. JR walked next to it.

"How did he know to do that?" she asked Noah. "Did you call him?"

Noah shook his head. "Didn't have to. He was told what he needed to do when he prayed at sun-up.

Our spirit helpers tell us everything we need to know if we just listen and believe. JR's a listener, and a believer."

In a few minutes Noah and JR had the fire blazing and the three went back inside.

"Amanda will smudge everyone here and then do the house while I set up my altar in Annie's bedroom," Noah said. "Amanda," he turned to her. "Do that room first." He pointed with his lips to the back room. "Then come do them." He tipped his head toward those in the kitchen. "When you finish, join me."

Amanda nodded and took the shell he held out. She recognized this ritual for protection; Gramma had done it often. She lit the rolled ball of sage with the wooden match Ben came up with, and blew lightly to help it catch. Noah took the shell and smudged her. Following his example, she smudged him. He motioned with his chin for her to go. She went to the bedroom alone.

She directed the sage smoke into each corner, around the windows and doors, under the bed that was made today, and in the closet, leaving the door open. The presence hung heavily in the room and stirred the air as she smudged. The hair raised on Amanda's arms and the back of her neck She was glad to return to the kitchen. Without a word, Noah took his bag and went to Annie's bedroom.

The four elders, Annie, JR, and his wife Winnie, stood in a circle around Amanda, waiting. She smudged them one by one, starting with Annie.

"I'm so glad you're here, my friend. Thank you. I've missed you so." Annie's voice broke.

Amanda put her arms around her frail cousin. "Please help her," she prayed silently as she brushed sage smoke over Annie's head, and up and down her body with miigwan, her feather.

That done, Amanda smudged every nook and corner of the house, coming back to the kitchen once for more sage. Finished, she went to the bedroom where Noah had already begun. The room smelled of bear medicine and cedar. Unseen hands slipped an invisible shawl lightly around her shoulders as she entered the room. Noah ignored her so she knelt on the worn linoleum, slightly behind his left shoulder, resting her weight on her heels, waiting for a sign or a word. White and blue spirit lights zipped and danced around his head.

"There's more than one," he whispered. "Can you feel them?"

Amanda nodded. A male presence was strong, and there was at least one, softer, female presence. Her eyes were drawn to the left up into the farthest corner near the ceiling. She frowned.

"Yep, that's where he is," Noah said. "The others are afraid of that one. They're hiding. They're willing to go, I think, but he won't let them." Noah continued praying, first in Ojibwe, then in English. Using Annie's Indian name, he told the spirits to leave her house; told them they didn't belong here, told them they couldn't stay. He repeated this four times.

The air began moving, so slowly at first Amanda barely felt it, but it rapidly got stronger. She looked at Noah who didn't seem to notice. She felt, rather than heard, a high-pitched buzzing coming from somewhere inside the house.

"Go open the back door," Noah said. "Then stand aside. Keep the others away from the door too."

She moved to do as she was told. Halfway to her feet, she heard Noah laugh. "No, she can't go with you. She has to stay here. . . . *you* go!"

Amanda looked at him, confused. She was still half standing.

"That male spirit insists you go with him," Noah told her, chuckling. "Wanna take a trip?"

"You're kidding me, right?" she whispered.

He turned away from her and spoke to the spirit in the corner. This time the laughter had left his voice. It was stern, almost unrecognizable. "*Because she's alive,*" Noah said. "She still has many things to do in this world. She belongs here. You don't! You're not alive. . . . you can't stay. It's time for you to move on! She stays. . . . you go! She stays, *you* go."

Amanda's cramping legs began to shake. She knelt again. "What's happening?" Her constricted windpipe allowed only a squeak to escape. She wasn't sure he'd even heard her. Amanda gulped, cleared her throat, and tried again. "Noah, what the *hell* is going on?"

Again, Noah didn't answer. He repeated his earlier words to the spirit, then spoke, for what felt like a long time to Amanda, in Ojibwe. "Okay," he finally said. "Do as I told you. Go open the back door and stand back—way back. Tell the others to stay back too. But *you* especially. This guy still wants you. . . . *Go!*" he ordered when she hesitated.

She did what she was told, glancing backward as she limped from the bedroom babying muscles strained by her crouch. In a few minutes Noah followed, urging something forward, something invisible . . . guiding it toward the door with his eagle fan. He was praying in Ojibwe. A gust of wind ruffled Amanda's pant legs as he passed. He indicated he wanted the others to help. The four elders joined Noah's prayers.

On the back porch, Noah motioned to Amanda to stand beside him. They watched as JR stepped back quickly as the cold wind whirled past him and pushed tongues of flames out in several directions from the center of the fire.

"That should do it," Noah said. His voice was tired but his black eyes twinkled. JR looked at them for a second, then raised his fist in a silent gesture of triumph. He joined them on the steps. Together they went into the kitchen where everybody was hugging everybody else and laughing, wiping away tears.

"Can't ya feel the difference already, Ma?" Winnie asked. "I can! What a relief. Thank you Noah, thanks, Amanda. You don't know what Annie means to me." Suddenly the big woman's shoulders shook. She turned her back and sobbed into the crook of her elbow.

Yemmy put her arthritic arms around her. "We all feel it, Winnie. Annie will get better now, I just know it. You're gonna have her for a while yet."

JR hugged his wife. Together they went and sat next to his ma. Both of Annie's hands clamped on to her son's good one, unshed tears making her eyes shine. She smiled crookedly at the daughter-in-law.

Dan and Winky slapped each other on the back. "Well, when we gonna eat?" Winky asked. His tic had slowed considerably.

"Right now!" Dan answered. The two old men began setting the table with the paper plates Winky'd bought. Still sniffing, Winnie pulled venison out of the oven. JR grabbed a brown, grease-stained bag of fry bread off the top of the refrigerator. With Winky's vegetables and fruit and Dan's wild rice, the feast was ready in five minutes. Ben offered thanks for the meal and ceremony, then Annie filled a dish of food as an offering for the spirits who'd come to help.

Noah took it to the other room. "Don't want to put this outside. . . . that guy might see this as an invitation and decide to come back," he said. Amanda threw him a look he chose to ignore.

The celebrants ate like they'd been fasting forever. Even Annie. Noah livened up the already jubilant atmosphere in the kitchen with his story about Amanda's spirit admirer. As much as Amanda wanted to enjoy the story with the others, she was too busy nervously watching the door, unaware that she was chewing on her thumbnail.

By nine-thirty the meal was finished and Annie's kitchen cleaned. Amanda's whole body screamed for sleep. The elders took turns yawning loudly; no one objected when Noah said, "Time to rest, we all earned it."

Noah and Amanda waved at Dan and Winky as they drove off in Winky's noisy pickup. Amanda noticed that he still hadn't fixed his tail light. Noah turned to Amanda. "I'll call you Thursday morning and we'll talk about a movie. Right now I'm too tired to even think, " he told her at her car. "You'll sleep tomorrow, and so will I."

"I won't sleep all day!" she said.

"Sure you will," he laughed. "It's okay, I will too." He hugged her quickly. "Sweet dreams."

"You too," Amanda said. She yawned, then smiled at him. "Well, maybe you're right."

Amanda couldn't help herself. As he walked to his Bronco she called to him.

"Noah?"

He turned.

"You were kidding about that spirit, weren't you? I mean, that really didn't happen did it?"

"Yeah, it did. Probably I shouldn't have said nothing. I didn't think it would scare you so bad."

"Why wouldn't it?" She hadn't meant to sound so nasty. "I mean, well, couldn't he follow me home?"

Noah walked back to her. "No, he's gone. Look," he put his hand on her shoulder. "I'm sorry I told you. It's just that when you came into the room, he wanted to negotiate, to delay, but he liked you too. I thought you'd enjoy that. Not everyone can turn a spirit's head." He laughed and brushed a stray lock of hair from her face. "But remember, a spirit can't take a living being any place that human doesn't want to go. So stop worrying." He watched her face. "You gonna be all right?"

"Yeah, I guess. It was just a shock, is all." The night eagle, an owl, hooted—a sound that had scared a young Amanda until Hobo assured her that owls were simply the Creator's night messengers and their cry was just to let people know they were around. The unseen hand tugged at the invisible shawl reminding her of the protection that was still around her. She felt Hobo's presence in the night and smiled.

"I'm okay," she said. Suddenly she knew she was.

Dreaming Home

⟨XI⟩X⟨

The Dream of the Golden Arrow

Gordon Henry, Jr.

When Ahwosso spoke of big casino dreams, some of us thought we could light up the whole visible world, as far as we knew it. To be sure, we rarely doubted Ahwosso on such matters. Over the years we had known him to be fair and just. Since he was a listener who had a balanced way of letting people speak and since he had a way of weighing decisions, without the nepotic burdens of a tribal leader, or the cashed out mentality of the model American politician, we trusted his motives. Some people believe this balance came from the season of his birth: he was one of those people born between changes, in a time of cool transition between the inviting song of live summer and the brusque wail of sleeping dead winter; he was an Autumn child.

Also, Ahwosso seemed capable of walking between us. Traditionals liked him. He participated in Big Drum and Powwows and he sweat with the old men. Political radicals liked him, he supported their rallies, gave them permission to use tribal facilities for meetings, offered them free xerox privileges and he listened to them, sometimes acting on their views when he thought they were right. Christians liked him, too. He was baptized. He made fry bread for socials and he donated venison every year for the Methodist camp meeting—he even sat and listened to the preachers at those meetings.

Some people looked back to a complicated lineage and his upbringing to explain him. Ahwosso, like his paternal grandmother, was descended from Eagle dodem people. He was also descended from fur trade marriages on his mother's side. So, Ahwosso was neither short nor tall, wide nor thin, dark nor light and he never dressed in ways which would consistently point to him being for or against someone or something. Even when he became chairman he still wore rummage sale clothes. Most often that meant a dark suitcoat with a plaid shirt underneath (in fall and winter) and tee shirts with "It's a Fine day in White Clay," written over the top of the White Clay tribal logo (in spring and summer). Almost always he wore those secondhand clothes with jeans and steel toe workboots. "In case I got to put my foot into someone or something," he would say.

Still the clothes fit. Ahwosso was after all almost an orphan. His father died in Nam, on a recon mission. His mother, she went urban and dropped him off when she exchanged vows with a Finnish carpenter. He was raised then, by his grandmother, Obahbaum, an old Bush woman, who chopped wood, raised a garden, gathered maple syrup and berries, trapped rabbits and hunted partridge, deer, and sometimes moose. Even into his adult years Ahwosso dreamt of her rhubarb pie and rabbit stew. Sometimes in the morning when he reached into his bathroom sink to gather water into his flat white palms, he would see himself, as a child, reflected in the enamel wash basin just outside the door to the kitchen of the old woman's cabin. She used to call him Geeshisohns (Little Sun) and every Sunday she held him to her breast before she sent him down the road to the Holy Family Catholic church. There he was inducted into the John the Baptist Society and once in, he immediately organized a group of boys and girls to go around helping elders and disabled people of White Clay. The John the Baptist Society youth ran errands, fed animals, weeded gardens, cooked, carried wood, lit woodstoves, and delivered books among other things.

More than that we loved Ahwosso. He was humble, gracious, and deep with humor—which he cast with such undecipherable monotony that he sometimes left us not knowing whether to laugh or change our attitudes. Further, he exuded a light, an aura of his own love for us which he demonstrated daily in his concern for the welfare of our children and our elders. Besides all that, we saw results in our day-to-day lives. Under Ahwosso's gentle leadership the council had done a lot, for the people, with the people. Over seven years we had built a preschool, an elementary school and a high school; we had staffed those schools with native people and we had developed curricula, with input and feedback from traditional and Christian, from elders and children, from BIA and AIM operative, from agnostic and burned-out shinaabes alike. We had also opened the Thunder Day clinic, where traditional healers worked side by side with medical doctors. It was true we had done most of this with money from gaming, first from bingo and then a casino. But all the positive change, though funded by gambling, had been part of a larger vision, of reconciliation and cooperation among all the different reservation communities.

Still, the big light idea had come to Ahwosso the way many of his big ideas came to him, through his wife—the one person he learned to trust without question, especially when the answers came to her through the spirit, like a child through a sunlit doorway. Sophia was the daughter of Oshaawaanong, who was descended from Geezhigoong Kamikag. She was descended from a long line of tribal dreamers, some of whom, like her sisters, needed no more than a cup of warm swamp tea and a half breed romance novel to enter the world of spiritual dreams. In that world the dreamers became a part of a drama of seeing and speaking which gave them foresight and allowed them to enter those invisible implicit facets of gesture, face and material presence which most of us have neither the openness nor the time to encounter. When she slept Sophia spoke in the spirit, a rapid alchemy of tongues, part Ojibwe, part Pottawottami, part Canadian French and part fur trade English. In his wife's case, if somebody was awake there when she was sleeping, they could hear what she was saying about the dream. From English Ahwosso gave us this version of Sophia's dream of the golden arrow.

"My wife she had a big vision. She had a bath and she fell asleep there. Scared the hell out of me when I opened the door. I went in there and it was like she was floating. I knew what was coming then because every time she dreams like that the spirit gives notice, sings a little song real fast. I won't sing that for you, though, I don't want to take anything away from the spirit."

At this point the seven elders who we invited to every council meeting nodded favorably, Ahwosso was right again.

"But after the song, my wife talked of a big golden light on the highest hill. She said the light was hundreds of feet high and as wide as eight Chevies, so it shined out in every direction for people, for all to see. She also said the light was shaped like an arrow and that arrow would tell people that we were here and that we had something to give people. Then my wife woke up and began shaving her legs."

Ahwosso went on, "I was thinking about this, and this dream is right. When we make our casino here, we need to build a big light in the shape of an arrow. This light will indicate our presence here and it will lead people to our casino. People from miles around will come to our casino. This should also be the name of our casino—the golden arrow. In this way we will be connected inside and outside to the world of dreams and our vision of the future will be perfectly aligned to those dreams. With the consent of the council I'd like to make a resolution which calls for building the golden arrow and which simultaneously calls for the creation of our new, larger casino.

Leaving Skin

One month after the Golden Arrow Casino opened, Ahwosso left his skin. He turned off the road from the tribal offices in White Clay and started west to Megis, on the road to the Casino. He wanted to go home, where his wife Sophia stirred ground venison into a macaroni dish. He wanted to arrive as he always arrived, his blue pickup dancing up the gravel drive; there the yellow dog would stand without barking and follow him as he went inside of the red house in the village where his grandmother raised him, long before he saw her go into the ground four summers back.

He thought then of night falling, of being alone with Sophia.

He thought of her warm skin, of her breath naming him over his own skin as they drew each other beyond the turnings and embrace of body upon body. But he took the road west instead and entered the refuge, distracted by visions of home, inattentive to the country tune whispering through the radio, from the reservation station, tired of chasing down people and relatives, especially his brother-in-law, Boose, the keeper of the Golden Arrow.

As he thought of his brother-in-law, the animal appeared, suddenly, from the side of the road, like a gust of instant fog, huge and white. After impact he saw the animal bend, twisting up and over the hood of his truck, the face, antlers, pushing forward into the windshield, one huge dark eye of the animal drawing toward him alive with light, as the windshield exploded in specks of glass, into dusk sequences of light and fluttering coruscations, like small charges given off in memory, by memory, until remembrance acts on its own, at random, with the force to call image, until Ahwosso felt himself drawn backward, away from himself, a rolling ball of energy, beyond his own limp shape in the vehicle. He looked back, tried to reconnect with the shape in the truck, with the one he knew was himself, the dark eyes, the dark hair, under the hat with the tribal logo. He tried to go back into the form of the man, staring vacantly, through a jagged space, to a world turned on its side, but somehow he could not meet himself and he passed over the truck on its side; he passed over where the broken white moose had stumbled back into the ditch and he felt himself moving, traveling away from his skin, toward the sun, on the road into the sun.

Ahwosso—Past

I am alone and poor, seeking a dream to carry me, a hawk wind, or a bird with a human voice, clear, resolute, with instruc- tions, or an act of some kind, a motion in trees, a moving star, a band of light on a stone face, or a painted old man, or woman, or child, walking toward me, human to bear to human. These things may not come, but I wait, alone and poor.

I chose to blacken my face with sweat fire ashes, seeking space where undergrowth shadow blossoms into ridge hill, morning light, where I find an ascendable arboreal ancestor, as invisibly earth rooted as visibly sky branched, less like a family than an explosion of dark heavy aspirations, checked by wind crossing, the weight of birds, the seed end of flowers, the brittle end of leaves.

Who will you become
will you become
What name
will you carry
What song
will you bring back
Who will you become

I am tired of dreaming, tired of the hot wind, the cold wind, who takes away my face with each breath.

The animal came first, out of the mist, separating from vaporous dawn, running, full of life, then struck suddenly inert, it fell, legs buckling, the body turning, even as it met earth, on an incline and gave up in gasps, through the smoking wound in the flank, through air from black nostrils.

The old man walked up later, to the crest of the incline where the animal had fallen. When he came to the deer, he set down his rifle and took a pack from his back. He spoke words I could not hear from where I sat in my nest in the tree. Then he moved the animal, placed it on the incline on its back, the head uphill. The old man made his way around to the animal head, he kneeled and looked into the eyes. He went on talking as he drew out tobacco, held it to the sky. He sprinkled the offering on the ground, in front of the eyes of the dead animal. He stood then and dropped more tobacco along the body, over the head. He covered the head with black cloth, went silent for a moment and he began singing. This much I could hear, though parts were whispers and parts were drawn into thin wind breaths with the calls of crows and whistling of jays.

Waskesh
it has been
a good life
Washkesh
i give thanks
for your life.
Waskesh
for all the days
you have lived
Washkesh
i give thanks
Washkesh
for the good life
you have lived
i give thanks

Then the old man drew a knife blade and he began to cut into the deer. He cut a circle around the anus, and tied that off with a thin cord. He slit the skin down from the breast, along the abdomen, cutting cautiously between the hide and the animal inside. He rolled the animal on its side, pulled out intestines, innards, the windpipe, he took away from the steaming insides of the animal, precisely and carefully. What he took he placed on the grass beside him, parts of the animal he would leave behind for other animals, who would come later.

When the old man finished inside, he reached for the heart, and cut it free from connecting organs piled in the grass. He stood up. The heart was dripping, a shining dead violet, dripping, almost black, a whisper of steam in his hands. The old man spoke again, his words rolled over the glistening face of the heart in cool fog dissipations of his breath. He reached into his bag, gathered more material, spread red cloth out on the ground. He rolled the heart into the material with the tobacco and tied them together with strips of blue cloth.

After that, he walked to a place where a big gray stone rose out of the earth. The old man took the heart over there: he talked to the sky, he held the heart to the sun, he turned in many directions; he looked down to the earth under his feet. When he quit talking the old man set the heart on the stone. He placed more tobacco there in a circle around the heart. He circled the stone with tobacco.

Then the old man was gone, a trudging backlit memory, dragging the dead animal behind him.

I had been in the tree for a long time. I had had no vision. Yes, the days were more gradual than the days back at home, but the fast had become full of ordinary sound and sense, of sun crossings, shadow extensions and animal movements. I had grown tired of watching and soon I went to sleep.

My dreams took me out of myself again. I found myself looking into faces around a fire. There were old people speaking, casting blue sparks into glowing rings of words. I was looking back at the earth, at villages in autumn, at the people moving across the earth in families. I drew closer to people, I became one of them, a child with a face blackened with ashes, walking into the village after having been gone a long, long time.

Loud echoes woke me. In full sun crows floated overhead, drifting like black paper ashes, communicating shadow crossings with other crows in tree branches. A crow came out of the sky then and landed on the gray stone where the heart lay. The crow nudged the heart and began pecking at the cloth. I came down from the tree and ran to the stone, calling back to the crows. "Go," I yelled, "get away, go, go, go." I made a song out of "go" and go echoes of go and I ran in circles around the stone as I sang, waving my arms and jumping.

Maybe I was wrong then. Maybe I should have stayed in the tree. But I sang the crows away and the heart remained on the stone. And I didn't go back to the tree. Maybe that was wrong. Instead, I remained there, circling the stone, watching, protecting the old man's offering, keeping the animals away from the heart..

When I tired of walking, of circling, I slept on the ground next to the stone. I don't know how many days passed, suns came and went and no one came for me. In time, air cooled, leaves drifted in the woods around the clearing there. No one came for me. Sun to sun. I just kept circling the heart on the stone.

Returns

David Pego

Ellen walked into Wilson's room and crept quietly to his bedside. As a shaft of morning sunlight fell across his forehead from between the venetian blinds, she reached down and pulled a worn patchwork quilt over his shoulders. She was surprised when he suddenly spoke to her.

"Is he here yet?" he asked in a thin, weak voice.

"Who?" she said.

Ellen could see that it was taking almost all of the energy that Wilson Walkingdeer had left to talk. He couldn't even open his eyes. The breathing through his nostrils grew louder as he tried to talk to her again.

"Is he here yet?" he asked. "I cannot go until he comes."

Ellen did not understand. Who was he calling? What did he want? She had not told him about any visitors, although a few relatives and friends had been asking if they could come by to see Wilson. But she had discouraged them because of his condition. After all, she still believed there was a slim chance that he could pull through all of this.

"Ellen, please answer me," Wilson said again. "Is he here yet?"

Ellen leaned over and kissed her father on his stubbled cheek. She left a bright red smudge of lipstick on his skin, which looked paler now than she had ever seen it.

"Daddy, I don't know who you are waiting for," she whispered. "Please tell me who it is that you expect to see."

Wilson's eyes opened narrowly until he could barely see Ellen through his long lashes. Girls had always loved his long lashes, he had been fond of telling Ellen as well as other friends who would listen to him talk about the proud days of his youth. Indian girls and non-Indian girls alike had loved his deep brown eyes and those long dark lashes. At least, that's what they had told him over and over. Ellen had no doubt that it was all true. Photos of her dad taken during his softball playing days had shown a much different figure than the one who was lying here in this darkened room. He had been one of the most handsome men in the tribe. It's no wonder that Ellen's mother had fallen in love with him so quickly and deeply. And once she had confided to Ellen while the two were washing the evening dishes that it was indeed her father's long, lovely lashes that had first caught her attention.

"Jack Frost, of course," Wilson said, finally answering her question before shutting his eyes again.

Like a hammer slamming into her locked memory, it all came rushing back. There was only one thing that Wilson had loved as much as Ellen and her mother—the fall and its amazing color display as the leaves changed. She had grown up walking hand in hand with him through the woods that surrounded their small house. They hadn't taken time to do that for years and suddenly she was very sorry. She remembered quite clearly that the mission of those walks in late summer had been to look for evidence that the heat of August and September was giving way to cool nights. And it was on such occasions, he had explained to her many times, that Jack Frost would slip silently through the forest, painting by hand the millions of green leaves until all of the oaks were wearing fine coats of gold, orange, crimson and brown.

Why did Wilson love the fall so much? Ellen could only guess. As with many other things, he never fully explained himself. But Ellen could guess that fall to Wilson meant this drab world was taking on new colors. She also knew that Wilson and many of the Creek elders had been taught to pay close attention to nature. In that way, the changing of the leaves signaled respite from searing Oklahoma heat. That was an important moment for someone who had never been in an air-conditioned house until he was in his late 40s. And even after his own house had been shut up so he could take advantage of refrigerated air, Wilson still liked to throw his windows open during the fall. For the past several autumns, he had sat by the window of his room in his wheelchair, one ear catching the baseball play-by-play that spilled out of his ancient, scratchy-sounding Philco radio on the dresser and the other ear cocked to hear the songs of the birds as they helped each other prepare for the long trip south. She also suspected that the coming of fall meant another World Series was on its way. Wilson lived for Series week. He had told her many times how he wished he had been good enough to make it to baseball's fall classic.

Wilson had lost all track of time, Ellen thought to herself as she heard him talking about Jack Frost. The season when leaves would start to change color one by one was a month or more away.

"Jack's not here, Daddy," she said softly. A tear streaked down the left side of her face, slowing down only long enough to leave a salty taste on the corner of her mouth.

Wilson did not respond other than to pull his eyes a little tighter. Ellen reached down underneath the quilt and grabbed his right hand. It wasn't the hand she had known even a few months before. As his appetite had disappeared, so had the last remnants of the powerful man who had reared her. A massive hand that could once put indentations in a tightly-wrapped softball as easily as squeezing a grapefruit now seemed like a bundle of brittle bones.

"I don't know when Jack is going to get here, Daddy," Ellen said. "You've got to hang on. He wants to see you, too."

Wilson's breathing was soft and steady. Ellen saw that he had fallen asleep again. She carefully pulled her fingers away from his hand, then she slipped her hand back out from under the quilt. Wilson did not stir.

"Good, Daddy," she said in a voice too soft to be heard by anyone other than herself. "Get your rest. You've got to be strong so you can see Jack again."

Ellen then slipped out of the room and went back to the day's chores. There was much to do, as there always was. It was also wash day, so it was shaping up to be a busy morning and afternoon. She wanted to get a lot done while Wilson was asleep so she could be by his side when he awakened. She did not want to waste a precious second of his consciousness.

Before putting the week's laundry in a vintage washer that sat on the screened back porch, Ellen phoned Virginia Salazar to give her an update on Wilson. Virginia was the head nurse at the tribal center and insisted on getting regular updates from the families of all of her patients. Ellen respected Virginia for her care and concern. Though her father's life was rapidly vanishing and both she and Virginia knew that the end was almost at hand, Virginia insisted on carrying on with the regular updates, maybe more for Ellen's sake than for Wilson's. If nothing else, it gave Ellen one more caring voice that could understand what she was going through.

After talking with Virginia for about two minutes, Ellen sat at the kitchen table and drank the last cup from the coffee pot that used to be entirely in Wilson's care. Even after he had lost his legs, he had loved being in charge of the mid-morning coffee and toast. When visitors dropped by, it was Wilson who would ceremoniously drop new coffee grounds into the top of his tarnished coffee pot and pour water into it. Then he would plug it into an uncovered electrical outlet underneath his corner chair. Back then, just a few years ago, he would also ask morning visitors how they would like their toast. He could only make the toast one piece at a time because the heating elements on one side of the old toaster had given out. After making the bread a golden brown or almost jet black, depending on his guest's preference, he would skim the surface with a light layer of butter. And if there was jelly or honey in the house, he would apply a dab in the corner of the toasted bread, then work the sweet substance over the rest of the brown surface in small circles with a knife, just the way he used to apply machine oil to the palm of his beloved softball glove.

Ellen rose and was going to place her empty coffee cup in the kitchen sink when she heard a commotion erupt in Wilson's room down the hallway. At first she thought something had fallen, then she realized it was the sound of rattling venetian blinds.

She ran down the hallway and burst into Wilson's room. He had pulled himself to the edge of the bed and had pulled the blinds halfway down. He was on his side, propped up on his left elbow with his eyes wide open, trying to peer out the dust-streaked glass and rusty window screen. As Ellen walked across the room, she saw the excited grin on his face.

"Jack's here," he said. "I knew he would come."

Wilson laid his head back on his pillow. Clearly, the effort he had made to see out the window had taken a great toll on his seriously weakened body. He was smiling, but his happiness was slowly giving way to great pain. He closed his eyes, then called to Ellen in a thin voice.

"Honey, they're here."

Ellen rushed to the side of his bed, but it was already too late. She threw herself across the top of his body and could feel the warmth of his being sliding away. She cried loudly, then caught herself. Then she put her hand over his frail right hand and closed his fingers into a ball. And, for the first time, she looked out the window and saw the branches of the oak tree that had for so many years given them cool relief from the scorching summer sun.

"You were right, Daddy," she said, her voice breaking as she spoke to him, hoping he would somehow hear her words before he went on his spirit journey. "Jack did come."

She pulled the quilt back over Wilson's shoulders, as if he were just taking a little nap. Then she rose and backed away from the bed.

There was a curious expression on her face as she rounded the bed and peered outside. How could it be? The tree that had been bright green with summer leaves was now dotted with brilliant flashes of orange, brown and gold. The colors seemed to sparkle in the wind. In fact, one leaf suddenly dropped to the ground, perhaps to officially begin the fall season, thought Ellen to herself. How lucky her father had been, but how could this have happened? There had been no cool nights. By experience, she knew it would be another month or so before the Oklahoma hillsides would explode in bright colors that often attracted long lines of slow-moving cars from the city. Just how had this happened? Had Jack Frost really come for her dad?

As she was trying to figure out how this had all come to be, the single leaf that had fallen to the ground suddenly shot straight up into the air, as if it had been plucked from the ground by a single shaft of wind. That's when Ellen decided she would go outside to see what in the world was going on outside her father's window.

She stepped through the front screen door and through what seemed like a wall of late-summer heat. The first thing she noticed was that there was no wind. So how was it that the leaves were rustling and that the fallen leaf had been blown straight up into the sky?

But it was true. The tree was covered by a beautiful brown and orange coat. From a distance, it appeared as though the branches were dancing in the breeze. As Ellen moved closer, she realized the truth of what was happening. It became abundantly obvious as another leaf blew abruptly from the tree, then flew through the air to land on her shoulder.

It wasn't Jack frost. It was a butterfly. Monarch butterflies. Tens of thousands of monarch butterflies. They were sitting in almost every branch of the oak tree as well as in many other trees in the back yard.

Undoubtedly they were taking a break while winging their way to their winter grounds in Mexico. But why they had chosen this moment to wind up outside her father's window had to be more than just coincidence. It was as if they had come to escort her father's spirit home to the warm southlands.

Ellen looked upward and circled the tree in wonderment. Most of the butterflies were flapping their colorful wings, as if they were all waving to get her attention.

"How did you know?" she said to them. "How did you know?"

Her head turned as another butterfly seemed to dart down

from the clouds and landed on the tree.

Then she remembered what her mother had told her many years ago. That was the day she and a couple of friends were throwing rocks at several yellow butterflies flitting from flower to flower.

"Don't bother them," her mother had told her and the other children. "The winged ones are your relatives. They are everyone who has gone on before."

Ellen and her friends had quit throwing rocks on that day, embarrassed by the fact that they had been caught trying to hurt poor, helpless creatures.

But it wasn't until now that she understood fully what her mother had said. She walked back to the house, shaking her head and wondering how big a winged creature had to be to qualify as an angel.

▶✕◀✕◀

Spider Dreams

kateri akiwenzie-damm

Pink-skinned mice frozen in a hollow of hay. Me, seven I'd guess, examining them for minutes through blurred eyes, fascinated by their delicacy, their hardness. Scooping them into the little snow shovel I'd gotten for Christmas, transferring them into a burlap sack and with great ceremony flinging them over the side of the hill behind the barn. Years later, tramping through the bush in early autumn, kicking leaves with steel-toed boots, I happened upon the sack, covered in years of debris, almost buried. Inside were the mummified bodies of the baby mice I'd mourned as a child. And I remembered the serious deliberateness of my thinking. And without knowing it at the time, I became aware that there are ceremonies of childhood that are as meaningful and exclusive as those we practice as adults.

With only the television for company, I drink myself into a temporary, fuck-it-all, joyousness. I've taken to buying imported beer. Somehow it doesn't seem as pathetic as sitting home alone, night after night, getting sloshed on Canadian. But the end result's nearly the same, apart from the wispy strand of dignity the imports dangle to one's self image. Delusions more likely. Or are they? No, not delusions—in the right light, in a certain detached frame of mind, I see it all for what it is. I can see the reality, I just choose not to.

But in the end you can't really hide your empty liquor bottles from yourself after all. You know they're there, wrapped in newspaper, hidden among the other trash you've created.

He is on top of me. Eyes closed, the trace of a smile pervading his face, his whole being. And we are making love. Making wildly energetic, passionate love. Loving and together and loving it. Skin against skin. Joining, melding, pushing and straining. Pulling each other in. Closer, tighter. I am not thinking, just feeling and knowing. Knowing the way each cell of his feels against each of mine, knowing the touch of him, the smell of him, his rhythm, his space, his look.

I want to laugh and cry and I cling to him, turning my face to tell him. To tell him everything. When I move my mouth to speak, his face turns gray and begins to drip like a reflection on a rain-pelted window. In that instant I can no longer feel him. And when I reach my hand to his cheek he vaporizes. I cannot move. I am the anti-Medusa and have turned only myself, all but my own eyes, to stone. I know I am crying but cannot feel the tears on my stone cheeks.

Overhead, a buzzard is circling. My eyes. Oh god, my eyes. At once the bird is here, standing on my face, ready to pluck my eyes from their stone sockets. I can't scream except in the way stones do.

Then I am running. My heart is pounding as though my blood will explode through my skin. All is black. So black I cannot see myself and keep running. Suddenly I am aware that this body is not my body. Not human. There are too many legs, no fingers, no thumbs. No tear ducts.

My heart is pounding, racing when I awake. Was I screaming? I look around as if there will be signs of it clinging to the bedroom walls. My heart is slowing. I don't want to remember the dream. Don't want to remember the first part especially because it hurts the most and takes the longest to shake loose.

I don't want to fall back to sleep so I rise, pulling on track pants and T-shirt. I can't bear to see my naked body. In the shower I bathe without seeing anything but fingers, forearms and toes. It's a trick I taught myself early on. And now I do it without thinking. It works best that way. The lights must be off and the temperature of the water lukewarm. Too cold, the skin comes alive in bumps and shivers. Too hot, the skin opens and every muscle in the body relaxes. The right degree of lukewarm causes the least reaction. As though the air has turned liquid.

For a while I didn't bathe at all. But that doesn't work either. Not with all the itches and tingles and smells that are like a kick in the gut. Lukewarm water was the solution. And nobody has to know.

Making coffee, I notice a spider in the jar beside the sink. I look at it. I have an aversion to squishing spiders developed in childhood. It will rain. An awesome responsibility for a child. Even one that is my age. I pick up the jar and place it outside in the snow, in the minus 30 degree air, and return to the coffee pot. But the spider is tangled in my thoughts, and minutes later I am retrieving the jar. The spider is stiff on the bottom and his strands of webbing crisscrossing the jar have frozen and frosted and are now visible. I place the jar on the vent inside the door. Miraculously, the spider thaws and begins moving, slowly at first, then with increasing ease. Now what? I watch the spider. If it was a different season I would throw it out the door with a respectful admonition that spiders belong outside.. But it has no chance in the heart of a Saugeen Peninsula February. Then again, I don't really want to open my house to every six or eight-legged either. Enough come without the invitation. Well, spiders do belong outside. I place the jar outside again. Minutes later, I am back setting it on the vent, not knowing if I want the spider to move or not. It doesn't and I feel sad and relieved and outrageously, rationally, humanly cruel. I stare at the spider, its legs curled into itself, for a good long while. Then I dump it in the snowdrift outside and close the door.

The coffee is bitter.

I decide to go for a walk, putter around outside, let the wind blow the cobwebs out of my head. I pull on clean underwear. (What if I freeze out there and they find me wearing yesterday's underwear?) then leggings, cotton socks, woolen socks, undershirt, T-shirt, sweatshirt, jacket, hat, boots, gloves, scarf. Despite this, standing in the doorway I'm already shivering and I haven't even stepped outside. When did I become this weak thing?

Skin stiffens on contact with the ice vapor. I roam around the perimeter of the house, looking for something useful to do. I halfheartedly shovel the laneway knowing how pointless it is in this wind. I carry wood from the woodpile, stacking it by the door. And I traipse inside, trailing snow all over the house. It pleases me. Even though I know I will step in small puddles later or, less likely, be forced to crawl around the floor wiping them up. To hell with that. I stomp my boots extra hard to be sure all the snow falls off before I go out for more wood.

The fire rages in the woodstove. The small house is sweltering. I open a window. Watch my breath float.

As a child I could spend hours outside on a day like this. Now if I can't find any work to do I rush back inside. Like so many other things, this too saddens me. I consider going back outside. I could make a snowman (wrong kind of snow), I could make snow angels (probably just blow away), I could get a piece of cardboard and slide down the driveway (where would I get a piece of cardboard big enough?). It's no fun playing outside alone anyway.

We used to play outside in the snow. Throw snowballs and chase each other. Slide on the ice. And laugh. We were always laughing together.

Once, not long before the time, the time I can neither remember nor forget, we built snow forts and started a snow fight. We recruited cousins and nieces and nephews, planned strategy, built munitions supplies. The battle raged all afternoon with each side winning in turn. Finally it was growing dark and the troops were called in for dinner. A grudging, reluctant truce was called and shortly afterwards, with battalions of sleepy-eyed, red cheeked warriors urging it on, a fragile peace was proclaimed over steaming mugs of hot chocolate. It was too tenuous to last though and later, left to our own devices, we broke out in a skirmish in the kitchen. The children, now quite peaceful and content, watched laughing and scolding us war mongering old folks as dishwater and tea towels flew.

"Hey, give peace a chance," one of the older ones called, laughing.

"Yeah, you two," they shouted, "war's over."

"Yeah, give it a rest."

We were still slipping and sliding around the kitchen when they called out their goodnights and headed off to bed. But shortly afterwards, in a tangled, watery heap on the floor, the peace negotiations began in earnest and lasted well into the night.

Is it what I miss most, his body curving into mine? His tongue against mine, him inside me?

My muscles remember and mourn.

Lately though it is the small things that cause the pointed intake of breath, the sudden welling of water in the eyes. A few lines of the song that we sang as we walked the road from the store, kicking gravel and eating ice cream. The drawling way he'd say "yeah, yeah" when someone's insistence amused him. The way he'd close his eyes when I touched his face. The way I would awaken with his eyes on me, watching.

The small things. The small things that fall bit by bit into the whole of life, that take shape and find meaning, that shift and twist, spinning us off into new directions.

Yes, it is the small things that make me weep now. Like the memory of him rising before dawn to cover me with an extra blanket that early autumn weekend we went camping. Tucking it around my body.

Now every love song makes me cry, every story of lost love, every lament, every sonnet. I am imploding, falling into this growing emptiness in the heart of my being, this nightmare. And I know he would not want this for me.

Shadows stretch across the room. The sun is at a lazy angle, drifting toward the horizon. The dullness in my head reminds me I have not eaten. I cook macaroni, then dump a can of tomatoes in the pot. Macaroni and tomato. Hangover soup. Standard rez fare for drinkers and nondrinkers alike. I eat from a mug, standing by the glass doors watching the shadows lengthen. The phone has not rung once today and the sun is ready to set.

We talked about having children. Four of them, two boys, two girls. We know what they will look like and the sounds of their voices and we know their names. When I am not pregnant after the first year, he cries. We hold each other and cry together. "In time," we finally decide. It will happen in time because we already know and love them.

I weep now when I hear mothers calling those names in the playground or at the mall. I weep when I see a man smiling at a baby or walking with his young children.

I weep for him and for our babies who have names that will never be spoken.

When I was a little girl my mother would hold me when I was scared. I was afraid of the dark and would lie awake at night, imagining something nameless and faceless and murderous. And I would sleep fitfully, waking terrified and screaming, the fingers of those dark thoughts still clutching my head. Then my mother would hold me and stroke my forehead until the fear was loosened and I could sleep through the night.

The winter I was four years old I was visiting my grandparents when the nightmares came as usual and the house was kept awake with my fear. The following morning I watched my grandfather give my grandmother four small feathers, a piece of buckskin, a red willow hoop and a small red stone. Then Nokomis sat by the front window, and while she worked I watched silently, hanging on to her knees. As her hands worked she told a story about an old granny and a spider. When she finished, she handed me a gift, smiling and rubbing her hand over my hair. A dreamcatcher.

"Hang it over your pillow, little one."

"I will," I said swallowing hard. "Thank you Granny. Meegwetch Nokomis," I called, running to hang it over my bed.

From that day forward, my childhood was freed of bad dreams.

Now I search through closets and drawers and boxes. I uncover all of the bits and pieces of him I had hidden from view.

The photos, the cards, the poems, the love letters, his favorite shirts—all are exhumed and wet again with grief. But I cannot find what I am looking for.

How can something just disappear, I rage. Wouldn't there have to be some trace somewhere? Wouldn't there? I am so angry I bash things about, swearing. Damn it to hell! Where is it? Where, goddam it!

In my rage I carelessly break a hawk feather in two. A gift from a friend. And I am immediately sorry, my anger vanquished. I sit until my chest stops heaving. I know the anger is useless.

His blue and gray flannel shirt calls to me from where it has been flung on the bed. There is a smell of him clinging to it and I put it on, closing my eyes and imagining that he is embracing me. I smile, hugging myself tightly. Then a tingle scampers down my arm. I open my eyes and a small red spider crawls from under the shirt sleeve across my wrist and drops to the floor. I rip the shirt off and fling it into the dressing table.

I stare at the shirt, heaped on the floor.

My hair is getting long again.

Sun drenched the room. It was early morning, a Saturday in late February. He rose before me. I could hear the rustle of him dressing and making coffee. Before leaving he sat on the edge of the bed and watched me sleep. I shivered feeling his eyes on me. Then he tucked the blankets around me and kissed my forehead, breathing deeply as if he was breathing me in, as if trying to hold a bit of my breath for safekeeping. I sighed and smiled but did not open my eyes, did not make any move to rise. His hand stroked my cheek. I heard the door close, the snowmobile engine idle and roar. And he was gone.

Gone.

This is what I have not been able to release. What has wrapped my spirit in silky strands, what has been slowly devouring it.

Now, suddenly, it hits me.

The dressing table.

A shoebox in the right side of the dressing table. After Nokomis died I had wrapped my dreamcatcher in tissue paper, placed it in the shoebox and stored it in the dressing table. I was twenty years old at the time and, thinking I no longer needed it, planned to save the dreamcatcher for my firstborn.

I unfold the tissue paper and it is there, perfect. I stroke the feathers, spin the stone in the webbing. I say a prayer and talk a good long time to my grandmother.

Later I am a little embarrassed and ashamed when I hang the dreamcatcher above my bed. The gift of the spider to my people. And just today I have committed arachnocide. Yet here I am expecting protection from my bad dreams, expecting guidance. Sometimes my humanity appalls me and I offer another prayer of thanks to the spider.

Later, I pour the beer down the kitchen sink until the bottles are empty. And I place his photographs back on the mantel before going to bed.

In the dark I wonder if I will dream of him at all now. And can I bear it if he isn't there in the good dreams?

I close my eyes and wait for the dreaming to begin.

Learning to Fly

Joyce carlEtta Mandrake

Opal wore long stockings and long sleeves with her long dress. A scarf covered her head. All the other girls and the women wore the same wrappings. All the women changed their clothes in a small dark room that was in each house. Everyone always changed alone. No one smiled or laughed unless you were not a girl or woman. Opal's memories were of silence since no one was allowed to talk with another unless you were not a girl or woman.

One day, something wonderful happened to Opal. A small white feather floated down from the sky and landed on the back of her hand. It tickled and Opal felt a stirring in her heart. A shudder ran up from her hand to her body. The corner of her lips started to turn upwards in a smile. A small laugh came out; it sang like chimes in the wind. Opal looked around. No one had seen the feather or heard her laughter. The girl gently covered the feather with her hand and wondered.

One day when the men and boys left the town to do whatever they did, Opal did a brave thing. She took the feather and walked down to the river. She removed her shoes and stockings and touched her feet and legs with the feather. It tickled. Her lips smiled and the small laugh returned, tinkling like bells hung on a string. Opal removed her scarf and a little breeze played on her hair. Another laugh struggled out. Her long dress followed the scarf and remained on the ground. Opal held the feather in one hand and stretched her arms up to the sky. She felt different.

The girl noticed for the first time the soft hair on her arms and legs. The wind felt delicious as it blew across her body.

Opal was smiling and laughing. She was unaware of the girls and women that were huddled in a group near her. Their eyes were full of awe and confusion. They came closer. The soft "ohs" coming from their throats began to grow into a long note of joy as they began to remove their wrappings. The air was filled with flowing hair and singing laughter. The girls and the women surrounded Opal in a large circle and joined hands. They felt different.

They were unaware of the men and the boys who were beginning to stand around them. Their faces were full of dismay and anger. They wanted to stop the women. They shouted. Opal and the girls and the women began to sway and to dance in their circle. They could not see the men's and boys' anger or hear their shouting. The songs of joy were so loud that the men and boys put their hands over their ears to stop from hearing the songs.

Opal grew brighter and taller, the girls and the women grew brighter and taller. The men and the boys covered their eyes to keep from seeing the girls and the women grow brighter. Opal and the girls and the women grew brighter. They were different. They marveled that they could feel so light and felt themselves slowly drift upward into the sky. The men and the boys cried for them to return but Opal and the girls and the women drifted higher into the sky, for they were different and learning to fly.

The Deer Dreams Were Always There

Michelle Boursaw

N'mudeben zhindu kashiigo ku giigudosii. Sit here but don't talk. It was my auntie's way of letting me listen. She said it so much it stuck in my thick head, long after the schooling took most of the language out. Stuck in my head there—one of the few things she got through to me. Maybe not, though. Or she wouldn't have had to keep repeatin' herself, eh? I can sing *Amazing Grace* and a few of the ol' fiddle tunes there, all in the language. *Migwetch, Gitcham 'nido* for that much, eh? But what's lost will come back around to us, see. Yeah, that's for sure—all lessons lost make their way known to us again. That's the trick.

My auntie gave me my name, she did. *Waawaashkeshkwe*— Deer Woman. But Auntie's gone, some twelve years ago she left this shadow of the real world. Not many call me by how I'm known now. My brother Giizhig used to call me Little Doe to tease me. Anything for a buck, he'd say. I used to knock him down for that one.

She gave it to me 'cause she said I was always walkin' in a dream after the deer, that my dreams and my walkin' was the same. I remember those dreams. As a girl I used to follow the deer paths, for hours I did this. I ate berries, took a nap in their grassy spots they'd slept in the day before, followed the wedge of their footprints everywhere. I did this for hours, days. In that time it was my real education, before the nuns got hold of me.

First, they came into my auntie's house there, told her I

138

looked smarter than they expected, seein' how I missed so many years without their school. Neglect, they said, was a crime my auntie did, she should get down on her knees against this sin. I was way past legal age, they said, so they would take me away from her.

I had the look of bein' smart, they said. Then, all the time they had me there, tried to tell me I wasn't smart enough. All them years they kept me there, tellin' me I was too slow.

Forgive me for swearin', but one of those black-robed bitches got ahold of me so good she knocked the words right outta me, she did. That's how come I was speechless for those early years. I had nothing left to say, no, I figured I was talkin' too much for them. It was those Indian words, she said, was wrong in me. It wasn't the good English; it was the devil's tongue coming outta me, she said.

They changed our names, making us Christians with them. Before that, we knew what *Anishinaabemowin* meant, what our given names meant for us. We knew what it meant to be Ojibwe: we were the fire and heat that is so strong, like those Grandfathers in the Lodge, they say. So strong, the heat will go right through you, make the cedar crackle and dance. Those lessons you learn, the Grandfathers teach you. You don't wait for the end of the world to get ready for them lessons.

My name. They changed it, gave me a new name. Called me Dorothy. My friends and family called me Doe, and that got around, you see. I tried not to forget who I was, those years at the school. They wanted us to forget.

That one Sister, the one who knocked the words outta me, she was bad like a snake, she was. Although to say so was a sin. Even now, but I've long since tried to give up those thoughts. An Elder, my auntie once said, can't hold a Bible and put tobacco down at the same time, no, you'd be dropping one for the other. You need two hands for a Bible, one to hold, one to turn the page. Same with the pipe, you need two hands for that, too.

Then that one Sister, she took that Bible with both hands and made us do the same. At first it made no sense to me, what it was all about. She always caught me staring out the window, caught me daydreaming one time too many. Woke me up with her eraser, or worse, her stick. She sure had an arm on her, hit her target from anywhere in the room, she could. By the end of the day my hair was more white than black and my hands swollen red to blue.

That one Sister was enough to scare anyone into the heart of Jesus, and he in you. When I first learned how to pray their way, those prayers of protection made more sense than most. I used 'em on her, I did, to see if they'd work. They didn't keep that eraser of hers from flying 'cross the room, or that stick away from my knuckles, I'll tell you that much.

Maybe they did, maybe those prayers worked after all, I can't say for sure. I'm still here, and those lessons keep coming back, those words I hear out in the woods there, when I follow the deer path. Like Auntie used to say: sit here, but don't talk. Listen.

There were times at the school, my dreams all but left me. There were other things at night, most of us tryin' to cry without noise. Then one loud homesick kid would start the whole room bawlin'. I saw what happened to those who were restless, couldn't stop bawlin', or worse, wet the bed. I did that too, when I first came. They'd come in, hit you with that stick. I thought I'd never sleep again as long as I lived.

Then that place started to give me their kind of dreams. They talked and talked of this devil that would come for us always, and finally he came for me.

One morning, I woke up to the Sister hovering over me. All over was my pee smell. She started beatin' me worse than ever. It was the first time I ever did that, like a dog she said I couldn't control myself. Boy, she'd learn me right off the bat. God told her to save me from those devil hands, and by God she would.

I had to wear that sheet all day, during chapel and lessons to show my shame. That's what they did, see, all of us like that, for bein' savage in our ways. There were things those nuns came at you for, and some things so bad they took you to see the Father himself. This was one of those things.

By day, Father was like them all, covered and floatin' black in his robe. Except he had hair. But in that dream he turned into the devil they talked about, and I was the one they said called him to me for what I did. I thought I would die and go under the ground to live in that place they said was always on fire. They were takin' me to that hell.

That one Sister, she brought me to Father and told him of my bad ways, and how I still spoke Indian, and the savage pagan soul I still clung to that was inside me. Father listened, said I had to go to that basement room and say Hail Marys until they came for me. That was their way, to help me learn that taste of hell so I wouldn't go to the devil but to Jesus.

I remember that darkness, so strong it turned red. I knew they sent me down there, down so deep into that place that smelled like me, full of pee and stale breath and dust. I cried until I couldn't hear myself no longer. I cried until all I could taste was that dust. Surely the devil would come, I thought. Surely he lives here.

The deer dreams were always there. The deer dreams, they still come to me, to warn me; even now they do.

Something was comin', and it said so:

Here I am   I am coming   for you to follow

I was still. I was awake, but unsure I was. I thought I was looking out my auntie's window, to where a spruce grouse was the night before. She was as still as I, sittin' in her nest; I thought she heard it too. I wrapped a blanket around me and walked through the door quietly, into night air. I sat still on the ground, far enough away from the grouse, but still watching her. I did this for a long time, I think.

Then I heard two loud stompin' steps, beatin' like a drum. When I looked up, there she was. She came runnin', jumped right over me. I could see the white of her belly as she leaped. I turned to see her tail waggin', the sound of her hooves beat in running rhythm, then slow to a stop. Nokomis Waawaashkesh turned, looked me straight in the eye. We were like this for what seemed like a long time. I have kept this picture in my heart, always.

Then more voices came from behind me. Nokomis Waawaashkesh disappeared into the woods. I heard steps again. I went to run after her. But now I was so full of fear, 'cause you see I turned to see these floating black women comin' for me. I ran wild, but only so far, until my little legs tripped me up. Then I was surrounded by these black skirts, their cold hands grabbin' me.

I awoke, knowing I had to go. I was theirs.

Wintering and
Returning

Indians Who've Been to Paris

Heid E. Erdrich

G inny's boyfriend rented three small rooms under the roof, six floors up, above the larger family apartments in Paris. Several stairways wound through the building—a wide, red-carpeted flight flowed like a rich vein through the middle but did not lead to their attic rooms. That first night Ginny followed Kirk up a narrow twist of steps off the courtyard, past the trash bins. Three flights up, those stairs ended. They crossed over a red-carpeted landing, opened a narrow door in the paneled wall and proceeded up three more flights of metal stairs. Open windows set up high above the rail let in light and cold. Ginny could see only brick through them as they faced a shaft.

"You're going to love this place," Kirk said. At the top of the stairs, he directed her down a corridor. "We're lucky to get it, it's illegal to sublet."

Ginny learned that in Paris it was not unusual to have no elevator, no heat, no toilet, no shower. After a while she was surprised to think how essential heat, showers and toilets once seemed. There was a space heater, hot water and a tiny sink and stove after all. Ginny reminded herself that her old auntie had gotten along just fine with an outhouse until a few years ago. Lots of people on her reservation were still waiting for water lines. Ginny knew she could manage. Still, an outhouse would have seemed luxurious compared to what she had to contend with—the thing down the hall—a closet with something like a drain. This, she learned, passed for a toilet in Paris. It took balance to use and that first night, after the red wine and lovemaking, when Ginny had to attempt it, she swayed, crouched, laughing until she was so weak she leaned against the filthy wall. But she took it as a challenge, really, and when she left France she could pee on a dime.

Ginny did not speak French and had never dreamed of visiting Paris. She had never, and this gave her a slight sense of shame, even wanted to go. That was un-American, she knew. On the flight over she tried to imagine herself where winding streets had been marched by great figures of war, where painted faces peered out from the art of centuries past. But she couldn't see herself there. She kept hearing her best friend, Critter, who was proud to say he had never left his *native ground*. Maybe he was right, she thought, because from the moment she arrived, she had the sensation of being untethered, ungrounded, like she had stepped right off the earth.

And yet she agreed to join Kirk in Paris for the year. He was a scholar from the French-speaking area of Canada on a fellowship to teach English literature. Ginny was through with long distance love. She'd tried it before and it never worked. She got lonely. This time she would give up something for a man for once, that might make it work. They hadn't been together long so there was a lot of passion between them. Ginny imagined Paris would fan their fire. And so she went with a head full of those kinds of ideas and very little money.

At first she thought she could take a job but, not speaking French, there was not much she could do. Her boyfriend showed her an ad he had plucked from a bulletin board. He had it all arranged, she just had to call and the job was hers. An American couple wanted an English-speaking woman to tutor their three-year-old child. Ginny contemplated the oddly long phone number, gazed at the squat phone, its tiny buttons, like an intercom. She wasn't even sure how to make the call, and she worried. She had taken care of children. She was aware of the many small moments of crisis that might arise. She imagined the child deathly ill—she alone must summon help. All one morning she ran the scenario through her head, commanding scraps of French and utilizing her phrase book, but her terrible fantasy always ended with the child turning blue in her arms. She was as good as mute. That's when Ginny told her first lie in Europe. She phoned the couple to say she had taken another job.

Kirk didn't bring up the subject of employment, so she just let it drop. He was full of plans for short trips. "We could go to Spain," he suggested. "Or Belgium?" She didn't know what to say, they had been there less than a month and she was hardly used to the city. But she wanted to sound game.

"How about England?" Ginny said. "Pocahontas died in England, maybe I could visit her grave?"

"England?" he laughed. "That would be just like going home."

They didn't disagree often, they just let things slide, which worked out OK for Ginny. She was still adjusting to sharing an apartment. Before, she had always insisted her sleep-in boyfriends maintain their own address. At first she felt like she and Kirk were playing house and she enjoyed it. They cooked a great deal in the small kitchen. He made fries out of a variety of soft yellow potato they bought from a Moroccan vegetable stand. His fries were exceptional and Ginny liked this about him. He salted the oil just before he dumped in the cut potatoes. He also popped good popcorn using the same oil and salt principle. That was what had drawn her to him at the university where they both worked. Kirk had been a friend of a friend who came to a party and just started to cook. She made sure he was the last guest to leave that night and soon after, he moved into her apartment. But she traveled so much for her job that she hadn't felt they were living together until she found herself with him in Paris.

Ginny would kiss him good-bye at the door when he went off to teach in the mornings. Then she had the whole day and the three small rooms to herself. She had never lived in a city and didn't like to walk alone. Just remembering which stairs to take down to the street was confusing and the streets tangled and circled back endlessly. She was sure she would get lost. If she had to speak French she knew she would freeze, although she understood it well.

So she would stay in, write letters to her mother, listen to the Arabic radio station, read Kirk's anthologies, stare out the kitchen window into the courtyard, and wait for him to return.

Often he picked up a bottle of cheap wine which they drank in the late afternoon. The next morning Ginny would wash the bottles. She began to stack them, one by one, in front of the window in the small alcove they called the sitting room. The bottles made a sort of stained glass window. The sun came through in the morning, when he was off teaching, and cast a pool in various shades of green on the floor. There she would rest, in a blanket, her thoughts at home.

One afternoon she woke to the tremendous beat of someone pounding on a door. She couldn't tell where the noise was coming from. There were no other rooms down the hall. She didn't dare investigate. There was a crack of wood like a door giving way, then quiet. Later, when Kirk came home, a policeman stopped him in the corridor. Ginny heard the detective ask if anyone was home that afternoon—a burglary had occurred. She expected Kirk to call for her, but he didn't. They spoke a few words more, but Ginny didn't listen. She gazed out the kitchen window over the rooftops at her familiar view: the domed building, a school with its fenced-in playground on the roof, the strange little mansard dormers across the courtyard. When Kirk came in he asked no questions, gave no explanations.

She stood at the window. "Will you teach me to speak French?" she asked.

"Oh," he laughed, "you want me to work at home, too?" She shook her head no and gave him her usual welcome. "No, no, you do so much for me," she said over his shoulder as she squeezed him. "Besides, who do I talk to?"

On his days off, they would walk miles and miles to save metro fare. The diesel fumes dazed her and the cold through her cheap boots made her miserable enough to appreciate great art. The huge halls and rich offerings exhausted Ginny, but she always found paintings of women bathers refreshing. Back at their little apartment, she too bathed standing in a basin, soaping her shoulders with a giant sea sponge. And she loved the paintings of Toulouse-Lautrec. For all their blue-green and yellow tones, his figures seemed so human. If Kirk had the price of coffee they would sit in a little cafe discussing what they had seen. At the end of the day they would take the metro back to their apartment.

Each time they went underground to catch a train, Ginny fought to keep herself oriented. The maze of the metro would branch before her in more directions than she thought possible. Like a gopher's tunnel, she always thought. Once, on the train she told Kirk how the metro reminded her of old Auntie's yard, of how she and Critter used to watch the gopher tease the cat by popping its head out one hole, then seconds later, peeping out another yards away. That's what made them impossible to catch—they had at least a dozen escape hatches. He smiled at her story but added, "Paris has the best subway in the world, you know."

Down the crowded metro hole one day, Ginny spotted a man coming toward them wearing a trade-blanket coat and black cowboy hat with a band beaded in Plains designs. She couldn't believe it—she had never imagined she would see another Indian in Paris! She tugged after Kirk's sleeve. There seemed to be a minimum speed limit in the tunnels so, like everyone else, he trotted through the metro. She never could keep pace with him. Her slowness often forced him to grab her hand, steer her through turnstiles, pull her up stairs to platforms just in time to catch the right train. And Ginny tried not to be distracted because she knew she would be lost without Kirk. But the Indian man—she wanted to go back to him, to ask where he was from, who his relatives were. She managed to stop Kirk for a second. A stream of huffy Parisians split and flowed on either side of them as though they were rocks in mid-water. Ginny pointed back at the Indian man. "He looks lost," she lied. "We should help him." When they looked back the Indian man had stopped and seemed to be studying the map printed on the wall. "Hurry!" they both yelled, Ginny because she wanted to go back and

Kirk because they had to step onto the moving sidewalk or miss the train. He grabbed her elbow, she fell toward him, then she felt the floor begin to carry her away. She kept glancing back at the man in the black hat, but the conveyor swept them forward and the figure quickly dwindled away.

That night, as they drank wine and ate bread and cheese, Ginny told him an Osage story she had heard from a friend. It took place in the early eighteen-hundreds. A party of Osage men were captured and brought to France to be displayed to wealthy ladies. These men were so beautiful, could sing and play flute so movingly, the great ladies tried to make them their lovers. But the Osage captives would have none of them. Many of their maids, however, managed to become pregnant by the Osage. The ladies sent the men back to their home, but wouldn't allow the servants to go with their lovers. They took the children and displayed them until they were no longer novelties.

"Imagine," Ginny finished the story by saying to Kirk, "somewhere in France there are Osage descendants, mixed bloods who've never been home."

"I doubt they think of it as home," Kirk remarked as he poured the rest of the wine in her glass, "but that's quite a story."

Most nights Kirk played chess alone and smoked after they ate. Ginny would wrap herself in a blanket and watch TV dubbed in French. She understood it quite well by then. Her favorite was Star Trek—she thought Kirk, because of the name he shared with the captain, might get a kick out of it. But when she asked him to come in he said he thought she should watch the French shows. "But there aren't any," she protested. Even Kirk had to admit that most of the shows were American: Dynasty, The Bionic Man, and re-run after re-run of Star Trek. She laughed hard to herself imagining what Critter would think of how the old doctor uttered his usual line, "He's dead, Jim." For some reason they had dubbed Bones in a heavy Parisian accent so it sounded like he said, "Lay Mort, Jhim."

During the day, many of the stations went blank—which was a good thing, or Ginny might have watched re-runs all day. The only place she dared go alone was to a little market across the street where the Polish shopkeepers didn't speak French and wouldn't question her. She pointed at what she wanted to buy and nodded when they asked if the amount was right. The Paris weather had turned cold and they were forced to stay near their little electric heater in the kitchen at night. They talked about their favorite foods. Every day Ginny would try to fix some favorite dish for Kirk. Using a wine bottle as a rolling pin, Ginny made biscuits and learned to roll a pie crust. She attempted her mother's fried green beans and, from memory, constructed a passable version of her grandmother's potato and cottage cheese dumplings. The Polish market sold the right kind of sauerkraut to go with the dumplings. It supplied the right pickles and a good vodka as well, but she didn't have the money for it. She had to ask Kirk when he came home. He was happy to run out to purchase a bottle.

For several days that winter heavy snows struck the city and a general strike was called. School was closed. The power went out so Ginny and Kirk stayed in bed to keep warm. One morning the wind blew in just the right direction to send gusts of snow through the skylight above their bed. When they woke to find their covers frosted in ice crystals, they just pulled the blankets back over their heads, slept and made love all day. Their mattress was low to the ground and Ginny could hear music coming from the floor below. All that day she heard the faint discord of students at voice and piano lessons. She wondered where the apartment was, directly below them or somewhere to the side—possibly in an adjoining building? And who were these teachers who argued at the top of their lungs between visits from pupils. There was no way for her to know.

In the evening, Kirk read aloud to her. They talked about the poems, but their discussion seemed formal to her, as though he were her teacher. Once Ginny found an Elizabeth Bishop poem in one of his anthologies and because it was about Paris she read it aloud to him. It was about looking down into the courtyard of houses built just like the one they lived in—with ornamental urns set on the mansard roof tops *where the pigeons take their walks.* The line Ginny liked best, about looking into the courtyard, she repeated to him: *It is like introspection to stare inside, or retrospection, a star inside a rectangle, a recollection.*

He said it was a beautiful example of alliteration—all those rr's. She said, "I have stared out at the mansard roof tops for hours."And he said, she thought to tease, "Are you sure you don't want a job?"

He drank espresso and glowered, grew silent. This is a problem she'd had with other men, after a while they didn't have much to say to one another. Except for Critter—when a conversation lapsed with Critter, they relied on a little game they had played for years. They quizzed each other. One would ask, "Do you know who's Indian?" and the other would suggest a famous American, like Elvis or Connie Stevens, of surprising Native ancestry.

She tried quizzing Kirk. He hardly said a word for days—she mentioned every Indian she knew of who'd been to Paris.

"Geronimo," she said. "Can you imagine what he thought of Paris?"

"And Dull Knife's son, and Black Elk?" She explained how those two Sioux had lived in Paris with the Wild West show, but had missed the Plains so much that they begged to be allowed to ride outside the city where they might hunt in the countryside. Their expedition caused quite a stir. And, she told Kirk, in the 1850s there had been a group of Ojibwe who visited several countries in Europe.

"They wrote a travel book," Ginny told Kirk, but he didn't seem impressed or amused.

"Why do you care?" he asked.

"Because," she paused, it seemed obvious, "I'm in Paris . . . I'm Indian."

"Not much," he said easily. Maybe he didn't know how that hurt her.

"Better not much of anything than a chameleon," she muttered.

But he didn't mind, he was happy to be turning French. He drank espresso, took up smoking French cigarettes with a sexy woman on the pack that embarrassed Ginny. He read French papers and played chess alone at night. In the morning he drank espresso before he went to teach. He rarely spoke to her anymore except to lecture from his books. He stopped cooking and instead bought liver pate and smoky olives, salads of bitter greens in sharp dressing. He bought cognac instead of wine. Ginny didn't drink it. He kept bringing home stronger and stronger foods until Ginny's tastes were eclipsed entirely.

She was relieved when the strikes ended, school resumed and the snow began to thaw. She got up the courage to go out walking alone. At first she kept to the block where they lived. There was enough to interest her—it was a long, three-sided block that bordered a little park along the river. On the corner away from their building she could peruse the neat rows of baked goods on the glass shelves of the patisserie.

In the next window hung a woodcut print of the tops of Paris buildings. It was almost the exact view from her apartment: the bell tower, the domed building, the mansard roofs—it was all there. Where the artist had seen this view Ginny could not imagine. She wasn't even sure of where her rooms were in relation to the building where she saw the print. She knew the entrance to the stairs she took from the tiled courtyard was on the other side of the block. Her view was of the inside, the courtyard. There were no other windows in the tiny apartment, so she had no idea what was outside.

Gazing at the woodcut, she thought of the Bishop poem again, *It is like introspection to stare inside, or retrospection, a star inside a rectangle, a recollection* . . . . Ginny asked herself what it meant to look out your window to the inside of your house. To see your house from the inside. She was beginning to realize she saw the whole world this way—a tribal stranger, looking out at her people from the inside. There at that window, staring at the woodcut she murmured to herself, "Oh, Critter," because she just then recognized how deeply she missed her home.

Every day for weeks after she saw that woodcut, she lied to Kirk about where she had been, what she had done while he taught. She hadn't ventured off the block, but she wanted him to think of her as independent, self-sufficient. Finally one day Ginny made a brave and solitary journey to the store by the river that sold English books. On its door a metal plaque etched with the bearded face of Walt Whitman welcomed them in

French. Ginny stood for a long while translating the Whitman back into English: *Stranger! If you passing, meet me, and desire to Speak to me, why should you not speak to me? And why should I not speak to you?*

On the way home she passed crews of men with long metal poles. They knocked ice off building roofs that slanted into the narrow streets. Their street was roped off. Ginny stepped over the rope to get to their building. A slab of ice two feet thick had slid off a roof and crushed one of those tiny French cars. Like a cartoon it was funny and frightening at once. She told Kirk all about it when he came home. When she got to the part about the car, she couldn't help herself, she laughed until she began to snort and sob. Kirk just glared at her. Then he got up and left the apartment. She hadn't even told him the most hysterical part— how, as she watched the men working on the car, she looked up to see another sheet of ice inching off the roof. The edge ran as it melted. She stood for a long time behind a curtain of water, enjoying the splash, thinking of the ice above, poised to fall.

Late that night he came home so drunk he had to stop in the toilet-closet. Ginny could hear him retching down the hall. Pity got the best of her and she went to him. He looked like one of Toulouse-Lautrec's paintings of drunks. He swayed against her, his face red, lips swollen, his hands clumsy. She put him to bed, then brought the heater into the sitting room and sat in the green light of the stacked wine bottles. She imagined herself as she was at thirteen, a junior Olympic swimmer, most at home in a swimming pool with Critter. She had gotten very drunk once and kissed him. They were camped out under the yard light at her auntie's place on the reservation. Critter was passed out when she did it. His lips, she remembered, were purple in the mercury light. He looked alien, painted—she pressed her lips against his. Critter kissed back, but didn't wake. She took that as a sign and quit.

That morning the thawing snow in the gutter lip of the roof leaked into their sitting room. Ginny removed the green wall of bottles and shoveled the slush into their bathing bucket. She threw the first bucket out the window. From the little balcony across the way a lady with a white towel wrapped around the waist of her dress called to her to stop, gesturing down into the courtyard below. Ginny could not see where the lady pointed, but guessed that whatever it was, she was dumping snow on it. Embarrassed, Ginny nodded and took the next bucketful to the sink, washing it down with hot water. As she bailed the snow out of the gutter, she glanced at the lady putting towels out to dry on a clothesline attached to the little iron railing. The lady leaned out to untie a nylon mesh bag of sausages hanging from the rail, something she had probably done every afternoon at cooking time, but this time the sausage snaked out and dropped. Across the way the lady leaned farther out to see where the meat had landed. From her own rail Ginny could see the bag in the courtyard. The lady, because of the angle, could not see what had become of her meal. She looked across to Ginny, then called to her in French. Unable to answer, Ginny stepped away from the window.

For several minutes the lady called, saying something about her sleeping baby. Ginny thought she should go down and bring the meat back up. But she couldn't imagine where the lady's apartment was in relation to theirs, how she would get there across the courtyard, which stairs to take. The best Ginny could manage was to go down into the courtyard and place the sausages where the lady, who was still leaning across her railing, could see them. As Ginny did this, the woman continued to call out, "Mon Dieu!" and "Non!" She must have thought Ginny was crazy. "Pardon!" Ginny yelled, then she ran into the street.

She did not know where she was going and before she knew it she was lost. Walking until she found the river, she managed to get her bearings. She made her way to the window with the woodcut. As she examined the carefully depicted roof-tops, the artist himself came out to greet her. He spoke English immediately, telling her that this was his studio. Everything he said came out in a small laugh. Ginny had noticed the French had small laughs. She had learned to contain her great loud chuckle which always came out when she talked to strangers. But today, she felt quite encouraged.

"Where was it you saw this view?" Ginny began. "The view from my room nearly matches the woodcut."

"Ah," he said, "And so does mine." He smiled at her warmly.

They stood in at the window for a few minutes, then Ginny explained that she entered the building farther down the block, it must be another building.

"It is the same building," he insisted. "This is the outside–you have an apartment on inside, no?"

Ginny still couldn't see it, so when this artist, this stranger, kindly said, "Allow me," Ginny let herself be shown into his studio. She followed him up five flights of stairs to a window which opened into her courtyard. Above, Ginny saw the rooms under the eaves with laundry flapping on their railings. This artist had lived below her all these months. At that moment she knew exactly where she fit inside the courtyard, how the stairs climbed to her rooms. She knew exactly where she was, and where she would rather be.

Kirk was in the little kitchen when she woke the next morning. He did not call out to her, so she went to the window.

She stood a long time choosing a roof-top whose building she might pass when she walked by herself later that day. Ginny was already moving down the streets that would take her to the train station, to the plane, and finally, some day soon, home. But then, in the three rooms, six floors up, she wandered only as far as the doorway before she turned. Ginny's eye caught Kirk drinking coffee, but, distracted, she saw him as a stranger, the way you can look right at a friend in a crowd and not know it because you didn't expect to see that person in that place. Ginny felt herself gliding away like that Indian guy in the metro. She held onto that sensation because it warmed her. She held it even as Kirk looked up to her. For as long as she could, she refused to recognize him, because it was so much better to be strangers.

East to West

Leslie Harper

Today it is about to rain. Norma stands in her doorway, wondering how many times she's yelled for Marcie to come in. This door she stands in does not face east, and she thinks maybe that's why Colin left her fifteen years ago with a baby too young to recognize yet. Today is a good day for remembering.

Norma remembers how on a muddy spring morning she woke to the words, "It's a good day to have a baby."

She opened her eyes to a tall, flat, black figure. Whose spirit was guiding this child's coming, Norma wondered. As she sat up, she realized it was her mother, Jeannette, standing in front of white curtains.

"Ma, what are you doing here?"

"I came to see you have that baby."

"Ma, how'd you get here?"

"The bus, how else?" Jeannette states, as if a three-hundred-mile bus trip off the reservation was absolutely common. It wasn't. Norma always went to see her mother when one or the other desired company.

"Couldn't Mary've brought you?"

"Oh, that boyfriend of hers. Thinks he knows all about cars, but he doesn't. We barely make it home from bingo some nights, it gets so cold sitting out there. Even in the summer."

"That's too bad."

"What's too bad is, she can't see you, can't be here to see you have that baby."

"Oh, Ma, not yet. I feel fine."

So Norma got out of bed to go to the store for breakfast. On the way home she slipped coming down the hill. Norma didn't want to scare her mother and tried to sneak into the bedroom to change her muddy clothes. Oh, but Jeannette was angry. She had seen it all from the window. She thinned her lips and said, "If there's anything wrong with that baby . . ."

An hour later Jeannette nudged her daughter on the couch, saying, "You're going to have that baby. I can feel it."

"Ma, you okay?" Jeannette was breathing hard, her face was puckered up.

"It's okay now, " Jeannette exhaled. "Come on. It's time."

Norma got her shoes and coat and they walked to the street. The women had to wait twenty minutes for a bus. There was no money for a cab. She was worried about her mother. Jeannette's spasms were coming pretty regularly now.

When they got to the Indian Health Service clinic, the woman at the reception window said, "Oh, no, is it time for you?"

"Time for me to what?" Norma asked.

"Time for you to have that baby," the woman answered.

"No, my ma's having some troubles. I don't know what's happening. My ma's gotta see a doctor. Now. Look at her."

Jeannette was sitting quietly in a corner. Every few minutes her face would knot up and she'd breathe deeply.

"Jesus Christ, I think my ma's having a heart attack. Get a doctor!"

Jeannette said she didn't need a doctor, that Norma needed one. Pretty soon some guys came out with a wheelchair. They wheeled Jeannette away to another room, one with a few less people in it. A woman asked what she was feeling. Jeannette said, "Labor pains."

A few people in the room looked at her like she was crazy. wondering if the old woman knew what she was saying. They checked Jeannette's vitals and concluded that nothing was wrong with her. The doctors were standing around, mumbling against themselves, when Norma's water broke.

"Jesus Christ," was all Norma could think to say. She didn't know what to do next. There had been no warning signals, and she was somewhat embarrassed. Wasn't a woman supposed to know these things? Jeannette's spasms stopped at this moment. The doctors would never understand how, but that woman bore her own daughter's labor pains.

The baby turned out to be a seven pound girl who needed a name. Norma wanted to call her Rainy Day, but Colin said, "What little girl wants a gray name like that?"

"Rainbows aren't gray," Norma came back quickly enough. Colin just looked at her like Alaska and unspoke the argument.

So she was called Marcie. Years later, Marcie would receive her great aunt's name, Chi-Ikwe (Big or Great Woman), and Norma would call her Marcie-Woman.

The summer of her first year, an old woman at the clinic leaned over and said, "Your baby's special. You can see it in her eyes." It was true. Marcie's eyes were shinier than the rings her Uncle George used to make before his fingers folded up—rivers of turquoise and coral set deep in the terra firma of silver.

The little family moved up north next door to Norma's ma, and before you could say gather, parch, winnow and jig, Colin was gone with the colors of the leaves.

They carried on just fine without him. Norma took Marcie outside after a too-long winter. On that day Marcie received a gift—an introduction to the earth. Marcie discovered dirt. How soft! Different from sticky linoleum. She plowed her fingers through the driveway, rolled around, over and through, and finally, spread-eagled on her back, fell asleep. After that Marcie was always the first to find berry patches; her plant from school turned into a whole row of beans in the garden. It seemed Norma could never get her daughter inside the house. She had learned well the trails her grandfather taught her, always knew what plants would settle her mother's stomach and sore throat. Evenings, Norma would yell, "Marcie-Woman! Time for dinner!"

When Marcie finally came in, she'd say, "It's about time. Your supper's nearly frozen." This was completely untrue. Norma always knew how long it would take her daughter to tear herself away from the moss and didn't put her food on a plate until the fourth time she called.

When it rained, Norma would send Marcie outside with a bar of soap and say, "Now get cleaned up," She'd watch through the screen door. Marcie danced around, giving herself completely to the storm. If she knew she wasn't being watched, she'd strip off her bathing suit and run around naked. Years later this would make Norma nervous, to see her daughter's hips wanting to shake, and her nipples so pink turning brown. She'd lie in the puddle, soak up her hair, stand under the gutter to rinse. No matter what, Marcie could not be caught at the door with a towel. She'd track around the kitchen and finally ended up in the big silver washtub.

Norma's memories are interrupted by a where-have-I-seen-this-before familiar looking car that pulls up and stops by the garbage cans. It is a reservation security man, the fat one with stringy hair.

"Hello, Kevin. What brings you out here? Are you just making sure I'm secure?" Norma calls out to him.

He looks at her like he'd like a Rolaid, his dry cracking fingers palming his forehead, "Uh, Norma . . ."

This is where Norma loses the story. She will never remember hearing the words: accident . . . a mile from here . . . Marcie . . . Merle, that boy she goes out with . . . alcohol . . . nothing could have been done. Norma sees only his jacket, ripped out at the armpit, stuffing piling out to cleaner air, his greasy lips alternately hiding and revealing the rotten front tooth to the rhythm of tragedy. She runs out the back door, falling down the steps, and rushes for the woods yelling, "Marcie! Marcie-Woman!" She does not come out for a long time.

Norma has passed a year waiting for the rain to bring her daughter back. She is again standing in this door that does not face east, looking at a bar of soap stuck behind the piece of plywood she once nailed to the screen door. Norma wants for all her life to yell, "Marcie! Time for dinner!" and to see her daughter's long thick legs unwind from the trees. The wind is picking up now and her nubby dog, Buzz, is hiding under an invalid car. The rain begins to fall, sounding like seven jingle dress dancers.

She finds herself out of the torn purple skirt and faded orange blouse. Past the concrete steps, she jumps in a puddle, runs the entire length of the yard. Norma, knowing her mother can see her, abandons her underpants and bra, dances around the plum tree that she knows will bear young, sweet purple plums soon. As she stands under the gutter to wet her hair, Norma thinks, "So this is what it must be like to feel your hips want to shake."

⋈⋈

Blackbird Women

Denise Sweet

I t was Aunt Gen who first raised my suspicions about the Sisters at Our Lady of Lourdes. Like at my first communion. She heard one of the Sisters say, "I think of the children as my very own." Aunt Gen had a fit when she heard that one. We had to leave in a hurry. She said to me on the way back to White Earth in Uncle Cece's truck, "They got their eyes on you, my girl." She was looking out the window at the time.

Aunt Gen and my mom don't see eye to eye about the Sisters. My Aunt Gen thinks like the old-timers on our reservation think and she don't like the parish school or the Sisters or nothing. "We're no match against that medicine of theirs," Aunt Gen says. "Look at us—our kids making signs across and forgetting about Wenabojho. Grown-ups ashamed of old ways."

My mom thinks parish school is the greatest thing since indoor toilets. She don't want me to go to no school that don't teach catechism. My Uncle Cece works at the sawmill in Winston so he drops me and my stupid brother off every morning at the school. I don't like the ride very much. Sometimes I get sick to my stomach and have to eat soda crackers. Uncle Cece keeps some in the glove box for me.

My mom don't want Aunt Gen to talk about witches to me either, but it don't matter. I'm only eleven but I've known for a long time about some people having powers and some not. Take me for example. I'm left-handed and my father was a full-blood.

162

I was also born with pierced ears. Aunt Gen says not to brag or your magic will turn on you or something will take it from you. So I'm careful, especially around the Sisters. They are all witches for sure, says Aunt Gen.

I've been thinking about the Sisters at Our Lady of Lourdes like they may be up to no good with me. For one thing, they try to make me write with my right hand when I do much nicer with my left. Aunt Gen says forcing someone to go against their natural direction is like trying to change the flow of a river. Uncle Cece says the Anglos can do that too.

And then there was the hair note I brung home last winter. Sister Stephanie's in charge of dress and personal grooming and one day she sent a note home with me. The note said Sister Stephanie found a creepy-crawler in my hair. It said the long hair had to go. My mom was so ashamed. I told her not to worry. Since the nights had been so cold, Makwa, that fleabag dog of ours had been crawling into my bed. That's where the bugs came from. My mom got over it, but she told me not to tell anyone about this. That made me mad. I wanted to tell my friends Jerry Hokanen and Patrick O'Grintz. Neither of them have dogs, much less creepy-crawlers.

When Aunt Gen saw my hair cut short, whoa was she mad! She let out a howl that sent Makwa barreling through the kitchen, scratching the door to go outside. Uncle Cece don't say too much, but he started yelling at Aunt Gen this time. He told her to sit down and listen while my mom explained. My mom seemed like she was expecting this kind of reaction from Aunt Gen. She told her my hair would grow back in time and besides short hair looked nice on me. It was no good. Hair is a big thing to Aunt Gen. When Aunt Gen looks at me now, she has this way of looking as though something was hovering over the top of my head. Makes her look as though she's just bit into a wormy apple. I don't know what it is. I'd never had a haircut before. The ends of my hair feel sharp and bristly. I do sort of miss my braid.

After the hair note, Aunt Gen started sitting me down and talking to me about those old blackbirds at Our Lady of Lourdes. Mostly she warns me not to believe anything the Sisters tell me especially when it comes to sinful acts. She also talks to me about the prayers. Aunt Gen says it just isn't a good idea to be a nag to the Creator about how bad you think you are and how bad you'll always be. To her, this is like bragging. Besides, calling for help all the time with only yourself in mind is false reverence, Aunt Gen says. Being grateful and giving thanks, now that's a different story. Keep your prayers for special, she tells me.

Here's where the word-songs come in handy. I say these for my own amusement during Mass or while I'm waiting for confession. Here's one I say instead of Our Father. You can use it, but if you say it out loud and catch heck, I'll deny I ever heard such a thing:

Cow fodder, warts and seven,
tallow plugs your brain,
thy king is dumb,
thy rope is rung,
an earthworm's in your navel.

Give us a dog to dunk or bread,
and fleabag our best guests,
as we fleabag those
who pass gas against us.

Now you are shabby,
and what a wide end (sometimes I whistle here)
amen. Way ah hey hey.

One night at bedtime prayers, I started my favorite "Half monkey, full of grapes," and my mom was standing in the hallway and overheard me. I do believe she thrashed me within an inch of my life. She don't think that kind of thing is funny. I'm more careful now.

At school, Patrick O'Grintz and Jerry Hokanen and I have this special club for witch-hunting. Like Aunt Gen says, you got to be on your guard and we're just the ones to do it. We keep watch over all the kids, especially the ones who play by themselves. See, when you're alone a lot, it's easy for a witch to raise heck with you.

Our second duty is to spy on the Sisters. This is the best part of being a witch hunter. During recess Jerry Hokanen, Patrick O'Grintz and I hide under the stairwell next to the Sisters' meeting room and wait for the last one of them to go in. When she shuts the door, we move in and listen for witch plans.

Sometimes it's hard to tell witch plans from teacher plans. Patrick said that the Sisters probably use a code language and we would have to break the master code to understand what's going on. It was his idea to put our songbooks for High Mass up to a mirror, but we deciphered nothing. Latin is Latin, even backwards in a mirror. But Patrick has not given up. He is good at this kind of thing. He's left-handed too.

Well, we've been listening for a couple of days straight and nothing has come of it. We're under the stairwell again and Jerry's telling about Nancy Laneri talking right out loud during her confession last Thursday when we hear this terrible rumbling up above us. It sounds as though someone has fallen the whole flight of stairs, head over teakettles. I don't dare move. I'm so scared of being found in the building during recess time that I can hear my own heart beating inside my skull. Then we hear someone say "goddammit" and really mean it. It was Sister Adelbert.

And then Patrick O'Grintz starts giggling. Patrick is my best friend and all, but he can't control himself very well. I want to see Sister Adelbert laid out on the floor as much as anyone, rubbing her fanny and cussing like my Uncle Cece, but laughing at the Sisters is inviting trouble. We were supposed to be out on the playground.

Patrick holds his breath and I pinch his nose but it don't help. He's hopeless. Next thing I know, he's cracking up, right out loud, and Jerry Hokanen can't help but laugh with him. I'm so mad at them both, I feel like crying.

It's too late. Sister Adelbert picks herself up off the floor and comes over to where we were hiding. The witch hunters of Our Lady of Lourdes have been found. Sister is so mad to see us inside during recess that her face is all white and puffed up like the underbelly of a catfish. The hair note was nothing compared to the note that was to come out of this.

Sister Adelbert is a whole lot stronger than any of us ever gave her credit for. She grabs me by one arm and lifts me up and out from under the stairwell like I was some scrawny chicken about to be butchered. She does the same to Patrick and Jerry until the three of us are standing in a row in front of her, wishing we had the magic enough to disappear into thin air.

She marches us up to fourth floor to see the principal, Sister Ignatia. I thought I saw her once at a school picnic. Sister Ignatia's got to be the skinniest nun I've ever seen. That stiff white habit sort of cuts into her forehead and her cheekbones stick out like chunks of ice. Her hands look like claws and her glasses set on the tip of her peaked nose, steaming up with every squawk that comes from her paper-thin lips. That day at the picnic, Sister Ignatia had been standing at the top of the stairs outside in front of the school, like some old scarecrow with her long black habit flapping around her legs. One of the eighth-grade boys said that one time the wind had whipped her habit high enough so's you could see she wore long johns, but I never believed it. In the middle of May?

Sister Ignatia whispers something to Sister Adelbert, and the next thing I know, I'm watching Jerry and Patrick walk away from me with Sister Adelbert holding the door for them. I try to follow, but Sister Ignatia steps in my way and closes the door behind them. I look around her office, trying to avoid her eyes. I remember Aunt Gen saying that if you lock gazes with a witch, they can steal your thoughts. This I didn't need. I look out the window at the playground and try to watch some kids play crack the whip.

Then Sister Ignatia tells me to go to the cupboard near the closet in her office. I'm to bring her the jar of beans. I open the cupboard and haul out a jar of black turtle beans and place them on her desk. She opens the jar and tells me to scatter them in a row on the floor. By now, I'm getting pretty scared. What sort of magic is this? Aunt Gen never told me much about beans, only that they're good in soup. Corn, butternut squash and black turtle beans. She calls it Three Sister's Soup.

Sister Ignatia wants me to kneel on the beans. I don't believe her at first. She says I'm harder to train than the others and that I have relatives that consort with the devil. She presses me to the floor and my knees settle into the hard black plugs. My knees begin to hurt so bad that I know for certain I will die from this penance. Sister Ignatia hands me her rosary and stands over me, holding the back of my neck. We begin. For the first time in my life, I say an Our Father as though I am a sinner.

When Aunt Gen heard of my punishment, she made Uncle Cece drive her to parish school to see Sister Ignatia. She came home and told my mom she was going to keep me away from those cussed blackbirds at the school. My mom just stood there and listened while Aunt Gen told her what they did to me. Aunt Gen made me go to my room. I try to listen but Makwa tries to scratch open my door and starts to whine. I can hear Aunt Gen and Uncle Cece talk Indian about what has happened.

Makwa pushes the door open and jumps on my bed. I am trying to study my catechism because tomorrow there will be a quiz on the Holy Days of Obligation. Aunt Gen brings me a cup of tea and sits on the bed to watch me drink it. She doesn't say anything for a long time. Then she takes a tiny bundle of cedar that she has made and puts it between my blankets like she was tucking a little kitten to sleep. Aunt Gen says that old witch is afraid. We have a strong medicine, she says and shakes her fist. All I want to know is why Sister Ignatia punished me and not Patrick or Jerry. But I don't ask Aunt Gen. I want to tell her that she was right. Sister Ignatia is sure enough an old witch blackbird with a magic stronger than anything I can muster. But it's hard to make the words come. Any magic left in me, I'd better save pretty much just to stay alive.

⧳⧳⧳

The Waiting

Marcie Rendon

In between the time of wake and asleep I listen to my mother's footsteps come up the stairs. I am so tired. I struggle to keep my eyes open until she reaches the top step.

Every morning I am disappointed that once again I haven't stayed awake until she could reach me. I know in my six-year-old heart that the only reason she doesn't take me with her is because when she gets to the top stair she sees that I am sleeping. She loves me so much she can't bear to wake me.

Each morning I swear that the next night I will try harder.

They haul me from psychiatrist to psychiatrist. My behavior puzzles them. Can someone explain why I try to sleep standing on my head? Why I dance on the railroad tracks, whirling, twirling in the sun as the engineer wildly sounds his horn? Can someone please explain to them why I wake at three in the morning and sneak into the attic and wrap myself in the tattered clothes the social worker brought me in?

The last psychiatrist tries to get me to play with a dollhouse. My seven-year-old brain knows he's looking for past abuse, some secret of my mother's and father's house to explain my strange behavior. I amuse him by throwing darts at a concrete floor, week after week, hour after hour creating sparks, an eighty-five-dollars-an-hour fireworks display. He never once straight out asks why I behave so strangely.

I would tell him it is my hope that if I behave badly, strangely enough, they will send me home.

During Advent the church sponsors a holiday bazaar. My tomboy body is dressed in scratchy tights and red plaid dress, braids shorn (I'm still not convinced I'm not going to die from this violation of my sacred being.) I see two women, ungirdled body rolls visible under calico print dresses, gray-streaked braids held back by beaded barrettes. As I approach the table of their wares, I am afraid to meet their eyes. If one of them is an auntie or cousin, my body will dissolve to ashes like the preacher says. Instead I run my hands over beaded medallions, feeling each bead come alive under my trembling fingertips. I give them time to recognize me first. But I am a lost child. As if they feel my pain, they call me "little one" and point with lips to my beaded moccasins. I run my homesick hands over tanned buckskin. From that spot I can smell wild rice and bacon grease, the smell of their hair carries me to pine groves and tarpaper shacks heated by wood stoves.

That night I dream of flying over treetops. In the distance I see a plume of smoke and circle down. Through a glowing window I see my parents and my brother and my sisters eating venison, laughing loudly at my mother's jokes. Before I join them, I decide to use the outhouse.

So begins a two-year cycle of shame as I awaken in a dampened bed.

It's also a cycle where I myself question my sanity. As I dream and fly nightly, sharing in my family's joys and sorrows, I become convinced that dreamtime is reality and waking hours are really when I'm sleeping.

And both realities are shattered when I'm told, not so gently, that my father has cancer and they've amputated his right arm. While I'm not allowed to see him, I am vaguely assured he isn't going to die.

Starting at eleven, I follow in my mother's footsteps and drink my pain away. Daily, weekly, nightly—I sneak every chance I get to numb the pain. My evening travels end as the nightmares of my days crowd my breaking heart. Physical abuse. Sexual abuse. Emotional abuse. But no one and nothing can touch the inner me.

Years pass. If they ever make a movie of my life it will be of a time warp. A deserted foreign planet, lacking in breathable atmosphere.

There are no dates for homecoming, junior/senior prom. Taunts (squaw, whore, squaw) delivered interchangeably in the school lunchroom line are more effective than any inner-city political redlining. Weekends are spent with boys, a twelve-pack (or a case), and suicide music airwaved in from Oklahoma City, Oklahoma. (Oklahoma, the final destination of the Trail of Tears).

Graduation happens. Into a paper bag I pack a pair of blue jeans, one red and one brown t-shirt. Without saying good-bye, without a backward look, I hitch-hike to my father's house. He gets up from the white, paint-chipped kitchen table. With his left arm, his only arm, slowly (to keep the coffee separate from the grounds) he pours me a cup of coffee. He says, "Come in, my girl, I was expecting you."

As we drink in silence he hands me a yellow telegram. Its short message tells me that my mother died two days earlier in Warm Springs, Montana. The alcohol finally did its job well enough to erase all her pain.

That night, between wake time and sleep time, I hear her footsteps on the stairs.

▷◁▷◁◁

Runnin' on Empty

Penny Olson

Runnin' on empty, runnin' blind,
I'm runnin' into the sun, but I'm
runnin' behind.

M ichael Ryan handed the salesman a cashier's check
for $2500, opened the door of the cherry-red 1965 rag-
top Mustang convertible, and taking a deep breath,
started the car. He waited for the joy to overtake him . . . nothing.
Driving off the car lot and shifting into third gear, he headed
out to the highway, California Highway 101. He shifted into
fourth and tried to match his mood to the accelerating Mustang.

The sun beat down on the sportscar. Michael had been out
of the Army since 1977, a little over two years, and still the
California sun surprised him with its December warmth. He
changed course, heading his Mustang for the mountains, longing
for the snow that he knew would be covering the ground at home
in the U.P.

The boys and I would be out on the snow machines right
now. We'd each have a pint of Schnapps to help keep us warm.
Suddenly Michael's thoughts changed tracks. Snow machines,
snow and Michigan were a lifetime ago. Nothing would ever be
that easy again. Winter, and all that went with it, were part of
Michael's memories of real life. Real life was Escanaba before
the six months he had spent in Viet Nam. California with its

171

year-round sunshine made it easier for him not to think of home. He just had to soak up the constant sunshine. If he returned, he might have to find his path again, as Gramps was so fond of saying, but he didn't feel up to attempting that kind of journey.

"Well, Gramps," Michael spoke aloud. "At least I've got my pony. You always said that a warrior needed to have a pony. I did it backwards though. I went into battle first, and then got my pony. What else is new? I never could do anything the right way."

Michael's father was Anishinaabe and Lakota. Gramps would joke that his heritage was at war with itself and that's why his descendants were all so different. And they were. Out of the seven Ryan children, Michael was the one who listened most to the old man's stories while growing up. He was the middle child like his grandfather had been, and maybe that's what created the bond they shared. Michael knew Gramps' stories held special truths for him. At one time, before Nam, the stories even gave his life direction, a path to follow.

Gramps was never in a hurry. One time when they were visiting the farm, Michael complained about how his older brother Jason would never wait for him.

"Gramps, I yell at him to wait," Michael almost whined, "and he just goes faster. If I speed up, he runs. If I stop to climb a tree, or blow the fluff from a dandelion like I do with you, Jason says, 'You're such a baby, I'm outta here.' Today he said he would only wait for me if I gave him my candy bar."

"Did you?"

Michael shook his head. Gramps smiled.

"First off," Gramps rumpled Michael's hair, "continue doing what you're doing. Don't be in such a hurry to grow up. We already have one Jason in our family; we need a Michael to keep things in balance."

Gramps stopped talking, picked up a shovel, handed it to Michael, grabbed a rake and motioned to a pile of fertilizer that needed to be spread around the garden. Michael worked silently next to Gramps and waited for him to continue. After a few minutes Michael's built-up frustration boiled over.

"Yeah, but why can't Jason wait for me just once? It wouldn't kill him, you know."

Gramps raked even more fertilizer into the soil before he answered. "If he did, my son," Gramps stopped and leaned on the rake's handle, "then he wouldn't be Jason."

Michael shook the memories from his head and tightly gripped the steering wheel. "Let's see how fast this pony can go," he said, stepping on the gas. "The speedometer says 150. I wonder if it'll make it."

The first time he had ever ridden a horse Gramps had taken him. He must have been four years old. Jason, who was eight, had balked about getting on Ryder, the old quarter horse that Gramps had saddled up.

"I'm not gettin' on any ol' horse, Gramps," Jason mumbled, scuffing up dust with the toe of his gym shoe. "I wanna drive the tractor. Mikie likes horses, take him for a ride."

"Lemme, Gramps," Michael tugged at his grandfather's arm. "Let me ride, please?"

Gramps lifted Michael up and set him on Ryder's back. Michael was so small that his feet dangled at least six inches short of the stirrups.

"Stay with Ryder," Gramps said as he led the horse around the corral. "A Lakota warrior always becomes one with his pony. If a warrior ever goes into battle, his pony can be the difference between life and death."

Later that afternoon while Jason helped with the tractor, Michael learned about brushing Ryder and the other work involved in taking care of a horse. When they were done, the boys went up to the loft to throw some hay down so Gramps wouldn't have to climb up and do it.

"Hey, Mikie, you were pretty good on ol' Ryder, but did you see me on that tractor? Gramps let me drive it all by myself."

"Someday I'll ride Ryder all by myself." Michael strutted with pride that his older brother had actually noticed something he had done.

"Yeah, sure, but you won't ever drive the tractor by yourself." Jason gave his little brother a friendly shove into a bale of hay. The two boys wrestled and tried to tickle each other before throwing the hay down for their grandfather. When the chore was finished Jason pretended to be a high wire aerialist on one of the beams of the barn's loft.

"Do you dare me to jump in the hay down there, Mikie?" Jason gave a lopsided grin. "Do you?"

Michael started to say yes, but he shook his head no instead. He saw that one of the horses was out of its stall, and he didn't want Jason to frighten it. The horse also gave him a good excuse to say no without making him appear chicken in Jason's eyes.

After that day Michael dreamed of being a warrior and quickly gained skill as a rider. When he was ten, he rode bareback. At 15, a little more than a year before he went to Nam, he helped Gramps train horses. He was always on the lookout for the one horse that would be his, the one Gramps said every warrior needed, the one that he could trust his life with.

But overnight Michael became interested in Jason's type of pony. He still rode horses, but they didn't go fast enough any more. He craved the speed of cars. Before, Jason had been the one covered in grease from tinkering with engines. Now Michael caught his fever. When, after high school Jason began work as a mechanic for Coynes, the Chevy dealer in Escanaba, Michael stopped by at least twice a week and washed all the cars on the lot just to be able to touch a red '65 Mustang he had fallen for. He stopped going out to the farm to help Gramps.

While he gave grudging acceptance or approval for something Michael accomplished, Jason never let him forget that he would always be older, stronger, smarter and better at everything than Michael was. "Finally figured out that a pony doesn't get the job done, huh, Little Brother?" Jason questioned Michael two weeks after his sixteenth birthday. "Why don't you take that Mustang out to Sioux Hill for a ride? Just to see what it's like? Afterwards, I swear to God, you'll never ride another horse."

"Won't we get in trouble for this?" Michael questioned Jason, wondering what his brother's ulterior motive was. "Won't your boss get mad?"

"I don't think so. He told me to take the car for a ride and open her up. You'll just owe me, Little Brother. Let's go."

Michael didn't wait for Jason to change his mind; he jumped into the passenger seat. Jason grinned and started the car. He pulled out onto the highway and headed for the back roads that would take them through the developing subdivision. Michael turned on the car radio. He punched buttons, listened for the right kind of music for cruising in the Mustang. Bubblegum Top 40 wouldn't do; he had to hear Pink Floyd, The Doors, Hendrix, Joplin. He quickly forgot about any ulterior motives Jason might have for being nice to him.

Jason turned onto a gravel road, accelerated into second. Michael watched the speedometer jump to thirty. Jason shifted to third, and as the speedometer came close to fifty, he punched it into fourth. Michael was mesmerized by the speedometer and he watched it as it jumped to 70, 85, 95, 110. He wondered if the tires were touching the ground. The speedometer went all the way up to 150; would Jason dare go that fast? Michael glanced out the back window; all he could see was white billowing out behind the car. He glanced at the speedometer again; it was pushing past 150 m.p.h.

"Woooh," Michael let out a rush of air. "I can't even hear the radio. This is great." The steady rat-tat-tat-tat-tat of gravel against the floor boards and tailpipe drowned out the radio cranked to blow a speaker. "Jason," he screamed. "Look at the needle; it's buried. This is almost like flying."

Just as Jason looked down at the speedometer, a white-tailed deer jumped out in front of them. The car hit its hindquarters and the sudden impact of deer and Mustang put the car in the air. Blood, fur, glass and metal became a tangled mess. The back half of the animal tore through the engine. Michael's head cracked the windshield. The Mustang finally came to a stop two-hundred yards beyond where it had hit the animal.

Michael opened his eyes, tried to wipe the blood that streamed from a gash in his forehead. "Jason, are you okay? Jason?"

No one sat in the driver's seat next to Michael. An opening gaped where the windshield had been on the driver's side a few seconds earlier. Michael tried the car door; it would not budge. He kicked with all his strength, heard metal grate against metal as the door gave way. He smelled blood mixed with gasoline as he searched for his brother.

"Jason? Where the hell are you? Answer me, damn it!" He saw a crumpled form lying on remains of the deer. "NO!" he screamed, and ran to his brother.

Michael tried to shake him, clutched at his coveralls, expected Jason to yell at him. He watched Jason's head roll in slow motion at an unnatural angle. Gently he laid his brother back down and unzipped his coverall zipper. He wiped the blood from his hands onto his jeans so he wouldn't get Jason's favorite flannel shirt dirty. He felt for a heartbeat. All he found was an envelope with "Draft Notice" printed on it.

Michael Ryan was found in shock, wandering down County Road 552, by a farmer an hour later. He still carried Jason's bloodied draft notice in his hand. Four days later he was let out of the hospital in time for his brother's funeral. A week later on June 17, 1971, Michael enlisted in the Army. One month later he left Escanaba for Fort Dix and Boot Camp. He requested overseas duty and received his orders for Nam four months to the day of the accident.

Until the war ended in April, 1973, Michael tried to take what he felt was Jason's place. He reacted to everything as though he was on auto pilot. Every time he came close to seeing what was actually going on around him, he would see Jason crumpled on the ground. He couldn't shake the vision for days. No matter how much dirt he covered himself with, he could only smell the horrible mixture of gas and blood. After he was shipped home, he remained in the service for another four years. Now two years after he had gotten out of the Army and seven years after the accident, he still heard Jason say, "You'll just owe me, Little Brother."

Michael walked onto the Ford lot looking for a used car to get him back and forth to work. He never expected to see a cherry red '65 Mustang waiting there for him. Once he saw the pony, he had to have it.

Maybe, Michael thought as he headed east toward the Sierra Nevadas, *maybe I can go home. It's been seven years. I've found another pony. Maybe . . .*

Michael turned on the radio. Jackson Browne's rough-edged voice blared out of the speaker. "Runnin' on empty; runnin' blind." Michael harmonized with the radio. "I'm runnin' into the sun, but I'm runnin' behind. He looked down at the speedometer. It remained steady at 90.

His foot pressed down on the accelerator; Jason would have to go at least 120. Jason would have the music louder. Jason would . . . and that's when Gramps' voice cut through the music. "We already have a Jason; we need a Michael to keep things in balance."

He eased off the accelerator. The speedometer rested between 85 and 90. *This is fast enough,* Michael told himself. *Gramps said it was a matter of working with, not conquering, the horse.*

He reached over to turn down the volume. Jackson Browne played his kind of music; he didn't need to blare it. As he looked down, reaching for the right button to turn, the blare of the semi's horn jolted him back to the highway. He crossed over the solid white line dividing traffic. He was headed straight for the oncoming semi.

Michael's only chance for survival would be to sandwich the Mustang between the semi and the narrow shoulder of the road where the cliff dropped into the valley. He yanked on the steering wheel and struggled to keep the Mustang under control. Eventually, he brought it to a jerky stop on the narrow strip of gravel on the opposite shoulder of the road. If he had been going any faster, if he had gone another six inches to the left, he would have been airborne.

At first he just sat in the car, afraid to get out, afraid to even breathe, let alone look out his window. His soaked shirt clung to his body. He closed his eyes and rested his head on the steering wheel. Finally he opened his door, carefully got out of the car, and looked over the precipice. His drawn-out sigh echoed back to him.

"I don't owe you anything anymore, Jason. I can't be you," he started in a whisper, but his voice gathered strength and momentum as he continued. "Gramps was right; we had a Jason in our family. We need Michael for balance."

Sovereign Motions

⋈⟩⋈

Giiwedahn: Coming Home
Summer 2000

Winona LaDuke

The ancestors were loud and getting louder. Moose Hanford could hear the ancestors even over the music from his tape deck and the roar of the road beneath the wheels as his ex-UPS delivery van hummed down the interstate through southern Illinois. There were forty-five ancestors in the back of the van. Resting. Now on their way home. Sometimes he could hear them sing, other times they were crying out. Now they just seemed to rattle.

The tape of Little Otter singing intertribals accompanied Moose on his journey. When Little Otter's drum stopped between songs, the sounds from the ancestors also ceased for a moment, but the rattling continued. Moose realized this noise was coming from his van. He turned off the cassette player and listened closely to the mechanical cacophony.

The van was an old UPS delivery van that had been virtually donated to Moose by the UPS driver who had had the misfortune of having White Earth on his route. The van had been well used by the time Moose had gotten his hands on it, and now it counted two hundred thousand miles more on the odometer before that too broke. Moose sifted through his mind, discarding various squeaks, rattles, and creaks that he had grown accustomed to in his van and focused his mind on a possible source for this new ailment.

He moved the van into the right lane and continued listening intently. He inadvertently drove over a pothole and the rattle became a scraping sound accompanied by the full-bore roar of the engine. Only one thing made that music: an exhaust system gone bad.

Moose quickly scanned the horizon for a place to pull over. *The last thing I need*, he told himself, *is for a cop to stop me, see I'm a skin, and give me a ticket for driving without an exhaust—and start asking me questions.* He sighted a rest stop a few miles ahead. He glanced in his sideview mirror to change lanes and to see if he had left any important parts of his van behind. He drummed his fingers on the door, slowed the van to thirty-five and set his sights on the rest stop, tiptoeing his van the last two miles.

Moose pulled the van into the rest area and killed the engine. He grabbed his pack of cigarettes from the dash, opened the door, and stepped down. He lifted his pony tail off his back and shook the back of his shirt for ventilation. *A bush Indian was not meant to travel the southland during the summer. It must be eighty-five degrees with no wind. Too warm for an Ojibwe.* He stopped for a moment and scanned the scene. The rest stop was vacant.

Moose lit a cigarette and walked toward the back of the van. With some effort, he bent over and examined the muffler, reaching his hand toward it. "Shit! It's hot," he inadvertently yelled. Sure enough, the hanging clips had broken and most of the exhaust system was hanging precariously from one remaining anchor. He realized duct tape would not fix this one.

There was a lot of responsibility in this journey and it weighed heavily on Moose.

People around White Earth joked that Moose must have been Mole Clan on account of his uncanny knack at finding things in the ground. The only problem was that there wasn't a Mole Clan on White Earth, and so his Marten Clan tendencies would have to account. Moose had discovered the grave diggings in the first place. Then, with Elaine and Danielle Wabun's help, they had come up with an amazing inventory of the people and belongings missing from the reservation through the years. Where they were now was anybody's guess, but they bet the Smithsonian Institution, Peabody Museum at Harvard, Minnesota Historical Society, and the University of Minnesota were the first places to look. The list of missing persons and their belongings ran to fifty typewritten pages comprising approximately two hundred and fifty ancestors.

With some digging of her own, Elaine traced the work of a Smithsonian researcher, one Dr. Ales Hrdlicka, who had made several "scholarly" forays to White Earth in the 1910s. He had dug up the remains of forty-five White Earth ancestors, labeled them, packed them away in wooden crates, and shipped them one thousand miles away to Washington so they could be measured, catalogued, and studied. And there they remained.

The White Earth Government, with the agreement of the *Midewiwin* Society, had drafted several polite letters to the Smithsonian. The *aanikoobijigan*, the ancestors, were to come home, the religious leaders wrote, as were all of the traditional objects of the *Anishinaabeg*, particularly those from White Earth. Finally, after years of wrangling, they succeeded in winning an agreement from the Smithsonian that the remains of some of the ancestors could be repatriated. Moose's journey was the first mission to bring back the ancestors, and it was not surprising that there were some technical difficulties.

The Smithsonian's was known to be the largest collection with more than thirty-two thousand remains in one location, not to mention a million or so "artifacts" that were held in various boxes, drawers, and warehouses at the museum. The Smithsonian's White Earth collection was a result of the physical and social anthropologists they had enthusiastically dispatched over the years.

The Peabody at Harvard had a similar number of "specimens," and over the past few years had also begun to return remains and objects to Indian tribes nationally, and to a lesser extent, internationally. The Maoris and Tasmanians had been picked over particularly badly and they had waged an aggressive campaign for the return of their objects that had been underway for almost twenty-five years.

Smaller public collections at state historical societies and universities were also under pressure, and both the Minnesota Historical Society and the University of Minnesota had joined with the various reservations to form local historical societies and museums so they had somewhere to return artifacts.

The curator at the Smithsonian had been courteous, even helpful. The Smithsonian, it seemed, had become a repository for all bastions of colonial and military expansion. In an era when collecting the heads of Indian men was a common practice of the military and anthropologists, the Smithsonian, over the years, had received the booty of ornithologists, generals, and anthropologists—men who literally lifted the human remains off burial scaffolds to send east for scientific journals and presentations.

Alanis Nordstrom, with her penchant for research, painstakingly reviewed the anthropologists' and Indian agents' records for White Earth and, after a few trips to Washington, had matched to the best of her ability people, documents, and sacred items. Under a new law, funerary objects, human remains, and objects of cultural patrimony were required to be made available to their people.

Moose and George Naganob took the trip to Washington. The Great White Father's closets were full. The Smithsonian's Office of Repatriation had twenty full-time staff members, all busy trying to sort out whose femur belonged with whose vertebrae or skull and where they might have come from. It was a complex task in the face of tens of thousands of cases.

Moose and George followed the lanky Smithsonian anthropologist through the maze of rooms in the immense building, the doors clanging shut in one airtight and fireproof section after another. The man with a clipboard led them on and on, through the rooms, while the air seemed increasingly more precious and less available. Thousands of green boxes lined shelves built from floor to ceiling and containing bones, birds squished behind glass, reptiles, insects, and dinosaur parts. Moose and George walked through rooms where ancestors languished. In small boxes. The size and length of a femur, the largest bone in a human skeleton.

At first it was a hum, somewhere in the back of Moose's mind. Slowly, death chants, lullabies, love songs and war songs became a composite of music, chants in his mind and ear, as their voices crescendoed. An immense graveyard of the unwilling dead, out of order. He broke into a cold sweat, beads dribbled down his face and back, as he followed the anthropologist and George Naganob through the vault.

George was single-minded and hummed a song to himself. In that way he kept the music of others at bay. Moose's eyes scanned the names written on the boxes: Inuit, Kiowa, Pawnee, Oklahoma, New Mexico, Florida, Florida, Florida. George, however, stared straight ahead until the anthropologist stopped. The boxes read, "Minnesota, White Earth Ojibwe." The Smithsonian man looked at his clipboard and flipped through the inventory list, running his fingers over the numbers in the aisle. George and Moose watched quietly.

"These are all of them," the anthropologist finally announced. "You can look them over if you want and we'll bring them out for you tomorrow."

George nodded. "*Miigwetch*," he whispered, "Thank you."

"I'll leave you now," the anthropologist said, looking at his watch. "Should I come back in an hour?"

"OK. Good."

It was in this vast warehouse of the collected remains of people from around the world that George Naganob, with shaking voice and trembling hands, made an initial inventory of the White Earth ancestors and those contents of their graves the Smithsonian would return to them. Moose gently moved the bones as George carefully placed medicine bags, clan markers, moccasins, and other articles of clothing in with the old people. Then George wrote it down as best as he could in his notebook, listing from what village or site the bones had originated, names if possible, and any other notes.

The men worked a full two days with the forty-five ancestors, and when they were done, they placed each femur-sized green box into a larger box for shipping. Finished, they went to a local Piscataway native man's sweat lodge, cried tears that were lost amid their sweat, and prayed to get the smell of death off their bodies before they headed home. Moose was designated to drive the ancestors home.

George flew back to attend to lengthy preparations at home. He was to arrange for a reburial ceremony as well as to determine what articles might go into the White Earth Museum.

The museum was located in the old St. Benedict's Mission in the community college complex. The museum had memorabilia from White Earth history, some ceremonial objects, copies of birchbark scrolls, and other aspects of the cultural traditions of the White Earth *Anishinaabeg*. Most of the religious objects, however, had been removed from the exhibits and were either in use or in "safekeeping" with various families. The pipes had previously been displayed in the museum in the bordertown of Detroit Lakes. Now all the pipes that belonged on White Earth were back in the correct place and as best as people were able, were presently in use in the different ceremonies in the villages.

The same was true of the *Midewiwin* water drums and the big drums, both of which were in use in the villages and not on display or stored away in a back room in the museum. Most of these drums had been stored for fifty or so odd years since the day they were taken by the priests or Indian agents. In later times, museum curators might have preserved the drums for observation, but not for use. The drums were now repaired by each of the families in charge of the twelve drums returned to White Earth.

The White Earth museum now played a different role: The displays and collections chronicled popular culture. For instance, the museum displayed the old fur press that the Northwest Company had used in trading with the Indians almost a century ago. The press had compressed furs so the trader could cheat Indians. Also on display were the black hats and some gambling sticks from an old moccasin game at White Earth.

The museum had a beaded outfit worn by Bugonaygeeshig when he traveled with a delegation of White Earth chiefs to

Washington to negotiate for better treatment. Bugonaygeeshig's outfit was displayed alongside Selam Big Bear's ribbon shirt and blue jeans, which he had worn to Washington to testify against the taking of the land in the White Earth Settlement Act in the 1980s, almost one hundred years later. The truth was, it was easier to get the ornately beaded outfit of the old headman than it was to get those jeans and the shirt. Moose had persuaded Selam's wife, Georgette, to make Selam a new, even fancier ribbon shirt and the museum budgeted for a new pair of Levis to replace the old ones.

There was also a display of shoes, illustrating traditional shoes and social shoes from different generations. When Georgette had suggested this to the White Earth Historical Society, people had laughed and said she had a "foot fetish," but after they saw the collection, everyone admitted that it was pretty damn interesting, all the kinds of shoes Indians had worn in one hundred and fifty years or so. Those were the kinds of things the Indians wanted in their own museum, and they were not necessarily the kind of things the white people liked to look at. These things made the people of White Earth feel a part of their history, not like their *aanikoobijiganag* were "objects" to look at and "things" to take apart.

So George Naganob had flown home leaving Moose with the responsibility of bringing the ancestors home. Moose had meticulously prepared his old UPS van for this trip. The van was fitted with shelves that were ideal to carry the ancestors. He had wrapped the wooden boxes in wool blankets and then strapped them onto the shelves so they were safe and secure. He slept in the cab when he stopped; he wasn't going to leave the ancestors on their own now. On one hand, he had to make sure that nothing else happened to them. On the other hand, it was out of respect for them. Someday, when he himself walked down the pathway of souls and met with the ancestors again, he wanted to at least be able to say that he tried to make their long journey home comfortable.

Moose took another puff on his cigarette and then focused his mind on repairing the van. His tool set was on board as his van was prone to odd noises, parts unceremoniously left behind on the road, and breakdowns. But what he needed now was a long piece of strong wire to rig up an exhaust system repair. He checked behind the seat of the van. Nothing. He put his cigarette out and slowly started walking around the van, looking at the ground, his eyes scanning his surroundings for any bit of wire or, ideally, a clothes hanger. Again nothing; the rest area was unusually clean. He started walking toward the restrooms, figuring the garbage can might yield some useful bits in the least. As he crossed the parking lot, Moose looked up at the sound of an approaching vehicle.

As if by some mysterious radar that attracts hippies to Indians, an aging Volkswagen van pulled up to the rest stop. Moose watched the van drive slowly by. It was painted brilliant purple from front bumper to tailpipe with rainbow mandalas on the side windows, American flags as curtains, *Free Leonard Peltier* and *Garcia Lives* stickers on the rear bumper alongside the Colorado license plate. Rock'n'roll drifted out the open windows like a trail of marijuana smoke. Moose observed the entrance of the Deadhead out of the corner of his eye as he began to dig through the garbage can. The van stopped, and Moose continued to scavenge, now acutely aware of being observed. He shrugged and picked up a stick to aid his search through the garbage. No hanger. He turned his back on the van and went to check the men's room. Nothing. With one eye on the van, he gingerly opened the door to the women's room and checked inside. No luck.

Moose exited the women's room and began walking slowly back toward his van just as a big hairy guy with a paunch covered by a tie-dyed T-shirt stepped out of the van. His reddish hair stuck out in all directions, absent of any wind. The man stretched his arms and wiggled his hips slightly to loosen up, most of his body continuing to move in several directions simultaneously even when he was standing still. His arms still outstretched, he looked to be poised for flight. Moose cringed and stopped in his tracks, still weighing the limits of his options.

With his radar lock on, the Deadhead moved toward Moose with a familiarity only Deadheads have for complete strangers. "How's it going, bro?" the Deadhead hailed him.

Moose winced and calculated quickly in his mind just how badly he needed that coat hanger. Besides, this guy did not look like someone who had hung up his clothes in quite a spell.

"Well," Moose said, "my tailpipe is falling off but besides that, I'm OK."

"Hmmm . . . Where you from?" The Deadhead was obviously less concerned about the present than the overall story.

"White Earth," Moose said. "Minnesota."

"Long way from home, eh?"

"Yup."

A pause.

"That'd be Ojibwe, right?"

"Yup." Moose was feeling cheap with his information.

Another pause as the Deadhead looked over Moose's ailing van from afar. Moose popped the question:

"You wouldn't happen to have any wire, like, say a coat hanger, would you?" He was both hopeful and skeptical.

"Let me take a look," the man offered. "By the way, my name's Mike," he said, offering a soul-brother's handshake to Moose.

"Moose," Moose said.

Mike dug into his van with a vigor that belied his paunchy build. He seemed hopeful that he could help an Indian. Tie dyed clothes were thrown in all directions and boxes of cassettes were dumped out. Finally, Mike blurted out from the depths of his van, "Hey, I've got it!" With a hard pull, a length of speaker wire came free in his hands. Mike appeared out the door, pregnant with the pleasure that he was valuable to his Indian brother.

"But your tunes . . ." Moose began.

"Worry not, bro. I've got six speakers set up in my van. I can live with only five."

Moose smiled and thanked him, turning now to the task of fixing his exhaust system. He walked back to his van with Mike following hopefully behind, wishing for a small morsel of Moose's affections. Moose lay down on the pavement and worked himself under his van to survey the damage. The scent of patchouli oil told him Mike had joined him under the vehicle.

"What ya got in the van, buddy?" Mike said as they worked side by side to lift the exhaust pipes back into place. "If you don't mind my asking, that is."

Moose had anticipated this question and now weighed his answers. Potatoes or bones were his two choices. He sensed Mike's earnestness and gave in.

"Bones," Moose said, grunting as he wrapped the speaker wire around a muffler.

Mike's face lifted up, privy to new information.

"How's that?" he asked.

"The bones of our ancestors," Moose explained.

"Wow!" the Deadhead responded. "Where did you get them?"

"We're going home from Washington. They were at a museum out there and we want them back." Moose generously offered the information to his ally.

Just then, another car pulled into the rest area and parked close to Moose's van—too close. A door opened and shut. Moose and Mike could hear the sound of footsteps on the pavement coming closer. They looked out from under the van to see two black, shiny boots.

"Uh oh," Mike said.

Moose held his breath.

The boots bent as their owner leaned down. Moose and Mike looked upside-down into the face of a highway patrolman. They could see themselves reflected in his mirror sunglasses, two grime-covered men on their backs with uncomfortable looks on their faces.

"What's going on here, boys?" said the patrolman in that expressionless drawl officers of the law have.

Moose looked over at Mike and Mike looked back at Moose. "I'll explain," Mike whispered to Moose, and then repeated it louder to the patrolman as he lumbered out from underneath the van.

Moose could hear them talking but could not understand anything they said from his listening post. Presently he heard the trunk of the patrol car open and then shut. *The cop's arrested him and thrown him in the trunk*, Moose worried to himself, concerned for a moment, wondering if he should intervene for his new ally.

Suddenly there was the high-pitched sound of squeaky wheels and the next thing Moose knew, the patrolman was next to him under the van with Mike sliding in on the other side. The officer had removed his hat and sunglasses and in his gloved hands he now carried pliers and a wirecutter. He was lying on a mechanic's dolly that he must have retrieved from the trunk.

"I've been reading up on this whole issue of repatriation," the patrolman said. "Let me see if I can lend a hand here."

As Mike held the exhaust pipe aloft, the officer ran the speaker wire around it and over a part of the chassis frame. Moose felt like a fifth wheel.

"Got any duct tape?" the patrolman asked.

"Yeah, sure," Moose said, somewhat confused at how he had been so quickly marginalized. He dragged himself out from under the van.

As he retrieved the duct tape from his toolbox, a fake-wood-sided station wagon with Pennsylvania license plates pulled into the rest area and parked on the other side of the van. All five doors swung open at once and a man, woman, four children and a golden retriever came spilling out. The man stretched, the woman yawned, and the children and the dogs raced for the restrooms.

"Howdy," the man said in his best frontier accent when he saw Moose. He looked around at Moose's van, the highway patrol car, and the brilliant purple VW van. "What's all the excitement about?"

"Well, my van's exhaust broke and we're fixing it . . ." Moose began, only to be interrupted by the patrolman who was suddenly standing beside him, wiping his sweating forehead with the back of one of his gloves.

"He's carrying an important load," the officer authoritatively told the family. "He's bringing back remains of his ancestors to be reburied."

The man and the woman looked surprised, then the woman asked Moose, "They're probably from the Smithsonian, I'll bet?" The man looked questioningly at his wife as she explained, "I heard all about this on public radio."

Moose looked at them both quizzically and said, "Yeah, they are."

"Is there anything we can do to help?" the man asked.

"No, sir," the officer said. "We're just finishing it up. Exhaust system's as good as some wire and duct tape can make it."

They all stood for a moment not knowing what to say next. Then the woman chimed in: "Well, have you all eaten?" She pulled a wicker picnic basket from the back of the station wagon. She began handing out sandwiches primly wrapped in waxed paper. "That one's tuna fish," she told Moose as she thrust the sandwich into his hands. He wanted to tell her he was not hungry but he suddenly realized he had not eaten all morning.

Before Moose knew what had happened he was sitting at a picnic bench with a red-checked tablecloth eating sandwiches with Mike the Deadhead, the patrolman, and the Walker family from Harrisburg, Pennsylvania, who were on their way to see the Grand Canyon. The officer and Mr. Walker were discussing repatriation while Mike ate tuna fish sandwiches with glee. The Walker children had just returned from under the van where they were inspecting the repairs. Exhaust grime now accompanied the Kool-aid mustaches on their faces.

"Well," Moose finally said. "I need to get going."

"Yes, you better," said the patrolman, nodding.

"*Miigwetch* to you all," Moose said.

The whole table responded with a chorus of *miigwetch* and Mike told Moose to look him up if he was ever in Colorado.

The big Indian extended his hand and walked toward his van. He jumped into the driver's seat and started it up. Everything sounded good. He looked into his sideview mirror to see the people at the picnic table waving to him and he stuck his hand out the window in return. He wheeled the van out onto the turnpike and north toward Champaign to take the ancestors home through Wisconsin. *That should be some smooth traveling*, he said to himself. *Besides, that's Ojibwe country so the old people will like that.*

Once he was out on the road and up to speed, it seemed to Moose as though he heard a lot of noise from the back of the van again. Noise, and even some singing. This time he realized that the new rattles were the old people, not the van. Once again, the ancestors were getting louder and louder.

That was why he decided to move his tape player into the back of the van. Moose had a good boombox cassette player and an excellent collection of music. On this trip he had tossed aside most of his country western and rock music and opted for his more traditional collection. This seemed to work out just fine with the old people.

He played grass dance songs part of the way back, and then started in with some special tapes he had made of "traveling songs" from Big Drum ceremonies. That's what he put in now, a nice tape of traveling songs from Leech Lake. *That should keep those old people happy*, he thought as he turned up the tape player in the back of the van. Then he shifted one more time and headed home.

Ethnic Derivatives:
Tricksterese Versus Anthropologetics

Gerald Vizenor

Almost Browne, that native savant of tricksterese, was invited by the student association to deliver the ethnic studies commencement lecture several years ago in Ishi Auditorium at the University of California.

Almost, you see, is almost brown; nearly, but not quite, an obvious trace of his native woodland ancestors. He bears the memories, the rush of native generations, the tease of wild shadows, the rue of heir and bone, in so many obscure stories. His traces are not terminal tragedies, his memories are not the strain of histories. The turn of his shadows must be *true*, but never borderline measures of civilization and reservations. His natural ties are chance, anything but the treason of absolutes. The native stories that overturn the burdens of the *real* are his beam.

Almost is an eternal brush of imagination, more than the real, but never the lonesome testimonies of mere victimry. The fealties of his house and motion are heard in the native tease of the seasons, and always in the summery solace of tricksterese.

Almost, in spite of his given name, derived, as you know, from a natal nickname, was the unconcerned choice of the students. The committee, more than eager to nominate a controversial speaker, had heard his wild lectures on reservation casinos at a recent conference. Tricksterese, his wise banter on

194

cultural envy and "testcross sovereignty," or the sovereignty of native traces and natural motions, aroused the students at the time, but his otherwise natural contradictions and ironies at the commencement ceremonies were too much to bear in an hour, as he was bound to tease the dominance of ethnic nationalism at the university.

I was there, at the back of the auditorium, the last faculty in native studies, and not ready to sit on stage with my colleagues in ethnic studies. Not that we were at war; we were not, except in the sense of contentious promotions, associations, and resources at the university, but it would have been unbearable to be perched in a medieval gown on stage as the last crossblood native on the faculty.

The dominance of untrue histories caught me once more at the university, as ethnic studies advanced and the native presence waned in another transethnic empire. We were burdened once more with historical ironies, those weary creases in our native remembrance. At the same time, our memories are sources of survivance, natural reason, and tricksterese. The auditorium, you see, was named in honor of Ishi, that obscure native other, who had been humanely secured in a museum, as the last of his tribe, by the anthropologist Alfred Kroeber at the University of California.

I sat next to a couple in the back row of the auditorium. They were handsomely dressed for an occasion that seemed to be more significant than the annual commencement of ceremonies. The man wore a new suit, and bright black shoes. He told me they were refugees, and that their daughter was the first in their ancient families to be educated, to earn a university degree. I must have made my own family proud in a similar way, and now, by chance, we were the heirs who had overcome the cruelties of racialism and the contradictions of nationalism. The horrors of war were in their near memories, as the massacres of natives were in mine, but our presence at graduation was an assurance of survivance, not victimry, in a constitutional democracy.

Almost, my distant cousin from the reservation, had given

me a copy of his lecture when he arrived on campus earlier
in the week. He seldom ever said what he wrote in advance,
as he would rather tease written words into an oral
performance, and he wanted to tease me in that way at
graduation.

The Vietnamese couple next to me could not, at first,
appreciate the summary tease of native humor. Later, when the
students protested, they were troubled, but they seemed to be
pleased to hear that the speaker said much more than he had
actually written. Almost was always more eloquent in sound
than in the silence of his written words.

The Vietnamese man turned and told me that his new name
was much the same, more than the words. His breath was
scented with mint. "Gio Nom, my nickname here, not my real
country name," he said as he printed his name in capital letters
next to the name of his daughter on the program. "My name
mean *south wind*, my freedom name." They were honored, of
course, by the achievements of their daughter, and, at the same
time, justly moved by the references to a constitutional
democracy.

Almost was not so honored by the faculty of historians,
literary theorists, social scientists, and others. They were
curious, to be sure, and wary, but that common academic pose
soon turned to anger, accusations, and summary evasion when
he announced in tricksterese that academic evidence was
"nothing more than a euphemism for anthropologism and the
colonial dominance over native memories and stories."

The "erstwhile ethnic identities," he shouted, "are fake
because we are tried, yes, *tried*, and feathered, by the racial
evidence of invented cultures, and the tricky trash, you heard
me, tricky *trash*, of ethnic nationalism and anthropologetics."
He coined such words as anthropologism, anthropologetics, and
tricky trash, to underscore his notion that the practices of
cultural anthropology were, as he said at commencement,
"colonial doctrines, and the deistic rue of dominance."

Almost could not see the seven faculty members seated in a
row behind him on stage. Later he told me they were circus

crows, "their sickle feathers trimmed to the metal chairs." Nearly every sentence in his lecture caused some bodily response in the faculty, a twitch, a frown, a turn, a murmur, and at least the sound of their shoes on the hardwood stage, the natural motion, as it turned out, to escape from the ceremonies.

"Listen to that trash, " said a stout sociologist to a historian.

"What, the rue?" said the historian on stage.

"Who is this clown, an evangelist?"

"The students' choice," said the historian.

"Choice, indeed, he sounds like an aborted anthropologist."

"Surely, no more than an invented native."

"Not really, he's the choice of the students to get even with the faculty," said the sociologist. "He might crow their sermon, but not on my time." Slowly he removed his gown and hood, folded them into a neat bundle, and then walked out at the back of the stage.

Almost was always in motion, his natural fealty, and seldom troubled by death or departures. Not much academic ever worried him either, but he pretended otherwise in some of his stories. Natives, he said "are almost always in constant motion, even in spirit after death, and that's what native sovereignty means, motion, not the curses and causes of manifest manners at universities."

The very moment that he raised his arms over the podium, and opened his wide mouth over the microphone that morning in the auditorium, only a few students could remember, without evasions or apologies, why on earth he had ever been invited to lecture at the commencement ceremonies. Even the couple next to me had their doubts until he mentioned native sovereignty and the "tricky motion of constitutional democracies."

Almost leaned closer to the microphone. He was in constant motion at the podium, an assurance of his sovereignty. The faculty was trained to listen, but they were more practiced at other academic maneuvers, and made wry faces as they sat at the back of the stage in borrowed nests, circus crows in their black gowns, velvet hoods, and bright ribbons. The students, who were once his promoters, shunned the very sound of his voice early in his lecture. Not that he was a terrible speaker, almost never less than a memorable contradiction. He was timely, and the tone of his voice was rich and dramatic, but he turned and traced words and sentences in such an ironic manner of survivance that no one could be sure what he meant. No one was ever sure that native tricksterese ever meant anything at anytime, anyway.

Almost teased the measures of civilization and the inventions of the native other, the abstruse other of dominance, as the extremes in his stories. "Besides," he said, "manners are more extreme at universities." Those students on the committee who dared to stand by their nomination, and that out of mere courtesy, did not understand extremes either, but in the end many students, and most of their parents, wanted to learn how to stand and deliver a lecture in native tricksterese.

Some students insisted that his lecture was a learned satire, and for that, unwise, given the ethnic politics of the audience, but they too were taken with the tricky notion and motion of tricksterese. Nonetheless, his notions were evaded at the time, and since then his words have been twisted, revised, and terminated in hundreds of extreme comments and critiques at the university. The faculty never understood why he was invited in the first place, but no one ever forgot that he was there.

Almost was embraced, hissed, and shunned, in turns, because of his obscure theories and conceit of ethnic histories, and, more than anything else, because of the ironies he meant in the title of his lecture, "ethnic derivatives." The students hissed when he said that their graduation gowns were "colonial drag, the happy hour of ethnic medievalism, ecclesiastical evidence of a dead letter degree in mere mimicry."

"How does he write that?" said Gio Nom.

"That's native tricksterese, an oral performance," I said. "As you can see, there's nothing like that here in the written lecture." The Vietnamese couple were astonished, at first, that he could create a lecture on his feet, and pretend that it was written. Later, they admired the practice and were pleased to follow the text and hear how he teased the printed words to dance on stage.

"Almost, a darn good man on his feet," said Gio Nom.

The ethnic faculty, moved by situational politics, shouted at the speaker and demanded that he explain what he meant by his hostile ironies, such as "colonial drag" and "happy hour." Seven faculty members were seated on stage at the beginning of the ceremonies, and at the end the metal chairs were empty, but for one. The ceremonies that year were memorable, to say the least, but more bent with ironies than the customary manners of such events. Since then the provocations of the faculty, the fickle rage of the students, and the dismay of parents, have been established as something of an ethnic tradition. Almost is remembered, in spite of everything, as the prime mover of the new agnostic commencement ceremonies at the University of California.

"The American Revolution, that celebrated war of independence, was not the *first*, but the *second* revolution on this continent," shouted Almost. His mouth touched the microphone closer than a rock singer, so close that he might have swallowed it with a sudden gasp for air. He raised his arms and turned his hands in tune with his words, each finger a gesture of tricksterese. His voice vibrated in the metal chairs and rushed to every secret pocket of sound in the auditorium. "These are the comparative chronicles of sovereignty, the motion and historical contradictions of our time, the everlasting traces of our resistance in a constitutional democracy."

"What constitution you talking about?" shouted a student.

"The end of colonial drag," said Almost.

"Man, get a new tune," said the student.

"What, transethnic nationalism?" said Almost.

"What kind of native are you?" shouted another student. She moved to the aisle at the side of the auditorium. Her black gown was decorated with ribbons, feathers, and beads. "Indian peoples talk for their communities, so where are you from to talk about colonial constitutions anyway?"

"Almost everywhere," said Almost.

"Mister, you better find yourself from somewhere."

"More than once a trick reservation."

"Constitutions are white reservations, and that's not our tradition," she said and folded her arms over the beads and ribbons. The audience turned to the aisle and praised the uncommon assertions of a native student. "So what's your native name?"

"Almost," said Almost.

"You're no Indian," said the native student.

"Almost Yosemite," said Almost.

"You're a white man."

"Almost," said Almost.

"Almost nothing," said the student.

"Almost true," said Almost.

"Who gave you that name?" asked the student.

"The *first* revolution was native, native, native," he shouted into the microphone. The power of his voice silenced the students. "The *first* was a war of independence from colonial domination and the rush of missionaries, and that was launched almost a century before the *second* historical revolution of the thirteen colonies and the formation of the United States."

"That's not our history, never," said another student. Others raised their hands and clenched their fists to support the statement of resistance, and several students in the front row moved to the back of the auditorium.

"The southwestern natives initiated the *first* united revolution on August 10, 1680, and defeated the Spanish Kingdom of New Mexico." Almost paused, brushed back his hair, and waited to hear the response of the audience. The students did not resist, so he continued. "Marc Simmons, in the introduction to his book *The Pueblo Revolt*, wrote that 'this dramatic episode represented one of the bloodiest defeats ever experienced by Spain in her overseas empire,' so that was the *first* revolution on this continent. 'And,' as historians are accustomed to say, 'it was the first successful battle for independence fought against a European colonial power in what was to become the United States.'"

"So what?" a student shouted from the back of the auditorium.

"So what, indeed," said one faculty member to another seated on stage. "The Spanish and Indian both lost their land in the end." Nearby, several other faculty members murmured and nodded their heads in agreement.

"Che Guevara, he was a true warrior," shouted a student.

"Che was a transethnic conquistador," said Almost.

"Che fought for the natives."

"Che was a transnational tourist," said Almost.

"Almost, you're a fascist, man," said another student.

"Che wrote in his travel journal that 'Cuzco invites you to don armour and, astride a sturdy powerful steed, cleave a path through the defenceless flesh of a flock of native Indians whose human wall crumbles and falls under the four hooves of the galloping beast.' "

"Che, who is this man?" asked Gio Nom.

"Ernesto Guevara, he was trained as a medical doctor in Argentina," I answered. "Later he became a revolutionary leader and one of the most important comrades of Fidel Castro in Cuba."

"Where is he?"

"Che was executed in Bolivia."

"No, no, here," said Gio Nom. He pointed to the manuscript. He followed the written lecture with his finger, but could not locate many of the words he heard.

"Almost never wrote that in his lecture," I said. "No, he probably just read the new translation of Che's journal, *The Motorcycle Diaries*, about his trip around South America." Gio Nom wrote the name and title on the side of the program.

"The unities of that native revolution, and others since then, are the foundational histories of survivance in this nation," shouted Almost. He turned from the podium and waved to the faculty who were seated on stage. The faculty, in turn, waved back, tiny, hesitant motions, as cautious children might wave to strangers. The audience laughed and then mocked the childlike gestures of the faculty. "Whatever the course of sovereignty, then and now, native resistance has been contrived too many times in aesthetic extremes, as either incertitude, necromancy, or mere victimry."

The students hissed over the last words in his lecture.

"Hissed again, what about this time?"

The hiss increased and rushed to the curtains on stage.

"What word, what's the hiss word now?"

The hiss circled the auditorium in harsh and uncertain waves.

"Incertitude, is that the hiss word?" shouted Almost.

The hiss seemed to weaken.

"Necromancy?"

The hiss heaved, rose louder, and became a demon wave.

"Victimry, how about pity, and tragic victimry?"

The demon hiss reached extreme overtones. The sound circled around and around and pierced every ear in the auditorium, but the intensities could not be sustained without some trace of humor. The hiss bounced, wavered, and weakened at last, and then the students laughed at their own hiss performance.

"The victims have it over the necromancers," said Almost.

"Never, never, never," chanted the students at the back.

"Why the students do that?" asked Gio Nom.

"The great cultural hiss, no one really knows why."

"So much to hear," said Gio Nom. He was troubled by the want of manners, and, at the same time, he seemed to be amused by the hiss play. I could not understand what he said to his wife about the students.

"Stay out of those word museums," warned Almost.

His mood had turned and the audience was silent. The students were uncertain and looked to each other for an answer. "So, who are you, the curator?" said a student in the first row. No one was sure what he meant by "word museums," but it had to be an ironic storehouse of native stories. A double irony because he teased the very words that created the museum. The faculty on stage raised their hands, shrugged their shoulders in casual doubt, and then laughed, artfully.

"The museums that hold our bones and stories," shouted Almost.

"No bones here," said Gio Nom.

"Bravo, bravo," shouted Ishmael Reed. The novelist, who wore sports earphones, had arrived late and was standing at the back of the auditorium. As the audience turned to see who had shouted such bravos of approval he walked down the center aisle toward the stage. Many children, the brothers and sisters, sons and daughters of the graduates, followed him and said their bravos in tune. "Tricksterese is the best street talk anybody ever heard at the university," said Reed. "We've heard too much from the tattlers, rattlers, and race talkers backlighted in museums, bank lobbies, and network news." The children danced in the aisles, and they were amused by his gestures, tangled gray hair, and bright orange earphones.

"The converse histories of dominance rather than native survivance have been secured in museums and at universities by several generations of academic masters and no one hissed about that," shouted Almost.

"Masters, who uses such a word?" said a woman in cultural studies.

"Who, indeed," said a political scientist out of the side of his mouth.

"I mean, the word is out the ruins of colonialism, the essence of dominance, at best an anachronism," she said and tapped the heels of her shoes on the hardwood floor. "Who does he think he is, a candidate for the senate?" She closed her backpack, raised her sunglasses in one hand, and left the stage.

Almost turned and saw one faculty member leave as another arrived. Ishmael walked on stage and sat in the empty chair next to the visiting faculty member. The children waved to him from the aisles. The audience was amused, and even the last of the faculty waved to the children.

"Now that's a civilized way to bear commencement," said Roberta Peel, a visiting scholar from the University of Kent at Canterbury. "Please, what's on the orange radio?"

"O.J. Simpson trial," said Reed.

"Americans are so demonstrative about crime," said Peel.

"What was that?" said Reed.

"Natives are forever studied, invented as abstruse cultures, and then embodied in motion pictures as the simulated burdens of civilization," said Almost. "These adversities became more grievous and caused a turn in the notions, courses, and literary canons at universities, but the treacheries and dominance of *anthropologism*, the obsessive, unmerciful studies of natives by social scientists, have *not* been overturned in comparative ethnic studies at this great university."

That much brought the students to their feet in anger, because most students, ethnic or not, were eager consumers of native feathers, leathers, turquoise, photographs, and mother earth memorabilia. The students raised their arms to protest the speaker, and black gowns spread out like sails with their gestures. Many students marched in the aisles and chanted, "natives are not unmerciful, never, never, never."

Several faculty members removed their hoods and walked out of the commencement. No one was sure, then or now, what word or notion so tormented the students, and so bored the faculty. One faculty member in education suggested that the students had no sense of what such words as necromancy meant and, rather than show their ignorance at the moment of their baccalaureates, the students protested, a common academic cover story.

"Almost, darn good on his feet," said Gio Nom.

"Now, back to anthropologetics," said Almost. He was unhurried. The faculty watched his every move, and they were much more critical in the end than the students. He wore no socks or tie, his shirt was too large, and his sports coat was stained on the sleeves, and torn at the back.

"Johannes Fabian wrote in *Time and the Other* that 'anthropology's alliance with the forces of oppression is neither a simple nor recent one,' not simple here in ethnic studies, not recent anywhere," said Almost. "Ethnic studies is no exception to that oppression because the 'relationships between anthropology and its object are inevitably political,' and the 'production of knowledge occurs in a public forum,' such as this one, right here: the parents, students, and the last of the faculty on stage."

Almost paused to hear the hisses, but he seemed surprised, as the faculty and students were silent. So, he hissed at them. "Fabian, you know, argued as everyone must, that 'among the historical conditions under which our discipline emerged and which affected its growth and differentiation were the rise of capitalism and its colonial-imperialist expansion into the very societies which became the target of our inquiries.' So, the historical alliance with anthropology and the social sciences is evermore political in ethnic studies, and you might say, that this graduation ceremony is a statement of that dominance."

"What does he mean?" asked Gio Nom.

"Anthropology is the natural enemy of natives."

Professor Simon Williams, a senior cultural anthropologist, one of the faculty members on stage, removed his black gown and walked toward the podium. A blush blotched his bald head and his face was double creased with rage. His shoes squeaked, and the moment of authoritarian surprise was lost to humor. Almost turned to the squeak and saluted the anthropologist.

"Browne, must you continue to malign everyone to make your point?" said the anthropologist. His wide mouth stretched back over his dark teeth, over the microphone, and his cheeks shivered as he spoke. "This is not the time to criticize the good work we have done to bring ethnic studies into the real world of the social sciences."

"Have you ever been in the military?" asked Almost.

"Have you ever been a professor?" countered Williams.

"Never, but we both know how to salute."

"Fabian is not relevant," said Williams.

"So, he's the squeaky name?" said Almost.

"He never wrote about ethnic studies anyway," said Williams.

"You mean, he never mentioned *your* name?"

"Almost, is that a traditional name?" asked Williams.

"Fabian wrote about the expansion of anthropologism, about the tragic curse of anthropologists, and he almost wrote about your squeaky shoes and the end of natives in the social sciences," said Almost.

"Never mind the insults, nothing you've said makes any sense, and that's my major objection, not that you were the students' choice, with no credentials, not even a traditional name, but that you think you can tear down what we have taken so many years to build," said the anthropologist.

"You mean the alliance with dominance?"

"Yes, someone must preserve the standards, and the best part of that alliance, as the students, faculty, and parents have already demonstrated so clearly, is your absence, your silence," shouted Williams. The shivers turned into a weak smile, a pathetic figure. The audience was never on his side, and the students were more critical of his dominance than they were of the obscure traces of tricksterese.

"Anthropology's on the ropes," said Almost.

"We *are* the ropes," said Williams.

"You can say that again."

"I have never, in more than thirty years of teaching, been so humiliated and angry at a graduation ceremony," said the anthropologist. "You may have the right to speak at graduation, but you will never have the right to my attention as a listener."

"So, what are you saying, then?" asked Almost.

"You should be silenced," said the anthropologist. He waved his arms, and the sudden motion tossed his gown over his face. The students laughed, and with that he marched to the back of the stage and vanished between the curtains. His shoes squeaked in the distance.

Indian Hands

Gail Moran Wawrzyniak

I sat on the floor, propped up against the green couch. My eleven-year-old legs straight out in front of me. My feet were swinging first left, then right, to the imaginary song keeping beat in my ears. Waiting. I heard the frying pan pushed across the metal burner, the spatula lifting the hamburger, silencing the sizzle for a few seconds until the fresh, uncooked side landed in the fat.

I watched the 5:30 news—Walter Cronkite, my dad, and me, all waiting for supper. I learned a lot by watching the news. I had learned earlier about Vietnam. While Walter droned on in his familiar, comfortable, and comforting voice, images of Vietnam flashed. I learned by experience how to listen for Walter for that second just before the image flashed so I could close my eyes, listening to the story until I was sure the images would be gone. Sometimes I guessed wrong and had to re-shut my eyes, holding them closed even tighter.

My dad didn't say much during the news except for a humph, tsk-tsk, or a sigh. He had settled in his chair, the recliner beside the couch. With his one leg crossed over the other, his dangling foot kept beat to a song different from mine.

That night Walter taught me about Wounded Knee. How many Indians, what the government was doing, how many gunshots were fired. And so many pictures of Indian men wearing bandana headbands, old and faded jeans, long hair braided, and always, it seemed, always these men were carrying guns. The camera zoomed in on one man's hands resting on the gun as he walked toward the camera. I looked at his Indian hands. They were dark brown with knotted veins rising from beneath the skin. I looked down at my hands, tan from the sun, tiny veins showing. I didn't know why these guys were at Wounded Knee. Walter wasn't offering to tell. But I knew scary things were happening because of the way the soldiers were running around. I closed my eyes until I heard no more gunshots and no more stories of Indians.

Mom had been standing in the doorway to the kitchen watching the news. Dad said, "God-damned radical Indians. They're just asking for it." Mom turned back into the kitchen, pushing more pans across the metal burner before she yelled, "Supper's ready."

Dad said, "Help me up, sweetheart." I'd grab his two hands in mine and pull. He'd pretend it was so hard to get out of the chair and try to pull me off-balance toward him and I'd pretend I was pulling as hard as I could trying to pull away from him. We'd both groan with our make-believe loads. We did this see-saw every night at suppertime. His hands in mine, I saw his pale Irish hands where arthritis was starting to grow knobs at the knuckles.

We sat down in the kitchen, Mom, Dad, my two sisters and me, to a supper of hamburgers, bread, salad and corn on the cob. Walter didn't seem to mind telling the news to the empty living room while we ate. From behind my hamburger I looked down at Dad's hands again, then I looked at Mom's hands as she ate her corn on the cob. I saw her dark Chippewa hands, brown with knotted veins rising through the skin. I remembered Walter in the living room and closed my eyes tightly. I opened them again when I heard the scraping of the chair on the yellow linoleum. Mom was getting up to get coffee, but before she walked away, she reached down, placed her hand over mine and squeezed.

◆⨯◆⨯◆

An Honest Brother

Janice Command

May 11, 1978. John Grandchamp woke that morning to the long bell, then echoes up and down the corridor as men woke and swore. The block's doors clanged. The lights hummed. The guard's heels struck the floor sharp and quick, like drips in a cave.

John saw the guard's shadow on the floor before he saw the guard himself. Then there was a young white man in uniform on the other side of the bars, his profile soft and blank. He didn't turn to look at John. He ran the nightstick across the bars of the next cell, apparently to rouse a man who didn't want to wake up.

John stepped into his prison slippers and up to the cell door. Old Maynard Lyle peered at him from across the corridor, his face severed by the iron bars. Maynard was the oldest Indian in the whole Wisconsin prison system. He smiled his crooked shadow-smile at John and nodded. John nodded back.

The guards stood at either end of the corridor after the count. The men filed out after another bell. When a guard diverted John away from the others somebody near the back of the line yelled, "See you at the Crow Fair, neezh!" Others grumbled obscenities as John departed. The guard stood back and told them all to shut up and hurry on. John didn't look back. He'd seen all he wanted to see in two years.

John's wife Annette and Patty, his cousin's girlfriend, waited in the release area. They looked like two versions of the same woman, ten years apart.

Patty was excited. She was still skinny and flashed plenty of white teeth. Long beaded earrings rattled on each ear and an AIM patch dominated the back of her denim jacket. Annette stood still and resolute. She wore a sweat shirt, jeans, and a floral barrette to restrain her long black hair. Except for the wedding band this was her only jewelry. She wore no make-up. John extended his arms to embrace her and she placed a nylon windbreaker in his hands.

"Here," she said. "Better take this. It's cold outside."

After an awkward pause Patty threw herself into John's arms and hugged him tight. "Daymond's outside," she said. "He can hardly wait to see you."

"Let's go then," said John when Patty released him. He made sure Annette's hand was in his before they walked through the doors.

Cool, damp air greeted John outside the prison doors, but he didn't stop to put on the windbreaker Annette had brought. Daymond started his car as soon as he saw them coming. Four other cars started up too, then maybe another five.

Indians occupied these cars. They were long-haired people, men and women, with a definite penchant for sunglasses, bones, beads, and the color red. Guards and administrators peeked apprehensively out of prison windows.

It surprised John to see this many people to meet him. He wasn't one of the big heavies, after all. He took his hand out of Annette's, smiled, and waved a little limply to all of those assembled. He had expected life to pass him by.

A horn honked in an old Plymouth behind Daymond's car. John looked to see the driver but saw only his own reflection on the windshield. The driver's window descended and there was Bruno's fat brown face smiling under a red beret. Then John saw his reflection again, this time on the lenses of Bruno's sunglasses.

"Hey, bro," Bruno said.

He extended his hand out the window the same way he used to offer a pint, gruff and persistent. Daring you not to take it. John shook his hand heartily, the AIM way, then raised his left fist in the air for the benefit of all the others. They honked their horns and yelled greetings from the windows,

"Say, John," said Bruno, a big smile on his face, "Ready for Bad River?"

John had heard something, but nothing concrete. Another tribal election contested.

"I gotta catch up," he admitted. His face burned.

"Next crisis in Indian Country," laughed Bruno. He rolled up the window, effectively terminating the conversation.

John and Annette boarded Daymond's car. They proceeded first, caravan fashion, to the prison gates. John noticed extra guards stationed at the gate as they left and several state troopers cruising the vicinity. Patty said she saw an eagle flying higher than the helicopter that appeared as soon as they got on the country road.

The windshield vibrated as the car accelerated toward the highway. John didn't feel in possession of himself until they were well on the road.

Patty exuded that barely contained, squirmy excitement she'd exhibited since she was a kid hopping around their neighborhood in the city. She kept lighting cigarettes and turning to talk to John and Annette in the back seat.

After nearly an hour on the road, John was finally able to listen. He had already heard some of what they told him in coded phone calls and hushed conversations while incarcerated. Indian and white newspapers carried half-stories, but now he got the real dirt uncensored. It was scary. Pigs everywhere and infighting.

"But there are really good people in the movement," said Daymond. "Good things are still happening."

Reservation people still called the movement when they wanted back-up in political disputes. And AIM went, like they were doing now, in Bad River.

"Pipe carriers are coming through to teach the people," added Patty. "Old Pius is gonna be at Bad River for sure."

Pius was a renowned pipe-carrier from South Dakota. Daymond and Patty participated in his ceremonies during their travels there.

"*Elderlies*, that's what they call old people in South Dakota," reminisced Patty.

"Yeah, they pray for prisoners and the 'Elderlies'," chuckled Daymond.

The car swerved around a bend in the highway and Daymond rested his hand on Patty's thigh. It was an automatic gesture. Patty and Daymond had an Indian marriage. They had been together so long they weren't just snags anymore. They obviously had good memories of their excursions to South Dakota, dangerous as it was. Daymond had an eight-track tape player, twelve years newer than the rest of his car, and he played grass dance music the whole drive.

"There'll be sweats at Bad River too," added Patty. "That'll be good for you." She smiled sweetly, oblivious of John. She took for granted that he wanted to go there.

John resented that Annette hadn't told him about this action. He resented that she hadn't spoken to him for six months. His mother's letters had become the link between him and his family. His mother notified him that his wife and cousin would pick him up. Mrs. Grandchamp liked Annette. He suspected she was working overtime to save his marriage.

After a couple of hours the gray city skyline appeared ahead. The car passed the familiar procession of exits before veering onto the one that took John home. John turned and saw the line of battered old Indian vehicles still behind them at the exit.

The city hadn't changed much, especially in their part of town. People had always laughed and argued both inside and outside of their doors. Kids and teens ran down the cracked sidewalks and rolled down the streets on bikes, even though it was still drizzling. Adults sat on their porches. More Vietnamese immigrants had moved in, Patty explained. They kept to themselves. But John saw that they lived outside too, the older ones squatting, elbows resting on their knees, as traffic went by.

The old neighborhood still smelled of beer. It always had. Huge breaths of it floated unseen from out of the brewery, like a radiation cloud, and it had rained down beer on all their childhoods. The beer dripped into their homes in amber bottles. Everyone in the neighborhood drank—black, brown, and white— but from early on it seemed to John that it was the Indians who got pissed on the most.

The irritating drizzle caused Daymond to cuss and run his wipers intermittently by hand. John looked out of the water-speckled windshield to see the new social service center that Annette and the others had started. It was a former second-hand shop that still needed a paint job. Red letters across the newly-curtained display window read: "Native American Assistance Center." Its primary focus was chemical dependency. Patty told in detail how there had been a fight over the name and mission of the center.

"A lot of people don't think Indians need to sober up," said Patty.

Patty added that there were also those who didn't want to be called "Native Americans" or work with the churches that funded the center, so they dropped out.

Annette lit a cigarette. She rolled her eyes and growled under her breath as she relived the controversies. She came close to actually addressing John.

"Native Americans, American Indians, Indigenous People— there was a strong push for Anishinaabe, but not everyone's Chippewa," she said, blowing smoke out of the side of her mouth.

"Thank you," said Patty, who was Oneida.

"And those same ones grabbed every church cent they could get back from Washington after the last national action," pronounced Annette. "Christians aren't the only hypocrites."

John saw first hand what others had suggested, that his wife had become a vocal woman.

"Can't please everybody," Annette continued. "You just do

the best you can and take the shit."

Absorbed in sarcasm, she accidentally glanced at John and then looked quickly away. Still stubborn, thought John, but now stubborn and strong. He liked looking at her. She had the same lidless black eyes, playful sometimes, like she was peeking through keyholes. Stunning thighs. The same prettiness. He could tell she felt his stare.

The caravan pulled up to the weather-worn house John had started buying years ago, when he had a steady job as a mechanic. He stared hard at the house as the rest of the caravan pulled up.

It was so different back then, ten or eleven years ago. White men called him "Chief." He wore the name embroidered on his garage uniform. Annette had a beehive and they both drank. Police batons beat Indians every weekend when the Indian bars closed. Paddy wagons pulled up to the beer delivery area like they were hauling off empty bottles.

These were the days before the Movement. Before John and Annette had words for what was wrong with their lives. John became speechmaker and ran around the Great Lakes stomping out fires. Annette got a job, then continued to piece together the house payments while he was in prison.

John was buried in the past until he saw his son run from the side of the house. John Junior laughed and yelled with about six other kids as a brown mongrel dog jumped all over them with muddy paws. A younger child saw the caravan first, but the other kids paid him no mind as he stuttered and pointed.

Daymond chuckled and honked his horn. The dog barked. The car door groaned as John got out. Junior looked up, screamed, and ran toward the car. His long hair flailed back. More kids burst out the front door, followed by adults.

John met Junior on the grass. His heels sank into the soft earth as he picked up his son and kissed him. Junior started to cry, but in a second was laughing again. Watery snot and tears ran towards his mouth.

Then John saw his mother on the porch. She leaned against the graying, bowed railing holding his youngest, Little Bird.

Bird sucked her thumb absently and watched with her grandmother's glistening eyes.

Junior held fast to his father's leg as John walked to the porch to embrace his mother and daughter. Tight gray and black pincurls framed Mrs. Grandchamp's face. She wore a stained apron and a flowered housedress that John recognized from before his incarceration. The old woman brushed tears out of the folds of her face with a pudgy hand.

"You lost weight," she said, and kissed him.

All the Grandchamps were fat. As he held his mother John saw quite a few fat people in the house gawking and smiling at him from behind the haze of the screen door. He saw a number of other people too. Their faces were both new and familiar, brown and white, and they betrayed all kinds of expectations.

Too many of the people in his living room treated John like some sort of celebrity. His mind grasped for the names of men and women who greeted him like old friends. Others cut in as he approached family members. A college reporter looked offended when John told him to talk to him later about Bad River.

The din of conversation increased each time the screen door slammed. Bruno caused a minor sensation as he and some other guys hauled in the drum.

"Drum coming through! Drum coming through!" bellowed Bruno, his fluffy white drumstick punctuating the air over the crowd. People evacuated to the porch at Bruno's behest. Bruno put the drumstick in his back pocket and set the drum down.

"We need chairs for the drummers," he pronounced. Guests scurried in all directions to fulfill the request.

Not everyone John expected or hoped to see was in the living room that afternoon. There were a few notable absences, primarily "those guys trying to take over" that Bruno had warned him about at the last prison powwow.

Absent too were many of John's relatives who couldn't tolerate his politics. They said movement people were all dopers, "militants," anti-Christian and un-Indian.

"Red Power means one thing," said one of John's uncles five

years before, "Communism." This had been John's favorite uncle, the only sober one. They never went hunting again after John came back from the Trail of Broken Treaties. He died while John was in prison.

The little house steamed from the cooking and the compression of bodies. Furniture and rugs absorbed the moisture. Movement posters and kids' pictures curled off the walls.

John Junior nagged his father as the adults greeted him with handshakes and bearhugs. Junior pulled John to the wall to show him his crayon rendition of an eagle. Gold sparkles affixed with Elmer's glue flaked off the beak and talons.

"That's really great," said John. Junior beamed as his father capped his head with his palm. The boy's hair was still wispy, like a baby's.

"An artist in the family," said a woman's voice behind John. He turned and recognized her.

"Trudy," he said, and he shook his head. A beaded wristband rattled on her wrist. "It's been a long time."

Trudy smiled, no secret behind it. John was glad. They had flirted years before, but nothing materialized. It wasn't because he had scruples. In those days he slept with women he didn't even like the looks of, just because they approached him. Things could be so out of control then. A lot of it had to do with the dope.

Trudy was still magazine pretty. John could detect tension from some of the Indian women as he shook her hand. Many didn't want her around, but she had friends among some of the older women. She always followed through on organizational work. And then she settled down with Bruno. These things made her a part of the community, whether there was consensus or not.

"She's been around for a long time. Maybe she isn't a groupie after all," ruminated Patty at the prison powwow. "But she does get pushy sometimes."

Trudy departed for the kitchen when John's aunt Bernie threw herself between them. You could hear the clank of pot lids in the kitchen, running water, and the floorboards creaking under heavy steps. Women laughed. Then there was a hush after Trudy announced that she would make gravy.

There was no dining room in the house, so they pushed kitchen and card tables together in the living room to make a banquet. Cooks dispatched steaming feast plates. The crowd parted as Mrs. Grandchamp waddled in with corn soup. Annette offered to relieve her of the heavy pot, but Mrs. Grandchamp shook her head no. Then Daymond sailed out with the turkey still in a roasting pan.

"The turkey has arrived and his name is Daymond," yelled Bruno, and the whole room erupted in laughter.

"What're ya talking about, Bruno?" howled Daymond. "You're the one with the drumstick!"

Bruno looked puzzled. When he got the joke he pulled the fluffy drumstick out of his back pocket and started flailing it above his head.

"That's right, Chief turkey right here!" he announced, and he started the beats for a song. Four drummers followed his lead.

"This one's for John, our AIM warrior," Bruno announced, but there was no immediate hush in the house. Furrows formed above Bruno's sunglasses.

"Women, show your brother some respect," he bellowed.

Many women's faces fell, sheepish, and the rattling evaporated in the kitchen. John saw Annette's eyes flare for a moment, but no one said anything. This was, after all, tradition.

Everyone stood. The kids finally piped down and stood on the perimeter of the drum, some leaning against their fathers' chairs. Women made a detachment and sang chorus. John's aunt Bernie sang the loudest. Her voice rose after and above the men's, self-possessed and generous. John folded his hands in front of his body and held his head up. He felt proud, but burdened. He knew they would want him to speak.

The screen door slammed during the song. John cocked his head to see Brad's bright face beaming in his direction. Still a hippie lawyer, only now a little fatter. The braid down his back was longer and there was a newborn asleep on his shoulder. No one had told John this, although some had implied other things. Things he had believed and over which he had confronted Annette in the prison visiting rooms.

In his living room Brad looked innocent, the way only the middle class and idealistic can. A white woman maneuvering a diaper bag and baby carrier joined him. They both looked really happy to see him.

Annette's eyes skewered John for a second. When the song was over there was a short silence, then Annette raised her voice.

"I want to thank the drum," she said. "And also the cooks and people who brought food. All of you who have come to welcome my husband home. . . ."

Annette was a public speaker now, but she didn't speak for long. She asked someone to prepare the spirit plate and laid out the sequence of speakers. First John, then Reverend Whitecrane to say an Ojibwe prayer before the feast.

John knew he would have to speak, but he wasn't prepared. He felt the speech unravel as soon as it began and sensed a letdown when he finished. People hooted and clapped in spite of this.

Then Reverend Whitecrane, a man as old as his uncle would have been, delivered the prayer in Ojibwe.

John, like the rest of those assembled, understood little of the language, but the words embraced him like water. They carried him through the history of his heart, starting that morning, and revisited every fluorescent sunrise that greeted him for two years, along with the iron bars and prison bell.

John chastised his mind for wandering, but the Ojibwe prayer took him back to his old oratory, when he used words like "sellout" and "apple" to try to control other people. He saw Indians divert their eyes in shame for being fearful or indecisive, or different from what he thought they were supposed to be. He knew now that he had not been the kind of leader needed then, and not the kind of leader needed now.

John would have liked to have told the people this, but he was just learning himself about the recesses you hit on the Red Road. More honest brothers, the non-elite, showed him the difference between pomposity and prayer in the prison sweats that Whitecrane and the women had fought to get. John took his delusions there, then wept them out in front of red and frowning rocks. It's the same for everyone. Silence is broken in the dark, when people speak without faces. When men cry out for their mothers and own the shame they've exploited to elevate themselves.

Reverend Whitecrane finished his prayer. The old people got served first, instead of the men. Something new. Everyone ate and laughed and sang. John's little girl didn't want to let him hold her. When she finally did he told the university reporter to talk to Bruno about Bad River.

The singers wrapped the drum in the old pink blanket and carried it out to Bruno's car. Other guests followed the drum's lead, trickling out in twos and threes, sharing the last, formal laughs before departing. Only those closest to him, the ones who visited and wrote often during his incarceration, dispensed with the pretense of celebration. They shook his hand and hugged him calmly.

"Give it up to God. You know . . . throw it into the fire," whispered Reverend Whitecrane. He trudged down the walk on bowed legs, wrenched the car door open and drove away.

The night was warmer than the day, and the sky clearer. Stars sparkled even through the filter of city lights. Before long it was just Bruno, John and Daymond on the porch. They could hear the women washing dishes and readying the children for bed behind the screen door.

Bruno looked a little fidgety, like he needed a drink. "Hey Neezh, wanna go in back for a joint?" he asked.

"I got enough to settle with Annette," John said. "No use starting another argument. Not yet."

John hadn't smoked in four months and was resolved to quit. Daymond declined too, so Bruno went back to the tool shed by himself.

"That guy gives me the creeps," said John. "I think he always did, but I never noticed it 'til now."

"Oh yeah?" said Daymond.

"Think it's the glasses," said John. "Reminds me of prison mirrors."

"Bad business, to have dope and drum in your car, too," said Daymond.

"You got principles," chided John.

"I got a eagle feather. You know about that," said Daymond and he told John again how he got it, and how it protected him in South Dakota.

"I backslide sometimes with the dope," he admitted. "But not the booze. Christ, you hear guys drunk singing the forty-nines. Patty says it sounds like they're beating a woman. She's right. You notice stuff like that when you sober up."

Bruno returned, confident again. He put on his sunglasses and sat beside the other two men.

"So chief," Bruno said, "when's the caravan going out tomorrow?"

"You're the one up on that," said John.

"Yeah, but when do you say it goes?" asked Bruno. He looked a little irritated. John saw his face on the black holes over Bruno's eyes.

"I'm not going Bruno. I gotta wind down."

"Man, you been winding down for two years," said Bruno. "Thought you'd be ready for action, not retirement."

"Bruno, you think I was on some kind of vacation? Shit. . . ."

"You gotta go," said Bruno with finality. "That Ricardo Rodale and all the others are trying to take over. Jesus, they're not even Chipps."

"Look, I just got out," said John. "My daughter doesn't even call me Daddy."

"You're soft," growled Bruno. John was fed up.

"I did hard time, man. Don't fuck with me."

"I'm just telling you, man to man," said Bruno. "Your woman's been trying to run the show around here and nobody follows a woman. People been waiting for you.

"I don't wanna be chief no more," said John. "I just wanna be an Indian."

"Indians are going to Bad River," declared Bruno. "AIM Indians."

John surged with shame. He took a deep drag from his cigarette and wished, for the life of him, that it was a bottle or a joint.

"Lay off him," whined Daymond. "The guy's paid his dues, he don't owe nothing to nobody."

Bruno ignored Daymond and kept up at John. "Rick and them guys are gonna bring the chapter down if you let them."

"I'm not young anymore," said John.

"Hell, I'm older than you," said Bruno.

"Then you be chief," said John.

"Then I will," said Bruno. He leaped to his feet.

"I'm finished defending you," he spat. "You are a used-to-be warrior, just like they say. I'm telling them you're a sellout too. . . ."

Daymond jumped up and then John did too.

"Don't you call my cousin a sellout, motherfucker. He did time. . . . " Daymond shouted.

Bruno backed off and froze. His fists were clenched and he looked stupid and scared. Maybe it was the dope that made Bruno look like he was thinking in slow motion about how to respond. John held his cousin back because, as sure as he knew Bruno had a joint in his hatband, he knew he had a gun under his car seat.

"This is my goddam front yard!" John yelled.

"Sellout my ass!" cried Daymond, behind John's arm. "Bruno, you walked out of that occupation with two white lawyers either side of you, that's the kind of kissass you always been. . . ."

The screen door cracked open and Trudy and some other women appeared. "Hey, what's up, Turkey Chief?" Trudy asked.

"We're getting the hell outta here," he pronounced. He grabbed Trudy's arm roughly and began to drag her down the steps.

"Hey, my purse is in there," Trudy protested.

Annette appeared at the door and threw Trudy's tooled

leather handbag to her. Trudy whispered hoarsely to Bruno as he rushed her to the car. Everyone heard him tell her to shut-up. Bruno slammed his car door belligerently. The car backfired as Bruno revved the engine.

"Red apple," yelled Bruno, barely audible over his muffler, then he sped off.

The Polish neighbors across the street were peeking out their windows as he drove away. Annette and the other women went back inside the house.

Daymond looked angry and puzzled. "Why'd you let him talk like that to you?" he asked. For the first time John noticed how lean and young Daymond looked.

"I've seen enough blood and bullshit for two lifetimes," John said earnestly.

Daymond looked into his cousin's sad old eyes and knew it was true. There was a silence, then Daymond spoke up.

"Turkey Chief's a good name for that Bruno," he chuckled. "Bet it sticks."

"Crazy as hell, always was," reflected John. "Well, you can't say he ain't AIM. . . ."

"He's a asshole," said Daymond, and the two men stomped up the old gray steps into the house.

▶️◀️

Congenial Heart Failure

Loriene Roy

J
ust like a goddamned squirrel!" she said when she
discovered he had lined the seldom-cleaned lower
dresser drawer with nut-filled stockings. Hazel nuts, al-
monds, Brazil nuts: select pickings of the holiday trays. And
here it was, late fall. Those nuts had been his secret since last
Christmas. She understood this act of defiance; she set her jaw
and narrowed her eyes. She remembered how, at that family
gathering, her grown children had laughed and scattered as he
hobbled, grinning, from room to room, the yellowed circle of bark-
covered hardwood that held the nuts, nut picks and nut crackers tucked under his one good arm. Now, this uncovered cache
was a sign of his continued selfishness and optimism. Selfishness that he would hide the plenty from others when he himself
could not eat his fill. Optimism in that he was planning to live
long enough to find a sympathetic ally who would crack the
shells and hand feed him. His aim, again, was to triumph, at
the expense of the family she had managed to hold together for
forty years.

Henry, Edith's husband, had been left gnarled and stare-eyed
by strokes. The years of hard drinking had stretched his arteries
paper-thin, had allowed the blood to thicken. Then clots, silent
and impartial, had measured an ironic justice. His fists, no longer
capable of their sure but unpredictable violence, were   now
dependent. She should have prayed for his death, not vengeance.
The small strokes confused and frightened him; he hid these

223

episodes until the tell-tale signs were too obvious: the left eye appeared to grow and soften, he had headaches and was dizzy even when sober.

Words and especially numbers were lost. His handwriting, the one talent she had been proud of, lost its engraving-quality cursive. Later, he no longer could hold the pencil.

The strokes also brought Henry closer to the older world. In the long recuperation from the surgery his surprise companion was the return of a long lost childlike humor. She thought he had returned, in his mind, to the reservation of his youth. He stared for hours at the backyard as the slowly receding snow mounds uncovered first the frames of several rusting automobiles, then strata upon strata of dissolving dog excrement. When the robins returned, his laughter erupted in short bursts of giggles. The birds would sprint and stop on their thinnest of limbs, heads held straight and fixed. Sprint and giggle; sprint and giggle.

He saw ghosts. First, a herd of little people marched out from under crawl spaces in the attic and under the stairs. He kept asking where they went. Then, she would awaken on moonless nights to find him sitting on the end of the bed, staring into the dresser mirror. His long dead brother-in-law, L. C., had come again to take him. On those dark nights, she would mutter, "Oh, for dumb" under her breath and roll over under the quilts. These episodes were more disappointing than chilling. The little people made work for her: she hammered shut the boards over the crawl spaces and tucked scatter rugs into the gaps near baseboards. L. C. was a different matter. Henry kept turning him down.

It was his laughter that angered her most: it was unjust that the animals would humor him. Disloyalty she believed was the greatest offense. Over those many hard years she kept the family secrets. For that she thought she was granted a special intuitive sense to which the animals responded. True, it was he not she who looked more Indian, but she had the gift. Year after year, season after season, they came to her: raccoon, squirrel, deer, and birds of great variety—chickadee, grackle, pileated woodpecker, hummingbird, quail, robin, jay. Once a young eagle perched on a nearby juniper tree, jerking its head in rapt attention when a neighbor's gray-and-white tom cat loped across the backyard. Others—bear, moose, and beaver—waited for her nightly walks along the paved trail from through the nearby state park. Fish the size of keepers swam circles around her ankles when she waded in small lakes, combing the sand for broken glass and tin cans. In their knowing looks they informed her that long suffering had singled her out for their benevolence. In turn, she packed the tree hollows with peanut butter and the bird feeder with the black sunflower seeds the cardinals favored. Now, they entertained him and would not meet her gaze. The bird seed lay untouched. The jays no longer chased the cat from the bird feeder where in his feline patience the cat would gorge himself on the smallest seeds, only to leave mounds of yellow, grainy vomit on the middle of the sidewalk.

For years the only laughter they heard was his sadistic mockery as he knocked them down, mother, sons and daughters, and slapped their faces from side to side until he tired. To a one, they never cried, waiting dry-eyed until his thirst drove him away to find more alcohol.

Henry's job at the paper mill brought him $600 a month, $100 of which he meted out to Edith for groceries, clothing and bills. She did not know what he did with the rest of the money. Some went to drink, to cigarettes, to cards. Some to his distant family in response to appeals. Strangers thanked her on the street for Henry's largesse, the T-bone steaks he purchased for them at local bars. Local shopkeepers smiled her way; they overpriced their outdated stock, knowing Henry favored local business and was an easy mark when he was drunk.

While their children never starved, neither did they flourish. Once a season, some member of Edith's family drove the three hundred miles from the reservation to leave a stock of commodities: five pound cans of honey, dried pinto beans, corn meal, condensed milk, powdered milk and powdered eggs, all labeled with the United States Department of Agriculture slogan: Not for Sale or Exchange. She supplemented these staples with wild berries, pit fruits, and vegetables canned in season and purchased cheaply from roadside stands or given in silent understanding by women in the Catholic Church's Ladies Home Auxiliary. She learned to follow recipes designed for large quantity consumption, bland food created by extending the flavorful ingredients. Soup from one can of cream-style corn and a half gallon of milk, a carton of elbow macaroni and butter, a tall stack of pancakes in the shape of round, brown teddy bears.

The first two of the eight children, born after Henry returned from Korea, remembered the early, hard years of the family. They lived first in a tourist camp at the outskirts of the state park while Edith tested the receptivity of the town. The neighbors were neither friendly nor openly hostile, though Edith learned later of the paper petition with its column of signatures attesting to the sentiments of some that the Indian family be asked to leave. After they made the down payment on the green asphalt-shingled house, Edith found the Singer sewing machine in the attic. She traced outlines of the children's overalls on ruled brown paper sacks, cut remnant upholstery cloth and arrived, with surprisingly little effort, at two new pair of facsimile overalls.

When the oldest children reached junior high, she bought an electric Swedish sewing machine at the county fair. For the first time she used commercially printed paper patterns, starting with simplistic A-line jumpers. She found comfort in handling large bolts of fabric as she produced darts, gathers and ruffles, buttonholes, necklines and sleeves. Only the zippers evaded her. It had something to do with laying straight the metal teeth; they never drew together without puckering. She paid a professional seamstress a quarter a zipper, grateful to find someone else who violated the smooth unblemished fabric without compunction.

Edith then took sewing classes and learned the technique of handling double knits and lingerie. She sewed on the sly— gingham curtains for the VFW club, circle skirts for cheerleader tryouts, empire waisted homecoming gowns, pastel tricot underwear and baby doll pajamas. Neighborhood women paid her for materials and a little more for her time. This allowed her to purchase the special all-fabric plastic thread wound on long wooden spools. Once Mrs. Olson inadvertently paid Henry instead. After that Henry reduced her monthly allowance to $90. Thus began their economic competition. Henry would pause at her sewing station in the living room bay window. Several times a week he would unexpectedly drive home from work for lunch, again to check her sewing or look for different fabric scraps. He left mending for her in the evenings and watched the length of thread diminish on the spool.

The children joined their mother willingly in the struggle. They searched couch cushions and inflated the amount they said they paid paper boys when asking for reimbursement. The most favorable opportunity was when their father lay in bed after a pay-day binge. The children would comb carefully through the car, knowing he would have no recall of where he spent his money, for what, or for whom. Once they found a roll of ten and twenty dollar bills wedged in between the front passenger seats. Other times the worn station wagon yielded strange and unexplained booty: ladies store-bought underwear and a pliable and purring two-foot-long cat.

One year she opened separate bank accounts for the children and gave them each a small plaid bank book in which to record their deposits. For months she carefully rotated her sewing earnings across their accounts. She warned the children to hide the books under their mattresses. Still, after nearly a year Henry found out about the money and withdrew it. That week he drove home in a new Skidoo, his smile broad under his snowmobile helmet.

His gait was parodied within the family, most frequently by a rebellious son-in-law and, unknowingly, by the natural mimicry of a three-year-old grandson. The son-in-law, Jim, had too much time on his hands. A libertarian student of the human condition, he spouted assassination theories and tirades against elected officials and the federal income tax. Henry's brain revolved on a new biorhythm; at dusk he stripped down to his union suit, a long, slow ritual that occurred in front of the living room picture window. When Henry retired to bed, Jim slid over to Henry's dais—a well-worn corner of the couch. There, Jim transformed himself into Henry, assuming his characteristic lean, horn-rimmed glasses askew at the end of his nose, greasy Gimme cap perched on top of his slicked back hair, and one hand poised in the air, like Lassie waiting for a good-boy hand shake. Christopher, the three-year-old, was his grandfather's shadow during the day, limping in time, two steps behind him, one hand also held stiffly aloft. While Henry did not hear the laughter, Edith did and was wounded. Before the strokes, the white men set upon him when he drank. They laughed as they kicked him until his fringed buckskin jacket was sprayed with blood. She sometimes laughed when she found him, crumpled on the front step, his hair matted with blood and his nose or eyes swollen. But now that his gait was, when sober, unsteady, she no longer sought laughter at his expense. His weakness also enabled her to favor him again, in little ways.

She emptied the nuts into old green-tinged glass Ball jars and screwed the metal lids on tight, too tight for his claw-like wrists to loosen. Just so he would know, should his memory hold steady enough to recall the hidden bounty, she replaced the nuts with empty wooden thread spools and closed the drawer.

Home Tellings

The Rez Road Follies
Stage Version: An Excerpt

Jim Northrup

As the audience enters, they see a dimly lit set and hear selections of Native American powwow music. As lights come up to begin the play, Luke Warmwater is discovered smoking a cigarette, sipping coffee, & listening to "Free Bird" by Lynurd Skynurd. The telephone rings.

Luke (Answering the telephone) Boozhoo. (Listens) Yeah, I'm Luke Warmwater. A Minneapolis newspaper? Great. Interview away! (Listens) Am I an Indian? No, I'm Anishinaabe. . . Yeah, A-N-I-S-H-I-N-A-A-B-E. (Listens) How long have I been Indian? Fifty years, it would have been 51 but I was sick a year. Yeah, that's right. Did we always live in a tarpaper shack? No, but as soon as we could afford it, we moved into one. Do I speak my language? Yup, and yours too. How long have I been I . . . You already asked me that. . . All fucking day!

Luke drops the receiver in its cradle, stares at it. He turns to his word processor and talks out loud as he types:

Thank you Christopher Columbus. The 1992 Quincentennial celebrations have meant a lot more work for me. All the thanks shouldn't go to you alone, however. The tomahawk chop and the Super Bowl mascot issues have helped, and the extremists opposed to treaty rights have kept Native American issues in the public eye.

Luke speaks directly to the audience.

I used to be known as a "bull shitter." It's true. But that didn't pay anything so I decided to say I was a "story teller." That was a little better . . . a little more prestige. That didn't pay so much so I decided to be a free-lance writer. At first it was more "free" than "lance" but pretty soon, I started getting money for my words. But when I became an "author". . . that's when I could start charging consultant's fees.

He stands up and sits on edge of desk.

I'm fifty-one years old. I'm finally at the age when it doesn't matter whether my belly bulges a bit. No matter how many sit-ups I do, the bulge is still there. I did one just the other week — it didn't change a thing. When I was young, I'd take off running and be at top speed in a step or two. Over the years, I've noticed that it takes longer and longer to get there. Right now, we're up to an hour and a half. By that time, I've forgotten why I wanted to run in the first place. As I get older, I find fewer and fewer reasons to run at full speed.

Luke crosses to down center stage.

I am not Indian. I am Anishinaabe. For over 500 years, my ancestors and I have been called something we're not. It started with Columbus, then continued with the Puritans and Cotton Mather. Along the way the United States government started using that word to describe us. It's become so common we internalized it, we began to think of ourselves as "Indians." I'm not Indian; I am Anishinaabe.

It has been over 500 years since Native People discovered Columbus wading ashore. Over 500 years of being known by the wrong name.

As my way of de-celebrating the Columbus event, the word Indian will not cross my lips for one year. Instead of saying the word, I will use silence. Instead of writing the word out, I will use dashes. I am banishing the word from my vocabulary for one year. Let's see, how would that work? That sign on the edge of the Rez would read "The Fond du Lac— (uses a gesture to fill in the blank for the word "Indian) Reservation. Yeah, that's good. If I went down to Minneapolis and saw Clyde and Vern Bellecourt, I'd be talking to members of the American— Movement. If I went down to the Federal Building, I'd be talking to the Bureau of—Affairs. My kids could still play, only now they'd be Cowboys and —. Yeah, not bad.

Powwow music comes up under Luke. As he hears it, he moves across the stage & picks up a cradle board.

The Anishinaabe have been here for a long time. So long, that we've got a "great flood" story, just like in the Bible or in the Epic of Gilgamesh. We've been telling that story long before the Bible came to this continent. I can tell you stories about my great-great-great-great-great-grandfather Mikinok who was walking around in 1740—some 30 years before there was a United States. He was living his life with the seasons, probably carrying around a baby in a cradle board just like this one. And I can tell you stories about each generation since then.

Luke moves to the storytelling area.

Now, me, I've only been here since 1943. In late April of that year, Luke and Alice Warmwater had their second child. I was named for my dad. I like to say that I was born at a very early age at the government hospital on the Fond du Lac Reservation.

When I was young, I used to hear the average age of death for I— was 44 years. I adopted an attitude that anything over that many years was pure gravy, just juice. It was a bonus for trying to live a good life. Today, one-third of us exist below the poverty line. Our children kill themselves four times more often than any other ethnic group. We have the highest rates of diabetes, TB, and fetal alcohol syndrome. (Pause) I bet you're wondering why I'm still here?

My early years were spent in the warmth of the family. Grammas and grannpas, aunts and uncles. Cousins by the carload lived in Sawyer. I had enough brothers and sisters to make two basketball teams—with substitutes. It was good living in that small village. But reality struck at age six. I was sent to a Federal boarding school 300 miles away. It was a policy at the time—educate the heathens.

Luke moves to the microphone stage right and recites the poem, "Ditched."

Ditched

A first grader
A Federal Boarding School
Pipestone
Said Anin to the first grown up
Got an icy blue eyed stare in return.
Got a beating from a second grader
for crying about the stare.
Couldn't tell ma or dad
Both were 300 miles away.
Couldn't write, didn't know how.
Couldn't mail, didn't know how.
Runaway, got caught
Got an icy blue stare and a beating
Got another beating from a second grader
for crying about the blue eyed beating
Institutionalized, toughed it out
survived.

The lights slowly revert to their "pre-poem" look. Luke focuses on the audience.

I remember asking my mother why we were the only ones who had to go away to school . . .why didn't white people have to leave their homes when they were in the first grade? She couldn't answer, she just looked away but not before I'd seen the pain in her eyes.

The sound of Christmas music is heard. Luke crosses up to get a cup of coffee. He sits on the edge of the desk.

Christmas—what a bummer. My earliest memories of Christmas were formed at the Federal Boarding School at Pipestone. We were given presents of ribbon candy and fruit. All it meant to me was some big guy was going to beat me up and take my present. In the Christian boarding school, I was older so no one beat me up but the season was still a disappointment. I learned at about that time that there was no such thing as goodwill towards man.

When my son was in the first grade he told the teacher we didn't celebrate Christmas. She went out of her way and bought him a fake tree. We thanked her but left it in the box and later gave it to someone who does Christmas.

Today there is no tree inside my house. We leave them outside where they continue to grow. No tinsel, angels, stars or cute manger scenes. My light bill stays the same because we don't outline the house in colored lights. I could never make the connection between lights and the birth of the Christ child. The only real connection I can figure out is that power companies sponsor lighting contests every year.

Psst, hey buddy, do you know where we can score a couple of Pilgrims? Thanksgiving is coming and, once again, we're looking for Pilgrims to help us celebrate our feast. In years past, we always started looking too late and found ourselves without Pilgrims for the holiday. We couldn't hold our heads up among family because we were pilgrimless on Turkey day.

Some historians say that Thanksgiving started with Governor Bradford of Plymouth Colony in 1621. That's one version. We know from our stories that the first people of this continent were having Thanksgiving feasts long before the newcomers waded ashore. As if this continent's history started when the

Pilgrims got here after the boat ride. My cousin calls Pilgrims the first boat people. Alas, America seems to have forgotten the original reason for the holiday. Today it means football games and shopping for that next one called Christmas.

Easter. I grew up hearing the Christian reasons for that holiday, but the way it's celebrated now confuses me. Let me see if I got this straight. It starts with a pre-Easter sale in the retail store. Then, this unusual rabbit—of unknown gender—lays and delivers pastel-colored chicken eggs. Sometimes chocolate eggs. Then there's green, plastic grass—that's part of it someplace. The kids are teased by hiding the food. Sometimes, the pastel-colored chicken eggs are rolled down the White House lawn. The ladies get a bonnet to wear in the Easter parade, and the whole thing is concluded with an after-Easter sale in the retail stores. I wish that Easter bunny would come hop, hopping by my rez. I got a snare with its name on it.

Luke is interrupted by the Marine Corps Hymn. He jumps to attention, then catches himself.

I don't have to do that anymore.

Crosses back down to the story-telling area.

I was still in boarding school when the Korean War was fought. My older cousins came home and told stories about the war. Other uncles told stories about their own experience in war, and of the Anishinabe as great warriors. So, after high school I joined the Marine Corps. Boarding schools were just practice for reform school which was a rehearsal for U.S. Marine Corps boot camp.

I went through the Panama Canal during the Cuban Missile Crisis. We didn't invade Cuba and just visited Puerto Rico and Jamaica. From there we went across the Pacific to practice war in Okinawa, Japan, Taiwan and the Philippines. I was in Subic Bay when Kennedy was killed. In 1965 I went to Vietnam as an infantryman, a grunt, with the 3rd Battalion of the 9th Marines.

*SFX: "I Can't Get No Satisfaction." Luke moves into "The
Duke."*

"Hold up on that patrol,
we got a chopper coming in,"
Good, no reason to stand so
we all sat down.
The slapping sound of the rotor
blades told us a landing was
near. Two gunships went over,
suspicious, looking for danger
to the chopper they were
escorting.
The chopper landed,
they walked in our direction.
Starched jungle utilities,
spitshined boots,
shiny rank insignia
told us these were rear
echelon Marines.
They surrounded a large
green-clad man.
"It's John Fucking Wayne,"
one grunt said.
The Duke centered himself in
the circle of men.
Smiling, posing for pictures
and signing autographs,
he was enjoying himself until
the Shinnob patrol leader
invited him for a walk
with the grunts.
The Duke patted his ample
belly and said, "Heh,heh,heh
I'll leave that to you professionals."

John Fucking Wayne, who killed
Native Americans by the dozens with his
movie sixshooter, refused.
The ranking officers looked
at the disrespectful Marines.
Court martials and other
punishments filtered through
their rear echelon brains.
The grunts looked back with:
"Whatcha gonna do, cut my hair
and send me to Vietnam?
I'm already here, maybe for
the rest of my life."
The Duke looked troubled when
he saw the killing etched in
the eyes of the grunts.
More killing than he had seen
in a quarter century of
movie killing.
Duke gave some excuse about
lung cancer and was excused
from the rest of the war.
Derisive laughter lifted the
chopper away from the young
grunts.
"What a pussy, wouldn't even
go on a little walk with us."

*The sound of a Huey helicopter has come up under the last few
lines of the poem. As it gets louder, Luke remembers another time.*

It was really crazy at times. One time we were caught out
in this big rice paddy. They started shooting at us. I was close to
the front of the formation so I got inside the treeline quick. The
bad guys couldn't see me. When I leaned over to catch my breath,
I heard the snick, snick bang sound of someone firing a bolt
action rifle. The enemy soldier was firing at the guys still out in

the rice paddy. I figured out where the bad guy was from the sound—snick, snick, bang. I fired a three-round burst at the sound. That asshole turned and fired at me. I remember the muzzle flash and the bullet going by together. I fired again as I moved closer. Through a little opening in the brush, I could see what looked like a pile of rags, bloody rags. I fired another round in his head. We used to do that all the time—one in the head to make sure. The 7.62 bullet knocked his hat off. When the hat came off hair came spilling out. (Pause) It was a woman. Her hair looked just like my gramma's.

Luke stops, lights a cigarette and catches his breath. We hear an erie voice (SFX) asking Luke questions about the war. He replies, all in voice over.

SFX: Were you in the war?
LUKE: Yes.
SFX: What was it like?
LUKE: Like nothing you can imagine.
SFX: Did you kill anyone?
LUKE: Yes.
SFX: How did that feel?
LUKE: I felt like a murderer, a savior, a cog in a machine.
SFX: Did any of your friends get killed?
LUKE: Yes.
SFX: How did that feel?
LUKE: Get the FUCK out of my face.
After the war, life settled down to a struggle. The jobs varied, deputy sheriff to floor sweeper, ironworker to chief investigator, factory hand to fork lift driver. A lot of different jobs, whatever it took.

Luke moves to the mic, recites "Shrinking Away."

Survived the war, but was
having trouble surviving the peace
couldn't sleep more than two hours

was scared to be without a gun
Nightmares, daymares, guilt and remorse
wanted to stay drunk all the time
1966 and the VA said
Vietnam wasn't a war
they couldn't help but
did give me a copy of the Yellow Pages
Picked a shrink off the list
50 bucks an hour
I was making 125 a week
We spent six sessions establishing rapport
I heard about his military life
his homosexuality
his fights with his mother
and anything else he wanted to talk about
At this rate we would have
got to me in 1999
Gave up on that shrink, couldn't afford him
wasn't doing me any good
Six weeks later my shrink killed himself
Great
not only guilt about the war but
new guilt about my dead shrink
If only I had a better job
I could have kept on seeing him
I thought we were making real progress
Maybe in another six sessions
I could have helped him
I realized then that surviving the peace
was up to me.

By this time I had been gone for years from the Fond du Lac
Reservation. I was working in a public defender's office as an
investigator, working for people like Johnny Cochran and Rob-
ert Shapiro. I got tired of talking to robbers and rapists and
murderers. I looked at my appointment book one day. At nine
o'clock, I had to talk to a guy who was charged with the shotgun

slaying of his girlfriend. At eleven o'clock I was scheduled to meet a guy who was charged with raping an eight-year-old boy. After lunch, I was supposed to talk to a guy charged with armed robbery. I got tired of walking in the sewers of humanity.

So, just after America's Bicentennial, I quit the city and went home to the Rez. I always knew I would, I just didn't know when. But when I got there, there were no jobs, no place to live. I solved my housing problem. I found a tipi advertised in the back of *Mother Earth News*. I sent them my 700 dollars, they sent me a 22-foot tipi.

Luke recites "Tipi Reflections" as he places another tipi pole up along the edge of the circular platform.

I moved into a tipi
my friends think I am strange
my family thinks I am nuts
Both friends and family wish
they were nuts enough to do it

The design is thousands of years
of a man wondering—Will this work?

The canvas is strong enough to
stop the north wind
yet delicate enough to cast
shadows from the cooking fire
Grandpa called it bajeeshkoagan
and knew all about it
before I was born

The poles, rising up and carrying
your eyes, thoughts and prayers
to the sky and beyond

The tipi contained people
eating freshly roasted meat
It could have been yesterday
or eons ago.

The tipi also contained a small boy
excited by the duty of tending the fire
staring at the flames for hours
making good childhood memories

For fun, telling the misbehaving
children they will soon have to
stand in the corner

The smell of wood smoke
clings to me when I have
to go to the city. It is a reminder
of where I come from and
where I am going

Meanwhile the loons sing to me
and get just as excited
when the bald eagle flies over
although for different reasons

The idea of living in a tipi
always brings out the
what you should do is
in people who visit

How many men have stood where
I stand thinking
what a fine place to live.

*As the last words of the poem are spoken, Luke pauses to listen
to the distant screams of an eagle.*

I lived in the tipi for several years. Three seasons of the year were great. Winter was just a bitch. I had a fire this high (holds hands waist high) all the time. But when it got really cold, I'd go visit *any* of my relatives. I'd say, "I've come to borrow your shower ..." and then stay for two weeks. I was the house guest that never left.

The tipi was set up on the shores of Perch Lake, a suburb of Sawyer. There were many visitors to the only telephone equipped tipi on the Fond du Lac Reservation. Stories were told while watching the sun go down or starting a fire. Whoever told the best story "took the cake." It was primitive but the pace of life was slow. Slow enough to begin writing stories about life on the Fond du Lac Reservation.

One of the visitors was a Dakota woman named "Pannequay." She was from the Lower Sioux Rez. I liked that visitor so much, we got married. But she said, "I'm not living in a tipi." So, we got a house and blended our families. Now there are seven children. And these kids are mostly grown up now, and starting to give us grandchildren. As of today's date, there are four of them—Ezigaag, Mato, Neewin, and Wiigwasequay. Ezigaag is the oldest, he's four, and he lives with us. His name means wood-tick. It describes the way he hugs.

Crosses up to desk, sits.

By this time, I was getting a little too old to work construction anymore. I figured out that lifting a pencil was a lot easier than swinging a three-pound hammer, or carrying 65-pound concrete block. So, I started to write stories. Went to work for a newspaper. In 1989, I started writing a column about life on the rez. It's kind of an irreverent look at the world through my eyes. Humor is a big part of my newspaper column. One of the parts that people really seem to like is the Question of the Month, where I answer the sometimes silly, mean, cruel, and mostly dumb questions that people ask about being Native American. For example, Question: Why do you call it a "rez" instead of a reservation? Answer: Because the white man owns most of it.

Or, Question: Are you a fullblooded Indian?

Luke mutters to himself as he puts a dollar in a jar on the
desk. Repeats the question.

Are you fullblooded? Answer: Pint low, just came back from
the blood bank. Here's one that was taped to my phone. Question: Do you have big mosquitos on your rez? Answer: On my
rez, the mosquitos have wood ticks.

The questions come from everywhere. I get them in the mail,
over the telephone. People leave them under my windshield
wiper. Sometimes, I dream them. Sometimes, I just make them
up.

It was then that I discovered how to make money as a writer.
(Says it slowly) Sin-di-ca-tion. Write once, get paid three times.

I know my grandfather would have been proud. His pen
name was Nodin. He was a writer back in the 1920s. When I
was a kid—nine or ten years old—I used to go up to the library
in Duluth and ask the librarian if she had anything written by
a man (pretends to forget it) "What was his name again? Oh,
yes. Nodin. He wrote under the name Nodin." She would duti-
fully look it up in the card catalog. When she'd find it, she'd tell
me they had a copy of a book called "Waweena." I'd say, "Thank
you. That's my grandpa," and walk out of the library. Now, my
grandchildren can do the same thing. Like my parents and
grandparents, I was born on the Rez, I live on the Rez, and will
probably die on the Rez.

Luke goes back to typing as we hear powwow music fade up. He
looks at his computer, then at log seats in the storytelling area.
Finally, Luke crosses to the fire pit and whittles on a sugar bush
tap as he talks about "living with the seasons."

The rez is called Fond du Lac in official circles. We call it
Nahgahchiwanang and home. My family and I live our lives
with the seasons. In the spring we spear fish and boil sap to
make maple syrup. We learned how to do these things when

we lived with our parents and grandparents. We teach our children and grandchildren what we've learned. This was Ezigaag's first time making maple syrup. His sugar bush began when he watched his grampa make taps for the trees. His eyes followed the maple sticks that were drilled, carved and turned into taps. His job was counting the completed taps as he put them into a coffee can . . . 1, 2, 13, 3, 7 . . . The numbers he used didn't match the taps he was counting. That didn't matter, he was counting. Ezigaag was learning sugar bush and math.

Luke goes to one of the log seats which has a pre-drilled hole for the tap to demonstrate.

I took him out in the woods and showed him how we tap the trees. We start by drilling a hole at an upward angle. Then, I pound in a tap. (He does so) In the old days, they just cut a slash in the tree and pounded a piece of wood into the bottom. The sap would drip down like clear water into the birchbark containers. Of course, our culture is ever-changing so in my grandfather's time, they started using number 10 cans to collect the sap. And we're still evolving.

Luke shows audience an example of the milk jug collector.

We use plastic milk jugs. They're great. They keep the rain and the snow out, leaves, bugs . . . and you don't have to worry about dogs visiting your sugar bush. When we're done with them for the year, we take them to the recycling center. (Pause) I don't know why they call it sugar *bush.* They're really trees. Anyway, we tap about 100 trees a year. That's enough work for my family. Ezigaag watched the sap drip from the taps. He watched for a long time before he tried tasting any of it. Ezigaag caught the drips of clear sap on his tongue. His smile was like warm sunshine to his grandparents.

The next day, we went back out to the sugar bush to see how much sap we had. At that time of year, the sun heats up the snow and I break through the crust up to my knees . . . just above the tops of my boots. It's kind of like trudging up stairs all day. But Ezigaag, with his 36 pounds, was able to dance across on the top of the snow from tree to tree without breaking through. He was a big help. He'd go and get the milk jug from each tree and bring it back to where I was lugging the big pails.

We finished gathering the sap and got ready to boil it. We boil the sap in our black cast iron kettle. That kettle has seen plenty of sugar bushing seasons. It's the same kind of kettle that's used to cook missionaries or explorers in cartoons. (Pause)

Ours is called a "treaty kettle." It was handed down from treaty-making times.

Ezigaag watched the boiling of the sap. We had a hot birch-maple fire and he learned to stay away from it. He also learned to stay upwind of the smoke. I use maple and birch because I think the smoke mixes with the syrup and adds to the flavor. The sap starts to simmer. The bubbling, boiling sap chuckles to itself once in a while as it cooks down. The sap, almost syrup, rolls in the kettle.

The fire invites participation. It begs to be poked and prodded so it burns better. Moving a piece of burning maple a quarter of an inch is sometimes necessary when tending a fire.

My grandfather used to rub a piece of salt pork around the top edge of the kettle to keep it from boiling over.

So, we boil it down, and we add more sap. Boil it down, add more sap. The fire burns on. The sound of the fire and the wind in the trees were the loudest noises we hear all day. The fire burns on for seven hours. We know that sitting around a fire is a good place to tell stories and hold a grandson in your lap.

We can tell when it's done by giving the sap a "taste test." If you taste it and it tastes like syrup . . . it's done. We take the syrup inside where we filter it. The golden brown syrup is warm as we pour it over pancakes. Ezigaag wants to go to the woods again. He's learning something he can teach his grandchildren.

Luke gets a smile on his face. He gets out his writer's notebook and creates a new "Question of the Month."

(To himself) How come some of our maple syrup is light colored and . . . No, how come some of your maple syrup is light and . . . Here we go . . . (To audience) Question: How come some of your maple syrup is light and some of it is dark colored? Answer: Because we boil some of it at night! (Searches notebook for another) Here's a good one . . . What is the unemployment rate on the rez? I don't know, that's not my job. (Deals with response) My wife hates this one . . . Why do Indian men . . .

Luke catches himself saying the word "Indian."

Damn.

He crosses to a jar on the table and places a dollar inside it. Crosses back.

Why do *Anishinaabe* men make better lovers? A lot of them don't have to get up and go to work in the morning. How did I—survive the Great Depression? We didn't know it was over.

We make a lot of jokes on the rez. Of course, some people believe that living on the rez is a rotten deal. That's because they're looking at it with "white eyes."

Luke crosses to the mic for "Brown and White Peek"

What's it like living on the Rez?
It's living near a lot of relatives
ready to help or gossip about your need for help
The word Reservation is a misnomer
Reserved for who?
The white man owns 80 percent of my Rez—Fond du Lac
Living there means finding something good
in something grim
Glad for our chronic unemployment when
the white guys get lung cancer
from breathing asbestos at the mill
We have TV, that window to America

We see you, you don't see us.
I watch the news every night, whenever they show
us, it's always the same tired tub of walleye
maybe some kind of bingo doings.
Surplus commodities are good for you, our nutritionist says;
right, they let your stomach know your swallower
still works, eat them for the bulk, not the taste.
Rice Crispies now come in commods, in addition
to the Spanish lesson printed on every box and can.
"Cereal de arroz tostado," anyone?
We live strong 'cause we know we're just one of
the generation of people called Anishinaabe.
Our spirituality protects us from the excesses
of the manifest destiny dominant society.
What's it like on the rez?
Come walk a mile in my moccasins
maybe we can pick up some commods.

At that moment we hear the loud barking of a dog from offstage.
Luke crosses up to the back of the stage.

    Quiet, Outside. I'm trying to work here. Pannequay, would
you let that dog out. Outside. Outside!

The dog stops barking.

    Good dog.

Luke turns his attention back to the audience.

    Our current dog is named "Outside." Ezigaag named him.
Now we can stand at the front door and say, "Inside, Outside."
Or, "Outside, Outside."
    We're kind of tough on dogs. We go through them like some
casinos go through managers. Some stay a day and others are
around for a year or more.
    Concrete was the product of a broken home. Neither one

wanted custody of the dog when the marriage failed. The big golden retriever came north to live with us on the rez. Since he was a city dog, he preferred sleeping on the front steps made of concrete. Thus he named himself. In the coldest weather he slept on the concrete, he refused offers of a dog house, a sheltered spot under the canoe or even inside. Concrete just lay on the concrete and protected the house.

When not on duty, Concrete liked to ride in the car; it didn't matter where it was going. He'd stick his head out the window, a goofy look on his face as he sampled the passing odors. His ears were windblown as he smelled the county. One day I had to go somewhere.

"Get in." I told the tail-wagging dog. Concrete jumped in and took his place in the back seat. I stopped a couple of miles from home because I recognized my brother's car. I parked and asked if he needed help. I let the dog out of the car to run around while we jumpstarted my brother's car. When his car was running, I yelled,

"Get in," and held the back door open. A big golden blur jumped into the car.

When we got home, I opened the back door and said, "Get out." The dog jumped out and went tail-wagging toward the house.

I looked closer at the dog. He didn't look right. I said, "Concrete, where did you get that collar?" He didn't have one on before we started our little trip.

"Who put it on you?" I knew he couldn't have done it himself.

"Concrete, you've gained weight, and who put that blond streak in your fur?"

This wasn't Concrete. It was some other golden retriever, an imposter. I asked him what he did to my dog. He didn't answer. I opened the back door and said,

"Get in." The strange dog jumped into the car.

I drove back to the scene of the crime. There was Concrete, sitting patiently on the side of the road. When he saw the familiar car he started wagging his tail. He was squealing with excitement. I stopped the car, opened the back door, and said, "Get out." The fake Concrete leaped out.

"*You* get in," I told Concrete, who was now licking my hand. We drove home. When we got there I said,

"Get out." Concrete walked up the sidewalk and lay down on the concrete.

He died one winter when he and a snowplow tried to be in the same place at the same time.

Then there was Speedbump. I forget what we first called him when he came to live with us. His name changed after an accident on the gravel road. We were just coming home from somewhere.

He was so happy to see us that he ran under the car. I hit the brakes and slid. The front wheel of the heavy Buick rode up and over him. I thought I had killed my dog. Then I could hear him thumping under the car. He was still alive. I cut the wheels sharp and slowly backed up. The front wheel passed over him again.

When he was finally clear of the car he took off howling for the woods. He didn't come home for three days but when he did, he had a new name—Speedbump.

We've tried different sizes, different breeds. Most were mixed breeds but their end was the same. They died so we could get to know a new dog.

▶◀▶◀

A Warrior with a Pen

Doyle Turner, Sr.

I read somewhere that the pen was mightier than the sword, so in a moment of simplistic optimism I picked up a pen and an old spiral bound notebook left by one of the kids and, bound to fight by the pen, I sat down at the table to write.

I have been sitting here for an hour now. The page is still blank. The simple thought was much easier than the doing. I look down at my old wrinkled, brown hand as if to offer encouragement. How quickly we become wrinkled, I think. How very quickly life goes by, one day you're young, full of piss and vinegar, and the next it seems, it hurts just to lie in bed. So quickly youth and its passion are gone.

I remember the burning passion in my young heart. I remember the anger. How unfair life is when you're an Indian. No one will ever make it right and no one cares. Lots of people say they care, but nothing ever changes. People are still living in slum housing, still living and dying in poverty, unable to affect any change in their lives. And people are still sitting out there saying, "what you people really need to do is . . . " or, "if you people could just . . ." God it makes me mad!

I was going to change all that. I was going to change the world. I would make people sit up and listen. By God things would change! If people were just told how we live poor in the midst of the richest nation in the world, things were bound to change. No one, I reasoned, wanted it this way. If people just understood the injustice they would surely act to change it. So I began writing letters to the senators and congressmen. I began driving to their offices asking for appointments and sitting in waiting rooms. I even went to Washington one time, taking our story to the people who had the power to change the course of history and make amends for what had been done.

How clearly I remember the blank looks, the words bouncing off blank faces and hard hearts. "I was not even born when all that happened to your people. . . ." or, "why do you people always try to make us feel guilty or responsible. . . ." "it's not my fault, why lay this on me. . . ." Five years older, broke, and unable to continue, I went home. "How's the politician," the people asked and chuckled.

Unable to make a small dent in the mountain of uncaring, I quit. The passion of my heart turned finally to anger, stark, smoldering, seething anger. The only relief was to numb my heart. If people don't care why should I.

I took up the bottle and began to drink. I am going to be the best damn drunken Indian there ever was, I thought. Years later, I quit that too. It made me sick. Every time I got drunk, I got sick. So sick I thought I was gonna die. But I had given it an honest try.

By the time I quit, I was alone, I sold my wife and kids for the numbness in the bottle. I live in an old shack out by the back of the lake. My health is still not too bad for an old rascal. I have been dry for many years. Now I care more for clear eyes than being sick all the time. I tried to make up to my family for my misspent life. But they had had enough of my lies long ago. Me too. I couldn't blame them; it was years before I even trusted myself again.

The kids are scattered all over the country. They have all done well for themselves. They all have good jobs and families. Two have college degrees. They must have got whatever it took from their mother. At the thought of her, the old pain comes flooding back. I remember too easily and too strongly what I regret losing most of all.

The image of Sari comes quickly to me. A tall, blond, blue-eyed, laughing woman with love in her eyes, trying hard to live with and understand the dark anger of a man with a passion for changing life for his people. Trying, trying, trying until there was no more trying left and then she left for her own sanity. She lives in Hawaii now. Her card comes once a year, bringing new pain and old memories. Light words, easy wishes, kindness at a distance, a great distance. Her cards are bundled together in a cardboard box under my bed, along with the remnants of my life and the memories of her love, beautiful, soaring memories of moonlit nights, of warm summer winds, of naked swims and carefree loving as the morning birds called for the light.

God, a man can make a mess of things. All the love in the world was unable to take away the burning anger. It left of its own accord suddenly one morning as I stood sick and alone in my empty house. My anger left that morning along with everything else. My love, my kids, my rage and my passion, too; all left me alone, sick and empty.

I finally understood then. I remember the stark clarity. I saw it all. I had stormed and raged my entire life and nothing had changed. The government hadn't changed; it is still bound to the notion that we are ignorant and simple children, unable to care for ourselves. The tribe hadn't changed; it still acts like a little federal government, tied to control and worried more about its pay than the well-being of its people. The people hadn't changed; they still act like it is an honor-bound duty to stay drunk and throw themselves, their lives, and their children's lives full speed against trees, other cars, and each other.

I guess in my bitterness I am not being totally fair. They are good people, a lot of them, who live good lives and who try the same as I tried to make changes and who are as frustrated as I am. They have coped better than I with their rage. They must be recognized as the good among us. For there is much good too. I know I am not being fair to the old people whose straight lives remember the old times and the old ways. They were the only ones who understood my rage; rage understands rage. Only they couldn't teach me to live with mine. I wouldn't listen; I couldn't hear. Mine was to be the greatest and the last of the rages ever needed. My spirit couldn't tolerate what their spirits had endured all their lives. Everything was going to change. There would be no more need for rage, ever, by anyone, period.

We would all live happily ever after. We would all live in peace and understanding with the long knife. We would live in peace and understanding with each other, and most importantly, we would live in peace and understanding with ourselves. Can you understand now the passion of my heart? Can you understand the rage at the trying and changing nothing? The beautiful vision turned slowly to dust, ashes to ashes, dust to dust, with each graveside litany. The realization came to me that never in my lifetime, nor anyone else's probably, would this beautiful life be a reality for the people. That truth fed the fire of rage until it became a towering mountain of fire.

I thought about the needless waste. Millions of lives wasted over hundreds of years. All the dreams of love and all the possibilities of life, all thrown away in the despair in which we lived. The remembered words of reality were a bitter slap in the face. "What do you want me to do . . . if you go to the third floor and talk to . . . I am calling security . . . you better leave!"

I remember the hollow sound of my own pacing in the dark, empty house and how it had finally brought me out of the bottle. I stormed out of the house with a new passion. I finally realized what it was that I needed most of all. I realized who it was that I had failed most of all.

I trailed my family as I trail the deer. A trace here, a track there, a word here, until I stood finally before them again, again the guilty begging for leniency. They too had been there before, too often. They couldn't see anything other than the old stale and bitter-tasting promises. They had eaten these until they were over-full, stuffed until they were fat with empty words.

They couldn't see into my wringing, panicked heart. Please, just once more. I mean it this time. Can't you understand? It's different now. God damn it, can't you see? They couldn't. Neither could I. I walked back slowly alone, no tears left, no rage left, no passion left, no Sari left, no kids left, no nothing left.

But then nothing needs nothing, so I moved out behind the lake and had nothing. Just a little shack in a clearing by the lake at the end of a two-rut road with grass growing between the ruts. To this the kids come back once or twice a year, sometimes more. The boys always land here for hunting. I love that; I never feel so alive as when I am out in the woods. They seem more peaceful and happy with me than ever before. The woods work magic, you see.

In the woods everything is predictable. If you do things in a certain way you get certain results. If you are respectful and thankful and careful the woods will always feed you. It is a pact the animals made among themselves to take care of us weak and helpless humans way back when the world was young.

The woods feed me now. My soul has never been so full, my heart has never been so empty of the rage. The woods gives me all I need now. If only Sari could walk with me again in the woods, if only . . . but then, hope for what cannot be is not a big item for me anymore. When I begin to dwell too much on that kind of hope, the old anger comes out to fight, and for sure I am too old for that. The real world is lived out in the woods anyhow. The Windigo we call civilization is a concept someone made up to keep the poor working for the rich, and who needs that? This Windigo is a creature who, in its greed, eats everything and everyone it comes across.

The Creator made things the way He wanted them to be. They are still like that out in the woods. If you're quiet in the late evening, just at the coming of darkness, you become a part of it. You can feel the Creator close by, walking in the woods. Everything is still and hushed. All the birds, animals, trees, rocks, and wind stop everything to drink in the beauty and stillness.

Perhaps this is the true vision, a vision which depends upon the changing of only one person instead of the whole world. Perhaps this is the real vision, meant for one person to live out in peace of soul and beauty. And maybe one other person will see this peace and beauty and be drawn in. The two people with a common vision make beautiful music. And one other person will listen and hear the music and the laughter and be drawn close. Pretty soon there will be one more and one more until the fullness of the vision is finally realized, one person at a time. Perhaps when all is said and done, beauty, peace and spirit will be more powerful and accomplish far more of the vision than the vain raging of one angry person.

Perhaps one day even Sari will come back, smiling, surrounded by kids and grandchildren, pulled by the beautiful strains of the far off music of yesterday. Perhaps . . .

I look at the clock. It is two am. I lay down my pen, drained from all of the memories, the relieved emotion and the dashed dreams. I look for a time at the blank sheet of paper. "Looks like you told them all you know," I say. I get up chuckling, and ignoring my cold supper walk stiffly back to my bed and sleep the dreamless sleep of a tired old man.

Day two

I come slowly down the trail and out of the woods to my shack. The sun is just peeking in dappled rays through the budding branches of the trees. The tinge of green brings a glorious change to the gray and white of the just passed winter. I like being out early. The birds are in full voice this time of the year, singing hymns of celebration for the new day and the warmth of the sun. They had been at it when I had my tea in the dark this morning, tentative voices of hope singing for the light before they could see it. Now it is different. Their voices are full and exuberant, holding nothing back, shrilly chirping out their joy, glad for the new day and the warmth that is upon them.

I feel the same, way down in my heart. In my pack is a big northern. I shot it in the grass along the river just as it was getting light. An old trick I learned from my father. I learned a lot of tricks from my father. I remember the time he left home with two shells, going to find something for supper. Late that afternoon, he returned smiling as he was always smiling, with a rabbit and two northerns. We ate well that night and I remember looking up at him and adoring a hunter who could take two shells and come back with three things.

It is good to be alive, I think; it is good to live in the moment. It is such an overwhelming high I have on, that my mind refuses to focus as I almost fall over the form of Scot bluelegs. He is sitting on step waiting for me. "Ho!" I sputter in surprise, scaring Scot who tries to jump up and falls to his knees in front of me.

"Blessing, my son," I say in my most pious voice. We both laugh, but Scot's laughter stops right in the middle and he bursts into tears. "Hey niijii," I say reaching out and helping him to his feet. "What's the matter?"

"Lori left me, Po, she took the kids and went to Minneapolis with her brother."

"When was this?" I ask him.

"Last night," he tells me, shaking his head miserably. "I came back from the game in town and she was gone."

"What time'd you get back?" I ask, as an old song begins to play.

"Must have been three, four o'clock this morning," he says, "I forget."

"Why do you forget, Scot?" I ask, looking him in the face.

Scot's head goes down. He looks at his shoes. After a long silence he looks up at me, his eyes full of pain. "I was drunk," he says softly.

"Did you fight her?" I ask, knowing their story.

"No, no, nothing like that. She was already gone when I got there."

"Come in, I'll fix you something to eat." We go on into the house. My mind is whirling fast. I don't need this, I think. The stale smell and the tears bring back old memories and feelings I try so hard to leave behind. They never stay behind for long, now they're back and I don't like it at all. Be calm, I fume to myself; if you blow up, you lose him. Scot is not only my *niijii* , my friend, but he is also my sister's middle boy. I don't want him to leave like this.

"What am I gonna do, Po?" Scot asks, "What's going to happen now?"

"Hold on, hold on, one thing at a time," I say, much louder and madder than I expected. Scot looks whipped and slumps down in the old soft chair by the window. "And get the hell out of that chair, that's my chair," I growl.

"I better go now, Po," Scot says jumping up and backing toward the door.

"Aw shit. Shit, shit, shit, sit down my boy. I'm sorry I blew up," I said softly. "But you just screwed up a beautiful morning."

"I'll come back tomorrow," he said.

"No, no, just sit quiet for a while, over there," I point to the couch. "I'll be okay. No, you better go to the lake and wash up; you stink like yesterday's breakfast. I'll cook something."

He is gone a long time. I think he hates to come back. I don't blame him, I wasn't too nice. The tea is bubbling away on the stove when he finally comes up from the lake. His hair is wet and he is wiping off his face with his shirt. His tee shirt has holes in it, lots of them. I laugh, "Scot, we should take your tee shirt down to the river and set it out," I tell him. "We could catch lots of fish." He looks down at it and laughs too. The laughter clears the air between us.

"Clean up this fish, Scot," I say, "and I'll get the spuds started." He leaves again, when he comes back he has a bowl of cleaned fish pieces. The spuds are frying loudly on the old gas stove and the other pan is hot, waiting for the fish.

We eat in silence, nothing to say, just good food. When it's gone we wipe the plates clean with pieces of bannock and wash it down with hot tea. I look over at Scot. He is a handsome boy and very young. "Go in the other room and get some sleep, neej, you need it." He smiles and goes through the curtain into the other room where my bed is. I hear the springs squeak for a few minutes then deep, peaceful breathing.

"Crisis over," I say to myself. Then I think, for now. The worst is still ahead.

I spend the rest of the day roaming. I carry my old .22 rifle and a half box of shells. I don't know why I carried so many shells. I never use more than two or three. Perhaps it comes from a time when there were few shells to have, a poorer time with little food and less money. My mind roams as I roam. Back through the smoky distance of memory to times and places I have not visited for a long time.

I have my old seamless feedsack pack on my back. I think back to where I first saw one of these packsacks. It lay in the woodbox at home where I was raised. My dad had one like it. He brought most of our food home in it. My dad was a hunter. A fine, fine, hunter proud of his craft yet keenly aware and appreciative of the sacrifice made for the food he brought.

In my mind I can see the old house where I lived when my memories began. It was a two story frame house. It had one room on each floor. The bottom floor was living space, the top floor was where we slept, four beds scattered around the big room with a tin stovepipe coming up through the middle from the stoves below.

I remember lying awake in the morning looking up at the images made up of the grain and swirls of the old rough pine boards which made up our roof, and the walls for that matter. It was just boards and tarpaper between us and forty below zero.

Dad was always up early when the cold still stung the nose, building fire in the dark. My day started by listening to the clanking and rattling of Dad waking up the coals in the stoves. There were two stoves, both wood, one for cooking and one for heating. Perhaps warming would be a better term, for it never really got hot. Yet today I can still hear the sounds coming up through the screen vent. The grates would vibrate as he shook the ashes down. The wood thumped and bumped as he put it in the stove. Dad coughed, the stove rattled and pretty soon the warmth spread out like a blanket as both stoves perked wide open. The door opened and closed as Dad headed out to the toilet some thirty cold yards from the house.

Then Mom got up, wrapped herself in a housecoat and went down to meet the day. There was the sound of the teakettle being filled and put on the stove for hot water. As the water warmed they talked. I could never quite hear the words but the tones were warm and reassuring. Laughter and teasing were going on, hearts being warmed as well as the water. Soon the breakfast smell wafted up through the vent. When the house was warm and the breakfast was on the way, then it was our turn to go down and meet the day.

One morning in particular I lay in bed and listened to the sounds coming up through the vent from the room below. Sounds of breakfast being made, sounds of talking and laughing, these were softly on my mind as I picked faces, eyes, noses and shapeless bodies out of the boards on the ceiling. It must have been Saturday morning; they were the only lazy ones I remember. Suddenly as clear as a picture taken by a camera there was Satan looking back at me from the ceiling. In a flash I was out of bed and down the stairs stumbling to get my pants on on the way down. I never forgot that morning. The old boy scared me so bad, I never lazed in bed again. When everyone else went downstairs there I was right with them or down before them. I laughed to myself as I went through the woods. Too bad Satan didn't look at our friend Scot; maybe he'd quit his drinking.

I get back well after dark and have my supper of cold fish, bannock and tea quietly to the sounds of snoring coming from the back bedroom. I build up my fire for the night and watch the news while I wait for the fire. The sleek face of our senator is front and center, right were he likes to be, I think. He is talking about the Washington struggle against the Republicans. They want to change everything, he says, including the way Washington does business with the Indian people. Senator Bond is doing a good job tap dancing his way over and around the issues. "Nothing is as simple as it seems," he is saying. You got that right, I think, especially when you have three reservations sitting right in the middle of your district.

It could get tough, I think. The tribes are feeling their oats from twenty years of good treatment from Washington and favorable court atmosphere. They are pushing hard for some borderline issues. There is a time to fight and a time to wait. We are clearly into a time to wait, but the tribes were not responding. It was full speed ahead. One day soon, I think, we may all be in for a tough awakening.

I spread my blanket over me in the chair and recline all the way back. Damn that Scot, I think. If he were smarter, I would have my nice warm bed to myself tonight. "Maybe I'll just have to smarten him up," I say aloud, "I'm not sleeping here another night." Scot mumbles something in his sleep at the sound of my voice. "Shut up!" I yell and make myself laugh, a fool arguing with a sleeping drunk—what next!

But the thought is still on my mind the next morning as I make coffee. I take a cup of coffee with its load of sugar and canned commodity milk and my pipe and go out to sit in my chair to watch the sunrise over the lake.

Maybe it's time we all begin to smarten up a little. We have been too long dragging our attitudes in the dust. We have been victims too long now. Maybe it's time to stand up, shake the dust off our attitudes, and walk a different road. We seem to wait until we're too old and it's too late before we begin to get wiser. Some never do. Some never even get too old. Some do get wise earlier than the rest of us, but they take their wisdom off the reservation instead of fighting it out here. We are not people to stand and fight. If we don't like what is happening we vote with our feet and leave. I light my pipe and let that sink in.

The sun is up, my pipe is out and my coffee is cold. I have a stale, bitter taste in my mouth. Come to think of it the taste has been there since Scot came yesterday. It is the taste of waste. It is the taste of having given up; it is the taste of empty where full should be. I am one who had voted with my feet. I am not proud of it. If anything is ever going to change, I would have to get up off my behind and walk down that road first.

Scot comes out of the house stretching and scratching. He sees me down by the lake and yells, "Po, y'got any brandy?"

"What?" I answer.

"Brandy for the coffee, do-you-have-any-brandy," Scot says slowly and distinctly.

"I hear what you said," I say loudly back, "but I can't believe what I'm hearing."

"You're pissed again, huh? What the hell'd I do now?" comes the pouty reply.

"Scot, my boy, bring your coffee out here and sit down with me," I say. Scot comes out dressed, bright eyed and clean. "Sit here," I say motioning to the porch.

He sits uneasy, looking at me from the side of his eyes. "Lecture time I guess, huh?" He is nervous, so his macho comes out to cover up his weakness.

"I just want to talk to you, m'boy, no harm in that, is there?"

"Ma said you'd try to preach to me if I came out here," Scot says.

"Well then, why did you come?" I ask softly.

He looks up at me with big eyes. "I know this happened to you a long time ago; I thought you could help."

"I sure ain't going to help you by giving you any brandy, if I even had any."

He smiles a weak smile. "I'm sorry Po, that was dumb."

"Aw, forget it," I tell him, "we all do dumb things, that's why you and I are alone."

A hurt look fleetingly crosses his face, followed closely by the macho man. "I'm glad I am alone now, at least I will have my freedom, like you," he says, pointing at me with his lips.

"I curse the day I became alone," I say huskily, "I would give anything in the world to have Sari back."

He looks startled, confused. "I don't understand," he says, "I thought you were happy out here."

"I am," I say, "but not as happy as I would be if Sari was here with me. Scot . . . look," I say, "it is a dirty shame that we screw up our lives of our families."

"I . . . I," Scot stammers.

"We do," I say, "we screw it all up with our damned drinking, and what for, so our friends will be glad with us that we are man enough to cut the strings to our wife's apron? Think about it. We can't go out and have a good time without getting shit-faced, we can't have one or two and go home to the ones we really love. Instead we stick around, get drunk, get beat up and then go home and beat up the one person who really cares for

us. We got something all wrong, Scot m'boy. Something is really
screwed up."

"Wha, what are we supposed to do, Po?" Scot asks, "We're
Indians and Indians drink."

"Right, right, right, but we don't drink because we're Indians,
we drink because we can't stand being Indians, not the way we
have to be Indians, anyway."

"What do you mean?" Scot says, truly bewildered.

"If we are so damn proud of being Indians and if we are
really so damn happy to be Indians, then why in the hell would
we be trying to escape by drink from something we are really
happy and proud of being? Does that make any sense, Scot?" I
ask, ending just a little too loud. "Well does it?"

"I never thought of it like that," Scot says frowning, "it really
don't make no sense does it?"

"Nothing makes no sense. Almost everything we do don't
make no sense, yet we keep on doing it. It's time, Scot, that
someone gave us a kick in the ass and said, straighten up, you're
screwing everything up. Of course we wouldn't listen, we would
just say, screw you, and go on our merry way, drinking ourselves
and our wives and our kids right down into the dirt, and laughing
all the while, saying Indians drink and Indians laugh while their
lives fall apart."

"Geez, Po, take it easy." The uncertainty in Scot's voice makes
me lose my mad and I laugh. "I never even heard you swear
before," Scot says.

I laugh like a maniac. "Sorry, Scotty, m'boy, but I had a long
talk with myself this morning. I'm taking myself waaay too
serious today. It's just that sometimes things get a little too much.
I wonder if anyone else ever thinks about what I just said, or if
it is just one big happy party and damn the consequences."

"Do you want Lori back, Scot, down inside where only you
know, do you really want her back?" Long silence; none of my
business he will tell me, I think, then he will walk away and I
won't see him again. Everyone will walk way around me when I
go to the store, scared that I may begin to preach at them, too.

"Yah." It was said so softly I hardly even heard it, I was busy directing my own little movie in my head.

"What?" I ask, more to myself than to Scot.

"Yah, Po, yah, I really want Lori back."

"Then listen," I say, not really knowing what I was going to say next. "Listen close. If you really want her back, you're gonna have to change some things, okay?" Scot nods, all serious now. "Number one, you will dry yourself out (not bad). Number two, you will write her a letter saying you are drying out and that you want her back more than anything else in the world (all right). Number three, number three, number three . . . (It was Scot who broke and laughed). Shut up! Number three is just shut up and learn to let your spirit talk (wow). You just listen and learn."

"When will I get Lori back?" he asks seriously.

"You will get her back when you have changed, Scot, and when Lori believes that you have changed just for her. Then she will come back." Long silence, I knew what was coming, I got up quickly to go into the house.

Not quickly enough. "Po," Scot says softly, "Did this work for you?"

I turn and look long at Scot, an honest question deserved an honest answer, "I'm still on number one." I go in the house.

I am sitting hunched over a bowl of Wheaties when Scot comes in. He has been doing some hard thinking while I have been trying to do some hard forgetting. "Po," he says, "I been thinking."

"Wah!" I answer, "and now you got a headache."

"No, really. I really been thinking, y'know about what you said out there. It makes sense. It all makes sense." Long silence. "Why didn't you ever do what you told me to do?"

"None of your damn business," I say, a little too quickly. "Scot, none of your damn business."

"Po, it is my business now," he states, braver than I ever saw him before. "If I'm gonna do this, I gotta know if it works. I don't want to just be fartin' in the wind. Po, did you ever try what you said?"

"No," I reply, "I never tried that. Now are you happy?"

"Why not?" he asks simply. "It sounds good, why haven't you tried it?"

"Because I just now thought of it, that's why not," I say looking right into his face.

There is a surprised look of incredible disbelief, then it slowly crinkles all up. First just a big smile, then his eyes wrinkle almost shut, then he just loses it and roars, "Hee, hee, hee," until he loses his breath. "Ho, ho." Soon tears are streaming down his face. He can't quit. "You just now thought of it," he roars. "Some wise man you are."

"I'm just a slow learner," I say and join in the laughter. "A damn slow learner."

⋈⬦⋈

Fancy Dog Contest

Kimberly M. Blaeser

T he dog stories started again last October in the Corner
Store. I was working after school, just like I had been
doing since I was ten. It's my auntie's store and she sells
most everything the folks in Pudge Lakes want that they don't
go to town for. The Post Office is right in there, too, and Auntie
has a gas pump outside. So it's a pretty busy place. Weekends
and most evenings she has coffee made for those who want to
sit and visit, which is just about everybody who comes in. You
know how it is. The talk is free and that makes up for the prices
on everything else.

Well that evening there was a table full of leechers that
should have been out checking their traps, but once Ronny Two
Mink's dog wandered in and started the stories, wasn't anyone
there going to leave. That's what I like about working for Auntie
Todd—you can hear all kinds of village news and old time tales,
too, without anybody paying you a bit of notice. I was unpacking
canned goods, wiping off their lids, and putting them away,
practicing my whistle while I did it. Maybe that's what brought
that fat Martha Beth into the store or maybe she just followed
someone in because she liked the smell of them.

Anyway, in she came and right away started making the
rounds at the leech table, offering to shake hands. She went
from one guy to the next, waiting by their chairs, pawing up
and down. All the guys shook just polite as you please. And then
Martha Beth started her tricks. She puts on quite an act. You

266

ought to come see. Sits up to beg, prances across the floor, and rolls over and over. She's really pretty good at it, but nowadays sometimes old age and her belly get in the way. Still, she keeps it up until someone feeds her. So that bearded guy, Truck, yelled to me to bring them some beef jerky and that's what Martha Beth carried off.

Then they started explaining to the new boy from the city— everyone likes to show off like that with city folks. I heard this guy called "Ringworm" and "Raymond" so I don't know what name he's gonna end up with, but he was a good listener. "Martha's one of the new *educated* reservation dogs," one of the leechers told him and they all laughed, because they knew good stories were coming. I knew it, too, and I was anxious. I wanted to hear about the Bush brothers. But of course, it starts with the dogs.

Outsiders have a hard time understanding the way Indians are with their dogs, just like they are always puzzled about Indians and their kids. Maybe in some ways the two patterns are alike. Dogs in Indian communities are lavished one minute and kicked under the table the next. And children, well, they're prized beyond almost any material thing, but then they have the air knocked out of them when they least expect it. I don't mean physically, necessarily, although that's true, too, sometimes. I mean the way you feel when something happens that suddenly makes you go limp with loss. My Uncle William once told me about a drunk hunter who shot his own dog when it got beat out in retrieving. "I can still see the betrayal in the eyes of that animal as it looked at the barrel," he said. "It turned away and went dead before that fool even pulled the trigger." Well, I've seen plenty of children wearing that look, and with reason enough.

But it's not the alcohol cruelty that makes reservations different from any other place, it's the strange loyalties. And the way they flow back and forth between children and parents, animals and humans. I don't know if you can understand, but it's like what happened between my grandma and her old dog Larky. Grandma and that dog had been together through two moves and ten kids. Larky didn't have a fancy life. She lived under the house, protected in winter by bales of hay piled around the skirting. And she survived mostly on scraps and table slop. I don't even remember Grandma spending very much time with Larky, just a quick scratch on her way to the woodpile or a pat while shucking corn. But they were friends. I knew that because Grandma could set Larky's tail to wagging more than anyone and Larky always started Grandma on a mumbling conversation. Well, that dog was old and beginning to suffer, her hind legs almost too weak to hold her up. My grandma finally told one of the boys to build a box and ready his gun. But the next morning they found Larky had just died. You see, that's what those two would do for one another.

And it's because Indians are loyal to their dogs in that way and their dogs are loyal to them even if it means sharing their poverty, that the dog population is always high around the village. And just like extra relatives are found in almost every house in the village, extra dogs seemed to attach themselves to every family, too. Used to be you couldn't walk to the outhouse around here without three or four dogs starting to bark. Wasn't anybody getting a full night's sleep and they were always scaring someone. My mom lost more than one pail of hazelnuts when someone's dog had a bark too close to her. Could be somebody complained. But more than likely the federal health people just showed up by themselves. My Uncle Timberwolf used to say the federal agents were like poison ivy, popping up every year, always right in your path, and good at starting an itch that would keep spreading until everyone was uncomfortable whether they were scratching or watching.

Anyway some officials started saying the mongrels were a nuisance and a hazard, carried diseases, and were dangerous. So they did what the government does best and started a program. They wanted all the dogs to get shots and licenses. But nobody was going to claim two or three animals when it meant it was gonna cost fifteen dollars a head. Far as I know there isn't a single licensed dog in the village yet. But they did get their shots. A big paddy wagon came in every weekend for a month and lots of young vet students chased around catching as many animals as they could, giving them shots, and tagging them. Sinner Jacob used to charge people five cents a piece to set up their lawn chairs in his yard and watch. He says he's got lots of good tales stored up from those days, but so far I haven't heard him telling them. Maybe he's gonna charge for stories, too. Anyway, those student veterinarians stopped coming after ticks progressed to grey and ready-to-pop.

Everything was quiet for awhile, except for the dogs kept barking. Then after a year or two some agency started *Phase Two*. But this time they must have asked around on how to get people to go along with it. So they put up posters—*Dog Training Classes. Learn to be in command.* They sponsored a contest that offered big prize money: *Win five hundred dollars for first place, two hundred for second, and one hundred for third!* They also started having food at training meetings, and somehow they got the two Bush brothers to enter their dogs. Those guys hadn't talked to one another for eighteen years and people started coming to the community center just to see what would happen with them both there at the same time. But the teacher didn't let you just hang around unless you brought a dog. So pretty soon almost all the dogs were being claimed. Sometimes if someone didn't have anything better to do and wanted to eat and gossip they would borrow a relative's dog for the night. And so the fancy dog contest replaced cribbage and friendship cakes the year I turned eight.

The first sign of craziness came after those people training dogs were told they had to have collars and leashes. It was almost like powwow time around here, with grandmas, aunties, and uncles all costuming the kids. A dog might have a few ribs showing, but you can bet it was going to wear one fine collar. No one was satisfied with a plain old Ben Franklin variety. You ain't never seen such fancy hunks of leather. Missus Manypoint made up the prettiest little deerskin collar edged with large blue trade beads for her Samantha Wolfe. Old Sid Cottonwood had his mum lazystitch an eighteen-inch collar and the whole length of the leash for his labrador. And just like Sid, all the folks started naming the breeds of their dogs or the breeds they imagined them to be in order to register them. Jim "Dandy" Trautner, who likes to call himself "The Fisherman," linked together a bunch of red spinners to make a collar for his *malamute* (which he used to just call a sled dog). English setter, blue dane, springer/poodle cross, terrier/fox mixed blood. Turned into another whole kind of contest I guess you could say, but one Indian people had lots of practice at anyways—bloodlines, stories, and invented identities.

Course it didn't stop there. One week after the dogs were issued numbers they started showing up in fancy outfits. Frank Rabbit's second wife Linda from Pine Ridge brought her husky in wearing sled boots decorated plains style. They were better than most moccasins. The story goes she had to carry that dog in because he couldn't get used to anything on his feet and kept trying to find a way to walk without stepping down on the leather. He kept at least one foot off the floor all the time, shaking his paws, walking on his two hind legs and then on the front ones like he was a circus poodle. Finally the poor critter just rolled over on his back and froze. Linda was sure put out at that dog which people started calling Possum after it stiffened itself out just like it was dead. And they say that dog ain't never walked the same since. I see him sometimes kind of slinking around, his tail drooping, stopping every step or two to hold up a paw like he has a thorn in it. Some things stay with you, I guess, for good or bad.

Well maybe Possum's getup didn't work out too well, but some of them dogs took to the fancying up like princes and princesses. Fat Martha Beth here had a little pendleton coat with a mink collar and Jimmy Sledge's terrier-cross Sun Dog had something like a grass dance outfit in rainbow colors. Both of them went round those training circles with their little black noses and stubby tails held real high. Beads, feather, tobacco cans, bones, skins—there's nothing you've seen stitched into a dance outfit that didn't end up on somebody's dog.

Of course, everyone watched the Bush brothers. But at first it seemed they weren't going to go to any trouble costuming their dogs. Folks call the brothers "Rusty" and "Dollar," the names they got about the same time their argument started. It was because of what the one brother did to the other one's pickup when they were just out of the service—drove it into Pickerel Lake one night. He did go through the trouble of towing it out, but then he just left it in the woods to rust. And he convinced his big brother that he had lost the truck himself in a bet with a Roy Laker. It was half a year before the truth got out. Meanwhile the second Bush brother bought a swanky blue pickup that he kept real clean and started using it to take his brother's girl to town. He got his name because he was always saying his truck was as shiny as a silver dollar. Until the truck thing, the brothers had always hung together. Story is Rusty washed and dressed Dollar from the time their Mum passed on. Later they were the only two Indians in their army platoon, so they had to keep each other remembering and believing they'd come home. I've seen pictures of them back then. In their uniforms you could hardly tell them apart, one standing like a reflection of the other. *Like two peas in a pod* my mom used to say. She says they still are and that's what made them so mad at one another. Course Rusty began to look his six years older once he started to carry his mad with him so long and now no one would mistake him for his slick-tongued brother.

Well anyway when they came to the second meeting their dogs had the plainest training collars of the whole bunch and Rusty had just an ordinary piece of clothesline rope instead of a real leash. Folks were kind of disappointed about that.

The Bush dogs had come from the same litter, but Dollar called his Spike a wolfhound and Rusty called Spitfire a borzoi. Neither one looked like those Irish or Russian dogs in the World Book encyclopedia except for being long-legged and pretty shaggy. At least at the beginning of the contest that's how they looked. Third meeting, Dollar brings in Spike all cut, brushed, and Brill-Creamed. Rusty sat real stony-eyed. Next week Spitfire comes in with his hair highlighted, honest-to-god, to look like flames on his flanks. From then on everyone began betting on the "Two Dog Match."

One day someone heard that someone else overheard Rusty
making a deal in Lengby for some bear claws. Didn't take long
until that got back to Dollar. Pretty soon he was out setting
traps and carving deer antler buttons. No one knew for sure
what those brothers were making, but the words *dog outfit* were
whispered back and forth. One night I heard my ma say
Snowflake was out getting wood when she saw that Old Shawl
Woman crossing the road real sneaky like, taking the path
towards Dollar's. *Probably helping him sew.* The rumors flew
for weeks as the suspense grew. Every Tuesday more people
were showing up at the center, but after the haircut and the
highlighting, neither brother was showing his hand.

Not that there was too much time for gawking anymore on
dog school days. The routines had become pretty intense. So
had the owners or trainers. Each week the dogs seemed more
and more in control, happier to come together for butt sniffing
and tail wagging. But at the other end of the leash the frown-
lines grew. Indians practiced their commands. Not just "sit" or
"come" like the teacher said, of course, but "seddown, you" and
"come 'ere" and lots more colorful variations, too. "Yadog" and
"animosh" were called by Pudge Lakers over and over no matter
how many times the dog extension class lady pleaded with them,
"Please, ladies and gentlemen, use your animal's proper name
so he or she doesn't become confused."

Towards the last some of us kids used to pile straw bales
below the windows so we could watch the doings. It was pitiful
really. All those mutts with new haircuts, new collars, and the
craziest, most colorful regalia you could imagine being led around
the arena by a group of people dressed in hand-me-downs and
Goodwill bargains. The teachers (there were two by this time)
had clip boards and pens which they mostly used for heading
off the wayward dogs or pounding themselves on the head.

Only the Bush boys and three or four other owners seemed
able to walk their dogs through the routine. Folks had kind of
expected Rusty and Dollar would be two of the contenders. I
heard how their daddy used to have some fine coon hounds and
how their Uncle Benson trained and sold hunting dogs. Lots of

stuff gets passed around here like that—in the family blood.

There's so many parts of those contest days that get remembered and told, but the wildest and best part was when the skunk showed up at the competition. Most everybody from the village had turned out and the teachers were too nervous to object. Even us kids talked our way in. I was on my cousin Detroit's shoulders and had a real good view. What I saw looked like some Disney nightmare or maybe a dog-America pageant. Up and down the rows, they stood, sat, or slouched, pooches of every variety. Long-hairs, short-hairs, tailed and tailless, they wiggled with excitement, jingling or swishing, flashing the colors of their costumes. The dogs were supposed to heel in circles and in figure eights. They were to sit, lie down, stay, come. Shake hands, roll over, fetch, sit up and beg.

Well it happened in the finals, during the figure eights. Rusty, Dollar, Sid Cottonwood, Toni Mae Singer, and the little LaTreque girl were in it for the money. Those who had been eliminated joined the rest of the community folks on the sidelines. Sid had just stepped out for his turn with his dog Otis. Suddenly a gunny sack flew in through a window and a skunk fought its way out. Dogs went crazy, the skunk's tail went up, and everyone raced for the door. That would have been a pretty good trick, one person could claim after a month or so had passed. But someone must have dumped a smudge or dropped a lit cigarette in the mad dash to escape, because somehow a fire got started. Soon a couple of the dogs' costumes were flaming while the poor creatures yelped and ran in panic.

Out of the screaming and whirling colors the brothers stepped, seeming calm and walking into the very center of that tornado-force chaos. Maybe it was their army training, an instinct, or the old bond they shared, but some power entered them and stirred in them the same response. Like twin spirits they each grabbed an animal, tucked their body around it, and rolled. When they stood, marked by the smothered flames, the people in the room went silent. Just that one moment. That's how I remember it.

Then we all were outside smelling like skunk and singed

hair. The Bush brothers were offered drinks and handshakes. Everyone was already busy telling what they saw. The teachers came over and they gave all that prize money to the two men, four hundred dollars a piece.

That seems like a real nice end to the story, but funny thing is the story I'm trying to get straight keeps going from there. See, something happened to the Bush boys that night that made them brothers again. Some people tell how they shook hands or exchanged glances. Some say they brushed one another off or even spoke. I didn't see any of that happen.

What happened then,and now in my dreams, and sometimes in the stories is this: *Rusty gets up to go and Dollar follows. They walk, each with the same stride, out to Dollar's truck and he hands over a set of keys just like it hadn't been eighteen years.*

And so when folks start telling about tomato juice baths and burying all those fancy dog costumes at the dump, when I see Martha Beth performing or Possum limping down the road, I think about brooding memory and blood. I try to figure what transforms boys into brothers or fueding brothers into heroes. I wonder what that fire purified in those two men, what burned off and what remained.

◤◢◤◢◤

Spirit Sticks

E. Donald Two-Rivers

*S*o what the hell are spirit sticks? I asked, because I didn't
have a clue and I really wanted to know. For the last
hour—and half a bottle of Southern Comfort later—he'd
kept repeating that he had to tell me about these spirit sticks.

He grinned one of those grins that said something was up
and then he started talkin' his shit. I had been told that this
dude was good and I wanted to find out if that was true.

"Well you know spirit sticks ain't nothin' . . . just a figment
of someone's imagination, but if it works? Well, what the hey!"
He stopped and lit the cigarette he'd been rolling with tobacco
that he took from a can that said "Black Cat" on the side of it,
then he continued. "Are you with me on this?"

I nodded to indicate that I was. He reached across the kitchen
table and helped himself to a drink of the Southern Comfort I
was nursing. I frowned; he grinned. He asked me if I minded,
but what could I say? He's my distant uncle or cousin or
something, or so he claims. I knew damned well that he knew
that any self-respecting Indian wouldn't think of denying a
relative.

"Now according to a rumor, this Indian guy, Bobby-Joe
McMillan, from out of Chicago found work as a guide in the
Ontario bush for some man who had a small tourist camp near
Sapawe Lake. Like spirit sticks he is non-real," he said, then let
out this high-pitched laugh. "Do you get it? They ain't no Indian
named that. Least wise not from around here. And this chick,

Margo Balledoften is just like him. She ain't a real broad either, but in your imagination let her be one of those pretty Georgia peaches from down in Atlanta. She's a natural born victim—a sure enough dilemma. That's how this story starts. Now remember, it ain't nothin' but a hallucination so don't get up tight about it. It probably ain't politically correct either, but what the hell, being born Indian ain't so politically correct neither, aye. Well anyway, this story starts in Georgia with this woman, see? And she's talking to her friend about their upcoming trip up here."

" 'I am so looking forward to this trip up to Canada. I'm hoping for spiritual uplifting. I hear tell that those Indian guides up there are so connected to the earth. I called the lodge and requested that they make one available to us.' "

"That's what she said, that woman from Georgia. You know the one I called Margo Balledoften." He smiled then spit into an empty coffee can that sat by the pot bellied stove. He told me it was there especially for that reason, when he noticed my look of disgust. I smiled to reassure him that I understood.

"The guide that was assigned to these five ladies out of Georgia was no other than this unemployed Indian comedian, Bobby-Joe McMillan. So what have we got here? We have this Georgia peach who's an accident waiting to happen and this red skinned jokester who likes to make them happen. They're stuck together for five days out in the bush. Soon's the guy laid his beady peepers on the broad he knows what her story is. Can you picture this now?

He got up and fetched himself a big ole water-glass and then proceeded to pour himself a stiff drink from my Southern Comfort. I remind him that it's more than twenty miles to the bootleggers house, but it doesn't phase him and he just winks at me. I'm his long-lost relative come from the city to visit with family on the rez and so he thinks that makes me a live one. He thinks that I have money to burn. He's hustling me and I know it, but what the hell, he tells good stories.

"When they get introduced, Bobby-Joe hands these two hand-carved sticks, sort of like chop sticks cut out of jack pine, to Margo and tells her that they're spirit sticks. Of course she wanted to know all about them, being that she was already looking for some kinda spiritual experience from any Indian who happened to come along. He informs her that spirit sticks are an old Indian custom used by young girls, generally virgins, but not necessarily so, especially in this day and age, to ward off evil spirits and hungry bears. Then he tells her that they should be utilized when using the bathroom. Well the clowning bugger sees that she's going for it aye—hook, line and sinker and so he adds a little more detail. He tells her that sometimes they're used on mosquitoes, but that usually wouldn't work unless the woman was a real virgin. Even a finger or two would disqualify her." He laughed a hearty laugh and I smiled at his vulgarity. I'd been told he was a pretty good storyteller. "To make things more interesting," he continued to talk, "Bobby-Joe tells her that it was a real bad omen if one of those bugs landed on her ass and didn't bite. Then it was doing something else. Something he wouldn't divulge in mixed company. You see what he was setting up? What a dirty bugger aye?"

He looked over at my bottle of Southern Comfort so I grabbed a hold of it and took myself a big swallow. To keep from insulting him I reached over and poured him a small drink. He looked at me for a minute then grinned a crooked smile and said it was good of me to share in the Indian way. I agreed, but didn't offer him any more. He made a mental note of that and kept talking.

"Well the first night that they're out in the bush they made camp and went to bed early because they're dead beat. As he laid on his sleeping bag McMillan heard someone get up. Pretty soon he could hear this tapping sound in the nearby bush followed by the gushing sound of water. Bobby-Joe was picturing her squatted down and trying to maintain her balance while at the same time tapping these sticks and slapping at an occasional mosquito who came a little too near her bared derriere. She didn't want no bad omens." He stopped talking so I handed him the bottle.

He took a drink then continued, "Suddenly she let out a yell and came running back into the camp just shaking. After they got her calmed down, and that took some doing, she explained what had happened. 'I was relieving myself and when I stood up to pull up my pants I saw it. It was lit up—and all I could think of was what Mr. McMillan had refused to tell me. I guess it could be said that I let my imagination run away with me.' "

He stopped talking a minute to relight the hand-rolled Black Cat, then continued his tale. "Well I tell you long lost cousin of mine, that lady freaked out because a lightening bug had landed in her bush and she thought he was doing the nasty to her and liking it enough to light up. That'd have to be one hot-assed bug, ain't it? It was more than Bobby-Joe and the rest of the campers could take. They all laughed themselves to sleep that night. Miss Balledoften, well she was getting a little skeptical about Bobby-Joe's spirituality. And who could blame her?"

I was beginning to wonder what the point of his story was. The way his eyes kept rolling to where the bottle of Southern Comfort was, I was positive that he would stretch the story out until it was empty. About the Southern Comfort, it was a round one. In Indian talk that means it was a one of those big bottles, as opposed to a flat one, which is a half pint. It was definitely meant to be consumed over a period of time. I had smuggled the thing across the border with me and I wasn't even sure if you could get that brand in Canada for anything less than an arm and a leg. I could plainly see he intended to polish the thing off right now. Just to be safe I poured him another shot so he would continue with the yarn that he had started.

"Well anyway, they got her calmed down and went to bed. I mean like these people were sleepy from all that fresh air. Shortly after midnight the Indian guide was awakened by this screaming and a loud grunting sound. He knew what it was. It was a bear. Nothing can wreck a campsite quicker than a hungry bear after food. It could be potentially dangerous as well. Bobby-Joe quickly told those campers to climb trees I tell you this much right now; he didn't have to tell them twice. Well once he had shimmied up a tree he took stock of the situation. The bear was a mess— flour all over himself and the campsite. He'd destroyed a tent and flung sleeping bags all over the place. Bobby-Joe was actually feeling lucky because no one had gotten hurt."

His cigarette had gone out so he stopped to light it again, then assured me the best part was yet to come. He waited while I poured him another small shot, which he quickly swallowed. "Well suddenly the bear stopped and stood on its hind legs. It looked up into this tree. You know bears can't see shit and this one probably had flour in its eyes. There on a branch was that broad Margo and to Bobby-Joe's surprise she was furiously tapping those sticks together and in this southern drawl cussing at the bear. I personally don't think that bears have the longest attention span or sense of humor, but the rumor says that the damned bear laughed, then farted. I don't know how true that is, but I do know that they will sometimes do the most unexpected things at times. This one shook his head, blinked his beady red eyes and then dropped to all fours and scrambled into the dense underbrush and wasn't seen or heard again that night. Margo just kept tapping and shaking."

He stopped talking and smiled. I realized that he had reached the end of his story. What happened to Bobby-Joe and the woman, I wanted to know.

This time he just reached for the bottle and took himself a long swallow, then told me the rest. "They say she returned to Georgia convinced that spirit sticks have power in them. Bobby-Joe," he continued—after another snort of my Southern Comfort, "well he quit the guiding business and went back to Chicago to work as a comedian in a strip joint on Mannheim Road. The bear—he's still somewhere around Sapawe Lake, and spirit sticks, well maybe they're real after all, aye?"

▷◁▷◁

Between Wilderness and Civilization

Pauline Brunette Danforth

I t all began with an old yellow school bus. Its faded mustard color was scratched like it had rubbed itself too close to some garage. The front fender was bent into a crooked smile. The windshield wipers were askew like crooked eyebrows. It sat in the used car lot, incongruous by its size next to the Novas, Chevies and Ford pickup trucks. Jake eyed it all winter, then finally stopped there one day for a closer look. He reported the engine purred like a kitten. "Nothing a little paint couldn't fix," he declared.

He didn't see it full of kids in rain slickers, but full of fry bread. He had an imagination, I'll give him that much credit, though to be blunt the bank wouldn't. How could they? Trapping beaver, his occupation, was chancy. You didn't file fat income tax returns on the occasional checks received for beautifully stretched and tanned beaver hides. No, it took a bit of luck for that bus to be ours.

It was Friday night and quitting time at the tribal offices where I worked. With my paycheck, I figured on paying rent and buying a few groceries to supplement our commodity supply. That left us $40.00 for gas, and dog food for Moose.

Jake picked me up that Friday night and we drove home past the Bingo Palace. Without asking me, he pulled in. Said he was feeling lucky. I said I wasn't and reluctantly offered him half of my cash. He was only gone for 20 minutes. He returned with $2,000.00. Just enough to buy that old bus plus some equipment.

Right away we headed for the car dealership and under the diffused glow of the yard light, Jake estimated with a few new belts and fresh oil, plus better tires he could get it running sweet in no time at all. Peering beneath the hood of the monstrous front end, he reassured me nothing was cracked and/or leaking. Inside the cavernous bus, he counted out seats. "The fridge will take two, the propane stoves maybe three, an extra long folding table will fit where these seats are, and supplies the whole other side." Toward the back, he decided we could store pop containers, vats of cooking oil and other heavy stuff. "Yep," he figured, "we are in business!"

A few days later he was jerking out green plastic seats while I knelt on the roof splashing it with a fry bread shade of yellow-brown paint. Occasionally he would shout out his renovation plans. That's the way we operated. He had the dreams and I went along, almost convinced they would pay off, but always fighting my skepticism. Last year he was sketching out plans for an Indian curio theme park next to the state park. Although he didn't figure out how we were going to buy that five acres, Jake had all the other details figured out, right down to how much lumber we would need for fencing.

I was the practical one, working 8-5 every day, while he concocted get-rich schemes. I rarely took chances, except by marrying him. He wasn't the sort mothers approved of—few apparent prospects, no bank account and big dreams. Except for the time he convinced me to elope, I approached life cautiously. I listened to the weather forecast every morning, brushed my teeth to fight plaque, and kept my mouth shut about tribal politics. And I didn't regret doing any of it, especially marrying Jake.

I'd met him out in the woods. He was walking to his trapline near Deer Lake and I was cross-country skiing on the state trail. He jogged along beside me awhile, his gangly, loose-jointed figure denying the muscles developed from hauling beaver. He invited me to his cabin for muskrat stew. Can't say I remember that stew, but our friendship began then and there. Turned out the cabin belonged to a friend and Jake had agreed to fix it up for free rent over the winter. That's how he preferred to do things— for barter, not money, whenever possible.

Although the bus was bought with cash, he did trade the scrap metal from the seats for a couple spare parts, a starter or something and a heavy duty jack from the junkyard. Out in our shed among the stuff he got in trade, he found a flying Pontiac Indian hood ornament that he welded onto the bus. We were going to follow that Pontiac to whatever powwow it took us, Jake solemnly pronounced.

Well, just two weeks after buying the Fry Bread Wagon, we decided to test it out on the highway and drive up to American Falls, 80 miles north toward Canada. It was a Saturday in April and still real chilly. Without any of our equipment or supplies, the bus rode like an empty tin can. Our sleeping bags, cooler and some loose tools rolled and rattled around in back. Jake sat behind the oversized steering wheel confidently shifting from low to high gear as we sped along the highway. Moose, our saggy mixed-blood bloodhound-mutt swayed on the floor in the middle and I sat in the only remaining seat on the right.

It was a glorious day. The sun glinted off the ice melting on the little lakes we passed. It teased us, cutting through the trees and splicing the Wagon's shadow on the road beside us. The breeze that came through the open windows promised spring.

Fifty miles up Highway 71, we heard "boom." Jake fought to keep the wheel straight as he quickly down shifted, then "boom" again. Luckily we were next to a rest stop overlooking one of those scenic lakes Minnesota is famous for. Of course, at the moment it wasn't scenery that had my attention. I clutched the rail in front of me and anxiously (and belatedly) asked about the condition of our spares, remembering we didn't have any.

Jake managed to stop the Wagon in record time, pulling into the little gravelled parking lot. We got out to assess the damage. Both rear tires were flatter than pancakes. I paced, Moose ambled off towards the lake, and Jake placidly sat down next to the bus and swigged on an orange soda. After a minute or two, I joined him. Somehow, I knew he would have a plan.

Finally, after I'd given up on him, he got up, dusted off his jeans, picked his tools out of the bus and said he was going for a little walk. He asked me to stay back with Moose. What choice did I have? I figured it was better to wait than walk five miles back to the last house we passed.

He was gone just over two hours. He returned in an old truck driven by a man in a greasy mechanics jumpsuit. The name tag in red letters said "Pete." Jake introduced us and I reluctantly shook Pete's oily hand with a couple fingers. Apparently Pete lived a couple miles off this main road. Jake trapped some beaver for him that were flooding the low part of his junkyard. From that time, Jake remembered seeing some old bus tires on his property. Pete just gave them to us, saying it was for the trapping Jake did for him.

Because it was getting dark fast, Jake said he would fix the tires in the morning and suggested we camp right there. The place had all we needed. A pump for water, an icy blue lake and lots of fallen branches for firewood.

That night we sat hunched under a blanket. We would reach out to the campfire to warm our faces and hands, then jump up to do a dance to warm our backsides. Huddled together again, with Moose squirming in, we boldly stretched out of our cocoon and admired the wondrous northern lights as they danced over the lake. Like paint on a giant canvas, the luminous northern lights streaked down the midnight-blue sky, shimmering and ever changing. Wolves howled in the distance. Closer by frogs croaked and raccoons stared at us from the woods, cracking twigs in their careless curiosity. Behind us, semi-trucks bound for Canada reminded us we were just on a wayside between wilderness and civilization.

Contributors

kateri akiwenzie-damm is a mixedblood writer from the Chippewas of Nawash First Nation who lives and works at Neyaashiinigmiing, Cape Croker Reserve in the Saugeen Peninsula in southwestern Ontario. Her work has been published in various anthologies and journals, and on audiocassette. She has given readings in Canada, the U.S., Australia, and Aotearoa and on national radio in Canada and Aotearoa. Readings have also been broadcast nationally in Canada on WTN (Women's Television Network). When not writing kateri works as a communications consultant and runs a small publishing company to support the work of indigenous writers. kateri says, "My work is fueled by love and rage and inspired by my community: the land and all of my relations who comfort me, support me, and give me strength."

Faith Allard is a member of the Sault Ste. Marie Tribe of Chippewa Indians. She completed her Associate's Degree in Teacher Education at Bay Mills community College in 1995. She has two children who enjoy listening to her writings as much as she enjoys writing them.

David Beaulieu currently serves as Director of the Office of Indian Education, U.S. Department of Education. He coordinates policy development and identifies research topics and priorities affecting American Indians and Alaska Natives within the Department of Education. Beaulieu has served as the Commissioner of Human Rights for the state of Minnesota. He is an enrolled member of the Minnesota Chippewa Tribe, White Earth Reservation, and the first American Indian to be appointed as a Commissioner in State Government. Beaulieu earned a Ph.D. in Education Administration from the University of Minnesota and is a former Post-Doctorate Fellow of the D'Arcy McNickle Center for the History of the American Indian, Newberry Library, Chicago. He has held faculty positions at Moorhead State University, The University of Illinois, Chicago, and the University of Minnesota where he was an Associate

Professor and Chairman of the department of Indian Studies. He was also Vice President of Sinte Gleska University, Rosebud, South Dakota, which is the first Tribally Chartered Indian-controlled college to achieve accreditation at the Bachelor and Master Degree granting level. Beaulieu is a member and former Chairman of the Board of Trustees of NAES College, an Indian-controlled college based in Chicago, with campuses at the Fort Peck and Menominee Reservations, and the Chicago and Twin Cities Indian communities. Beaulieu was appointed to the Indian Nations at Risk Task Force., has served as a member of the National Governing Board of Common Cause, a member of the National Governing Board for the University of Minnesota alumni association and as a member of the Board of Directors of the St. Paul Foundation, The Minnesota Foundation and the St. Paul Public Education Fund.

Michelle Boursaw (Dwaagiakikishkoodekwe, Autumn Earth Fire Woman) is a Turtle Clan member of the Mackinaw Band of Ojibwe, Sault Ste. Marie Tribe. She works as a staff writer and reporter for *Win Awenen Nisitotung*, the Sault Tribal Newspaper and is currently completing a master's degree in Creative Writing at Michigan State University. Boursaw is a member of the Wordcraft Circle of Native Writers and Storytellers and her poetry has been published in several places including *Moccasin Telegraph*. She also runs a small Ojibway Pottery and Design business.

Janice Command (Ojibwe and Potawatomi) is a Walpole Island enrollee currently working as a free-lance journalist in Minnesota. Her creative writing achievements include residencies with the Playwrights' Center and the Loft, regional writers' centers in Minneapolis. Several cabarets have produced her theatre work, and her prose has appeared in *Beaver Tail Journal*.

Pauline Brunette Danforth is from the White Earth Reservation, although she currently lives in the Twin Cities where she is writing her dissertation in American Studies and working as an academic advisor at the University of Minnesota. She is a graduate of Bemidji State University.

Anne M. Dunn is a creative writer, poet, essayist, editorial cartoonist, storyteller, educator, free-lance journalist and columnist for *News from Indian Country*. For five years she edited and published *The Beaver Trail Times*, a nine-page monthly newsletter promoting positive human values in an engaging and inspiring manner. She is presently an area correspondent for the Native American Press (NAP), a board member of Battered Women Services of Hubbard County Inc., and a founding member of the Northern Minnesota Religious Freedom Council. She served for three years on the Peace Lantern Committee which endeavors to promote peace and racial justice, and is also a founding member of Warriors In The Struggle (WITS). In 1996 she was one of 15 women selected nationwide to participate in the Pastors for Peace Women's Delegation to Chiapas, Mexico. Dunn has written *Our Relations Are Coming*, a three-act play which focuses on reconciliation among all nations; *Cora the Battered*, a one-act soliloquy which addresses the issues of domestic violence; and *Crow's Disgrace*, a four-act play based on a traditional Ojibwe myth. Dunn, with her mother Maefred Arey and daughter Annette Humphrey, has produced a cassette collection of Anishinaabe Grandmother Stories. Her first book, *When Beaver Was Very Great* (Midwest Traditions, Inc.), was nominated for the 1996 Minnesota Book Award. Her second book, *Grandmother's Gift*, was published by Holy Cow! Press.

Heid Erdrich grew up in Wahpeton, North Dakota, where her parents taught at the Bureau of Indian Affairs Boarding School. She is a member of the Turtle Mountain Band of Chippewa. Erdrich has degrees from Dartmouth College and Johns Hopkins University. Jobs she has held while writing include: seamstress, cleaning lady, court-scene reporter, teen counselor, police dispatcher, jail matron, bartender, teacher, and multicultural recruiter. She moved to Minnesota in 1992 and now teaches at the University of St. Thomas. Erdrich won a Minnesota Voices Award in 1995. Her poetry collection, *Fishing for Myth,* has been published by New Rivers Press, Minneapolis, Minnesota.

Lise Erdrich is a Turtle Mountain Chippewa. Her fiction has been included in various journals and collections including: *The North Dakota Quarterly, Special Report: Fiction* and *Tamaqua*. In 1989 she was the recipient of the John Hove Creative Writing Fellowship from the North Dakota Council of the Arts. Her short story, "XXL," won the 1996 Tamarack Award from *Minnesota Monthly*.

Louise Erdrich is of German and Anishinaabe descent and is a member of the Turtle Mountain Band of Ojibwe. Her mother, Rita Gourneau, is a noted Ojibwe artist. Her sisters are the writers Heid Erdrich and Lise Erdrich, and her brothers Louis and Ralph work in the hospital system at Red Lake, Minnesota. Angela Erdrich, her youngest sister, is an IHS physician practicing in Wisconsin. Louise has written *Love Medicine, The Beet Queen, Tracks*, and most recently *The Antelope Wife*.

Leslie Harper is a twenty-four-year old Ojibwe woman from Leech Lake Reservation who grew up in Cass Lake and now lives in Minneapolis. Currently she has a job in a coffee shop and is trying to reconcile herself and her family over her state of urban Indian-ness.

Gordon Henry, Jr. is Anishinaabe. He teaches in the English Department at Michigan State University. In 1995 he received an American Book Award for his first novel, *The Light People*. He lives in Big Rapids, Michigan, with his wife Mary Anne, daughters Kehli, Mira and Emily and animal skins Kota and Astoria. He has recently taken an apprenticeship with Dr. A.A. Gaween, a tribal artist/historian/custodian who recreates villages out of White Clay.

Danielle M. Hornett is a Bad River Chippewa and Oklahoma Cherokee. She is Associate Dean of Cultural Diversity at St. Norbert College, Wisconsin. She has had several poems and a textbook published.

Paul Kinville is currently working with Red Hawk Laboratory, Inc., a Native American owned engineering company in Alexandria, Virginia, as a technical writer/researcher. He lives in Washington, D.C., and is finishing his undergraduate degree in Journalism and English. This is his first publication.

Winona LaDuke is a White Earth enrollee known primarily as an environmental activist and the founder of the White Earth Land Recovery project. She has published numerous essays, interviews, and introductions. Her novel, *Last Standing Woman,* has been published by Voyageur Press.

Joyce carlEtta Mandrake was born in Salmon, Idaho, and grew up in the mountains of Idaho. She graduated from Idaho State University in Pocatello, Idaho, with a B.A. in Art. She is currently living on the central Oregon coast with her husband and son. "I spend a lot of time walking," she says. "During this time, I pray and visit with the creator; it is a time of recharging my spirit and soul. It is my moment of gratitude."

Paulette Fairbanks Molin is a member of the Chippewa Tribe from the White Earth Reservation. She serves as the Director of American Indian Educational Opportunities Program at Hampton University, Hampton, Virginia, which provides scholarship support and other services to participating students at the school. Her article about early Chippewa students who attended Hampton was published in *Minnesota History* (Fall 1988). She co-curated a photographic exhibition entitled *To Lead and to Serve: American Indian Education at Hampton Institute, 1878-1923* and co-authored the exhibition's catalog (Hampton University and the Virginia Foundation for the Humanities and Public Policy, 1989). Recent writings include co-authorship with W. Roger Buffalohead of an article for a special boarding school issue of the *Journal of American Indian Education* (Spring 1996). In 1997 she completed collaborative work on curriculum materials for the Native American/Hawaiian Women of Hope Project, sponsored by the Bread and Roses Foundation in New York City. Paulette serves as a board member of Wordcraft Circle of Native Writers & Storytellers.

Jim Northrup lives with his wife and family on the Fond du Lac Reservation in northern Minnesota. His column, "The Fond du Lac Follies," appears in several Native American newspapers. His first book, *Walking the Rez Road,* won the Minnesota Book Award and the Midwest States Achievement Award. His one-man show, *The Rez Road Follies,* has been performed widely, and a prose version has been published by Kodansha America, Inc.

Penny Olson is an Ojibwe from Sault Ste. Marie, Michigan. She lives in the Upper Peninsula with her husband and two children. She has a Masters in English with an Emphasis in Writing from Northern Michigan University where she is currently working as an adjunct instructor in English and Native American Studies. Penny also taught for three years at Bay Mills Indian Community College on the Bay Mills Reservation in Michigan. She is a founding member of Wordcraft Circle of Native Writers and Storytellers. She has had short stories published in *Earth Song, Sky Spirit* and *Blue Dawn, Red Earth* and has had poetry published by AISES. She is currently working on a novel and considering returning to college to work on her M.F.A.

David Pego is the director of educational services for the *Austin American-Statesman* newspaper in Austin, Texas. A career journalist, he previously held a variety of reporting and editing positions at the *American-Statesman*, the *Dallas Times Herald*, *The Daily Oklahoman*, the *Oklahoma City Times* and The Associated Press. A graduate of Leadership Austin, David is active in numerous professional and community organizations. He is the founding chair of the largest single-day school event, The Austin Independent School District Powwow and American Indian Heritage Festival. He was appointed by President Bush to represent Texas at the historic White House Conference on Indian Education and was named to the Texas Goals 2000 Committee by Governor Ann Richards and Governor George W. Bush. He writes for several magazines and has published two short stories from a novel in progress.

Marcie R. Rendon, White Earth Anishinaabe, is a mother, writer, and sometimes a performing artist. A former recipient of the Loft Inroads Writers of Color Award for Native Americans, she has also received a Multi-cultural Collaboration grant from the Playwright Center, and an Intermedia Arts Emerging Artists' Installation Award. Her first children's book, *Powwow Summer*, with photographs by Cheryl Walsh Bellville, was published by CarolRhoda, Inc.

Loriene Roy   was born in Cloquet, Minnesota, in 1954. Enrolled at White Earth Reservation, she is a member of the Pembina Band. She received undergraduate degrees from (Klamath Falls) Oregon Institute of Technology, a Master's degree from the University of Arizona, and a PH. D. from the University of Illinois. She has been on the faculty of the Graduate School of Library and Information Science at the University of Texas at Austin since 1987. She has published over 50 articles, chapters, reports, documents and book reviews, and given over 50 formal presentations in the U. S. and abroad. She is also a songwriter. Her professional writing covers a wide spectrum of issues including censorship, collection development, and library services to Indian populations.

Armand Garnet Ruffo was born in northern Ontario and is the great-great grandson of Chief Sahquakegick (Louis Eponiel) of the Ojibwe Nation. Ruffo now makes his home in Ottowa where he is a lecturer in the Department of English and the Associate Director for the Centre for Aboriginal Education, Research, and Culture at Carleton University. Strongly influenced by his Ojibwe heritage, his first collection of poetry, *Opening in the Sky* (Theytus Books, 1994), reveals an abiding interest in the complexities of Aboriginal identity in a multicultural society. His second book, a creative poetic biography, *Grey Owl: The Mystery of Archie Belamey* (Coteau Books, 1997), "raises difficult questions about voice and identity, aboriginal culture, human rights and the environment." In addition, he has published plays, stories and essays in various literary periodicals and anthologies, including the recent *An Anthology of Canadian Native Literature in English* (Oxford Press, 1998).

Denise Sweet is an Anishinaabe poet (White Earth) and a pro-fessor of Humanistic Studies at the University of Wisconsin, Green Bay. She teaches creative writing, literature and mythol-ogy, as well as a travel seminar involving fieldwork among the Mayan peoples of the Yucatan Peninsula and Guatemala. Sweet has presented nearly 100 public readings around the United States, in Canada, Mexico and Guatemala, and has served as poet-in-residence in public and tribal schools as well as at the Grand Marais Art Colony in northern Minnesota and at the Apostle Islands National Lakeshore. She is also a part of the staff of artists and writers at the Split Rock Arts program in Duluth, Minnesota. Her 1995 manuscript, *Songs for Discharming*, won the First Book Award from the Native Writers Circle of the Americas and was recently released by Greenfield Press of New York. Her poem, "Veteran's Dance," placed second at the Sante Fe Indian Market Poetry Competition, and her poetry has appeared in various journals and anthologies including *Reinventing the Enemy's Language, Sustaining the Forest, The People and the Spirit, Calyx, Sinister Wisdom, Akwekon, Another Chicago Magazine, Returning the Gift, Women Brave in the Face of Danger,* and *Days of Obsidion, Days of Grace: Four Native American Writers* (Poetry Harbor). Her work has been commissioned by Great Lakes Intertribal Council, and has appeared in museum art exhibits. Sweet is currently the chair for the American Indian Studies program at UW-Green Bay and director of "Who We Are, What Is Ours: Young Writer's Workshop," UW-GB's first self-sponsored pre-college program for students of color. In 1995 she received the "Outstanding Woman of Color" award from the UW System and the "Outstanding Indian Woman" award from the Positive Indian Development Center and the Wisconsin Women's Council. Sweet is currently working on a third collection of poems, *As Those With Faith Will Do*. She is the mother of two sons, Damon and Vaughn.

David Treuer, Ojibwe, grew up at Leech Lake, Minnesota. A graduate of Princeton University who is completing his Ph.D. in Anthropology at the University of Michigan, Treuer is currently a Lecturer in the Department of English at the University of Wisconsin-Milwaukee. Treuer's first novel, *Little*, won the Minnesota Book Award. He is completing a second book, *The Hiawatha*.

The Reverend Doyle Turner, Sr., a White Earth Ojibwe of the Mississippi Band, was born and lived most of his life on the White Earth Reservation. He has been married for 32 years to Mary Olsen Turner. They have one daughter, two sons, and three grandchildren. He graduated from Moorhead State University with a Bachelor of Science Degree in Personnel Psychology and from Seabury Western Theological Seminary with a Master of Divinity Degree. He has served the Episcopal Churches on White Earth since his graduation from seminary. He currently serves on the Staff of the Bishop of The Diocese of Minnesota as Canon Missionary for the nine Ojibwe Missions of Region I of their Diocese. Turner loves reading, writing historical fiction, hunting, fishing and traveling. He has been writing for a number of years but has submitted only three short stories for competition. One of these placed first and one third in the contests. He says, "I am of the firm belief that until we as Native writers tell our own stories we will continue to be marginalized or romanticized by those who write about us. We will claim our reality and our true identity by the stories we tell about ourselves."

E. Donald Two-Rivers is an Ojibwe Indian from the Seine River Band in Ontario, Canada. He moved to Chicago during the politically turbulent 60s. As a member of the American Indian Movement, much of his adult life has been spent in the Indian's struggle for equal rights. A journeyman machinist by trade, his passion is writing. As an environmentalist, his message is the red man's continuing plea to protect and take care of Mother Earth. As a worker, his work echoes the disenfranchised voice of the angry and frustrated workers everywhere. He records today's struggle of environmentalists, workers, homeless and Native Americans. Two-Rivers has authored a series of plays which were produced at local theaters and area colleges. In recent years he has begun directing plays and is the founding artistic director of Red Path Theater, Illinois, the only Native American theater touring troupe. His collection of short stories, *Survivor's Medicine,* has been published by the University of Oklahoma Press in the University's American Indian Literature and Critical Studies Series. His first publication, *A Dozen Cold Ones*, received a Dennis Brutus nomination for Socio/Political award.

Gerald Vizenor is professor of Native American Literature at the University of California, Berkeley. He is author of more than twenty books on native histories, literature, and critical studies, including *The People Named the Chippewa: Native Histories*, and *Crossbloods: Bone Courts, Bingo, and Other Reports*. His autobiography, *Interior Landscapes: Autobiographical Myths and Metaphors*, and his first novel, *Bearheart: The Heirship Chronicles*, were published by the University of Minnesota Press. Vizenor edited *Narrative Chance*, a collection of essays on Native American literature. *Manifest Manners: Postindian Warriors of Survivance*, critical studies; *The Heirs of Columbus*, a novel; and *Landfill Meditation*, a collection of short stories, were published by Wesleyan University Press. *Griever: An American Monkey King in China*, his second novel, won an American Book Award. *Dead Voices; Natural Agonies in the New World*, his fifth novel, was published by the University of Oklahoma Press. His recent books include *Shadow Distance: A Gerald Vizenor Reader*, and *Hotline Healers: An Almost Browne Novel*. He edited *Native American Literature*, an anthology published in the Literary Mosaic series by Harper Collins College Publishers. Vizenor is series editor of American Indian Literature and Critical Studies at the University of Oklahoma Press.

Gail Moran Wawrzyniak (Lac du Flambeau, Ojibwe) writes poetry and nonfiction and has been published in *Colors Magazine*, *The Hamline Literary Journal*, and *Native Woman Silent Vows*. She was profiled in *The Circle Newspaper* and was selected to participate in the Loft's Native American Inroads Program for Emerging Writers and S.A.S.E.'s The Poet Is In Program for Emerging Poets. She has an M.A. in Liberal Studies with an emphasis in Literature from Hamline University, is currently working toward an M.F.A. in Creative Writing, and teaches at North Hennepin Community College.

Kimberly M. Blaeser, Anishinaabe, is an enrolled member of the Minnesota Chippewa Tribe and grew up on the White Earth Reservation in northwestern Minnesota. Currently an Associate Professor of English at the University of Wisconsin-Milwaukee, Blaeser teaches Creative Writing, Native American Literature and American Nature Writing. She lives with her husband, son Gavin, and a menagerie of animals on six-and-a-half acres in rural Wisconsin. Her publications include a collection of poetry, *Trailing You*, which won the 1993 First Book Award from the Native Writers' Circle of the Americas, and a critical study, *Gerald Vizenor: Writing in the Oral Tradition*. Blaeser's poetry, fiction, personal essays and scholarly articles have been included in over fifty Canadian and American anthologies and journals including *Earth Song, Sky Spirit, Reinventing the Enemy's Language, Narrative Chance, Returning the Gift, Women on Hunting, Blue Dawn, Red Earth, The Colour of Resistance, Unsettling America, As We Are Now,* and *Other Sisterhoods.*